LEGACY

LEGACY

palm south university book 4

kandi steiner

Published by Kandi Steiner
Edited by Elaine York, Allusion Publishing
www.allusionpublishing.com

Cover Design by Kandi Steiner and Staci Hart
Formatting by Elaine York, Allusion Publishing
www.allusionpublishing.com

Legacy picks up right where *Pledge* left off. As this book is part of a series, you will need to read the other books in the series before beginning this one:

Rush, PSU #1
Anchor, PSU #2
Pledge, PSU #3

In addition, *Legacy* takes place during the same semester as another book of mine you might not have heard of yet: *Black Number Four*. The Palm South University series started as a prequel to this book, and finally, we've come to the part in our story where these worlds meet.

You do not have to read *Black Number Four* in order to read and completely understand *Legacy*. You can simply read this book and move right along in your Palm South University journey.

However, for those of you who want the all-around experience, who want to live in this world a little while longer, I have included a reading guide at the end of each episode to help you read *Legacy* and *Black Number Four* TOGETHER.

If you'd like to have that experience, you can grab *Black Number Four* here (http://amzn.to/2fSsQE1).

EPISODE 1

"SO, SHOULD WE START taking bets on which pledge will have the best game?" I ask Skyler as we make our way through the pledge tents. I balance our tray of cookies in one hand as I use the other to pull my strappy hoodie down and show off the girls a little more. It's chilly for Florida — hovering right around fifty-five — but it doesn't stop me from showing a little flesh.

I mean, I *do* have a reputation to uphold.

Flags with Greek letters fly high from all the tents around us as we weave between the different frats, the field lit up by the industrial-size lights that have been set up all week. The entire PSU Greek Life organization is out in full force, all of us donning our letters with pride, gathering like a bunch of hyenas at a damn watering hole. And I'm wearing the biggest smile on my face, passing out winks like candy, because I'm right back in my element.

It's fraternity rush, my favorite thing about coming back to Palm South University for spring semester.

And there are boys *everywhere*.

Rush used to be my mecca. It used to be my playground, jackpot, my pond full of fish, if you will.

There's always fresh meat to be found, and all the *current* brothers are at the top of their top game, too. Rush is a time of bromancing, of convincing other guys how great you are, how cool you are, how much they need you in their organization or, if you're already a brother, how much they need to be in *yours*.

Of course, part of that game is showing off what girls you can land. Back in my prime, I loved to play in the game, to be the arm candy hanging on a brother's arm or, sometimes, even the arm of a freshman. Hey, if I could help them get into the frat they wanted? Well, I saw it as my civic duty.

It was a simple game, one I dominated easily, and one I loved to be a part of.

But that was before Jarrett, and I realized over winter break that my life would forever be separated into those two categories: before Jarrett, and after him. I remembered easily what life was like before I met him, remembered the way I used to be, and I could still close my eyes and feel every ounce of happiness, and pain, that I'd felt while being *in* his arms — while being his.

But life after Jarrett? I don't understand that beast yet.

I'm like a baby gazelle, trying to figure out how to walk and run away from lions at the same time. All I can do is put one foot in front of the other and pray for a miracle.

"Aren't we a little old for freshmen, J-Love?" Skyler asks with a roll of her eyes. She's also wearing a Kappa Kappa Beta hoodie, but hers actually covers the goodies.

"Hey! Some of them are sophomores. I heard there are even a few juniors this year."

"What happened to Greg? I thought things were getting *serious*," she mocks, nudging me.

Hearing his name makes my stomach flip, like butterflies are trying to give it liftoff but fail halfway up so it just tumbles on top of itself.

Greg and I haven't talked since semi-formal, and though I had fun with him, I can't help but feel like he's part of the reason I lost Jarrett — even though I *know* that's not true. It isn't his fault I went into that bar on Thanksgiving on a mission and found him, and it definitely isn't his fault that he played into my hand exactly the way I wanted him to.

My plan had worked, and then it had backfired, and I'd lost the most important human to ever exist in my life.

I scoff, trying to play it off. "Yeah right. He was fun for semi-formal, but I lost interest over Christmas break."

That's a lie.

"I'm ready for a new toy."

Also a lie.

Skyler laughs. "You're relentless. You do realize you're the Recruitment Chair now, right? You should probably be setting the standard for our sorority, which I don't think includes scamming on fresh meat."

"There are more eyes on your Big than on me, Sky," I remind her. "Besides, maybe I'm trying to recruit all the skanks this semester." I shimmy my hips a little just to drive that point home, making Skyler laugh.

"Yeah, like that would ever fly with Ex or Lei."

Erin is president this year — the title she's been fighting for since she arrived at Palm South — and she's already taken her new position so seriously that I wonder if I'll ever get to see the *old* Erin again. Believe it or not, she did party once, and even though she's always had her eye on the prize when it came to getting president, she stiffened up even more than usual last semester.

Our recruiting styles would *definitely* be different.

"Come on," Skyler says as I link my arm in hers. "Let's go drop off these cookies and start making the rounds."

As we head toward the Omega Chi tent, I let my mind wonder over what Skyler just said as my eyes wander over the fresh meat at the fraternity rush buffet. She's right — I do need to keep my shit together. Erin won't settle for me getting into too much trouble, not now that I'm our recruitment chair. That thought also sobers me, because I'm officially in my last year at Palm South University.

Since I changed my major late and took a position with the sorority, I'll be graduating after fall semester instead of this May. Even still, that's less than three-hundred-and-fifty days until I walk across the stage and leave PSU behind, until I start a new chapter, a new life.

I thought I had it figured out.

It sounds ludicrous now, that I had hung up my dreams once I'd fallen in love with Jarrett, but it was true. I was perfectly content to graduate and move wherever the fuck he was — New York, Atlanta, Papua New Guinea — it didn't matter, as long as he was there.

But now, there is no Jarrett.

Now, there's just Jess Vonnegut, and that bitch is a mess.

Clinton starts in on Skyler as soon as we reach the Omega Chi tent, and I take the opportunity to pull out my phone while they banter back and forth. My finger finds Jarrett's text messages easily, and I stare at the last one I ever sent him.

- I will always love you. -

My stomach sinks, unlike the flip it did at the mention of Greg's name. No, this time it just falls like a thousand-pound anvil, crushing those poor butterflies beneath it and breaking all their wings in the process.

What everyone already knows is that I fucked up. I lost Jarrett, he broke up with me over a fucking video chat session, and I took Greg to semi-formal, basically only because I didn't want to sit home and sulk. They know I was devastated by losing him, and they know I've never loved a boy until him.

What they don't know is that over Christmas break, I flew to New York to try to see him. And I did.

But he didn't see me.

I had it all planned — the words I would say to win him back, the case I would plead, the promises I would make. But nothing mattered once I finally found him, because he was at a bar with another woman, the one I presumed to be Jenny, his co-worker he'd told me I was crazy for feeling any kind of jealousy toward.

His tongue being halfway down her throat assured me that feeling existed for a reason.

I'm not sure how long I stood there, staring at him from across the crowded bar, watching as they kissed, and held hands, and laughed. It was like he wasn't heartbroken at all, like he never had been, like I was so far in his past that he couldn't even recall my name.

When I left New York City, I vowed to leave my broken heart behind, too. I vowed to return to Palm South as the *old* Jess Vonnegut, the man eating, take-no-shit, bad-ass bitch.

But like I said before — that was *before* Jarrett, and this is after.

Everything is different now.

My attention snaps back to the Omega Chi tent when I hear Skyler talking about the poker tournament she entered that takes place at the end of this semester. Clinton makes some comment to the new pledges gathered around him about her winning every tournament, and she quickly corrects him.

"Not *every* tournament."

I see doubt creep in over her bright blue eyes, and I pull my shit together, eager to squash it.

"Not yet, you mean. We all know you're going to take it all this year," I say, and Clinton nods in agreement.

Skyler smiles, a little light coming back into her eyes, but I know we're all going to have to be there for her this semester. This is a tournament unlike any other she's entered before — higher entry fee, higher stakes — and we have to have her back.

The three of us make our way to the back of the tent, cookies in hand, and Skyler changes gears back to rush. Clinton is telling her all about the new guys rushing, including a few promising guys for the intramural football team, but it's not until he mentions the hot new transfer that both mine and Skyler's ears perk up.

"Transfer?" she asks. "Who the hell transfers to Palm South?"

Clinton laughs, his bright white teeth blazing against his dark skin as he shakes his head, just as confused as we are. "Right? That's what I said. But, apparently he's got a pretty impressive resume. I heard he's a Creative Writing major, though, so my money is on him going Alpha Sigma."

My eyes skirt to the Alpha Sigma tent as they continue talking, and I see a big crowd gathered around it. I can't help but think of Adam, of the legacy he's already built as president — hell, the one he started building *before* he even got the gig. Between his concerts and last year's Halloween party, they've really made a name for themselves.

One of Clinton's brothers, Willie, pops up beside Skyler, joining in the conversation about the all-mighty transfer. I swear, fraternity rush is the only time you'll ever hear guys getting all gooey over other dudes.

"Okay, where is this guy?" I finally ask, scanning the courtyard. "I need to see what all the fuss is about."

Skyler chuckles. "I'm going back to the house to see if my Little is done studying yet. Behave yourself, Jess," she says pointedly.

"No promises."

I'm still on my tiptoes scanning the crowd when she disappears into it, and Clinton and Willie go back to talking to the freshmen. Shrugging when I don't immediately spot some hypnotizingly hot transfer student, I give up, turning to make my way toward the Mu Beta Chi tent, and that's when I run straight into a brick wall.

Or rather, a man as hard as one.

Greg smiles at me, one corner of his mouth pulling up in a lazy, sexy smirk, which makes that damn dimple pop on his cheek. His dark hair blows a little in the wind, and he tucks his hands into his pockets easily, like he's not the least bit affected by my proximity.

I try to pretend the same.

I was serious about what I said to Skyler earlier, that Greg was just for fun, that he wasn't anything special to get my panties in a knot over. But the truth was that the last time I saw him, I was fresh off my break up, and he was just there to pick up the pieces.

Now, though the hole in my heart still gapes from where Jarrett used to be, I can't deny that those damn butterflies aren't trying their damnedest to sprout back to life under the weight of the anvil.

"Hey, stranger," he says, his eyes flicking down to my cleavage and back up again.

My cheeks heat, and I find my stupid gazelle legs standing a little taller, a little straighter — all at the sight of a beautiful boy with dark eyes.

He was just a distraction last semester, a fill for the void, a patch over the hole.

But maybe, just maybe, his job isn't done yet.

Cassie

I AM TOTALLY COOL.

The girls convinced me to come out of my study hole, even though classes haven't even officially started, and join them for fraternity rush. I was just trying to get ahead of my classes, to get a jump start.

I was totally *not* avoiding Adam.

And now that the party has moved from the courtyard to the Alpha Sigma house, I'm totally cool! My palms aren't sweating at *all,* and though my swinging legs with my hands tucked under them might make me *appear* nervous, I'm actually completely fine. I'm just sitting on the kitchen counter in the Alpha Sigma house in very close proximity to Adam and I'm not even concerned a little bit.

Totally cool.

Skyler, on the other hand, looks very concerned about the fact that there is a parade of sorority girls around the new transfer everyone is talking about.

I eye him from our vantage point in the kitchen, the steam from Skyler's skin making *me* a little hot in my long-sleeve shirt. It's not hard to see why he's causing a commotion — the kid is hot. His blue eyes are almost as bright as my Big's, his muscles lean and tanned, and his blond hair is tussled in that *maybe I just had sex, maybe I just woke up, maybe I used a ton of hair product to get it this way, but you'll never know* kind of way. He's also sporting a pair of black-framed glasses that, for some odd reason, really do it for me — and apparently every other girl here, too.

Kip Jackson is the new, shiny toy at Palm South University, and also the newest pledge to Alpha Sigma.

And currently, he's being circled like a bucket of chum, and the Zeta girls are the sharks.

"You know, I think I could rock those glasses he has on," I say after a moment, trying to get Skyler to talk about the very obvious elephant in the room. She hasn't been able to get into much of a conversation with me ever since Kip walked into the party, and the way she's staring at him, I know he's gotten under her skin.

"I think he looks ridiculous."

Liar, I think, but I just smirk.

"I love nerds. And do you see his arms? Something tells me he's not just a book reading, chess playing kind of nerd."

I know I'm pushing all the right buttons when Skyler bites her lip, leaning against the kitchen counter with her eyes still fixed on him. "I think you might be reading into this a little too much, Little Nug."

"Maybe," I agree. "But at least I'm not denying his hotness when I'm clearly affected."

Skyler fights against a smile, but in the end, it cracks her face in half like an egg. She snatches a ping pong ball off the counter next to her and tosses it at me. "Shut up."

I laugh, dodging her attack, but my feet keep swinging as I watch her digest her feelings. Suddenly, her eyes widen at a bottle of tequila sitting next to me, and she swipes it from the counter before heading toward the fridge.

"You know what?" she says. "You're right. He is delicious — like a cool slice of key lime pie on a hot summer day. And have you ever known me to turn down key lime pie?"

I laugh, shaking my head. "Nope, never."

"Exactly. Which is precisely why I can't start now. After all, I have a very demanding sweet tooth."

"Right," I agree, tossing her the shaker of salt from behind me. "I mean, you have a reputation to uphold. You can't let other girls go scamming on your pie."

"Indeed." Skyler winks at me, her feet already well on their way to the path toward the new kid. "I'm glad we talked this out, Little Nug. Thanks for being my voice of reason."

"What are Littles for?"

With one last grin in my direction, Skyler turns, her eyes locked on Kip. I can't hear what's said between them, but the next thing I know, the crowd is gathering around the two of them at the foosball table. And I may not know exactly what game they're playing yet, but I know without a doubt that there's no way in hell my Big won't be the one who wins in the end.

The crowd grows around where Kip and Skyler are setting up a game at the foosball table, so I hop down from the counter, making my way toward the commotion. But before I can get too close, the hairs on my arms stand at full attention, a familiar rush of emotion flooding me from head to toe.

I feel his eyes on me before I see them.

Swallowing, I lift my gaze to the table, and standing next to Jess in the center of the action is Adam.

His dark hair is flushed over in a soft wave, like he just ran his hands back through it, and those dark eyes I've been lost in more than once swallow me like a black hole from across the room. His skin is still bronze, though not quite as tan as it was before he left for winter break, and as my eyes roam over the lean muscles of his arms, a flash of our last night together before break hits me like a strike of lightning.

I feel his body, hard and warm, wrapped around me under the sheets that smelled like him. I hear his voice whispering my name, telling me it will all be okay, groaning against the urge to have me the way he wanted to. I see his dark, long lashes on the apples of his cheeks as I peeked my eyes open mid-kiss, his lips still on mine, his hands gripping my hips like he had to hold onto them for dear life so he wouldn't move those hands anywhere else.

We'd given in. He was right about Grayson, about the man I'd trusted with my heart, with my body, but he hadn't taken the opportunity to say *I told you so*. Instead, he'd held me, and kissed me, and cherished me like I was so precious, so fragile, that every move had to be planned and plotted and practiced before he could ever actually make it.

I'd always loved him, and I'd finally admitted it.

But after that amazing night, after he swore he was never letting go of me again, he disappeared.

I hadn't heard from him since.

The room snaps back like a warped rubber band and I take in a sharp breath, inhaling a burning gulp of oxygen with my eyes finding Adam's again. There's a pained bend in his eyebrows, an apology behind his eyes — or perhaps an explanation? He holds my gaze as long as he can, saying more in that silent stretch of time than he did all break.

That's the way it has always been with us — we spoke in longing glances, in soft, seemingly innocent touches, in the quietest of moments. Words could never say what we needed to so we let our actions and our eyes be our voices.

I can't be sure how much time passes as we stand there, staring across the room at one another like there's still some barrier between us, but after a few moments, or maybe a few years, Adam's expression softens.

And he smiles.

That smile, that soft, slow spread of his lips over his mesmerizing face, it's all I need to feel every tight muscle in my body unwind at the same time.

I exhale, smiling in return, the weight on my chest lifted like a cement block turned to a helium balloon in the snap of his fingers. He holds my eyes, that smile still in place, and holds up one finger, letting me know we'll talk when the game is over.

I still feel a slight pressure, the same one I always feel in his proximity, as he holds up the little white ball between Kip and Skyler. He drops it in after a moment, and the game begins.

I should be watching Skyler in her element as she whoops the new guy's butt in a game of foosball, should be laughing and cheering with the rest of the crowd, but I can't take my eyes off Adam. I can't stop the parade of questions storming through me, like his smile released the flood gates I hadn't even noticed were holding so much back.

How was his break? What did he do? Where did he go?

Did he think of me?

What are we now?

Are we anything at all?

It's not until the very last score that I even register what's happening, and I blink back into the moment just in time to see Skyler throw her hands up in victory. I rush to her, Jess and I engulfing her in a group hug at the same time as I finally tear my attention away from Adam — at least, for the moment.

Skyler won — and now, it's time for Kip Jackson to take a shot of tequila and accept his defeat.

"Grab me a knife, will you, Little Nug?" Skyler says, the bottle of tequila and a lime in her hands.

I skip off to the kitchen, returning to find my Big sitting on one of the tables that was just being used for beer pong. There are empty, red Solo cups scattered on the floor all around her, and Kip is just staring at her with one brow cocked in question.

Oh boy, this poor kid has no idea what he's gotten himself into.

Skyler takes the knife from me with a smirk still firmly in place. She slices the lime into four equal wedges, and then like no one else is in the room, she takes Kip's hand and licks the skin between his pointer finger and thumb with her eyes locked on his.

I swear, the guy practically falls to his knees right then and there.

"I said you had to take a shot of tequila if you lost," she says, lying back on the table. "I didn't say you'd get to shoot it out of a shot glass."

She pops one of the lime wedges in her mouth as the room erupts into a fit of cheers, and Kip just stands there with his mouth open. Jess and I start our sorority chant, the guys hooping and hollering as Skyler lifts her shirt up and tucks it under her bra, revealing her tight, toned stomach. She pours the tequila over her exposed skin, the liquid pooling in her navel, and once the bottle is back on the table, all eyes are on Kip.

He seems to be stuck in some sort of spell, standing there over Skyler, and I can't say I blame the poor sucker. I've seen my Big in action, both with Adam and plenty of other guys on campus, and I know how impossible it is for anyone — especially of the male persuasion — to say no to her. When one of his brothers smacks him on the arm, it seems to jolt him back to the moment, and he licks his hand to another roar from the crowd.

Then, his mouth is on Skyler's stomach, sucking up every drop of tequila before he sucks the lime in her mouth and kisses her like they're the only two in the room.

I laugh, cheering again as the crowd starts to disperse. Kip and Skyler continue making out, oblivious to the party still happening around them, and Jess nudges me as she heads toward the kitchen.

"Okay, I think *I* need a shot after that. You in?"

"Right behind ya."

She weaves through the crowd toward the kitchen, me on her heels, but before I can slip through the opening and join her, I feel a strong, warm hand graze my hip.

I close my eyes, that hand grounding me to the spot where I stand, paralyzing me.

His lips graze the back of my neck, his chest pressed against my back as he whispers the first words since the night I spent in his bed.

"Hey there, Red."

I fight against the smile cracking my face in two, spinning with his hand never leaving my hip, and then I'm face to face with the one guy I've always belonged to, yet never truly had.

I shove his shoulder, still smiling. "Don't even start with that," I warn, referring to the stupid nickname that every single person uses for the redheads in their life. He teased me with it the first semester we met, and never fails to use it to get under my skin when he gets the chance.

Adam just grins, his eyes a little glossy from drinking, the chocolate around his pupils shining in the dim light of the party. He swallows, tucking his hands in the pockets of his jeans, and then we stand there — staring, smiling, shaking a little like two middle schoolers who were just dared to do seven minutes in heaven.

After a moment, I laugh, tucking a strand of my wild, fiery hair behind one ear. "How was your break?"

Adam leans in, his brows pinched together as he yells over the music and cheers coming from the game of flip cup taking place behind us. "What?"

"I said, how was your break?" I yell in return.

He smiles, looking around at all the chaos surrounding us before he reaches forward and grabs my hand without a second thought. Adam turns, leading me through the crowd toward the back yard, all the while completely oblivious to the wave of electricity he just sent crashing through me with the touch of his hand.

I stare at his fingers laced with mine as he tugs me through the sea of students, smiling so big my cheeks hurt.

When we finally break through the crowd, Adam drops my hand to open the sliding glass door, and we step outside into the blissfully quiet night.

He shuts the door behind us, muffling the music and laughter from inside, and then it's just the two of us alone on the empty patio.

The night air seems to buzz to life, warm and sticky between us even though it's below fifty now and entirely too cold for any Floridian to be outside. The party rages on inside, but out here, it's just me and Adam.

"There," he says, guiding me over to where a small fire pit is going in the corner of the yard. "Maybe now we can actually hear each other."

"Yeah, it's a little crazy in there."

Adam plops down in one of the chairs around the fire, and I stand, unsure where to sit. Do I take the chair across the fire? The one next to him?

But I don't have time to make the decision before Adam makes it for me, reaching for my hand and pulling me easily down into his lap. He wraps his arms around me, blocking the cool wind, his eyes reflecting the low flicker of the fire.

"Hi," he says.

I let out a long breath, smiling like a fool again. "Hi."

"You're nervous."

"I am," I admit on a soft laugh. "I don't know why."

"It's just me."

"I know, but..." I bite my lower lip, eyes searching his as my stomach drops to my feet. The stinging reminder that he never called, never texted, never said anything to me after the night we spent together resurfaces, and my confidence shakes under the weight of it. "What happened? I never heard from you after... you know, after everything."

Adam's eyes widen, his arms tightening around me. "Oh, God, Cassie. I'm so sorry, I thought that's what you needed. I was just giving you some space," he says quickly.

My eyes fall to my lap, but he thumbs my chin quickly, pulling my gaze back to him.

"I meant every word I said that night," he says, sincerity laced through every word. "I'm here, Cassie, and I'm not going anywhere. I'm not letting go. But, I also don't want to rush things," he adds. "You've been through a lot, and I wanted to give you the time to process all of that."

"So, you don't want to be a rebound," I whisper.

Adam chuckles. "I know I'm not a rebound," he says, running one hand down my arm. He laces his fingers through my own, squeezing. "But, I also know that you've been hurt. Grayson hurt you. It's okay to admit that, and it's okay to take some time to sort through your feelings on all of it."

"I don't need time," I say quickly. "I need you."

"No, you don't."

My heart sinks further, in danger of drowning, but Adam squeezes my hand again.

"Cassie, you don't need me. You don't need anyone, because you're an incredible girl on your own. You're smart — *so* fucking smart — and beautiful, and funny, and charming." He offers me a soft smile. "You're unlike any girl I know. And *that's* why I think it's important for us to take this slow," he says. "Because I want you to take the time you need to remember all of those things, to get back to Cassie McBee."

My heart squeezes, and I smile, tears pooling in my eyes.

He's right.

All break long, instead of thinking about me, about my goals, about the things I want for myself this semester, I just sat around thinking about Adam. As soon as Grayson was gone, I filled that void with Adam, not even taking the time to process what happened, to let myself be hurt, or to stand on my own two feet again.

I was perfectly content crawling on bruised knees into Adam's arms, to let him hold me and lean on him instead of standing on my own first.

The fact that *he* won't let me do that shows me more than anything that he cares about me more than Grayson ever did.

"Don't worry about me right now, because you've got me — I'm right here, and I'm yours. I'm not going anywhere."

I sigh, nodding and leaning into his chest.

"I just missed you," I confess. "But you're right. We should take it slow." I shake my head against his chest. "I mean, Grayson stuff aside, you used to date my Big and she has no idea I even had a crush on you."

"You had a crush on me, huh?" Adam asks, smirking.

I pinch his side. "Shut up. I'm just saying, I should probably talk to her about everything before we make things official, too."

He shifts, pulling me close until my eyes are locked on his again. His hands frame my face, the tips of his fingers brushing back into my hair.

"Hey, don't worry about any of that right now, okay? Skyler will be fine, and you have plenty of time to tell her. Right now, I want you to focus on *you*."

I nod, leaning my forehead against his. My chest is still tight, anxiety gripping my ribcage with force, but I know Adam's right. It's only been a few weeks since my break up with Grayson, since I found out the man I said I loved cheated on me just because I wouldn't *give it up* fast enough.

My stomach turns.

Maybe I wanted to crawl to Adam because I knew it'd be easier, knew his arms would be waiting, and he'd know all the right words to say. I fled to his window that night because I knew he'd be there, just like he was the semester before, when Clay took my virginity and then slept with my roommate.

My dating record sucks.

A sigh flushes an anxious breath from my lips, and I nuzzle into Adam more, aching at the thought of taking thing slow with him when all I want is to lose myself in his warmth.

"Can I still kiss you?" I whisper after a moment.

Adam shakes his head, fingers gripping my hair a little tighter.

"You never have to ask. Kiss me anytime you want, Red."

I laugh, shoving my hands into his chest to push him away but he wraps his arms around me, pulling me in tighter, and then without warning, his lips cover mine.

That kiss steals my next breath, holding it hostage as my hands fist in Adam's hoodie. I tug and tug, wanting him closer, needing more of him — and he gives without question.

He always has.

One hand finds the back of my neck, pulling me into him as the other warms the exposed sliver of skin under the back of my sweatshirt. And he doesn't rush, doesn't devour me, his lips taking their time tasting and kissing and exploring. I'm reminded of the night spent in his sheets, and every nerve in my body begs me to pull him back into his room to relive that night, to take it to the next level.

But I can't.

Because Adam is right, and as much as I want his hands on every inch of my body, I want to feel okay again, more.

I want to stand again, to walk, to run free — on my own.

Then, when the time is right, I'll fall into Adam's arms.

And I know without a doubt that he'll be there to catch me when I do.

Skyler

"THESE SHOES ARE TOO much," I argue with Ashlei, who just wrangled me into a dress and wedges for the first day of class. She's dressed to the nines, of course, but she also has an internship downtown and a reason to be wearing stilettos.

I, however, do not find it at all necessary to wear shoes with a heel when I expect to walk at least a mile.

"Your legs look *killer* in those shoes paired with that dress," she argues, touching up her lipstick. "Please? Just try it. For me."

Turning in the mirror again, I can't say that I disagree with her. My legs are tan from all the paddle boarding time I got in over winter break, and the yellow dress with a simple sweetheart neckline she's dressed me in looks perfect with the wedges. I'm all legs and collarbone and toned arms, and my hair is down and softly curled.

Still, I feel a little overdressed.

"I'm just going to class."

"Yes, but you never know who you might run into."

A flash of the new guy I made out with at the Alpha Sigma house last night hits me, and I smile. *Maybe I'll run into* him.

"Here," Cassie says, popping up from her seat on Jess's bed to hand me the one and only strand of pearls I own. "Add these. They're the perfect accessory."

I do as she says, but it just makes me scrunch my nose up more. "This feels like a lot."

"They're perfect!" Cassie argues, her red hair bobbing a little as she bounces with excitement.

"It's syllabus week, it won't be that long of a day anyway." Ashlei pokes her bottom lip out as she tucks her lipstick back in her bag. "Pleeeease."

I huff. "Fine. But next time I want a drink at Ralph's at ten o'clock on an internship night, you both have to come."

"Deal," they agree in unison.

"Are you heading to your internship now?" I ask Ashlei, packing up my bag.

She shakes her head. "It's a later report for me today, since I don't have to do the orientation that all the new interns will have to do. I'm going to hang out with Erin for a bit and then I'll head downtown."

"I'll probably come back to the house between classes, so I'll see you in a bit."

"Sounds good! See ya later, Legs," she teases, swatting my ass as she skips out of mine and Jess's room. My Little does the same thing, and I laugh, waving them both off before I make my way downstairs.

I'm running late as I hobble-speedwalk across campus to my first class — Writing for Television. Once again, I have an eclectic mix of classes this semester, my feeble attempt to figure out what the hell I'm doing with my life after college.

If I'm being honest with myself, all I really thought about over break was the American Poker Club Tournament. I officially announced my entrance, and even though I haven't fully paid the fee to enter yet, the poker blogs and magazines are already eating it up. I'll be one of the few females in the tournament, and by far the youngest.

But for once — at least, for *now* — they're all talking about how I'm one to beat, not just a hot girl who plays cards, but an actual contender.

It's a step in the right direction, however small.

So, as much as I *do* want to figure out what my next steps are after college, all I've been able to think about is poker.

Well, at least, until the new transfer showed up.

I met Kip Jackson last night at fraternity rush, and about an hour after making fun of his glasses and his name, he was sucking tequila out of my belly button and licking lime juice from my lips.

I smile, biting my lower lip at the memory of that kiss. I'm no stranger to the buzz of a first kiss, of a first night with a guy, but this was different — it was *more*. The moment our lips met, I swear I felt a million bolts of electricity course through me in a smooth, vibrant wave. I'm not even sure how long we made out before he pulled away, but I know it was long enough for me to decide he is *absolutely* my new target for this semester.

I'll have Kip Jackson wrapped around my finger soon enough.

I ended up texting him late last night, thanks to Adam forking over his new pledge's number, but we haven't really talked since then. The ball is in his court. If he wants a date, he'll ask for it.

He better.

I skip into class right after the professor, who tosses his belongings down on his desk and starts writing on the whiteboard. Scanning the classroom, I try to find a place in the back, but sigh when I see all the seats are taken. I'm used to taking classes with at least one sorority sister, having someone to walk into class with and sit with all semester, not to mention, a study buddy. But with this class, I'm on my own.

At least, that's what I think — until I spot Kip a few rows back.

God, he's even sexier than I remember. I decided after I met him that it's not his hair, which is a soft, rugged blond styled messy and casual like I love. And I don't think it's necessarily his lean, toned arms or easy, confident smile that sets him apart, either.

No — it's his eyes. *Definitely* his eyes. They're an electric blue, ocean-like just like mine, and they're framed by black, plastic frames that make them impossible to ignore. Except, he's not wearing those glasses today. Instead, those eyes stand out all on their own, twinkling under the fluorescent light as he watches me from his desk.

I glance at his full lips, that memory of them being pressed against my own sparking to life again. Smirking, I make my way up the steps and slide into the open seat next to him.

"Where's mine?" I ask, eyeing the coffee cup at the corner of his desk.

He follows my gaze to the cup before giving me a smirk of his own. "Sorry, they didn't have tequila. I checked."

"Damn them," I exasperate. "I need to run for Student Council so I can change that."

I don't have time to flirt as much as I'd like, but Kip is still smiling at me when the professor claps his hands together and starts in on his lecture.

I feel a little uneasy being in a classroom full of writers, almost like a poser in some way. The first question Dr. O'Neal asks is, "Why do we write?" It only takes a couple of people being shot down with their attempts at responding to that question for me to know that I have no *chance* of offering any kind of worthy answer.

Kip watches me as I fidget with my pencil, silently begging the professor to move on from this and back to the syllabus. For some reason, I'm completely petrified that he'll decide to call on someone from the class roster or just spot my discomfort and shine it under a spotlight.

It's an unfounded anxiety, I realize, but I can't quiet it.

Luckily, I don't have to, because when Mr. Sexy Four Eyes opens his mouth to give *his* answer, I'm in a complete trance along with the rest of the class and the professor.

"I guess I can't speak for everyone in here," he starts, like he's unsure, though everything about the way he's sitting and speaking screams confidence. His shoulders are back, head high, easy smile in place as he drapes one ankle over the opposite knee. "But I write for a purpose — a purpose that changes each time. Sometimes it's to evoke laughter, sometimes to make people think, sometimes to bring a feeling to life like romance or pain, and always — no matter what the topic — to entertain."

The professor smiles, pointing his marker at Kip with approval before he drones on about something else. I don't even hear it, because I'm too busy staring at Kip's mouth again.

"You kind of have this all figured out, don't you?" I tease.

"I like to think I know what my passions are, yes," he answers, his aqua eyes skirting to mine.

"Passion can be a dangerous thing."

He smiles, turning his attention back to Dr. O'Neal. "What's life without a little danger?"

And just like that, our little game of cat and mouse is back on.

After class, the professor asks Kip to stay back, so I wait for him outside of the Visual Arts Building. I can't help myself

— he's just too delicious *not* to play with. When he emerges from the double doors, he grins at the sight of me, tucking his hands into the pockets of his hunter green shorts.

"You really are stalking me."

I shrug, still leaning casually against the brick of the building. "You should be so lucky, Four Eyes. Speaking of which, where are your specks today?"

"Contacts," he says. "I'm heading to the gym after my last class today, and they don't fare well with sweat."

The image of him sweating, the muscles in his arms bulging as he bench presses more than I weigh makes me chew my cheek.

How long until I can get him in bed with me?

"You're weird," I assess after a moment, because he is — he is truly a strange creature, one I've never experienced at Palm South University. Usually, the guys here fit easily into a box: Jock, Nerd, Frat Daddy, Rock Star Wannabe, Loser, etc. But Kip?

He doesn't fit in. He stands out.

And he owns that shit like a boss.

"You like it," he challenges, to which I just roll my eyes, turning on my heel for Greek Row.

"Skyler!" he calls out after me, and I smile, hiding it before I turn back to face him. "How do you take your coffee? For next week."

"Trying to be a gentleman now?"

He shrugs, and even though it's kind of a lame game to play, I can't resist the chance to toy with him more.

"I only like one thing on the Starbucks menu. You seem to have everything else figured out, let's see if you can guess what it is."

I turn just as another smile threatens to break on my face, and he calls out behind me again.

"Will I see you before then?"

I only offer him a glance over my shoulder, batting my long lashes with a soft shrug.

Who knows, Kip Jackson — maybe you'll see me before then, maybe you won't.

I'm still floating on the Kip Cloud when I make it back to the sorority house, thankful I survived the trek in my wedges. But before I have the time to kick the God-forsaken shoes off my feet, Jess grabs my arm, dragging me through the house.

"Ex just texted us and said to meet in her room ASAP. Sounds important."

"Crisis with Spring Break planning?"

Jess tries not to laugh, but fails. "I'm sure it's something equally as serious, knowing your Big."

I smile, grateful that I'm still at the point in my life where Spring Break is my biggest worry. At least, for now. It won't be long before all I'll be able to think about is the poker tournament, and how much is riding on it.

I love PSU, and I'm next in line to be president of Kappa Kappa Beta.

But in order for that to happen, I have to be able to *stay* at Palm South.

And in order for *that* to happen, I have to win this tournament.

No pressure.

Erin

WHAT THE HELL IS *this feeling?*

That's all I can think while I wait for the girls to get to my room.

My chest is prickly, like the air inside my lungs is electric, sending little waves of static through every breath. I can't stop smiling, and there's almost a little... dance? Skip? In every step I take. I know I've felt this feeling before, yet it's foreign and confusing, like my body forgot how to feel it and thus is having a hard time computing.

Is this... excitement? Hope? *Both?*

I smile, shaking my head against my own giddiness.

Calm down, Erin.

But how can I?

Kip Jackson is at Palm South University.

Kip Jackson — my first love, perhaps the *only* boy I've ever loved. Kip Jackson — the one I've wanted to lean on ever since we broke up, the one who always rushes back to my mind when the emotions get to be too much.

I lost him, and I've never forgiven myself for it. He's the best guy I've ever dated, and yet, I thought he was destined to be the one who got away.

But now, I finally have my second chance.

Because Kip Jackson is at Palm South University.

Ashlei and Cassie fly through my door first, Cassie hopping up on my bed as Ashlei tries as delicately as she can to sit in my bean bag chair.

"What's going on, Ex?" she asks, but I just pull up my desk chair to form a semi-circle.

"Let's wait until the other girls get here."

As if on cue, Jess pounces through my door next, taking the spot on my bed next to Cassie. Skyler is the last to join us, and she shuts my door behind her, kicking off her wedges before plopping down on the floor to complete our circle.

In a dress.

"Ew, put your snatch away, Little," I tease.

Jess throws a pillow at Skyler from where she sits on the bed, and my Little glances down at her exposed thong as a blush shades her cheeks.

"Did you just call my treasure box a snatch?"

"Did you just call it a treasure box?" Cassie counters.

"Would you prefer I say vagasaurus? That's my personal favorite nickname," Skyler says matter-of-factly, tucking the pillow Jess threw into her lap to shield her underwear from view.

The girls all chuckle, though Jess looks appalled.

"Do you really call it that?" she asks Skyler.

"Among many other things, yes."

"Like what?" Jess pokes, her brows still pinched together in a mixture of curiosity and disgust.

"I don't know... hoohah, muffin, pink canoe."

"Juice box, kitty, hot pocket," Cassie adds.

Ashlei sits up a little straighter, running her hands over her tight pencil skirt before chiming in. "Tampon tamer, magic bean, cubby hole. I heard someone call it a finger hut once. My personal favorite is vajayjay."

"Oh! That's another one I use frequently, Lei. Nice."

Skyler practically air-high-fives Ashlei from across the room, and what started off as a fun joke suddenly starts to annoy me. The skin on my neck tingles, and my left leg bounces where it rests over my right one.

Don't they realize we have more important things to discuss?

"I seriously have never used any of these," Jess says. "I say vagina. Or occasionally I get a little *Jersey Shore* and say co-cah."

"Or cho-cha like Missy Elliot?" Skyler asks.

"Yes!" Jess and Cassie say in unison, and then everyone explodes into another fit of laughter — me included.

"Can we stop talking about penis fly traps for like two seconds?" I finally say, but I can't deny that it feels good to laugh.

When was the last time I did?

"This is serious!" I add for good measure, but my straight face cracks into another smile which just makes all the girls laugh harder. Snatching a handful of highlighters off my desk, I peg each one of them with a different color to a chorus of more laughter.

Finally, Jess wipes tears from her eyes, settling the room. "Okay, Ex, what's going on?"

I exhale long and slow, folding my hands in my lap and sitting up straighter. Time to get down to business.

"Did I ever tell you guys about the summer before my senior year of high school?"

My Grand-Little stops digging around for snacks in my bedside table long enough to answer. "Isn't that the summer you spent with your grandparents?"

"Yes. It was the summer I wanted to find myself, that I wanted to sort of break free from everything I thought I was."

I close my eyes briefly, smiling a little at the memory of that summer — the Kansas wheat fields, the hot sun, the constant breeze that ruffled Kip's blond hair. I can still feel the way his calloused hands fit in mine after long days on harvest, can still smell the country air as we passed long nights on a blanket under the stars behind my grandparents' house.

"I had just ended a two-year relationship," I continue. "And I was in a strange place." My voice fades as I realize how tough I thought *that* time in my life had been...

If only I would have known what was still to happen to me in the future.

I shake my head. "Well, I met a boy that summer..."

"Oh!" Ashlei says, snapping her fingers. "I remember the story! He was the Army brat, right?"

"He wasn't a *brat,* you brat," I say, narrowing my eyes at her as I fight back a smile. "But yes, he did live on the base by my grandparents' house. He was amazing — everything I needed that summer. We spent practically every night together and as cliché as it sounds, I fell in love with him." I smile. "Well, as in love as I could be at that age. It was the perfect summer romance."

I'm still kind of lost in my memory when Skyler's voice breaks through the fog.

"Not that this isn't romantic and touching, but is there a reason you're telling us this?"

Standing, I let the warm light within me beam through. "You are not going to believe this," I say. "The boy I met that summer? He's *here*... like here, as in he's a student at Palm South!"

"What?" Ashlei pops up. "Isn't that impossible? We know pretty much everyone on this campus."

"Not the new students," I point out, waiting for them to catch on. When they don't, I sigh. "He's a *transfer!*"

My chest prickles with those damn bolts of electricity again, and I press a hand to the center of it, smiling.

"He just moved here. I heard Adam talking about his new pledges this morning outside of the Greek library and I just kind of casually asked about him — where he was from, what he was like — it's definitely him, girls!"

Ashlei's face lights up, but the room is quiet for me having just dropped such exciting news. Provided, I was *possibly* being a little dramatic about the whole thing, but it's been so long since I've been excited about — well, *anything* — that I kind of expected a little more gusto in the reaction to my news.

For some reason, Jess and Cassie are watching Skyler, who looks like she's about to throw up.

"What?" Ashlei asks before I can. "Why are you guys acting so weird?"

"Nothing," Skyler says quickly. "We know him. Well, we met him. Last night."

"At rush?!" I ask excitedly. My stomach flips at the thought of seeing him again, of just *casually* running into him with the girls.

"Oh my God, Kip? Is that you? How's it going? Oh, have you met our president, Erin Xanders? Oh, you HAVE?"

Skyler nods. "Yep. He was nice."

"That's one way to put it, Sky," Jess adds, snickering. She nudges Cassie, like there's some sort of inside joke under those words, but Cassie just coughs uncomfortably.

What the hell?

"Okay, what the hell happened, Little?" I ask, turning on Skyler.

She groans, face flopping into the pillow in her lap. Her next words are muffled through it. "Nothing. We played foosball."

"And he lost, so she made him take a shot of tequila..." Jess says.

My anxiety eases a little. So they met, and maybe they flirted a bit. Doesn't surprise me that my Little had the new kid taking a shot of tequila to welcome him to PSU.

But then Jess continues, and my stomach sinks with her words.

"...Off her body."

The first thought through my head is *school your features*. If I learned anything from my mother over last summer, it was that ninety-five percent of a woman's power comes from how well she responds to potentially emotional situations. *Think like a man,* she'd put it — though I like to think it's more thinking like a *woman* — a strong, logical woman not ruled by her emotions.

So, even though the thought of Kip running his tongue over my Little's stomach makes me want to punch her in the nose and then run off crying, I simply take a breath, and start thinking.

"Oh," I say first, as calmly as I can. I need something to do with my hands, so I walk toward my closet, running my fingers over the different Lily Pulitzer dresses inside. "Well, that's okay. I mean, you didn't know. How could you?"

And though those words shake as they leave my lips, they're true. Skyler wouldn't hurt me, and she definitely wouldn't have a guy I'm still obsessed over take a body shot off her.

Still, jealousy is an evil bitch, and she's got her claws in me deep now.

All I can think about is him touching her, and her touching him, and both of them smiling and laughing and... *God,* what if he liked it?

What if he likes *her*?

"I swear I didn't, Big," Skyler says. "You know I wouldn't have done it if I had known."

"No, no, it's okay," I say deftly, because now my wheels are turning over that last thought.

What if he likes her?

What if he likes her?

And just like that, an idea snaps into place like the last piece of a puzzle.

What. If. He. Likes. *Her.*

"Actually," I say, turning to face them all again as hope finds me. "No — this is good. This is perfect."

"Um, how is this even remotely in the same category as good?" Cassie asks.

I dart to the planner on my desk, flipping it open as I try my best to explain. The idea is a little crazy, but crazy just might work.

"Well, Kip and I didn't exactly have the best ending that summer. I may have acted a little immature, at best," I admit, thinking of how I would look through his phone, letting my jealousy get the better of me until I blew up on him.

I was young, emotional, naïve — I didn't know what I had until I lost it.

Finding the date I was looking for, I tap the highlighted event, spinning to face the girls again.

"This is perfect. I don't think he would want to talk to me, let alone get back together right now. I need him to come around more, to see how I've grown and how respected I am here. I want him to see that four years has done me well."

"Absolutely! You're the shit," Jess says, but she still looks concerned. "But, I'm lost on how this has anything to do with your Little having lover boy's tongue in her mouth."

Skyler groans, stuffing her head back into the pillow while I try again not to give into my urge to scratch her eyes out for so much as *looking* at Kip.

What the hell is wrong with me?

"Because," I say, calm again, my features smooth. I carefully take a seat on the floor in front of Skyler, knowing before I say the words how insane my little idea is. "She's going to be the one to get him to come back to me. She's the bait."

Skyler's head snaps up, her wide, blue eyes meeting mine.

"*What?* No way!" She jumps up from the floor, tossing the pillow she's been hiding behind on the bed. "I mistakenly made out with your high school... whatever he was, but I'm not involved in this."

I pop up, ready to plead my case. "You are now! He knows you now," I argue. "He's obviously interested, and you're the best shot I have at getting him to hang around me in a natural way without it looking like I'm insane. Or a creeper. Or both."

It's true. I had pulled the girls together to think of ways for me to get him back, to work out a plan. Though this isn't *exactly* how I pictured things going down, it just might be crazy enough to work.

"Big, you can't be serious," Skyler says. "What am I supposed to do... woo him? Flirt him into following me around like a puppy and then blow him off so you can pick up the pieces?"

I pause, digesting her suggestion. "I hadn't thought it out quite that far, but yes."

"No," Skyler says immediately, tossing her hands up. "I'm leaving this room and we can just pretend like last night and this conversation didn't happen."

She turns to leave, and like an out-of-body-experience, I watch in horror from the corner of the room as the next words leave my mouth.

"You want to be president next year, don't you?"

It's like all the air is sucked out of the room with that question. Skyler is stiff as a rod, and when I come to, back in my own body again, Jess is the first person I hear.

"Ex," she warns. She's telling me to back off, that I've gone too far, but she doesn't understand.

No one understands.

This is the only speck of joy I've managed to find since I was violated in the worst possible way a woman can be. It's been almost a year since it happened, and I still exist in a dark hole of nothingness, where the thought of being happy again feels so ludicrous I don't even allow myself to consider it.

But then, Kip showed up at Palm South University.

I won't let this chance pass me by.

"No, I'm serious," I say. "You have to make a lot of sacrifices as president, Little. You have to do a lot of stuff you really don't want to do. This position is not for the weak or the scared or the selfish."

The irony of that last sentence isn't lost on me, considering I *was* weak, I *am* scared, and right now, I'm also proving to be very, very selfish.

"You want to be next in line?" I ask her. "It's time to start proving you can take it, that you belong in this room when I leave. You need to step up, Little."

And just like that, I become the villain I never knew I could be.

Skyler's face crumples, but she nods. "Can I at least think about it?"

Thinking back to my original plan, I glance at the date still highlighted in the open planner on my desk. "I tell you what, the date auction is Saturday. Let's see if you made the impression I think you did. If he bids the highest and wins the date with you, then the game starts and you play him right into my hand."

"I have a tournament that night, Big," she complains. "I wasn't even going to go to the auction."

"Well, now you are going — and you're getting auctioned off. If he bids the highest, then you're doing this." My words are absolute — final.

"And if he doesn't?" she asks.

I shrug, confident enough in my assessment that I won't have to worry about that possibility. "Then you're off the hook. I want it to be easy for you to get him to come around, and bidding the highest at a date auction is pretty much the most simple way to get a girl on a date. If he doesn't try and succeed to do just that with you, then there's no point in you making it awkward and throwing yourself at him. But," I counter. "If he dragged his tongue up your stomach, I seriously doubt he'll let you go on a date with anyone else."

It's my attempt at a joke, to lighten the mood, but Skyler doesn't crack so much as a small smile.

Can I blame her? This is possibly *the* worst thing I've done in my life... and that's saying something, considering my actions after I slept with Clinton.

"Fine," Skyler concedes. "But if he doesn't make the highest bid, then I'm off the hook and you're on your own to reel in your fish."

Hope floods me again. *She's actually going to help!*

Well, not that I actually gave her an option, but whatever.

"Absolutely, no questions asked." I hold out my hand to shake Skyler's, and when the deal is sealed, I can't help the excitement that pours through me like liquid gold. I turn back to the other girls, practically squealing. "This is going to be fun!"

But even as I say the words, I know in my heart that this is going to be anything but fun for Skyler.

Her face falls again as she leaves the room, and I silently vow to make it up to her.

I owe you one, Little.

Ashlei

A COUPLE HOURS AFTER Erin's emergency meeting, I'm swinging through the doors to one of the tallest buildings downtown with the biggest smile on my face. The *click clack* of my stilettos on the marble floor of the lobby comfort me, a calm, soothing sense of home washing over me as I make my way toward the elevator. That elevator will take me all the way up to the thirty-second floor, back to *Okay, Cool*, back to a place where I feel confident and respected, back to opportunity.

And back to Brandon Church.

A shallow breath fills my lungs as I press a hand to my stomach at the thought of him. I run my fingers over the buttons on my rose-pink blouse, biting my lower lip against the smile threatening to break on my face. When the elevator doors open, I step inside confidently, a blush creeping over my cheeks at the memory of my first time inside it.

That was the day I met Brandon Church.

That was the day everything changed.

I sigh, giving into my smile as the doors start to close, but just like last semester, a hand darts in to stop them.

Only this one isn't the strong, dark hand of the CEO who makes my panties drip with want. It's a lighter hand, more feminine and delicate, with long, shiny, black pointy nails.

The silver doors open again, and the last person I expect to see greets me with a wicked smile.

"Hello, Ashlei."

"Kimberly," I manage as a response, straightening

as she steps onto the elevator with me. I wait for her to choose a different floor, to explain what the hell she's doing back in this building, but she simply smiles wider at my apparent confusion.

Kimberly Marks was an intern with me last semester, and it was no secret that she absolutely hated me. She started rumors about me and Brandon, and although they weren't completely *un*true, they also had no proof to back them up. Most of the associates couldn't stand Kimberly — me included.

So then *why* was she on her way back to *Okay, Cool* with me?

Kimberly had cut her hair since I'd last seen her, the long, brown locks of curls chopped high and tight into a masculine fade. It accents her high cheek bones and slender nose even more, and leaves her slender collarbone exposed in her simple, scoop-neck, black dress. Her heels are a matte black, too, making her entire appearance dark and commanding.

She's taller than me by several inches, even though my heels are higher than hers, and she seems to take pride in the way she gets to look down her nose at me to answer the questions I haven't even asked aloud.

"What?" she asks, one thin, dark eyebrow raised in pity. "Did you think you were the only intern they invited back for another semester?" She clucks her tongue, turning back toward the elevator doors. "They asked me to come back, too — and unlike you, *I* wasn't asked to extend because of the quality of my blow jobs."

The corner of her red-stained lips quirks up at her little comment, and though my first instinct is to shove my stiletto heel up her ass, I simply smile back in a *bless your heart* kind of way, just like Mom always taught me.

"Well, congratulations, Kimberly. I look forward to working with you again," I lie through my teeth. And just as the elevator dings, letting us know we hit the thirty-second floor, I step forward, making sure she understands her place *behind* me. "And thank you for the compliment on my skillset. It's *so nice* to have the support of another professional, mature businesswoman."

As the doors slide open, Kimberly steps up right behind me, her next threat hot on the skin of my neck.

"You were the top intern last semester, Daniels, but it should have been me. And now that I've been invited back for a second chance to prove that, you better believe I'll do whatever it takes. I'm on to you," she seethes. "So watch yourself, because I'm not backing down, and I won't be overshadowed by the office slut again this semester."

Her words sting, even though I try not to give them power. Still, I don't offer her so much as another glance, let alone more of my time. I simply *click* and *clack* my way off that elevator and back into the place that feels like home — and I don't bother holding the door open for her on my way in.

"ASHLEI!"

Mykayla throws her arms around me as soon as I make it inside, her ginormous breasts pressing against my stomach as she nuzzles into me.

"I'm so, *so* happy you're back. I've missed you so much! How was your break? How's the sorority? I love that skirt on you, and oh, my God, you're so *tan*."

I chuckle, pulling back from our embrace with a smile that mirrors hers. "I'm happy to see you, too, Mykayla."

Kimberly slinks by behind us, narrowing her eyes at me and Mykayla as she makes her way to our section of cubicles. Mykayla notices the ugly look and scoffs, pointing her thumb over her shoulder at where Kimberly's back just disappeared around the corner.

"What the hell? What is *she* doing back here?"

"Hell if I know," I say on a sigh. "She seems pretty fixated on my demise, though."

Mykayla snorts, rounding the welcome counter back to her chair and plopping down. She hands me my new name tag and office key fob with a gentle roll of her eyes. "Whatever. She's peanut butter and jealous — has been since the moment she met you. Anyway, the other interns are almost finished in their morning orientation and then we'll all break for lunch. Sit with me? Let's catch up before the afternoon briefing!"

"You got it. I think I'll walk around, say hi to everyone before then," I say, pulse ticking up speed as I glance down the hall at Brandon's office. The door is cracked, just enough for me to see his strong hand clicking away at his keyboard inside.

"Perfect. Holly should be back by the internship cubes already, if you want to start with her."

I nod, knowing my manager's desk *should* be the first place I stop, but ever since the last time Brandon's hands splayed the small of my back, since the night I ditched my own formal and opted for him plowing me over the side of his desk, instead — he's all I've been able to think about.

He said it was the last time he'd be able to touch me. He swore we'd have to behave ourselves, that we couldn't see each other again — not like that.

But it was like telling a bird not to fly, or urging the wind not to blow — impossible, ridiculous, and absolutely futile.

I would have Brandon Church again. Of that, I was sure.

"I'll make my way back there in a moment," I finally say, my eyes still on his office door. "Figure I might as well say hi to Mr. Church while I'm out this way."

Mykayla follows my gaze, shrugging. "Sure. He's been locked in there all day, I'm sure he'd be happy for a break and a chance to welcome you back." She smiles up at me, completely oblivious — *thank God*. "See you at lunch!"

Then, she gets right back to work like I'm no longer standing there, her little smile in place as she files through a massive stack of paper on her desk.

My throat is dry and sticky, my ability to swallow temporarily thwarted as I slowly make my way back to Brandon's office. Each step has my heart beating a little faster, and my hands do anything but stay at my sides — they slide over my long, slick pony tail, smooth down the sides of my pencil skirt, fidget with my necklace. By the time I make it to his door, my knuckles softly rapping on the sleek, cool metal, I'm not sure if I want to smile, dance, or throw up.

"Come in," Brandon says without looking up from his monitor.

I wedge my hip between the door and the glass of his office window, leaning against the silver pane and crossing my arms casually over my middle. "Good afternoon, Mr. Church."

His hands stop, his eyes still locked on his screen. I watch his face, searching for a sign of recognition, of delight, of want — of *anything*, but he keeps all of his features completely schooled. His fingers go back to typing, only the slightest tick in his dark, strong jaw letting me know he registered my words at all.

"Miss Daniels," he says calmly. "Nice to have you back. How was your winter break?"

"Uneventful," I say, lowering my voice a little. "I was pretty sore, after all the *dancing* I did the night of my formal. Spent a lot of time recovering from that."

There it is, I think, noting the slight twitch at the corner of Brandon's mouth. He wants to smile, wants to tease me back, but he doesn't. Instead, he clears his throat, keeping his eyes glued to his screen.

"Well, we're glad to have you back at *Okay, Cool.* I have to finish this report, but I'll see you at the briefing later?"

"Are you sure I can't help with your report?" I ask, voice seductive and laced with intention.

In the next second, I feel like a foolish little girl, because Brandon huffs, shaking his head as he pounds on the keys harder.

"No, Miss Daniels, you can't help. This is a report being crafted by the CEO, it's not exactly internship busy work material."

I snap back at the briskness of his tone, standing straight as shame shades my cheeks.

"Right. Of course. I didn't mean to... I apologize, Mr. Church."

He gives a curt nod. "No need to apologize. Have a good afternoon."

My heart deflates like a sad, whining balloon. Brandon still won't look at me, and though I knew he was serious when he said he wouldn't be touching me again, the bigger part of me assumed that was just a cover — a way for him to say he *tried* to stay away from me once he finally gave in.

Judging by the way he won't even look at me now, I realize I was wrong. He didn't say those words last semester as a tease, or a joke, or a challenge.

He meant what he said, and for the first time in my life, I wish a man would have lied to me.

"You, too," I say softly, dejected.

My heart beats too loudly in my ears as I shuffle my way back to the internship cubicles, my heels clicking along the marble once more.

But now, the sound doesn't bring me comfort.

It just breaks my heart.

Bear

"I KNOW IT'S UPSETTING, but remember how you got here in the first place," Alec says to a full, groaning chapter room on Friday night. He holds up his hands to try to silent my brothers, but it's a futile attempt. Everyone is already anxious to get out to the bars, being that it's our first weekend since rush, but with Alec's news, that anxiousness turns more to anger.

Alec is the most hated alumni of Omega Chi Beta, mostly because he was the one to deliver us our asses on a silver platter last year in the form of a chapter suspension. And with the news he just delivered, his reputation isn't getting any better.

Because even after minding our Ps and Qs last fall, we're *still* suspended.

And my brothers are pissed.

After a semester of good deeds, we all thought we'd be back in action this year. But it turns out one semester doesn't undo years of getting ourselves into trouble, and honestly, I can't say I'm surprised.

"Look," Alec says louder, calming the room. "You guys did great in the fall. Your philanthropic efforts were spot on, and you stayed out of trouble once the suspension was put into place. I know another semester feels like a lifetime, but if you can hold it together, you'll be back to full status next fall."

The room erupts in groans again, and I'm secretly thankful that our first chapter doesn't include any of the new guys who decided to pledge Omega Chi. They'd be changing their minds real quick if they saw us right now.

"What about the seniors?" one brother asks above the rest.

"Yeah, what about Spring Break?"

That causes another unified growl of disapproval, and Alec looks a little sorry then, scanning the faces of the other alumni advisors behind him. One of them says something to him that none of us can hear over all our brothers bitching and moaning, and Alec comes back to the mic with his hands up again.

"I'll try my best to get you permission for Spring Break, but even if you *can* do something as a chapter, it will most likely have to be with another fraternity, too." Alec kills the protests to that before they can even start. "OR, you can not go at all, the choice will be yours — *if* I can convince nationals that you deserve a Spring Break."

We all pack up our shit in relative silence when chapter ends, a solemn disappointment settling over all of us. The Omega Chi Beta brothers were the top fraternity on campus, until our suspension, and now we're quickly being replaced — or at least rivaled — by Alpha Sigma. My brothers hate it, and so do I, but there's not much we can do.

"This fucking blows," my Little, Josh, says as we push through the chapter doors and out into the cool night air. It's our first chapter, less than a week of classes under our belt in the new semester, and now that rush is over, there's not much for us to look forward to.

"It'll be alright," I assure him, adjusting my book bag on my shoulder. "We'll just have to party off campus or at other frat houses like we did last year."

"Oh yeah, let's just continue to go to Alpha Sigma parties and help them elevate their status above ours. Sounds great."

"Better than not partying at all, am I right?"

Josh frowns, not happy about that point. He runs a hand over his curly, ginger hair, a frustrated sigh leaving his lips.

"Whatever. I just hope we get to go on Spring Break."

"I think Alec is actually in our corner this semester," I say. "Let's just hope nationals will listen to him."

"We'll find out."

Josh looks at me, taking in my haggard appearance. I know I look haggard, because I slept half the day away and woke up just in time to throw on business slacks and a button up for chapter. It was my first chance to catch up on rest since last semester ended, after spending winter break up in Pittsburgh helping my little brother, Clayton, find a part-time job.

"You need to get laid," Josh says when we turn onto Greek Row.

I chuckle. "I don't think I have the energy to fuck anyone right now."

"Well, you better take a nap and find some. And fast. Because you look like shit."

"Thanks, Little."

"I'm serious," he continues, unapologetically. "You spent your entire winter break helping out your fam, which is admirable, man, and I think it's awesome that you're there for your little bro. But seriously dude, you're Clinton Pennington. You're M.O. is weightlifting, partying, and fucking — and I haven't seen you do much of any of that in a while."

I frown, considering his assessment. With Omega Chi being suspended, I have toned down on the partying, and after the little stunt I pulled with Shawna in front of Lacey last semester, I'm not getting any tail from her anymore.

The combination of worrying about my brother and feeling sick over treating Skyler like shit had me sitting in my room playing video games more than lifting weights at the end of last semester.

In a way, I guess you could say I'd let myself go.

"I'm just in a funk," I finally say. "I'll be fine."

"Here," Josh says, thumbing out a text on his phone. Mine pings in the next instant. "I just sent you an invite for this dating app everyone is talking about. It's exclusive to PSU, and it's literally like shopping for a fuck buddy. You just swipe right on a girl's picture if you're interested, and swipe left if you're not. If you match, then you can see their phone number and they can see yours. It's up to one of you to make a move then."

"Sounds creepy."

"It's efficient," he argues. "And I've already fucked three girls this week."

I raise my brows, and as sad as it is, he has my attention.

"I'll think about it."

Josh opens the door to our house, letting me in first before he holds up his phone again. "Don't think about it, do it. Seriously, Bear. You spend so much time taking care of everyone else — the fraternity, your family — but what you *need* to spend some time doing is getting your dick wet."

"That almost sounded sincere."

Josh just shrugs. "Hey, I'm nothing if not honest. Download the app. And come out to the Kappa Kappa Beta date auction tonight. You need to get out of your room."

He doesn't give me a chance to respond before he's jogging up the stairs to his room.

I sigh when I'm inside my own room down the hall, dropping my bag at the door and taking in the small space. It's the same room I've had since I joined Omega Chi, same bedspread, same décor. The same gaming system rests underneath the same TV, the same paddle with the same letters hanging above my bed.

So much in that room is exactly the same as it was the day I moved in, and yet the man who sleeps inside it every night couldn't be further from the boy he was that day.

I flop down on my bed, eyes on the ceiling as my Little's words play on repeat in my head.

In a way, he's right.

I can't help but take care of the people around me, it's just who I am. Between my brothers and my family, I haven't had energy for much else. Add in the fact that Erin *still* won't let me in to talk about what happened last year, and you could say the amount of space left in my energy tank for dating is pretty nonexistent.

But as much as I want to blame it on time and energy, the truth of why I've avoided anyone other than Lacy hovers over me like a blinking neon sign.

I'm not over Shawna.

Just bringing her memory to mind makes my chest tighten, and I roll on my side, staring at my phone on the bedside table.

Have I even *tried* to get over her? To forget her?

I know that answer before I even ask the question, but it doesn't make it hurt any less.

I don't do feelings. Before Shawna, the most a girl had ever gotten out of me was more than one night in my bed. But *after* her? Well, no girl had a shot in *hell* of getting anything at all from me. Lacy had been there, sure — but as a distraction, as a mutual understanding. We didn't talk, didn't hang out, didn't go on dates. We banged, and then she left. The end.

But I'd ruined that.

Huffing, I swipe my phone off the table, opening up Josh's text and clicking the link inside it.

I don't know if I'm ready for dating, or even finding a fuck buddy, but I decide to give it a shot, anyway.

My brother is fine — he's got a job now and still has plenty of cash leftover from the generous gift Skyler gave him last semester. My brothers are stuck on suspension, and there's nothing more I can do about that right now. And Erin? Well, she doesn't want my help — no matter how much I want to give it.

It's a new semester, a new year, and maybe it's time I get back to basics — back to Bear.

So, I make a new gym plan, order some protein powder online, and then I download the stupid motherfucking app and start swiping.

Adam

IT HAS NEVER BEEN so difficult to keep my damn hands to myself.

The Kappa Kappa Beta Date Auction will always remind me of Cassie, no matter what, because I can't help but think back to her first year when she was auctioned off. She was so shy and timid, so scared, so completely oblivious to the fact that she is seriously sexy and adorable and way too intelligent for any of the poor suckers here at PSU.

And now, watching her from the crowd while she scurries around Ralph's, helping Erin and the MC, Chelsea, with whatever they need, I practically have to sit on my hands to keep from rushing to her. All I want to do is shove her behind the stage curtains, hike one leg up, and slide my fingers under the tiny skirt she's wearing to find out what kind of panties are underneath it. Are they lace? Cotton? A thong or boy shorts?

Is she even wearing any at all?

I groan out loud at that possibility, which has Jeremy's eyes following mine to where Cassie is looking over a clipboard with her Grand Big.

He whistles, nudging my elbow with his. "Damn. Cassie's looking good tonight." He takes a tentative sip of his beer, watching me out of the corner of his eye. "Don't you think?"

"Shut up, Jeremy."

He chuckles. "Come on, man. You're watching her like you're something between a lovesick puppy and a possessive, ravenous bear that hasn't eaten since it went into hibernation."

I sigh, eyebrows lifting at the surprising accurateness of his assessment.

"Are you guys dating now or what?"

"Or what," I answer, taking a drink from my own bottle.

"What the hell is stopping you now? She's single, *you're* single, you both want to bang each other or eat the other's face off, depending on how you decipher those weird looks you give each other across the room. What's the issue?"

"There's no issue," I defend. "We're not together, but we're not *not* together either."

"Then what the fuck are you?"

"Complicated," I murmur, taking another drink.

Jeremy watches with me as Cassie scans the room, looking for something. She glances past us before doubling back, and when our eyes lock, a slow, dazzling smile spreads on her strawberry-pink lips. She waves, tucking a strand of her curly hair behind one ear, and I tip my bottle toward her in greeting with the same stupid grin on my face.

"She wants to fuck," Jeremy says, and I punch him hard in the chest. He bends with an *oof*, but just laughs it off. "I mean seriously, dude. Did you see her all playing with her hair and eye-fucking you from across the room? What is so complicated about that?"

"Look," I say with a sigh, pointing my bottle in his face. "Every single guy at PSU who has gone after Cassie has had one thing on their mind — getting in her pants. Clay took her virginity, and then embarrassed her in front of the entire Greek system by showing up to the end of the semester party with her *roommate*. Then," I say hurriedly, cutting off Jeremy's attempt to argue with me. "She falls in love with our closest thing to a campus rock star, and he swoons her out of her panties with his bullshit sensitivity and acoustic guitar, and she finds out he was cheating on her with some groupie the entire time."

Jeremy opens his mouth again, but I shake my head.

"I have wanted Cassie longer than I was even able to admit to myself, and yes, while all the doors are open right now, I also don't want to be just another guy on the long list of ones who have disappointed her. So, while I desperately want to sleep with her, I respect her more than that, and I know she needs some time to figure shit out after what happened last semester."

I swallow, thinking back to how hard Cassie cried in my arms that night she crawled through my window. I'll be damned if I'm ever the reason for tears like that.

"She's the most incredible girl I've ever known, Jeremy. I've fucked up in the past, lost her when I had the chance to have her, hurt her when all I wanted was to heal her. Now that we're both single, I have the chance to do this right. So, I'm moving slow, and I'm giving her space to find herself again before she finds who she is with me."

Jeremy half-smiles, his expression something between pity and understanding. "I get it, dude. And it's admirable. I don't envy you or your blue balls," he adds quickly. "But, I get it."

I nod, taking a longer pull from my beer before Chelsea takes the stage again, ready to auction off the next KKB sister.

She starts by talking about the philanthropy again, and as she reads off statistics of the past few years with how much their fundraising has helped the local chapter, I think over what I just said to Jeremy, memories of my talk with my aunt over the break still loud in my head.

"A good woman is worth waiting for," she'd told me after I'd spilled out my heart. My aunt was like a mother to me, just like my grandfather had been like a dad. Now that he was gone, she was all I had, and she'd listened patiently as I'd told her everything about Cassie.

It made sense, what she said, about Cassie needing to find herself again. I knew what it was like to emerge on the other end of a break up wondering who you even were without the person who'd been the other half of your life for so long. I'd felt it when I broke up with Skyler, and even more so when I'd split from my long-time high school girlfriend before coming to PSU.

It's tricky, navigating the waters post-relationship, and while I want nothing more than for Cassie to dive straight into me, I know she needs some space, some time to remember how to swim again. I don't want her to drown *in* me — I want her to thrive *with* me.

A loud roar from the crowd snaps me back to the present moment, and when my eyes find Skyler in a bright pink dress on stage, I can't help but laugh and cheer with them.

She looks wildly uncomfortable in that dress, but her confident *I'm Skyler Fucking Thorne* face is firmly in place, and more cat calls and whistles ring out as she does a little spin for the crowd. I'm surprised they convinced her to even participate in the auction, but it was a good call on their part — Skyler would easily be their biggest moneymaker.

After she lists off some of Skyler's "selling points," Chelsea starts the bidding at fifty bucks.

The first paddle belongs to Josh, Clinton's Little in Omega Chi Beta, and I roll my eyes. That kid has had a crush on Skyler since the beginning of time. He's also had absolutely zero chance of ever getting her on a date.

When Chelsea calls for one-hundred dollars, I put my own paddle up.

Skyler's eyes widen, but when she realizes it's me, she shakes her head, pointing at me with a smile. I just shrug. Hey, the least I can do is *try* to save her from the literal last person she would want to win her.

When he bids two-hundred, I shove my paddle up one more time to outbid him, someone in the back outbidding me next, and then it's back to Josh at four-hundred.

Too rich for my blood.

I bow out, throwing my hands up in surrender. Though Skyler and I discovered very quickly that we're much better as friends than anything else, I still love her — more like a sister, I suppose. I did my best to save her from having to go on a date with Clinton's beefhead little brother, but she might be screwed.

Suddenly, someone calls out from the back, and I turn to find one of our new pledges — Kip Jackson — holding up his beer as he becomes the new highest bidder at five-hundred dollars.

"Damn it, Kip," I murmur under my breath.

Jeremy turns, laughing when he sees Kip climbing up onto the bar. Josh bid it up to six-hundred dollars, but Kip swiftly defeats him when he thrusts his arm up again and bids one-thousand.

"Why do you look so upset?" Jeremy asks, cheersing Kip from afar as the bar erupts into cheers. "That's a lot of money to charity."

"He's a pledge," I remind Jeremy. "He should be laying low, learning the ropes before he's thrusting himself into the spotlight like that."

"Oh, come on." Jeremy scoffs. "He's a junior, not a freshmen like most pledges. And I like him. He's got guts. Reminds me of you when you first joined."

I grimace at the comparison, though I can't figure out exactly why. I'm the one who recruited Kip, who wanted him to rush Alpha Sigma. But along the way, I learned he's a little pretentious, and while Jeremy might see his attitude as *enthusiasm,* I saw it as him not knowing his place.

Ugh. I sound like Clay.

Thinking back to the douchebag who was president when I was trying to make strides for Alpha Sigma makes my lip curl even more, especially after what he did to Cassie. I don't want to be anything like him, and yet here I am, hating on a pledge who just did a pretty awesome thing not only for KKB and their charity, but for our organization, too.

"Going once? Going twice?" Chelsea bangs the gavel against the podium. "Sold! To the Alpha Sig pledge in the glasses!"

Everyone laughs a little as I sigh, shoving down my pride and clapping along with the rest of the bar. I frown a little at the sigh of Skyler fleeing the stage so quickly. She's smiling, waving at the crowd like she should, but something in her eyes says she's not happy about something.

Probably the fact that her Big made her do the auction at all.

She's never been the kind of girl to get all dolled up and stand on stage to be bid on. She's more of the ripped-up jeans and t-shirt kind of gal.

I'm still watching as Kip chases Skyler out the front doors, and if anything, I can at least be happy for *her* — even if I am annoyed at Kip. She made it clear he was her new target for the semester, and this is a sure way to make sure she gets more time with him. Skyler deserves to be happy, and if a new transfer with glasses is going to do it for her, then I wish her the best.

My eyes find Cassie's in the crowd again, and she's right back to work now that the auction is over, helping Erin collect the winning bids and organize clean-up. Even though she seems a bit overwhelmed, her smile is genuine, and I can feel her happiness from across the room. She's getting back to the old her, finding herself, and as much as I want to drag her back to my bedroom tonight, I don't mind watching that happiness from afar for a while.

When the time is right, we'll be together — but there's no need to rush.

I'm not going anywhere.

Skyler

KIP JACKSON IS ABOUT as subtle as a fog horn in a museum.

I somehow managed to make it to the small poker tournament I originally had planned *before* Erin saddled me into the date auction. The only problem is that Kip wiggled his way into my cab, too. And now, on top of my plan of getting Clinton's Little, Josh, to buy me tonight so that I wouldn't be stuck playing Erin's game anymore falling through, I'm also stuck with Kip distracting me from the bar while I'm trying to focus on winning the next hand.

He doesn't fit in, not in this little shit hole bar. It's closed off to the public, only accessible with a secret password, and the clientele are *far* from anything remotely close to Kip. Everything in here is dark — the lighting, the liquor, the tattoos on the guy sitting at the bar, eyeing me like a snake now that I've taken his money and booted him out of the tournament. It's okay that my bright pink dress stands out — hell, it even plays in my favor, since distracting the other players and playing up my naiveté is part of my poker game.

But Kip? He needs to blend in, to not cause a scene.

And he's failing.

Not too long into the game, I beat out one of the toughest players at the table with a flush, one he thought was a bluff. He, of course, threw a big fit about his loss, which I'm used to. But Kip looked like he was about to jump out of his skin and across the bar to pummel the guy when it all went down. I had to shoot lasers at him with my eyes to get him to sit back down.

Now, an hour later, and it's down to just me and the guy I've been strategically flirting with all night — Luke. He's dressed pretty fratty in his khaki shorts straight from The Gap and his bro tank, complete with dark Oakley sunglasses and a ball cap turned around backward on his fat head.

He's had his eyes on me all night, and though I've been playing into his flirting banter, it's pure strategy — he doesn't have a shot in hell with me.

Still, I'm a little nervous now that I've just called his bet. He's all in, which means if I win this hand, I win it all — one step closer to paying off my entry fee for the APC tournament. But if he wins, I'm down to just twelve-hundred dollars to try to battle back to the top with.

Luke's been making comments about me being Barbie all night — which I can't really blame him for, seeing as how I'm still sporting the bright pink dress the girls dressed me in for the auction. Still, I can't resist the urge to throw that shit back in his face when he lays his hand down, smug as hell.

He has a straight, and that's all fine and dandy.

But I've got a four of a kind.

"Oh, Ken," I tease. "Barbie never bluffs."

Spreading the cards out on the table, I reveal my hand, and my opponent's jaw drops as the tiny bar erupts in a mixture of laughter and applause. I graciously accept the congratulations from those who offer, quickly swiping up the envelope with my cash in it as soon as the dealer places it in front of me.

I need to get out of here — need to get *Kip* out of here — and fast.

"That was a good game," the dealer says as I stand and tuck the envelope of cash in my clutch. "You know, you look familiar. Do you play a lot around here?"

I quickly shake my head. "No, but I have a familiar face. A lot of people think they know me."

I know he doesn't believe me, but thankfully, he doesn't push further. "I guess that's it. Well, at any rate, good job tonight."

I thank him, glancing at Kip briefly to let him know it's time to go before I make my way toward the door.

My one, explicit rule for allowing him to come with me to the tournament was that he stay cool and pretend like he doesn't know me. If these guys found out it was me, Skyler Thorne, one of the hottest women in poker who came to clear out their pockets at a tiny little tournament, we'd have trouble. Somehow, we've managed to skate by without anyone noticing, but I still won't feel at ease until we're back in a cab.

"Wait a second," Luke says, blocking my exit as he grabs my arm. "You're Skyler, aren't you?"

Though my heart skips at his recognition, I rip my arm free, stepping around him with ease. "Nope, I'm Barbie, remember?"

Luke grabs my arm again, but before I can defend myself, Kip is sprinting across the room.

"Don't touch her," he growls out, and I internally groan.

Damn it, Kip.

While I want to admit that it's a little hot how possessive his icy blue eyes are as he pins Luke with them, I'm more than a little aggravated. We need to get out of this bar without causing a scene, and this is *not* how we do it.

"Who the fuck are you?" Luke asks when Kip steps into his space.

"He's leaving," I say quickly. "We both are. Let's go," I say to Kip next, shoving him toward the door.

"Hey, I thought we were going out after this," Luke says, his arm wrapping around my waist from behind. "You just hustled me, the least you can do is put out tonight."

I narrow my eyes, ready to lay into him, but my blond-haired, blue-eyed bull dog attacks before I can.

Kip shoves Luke back, *hard*, sending him flying into the poker table. The chips scatter in his wake, a drink splashing over the side and onto the felt, and then all hell breaks loose.

"Take that shit outside!" the dealer yells.

"Yeah, let's go, playboy." Luke pushes himself off the table, launching at Kip, who rushes toward him, too.

I throw my hands out just in time to catch Kip's advance, shoving him back toward the door as I grit through my teeth. "Go. Now."

"I'm not going to let this asshole put his hands all over you."

Swoon.

Ugh, stop it, Skyler.

I shove Kip harder, making him stumble back toward the door. Once we're safely outside, the little bit of weakness Kip gave me with his possessiveness morphs back into annoyed anger. There's a cab waiting, one Kip was instructed to call at the end of the tournament, and I climb inside it, immediately smacking his chest once the door is closed behind us.

"What the fuck, Kip?! You almost screwed everything up!"

"I wasn't just going to stand there and watch that shit happen, Skyler!" he says, his breath hot on my skin.

Our bodies are too close, and I scoot away, putting distance between us in the backseat.

"I don't care if you did take that douchebag's money, he shouldn't have put his hands on you."

Do not swoon. Do not give in.

"I told you, I can handle myself," I remind him, crossing my arms and looking out the window. I don't know if I'm more frustrated at the fact that he almost blew the tournament for me, or at the fact that I still desperately want him, except now, I'm not allowed to have him.

Now, I have to play him like a game of poker — right into my Big's hands.

"I don't need you to save me, Kip," I say quieter.

For a while, we sit in silence, and I try to let that truth sink in. Kip is not mine, he never *will* be mine. And now, I'm stuck in a game I never intended to play, with a heart who doesn't even realize it's in the game, too.

Great.

"Hey," Kip says after a while, reaching over to place one hand on my thigh. Warmth spreads from that point of contact down to my toes, and I fight the urge to shiver. "Listen, I'm sorry."

I smack his hand away. "Whatever."

"Shit, Skyler," he says, exasperated. "I don't know what you want from me. I'm into you, okay?"

My heart squeezes.

"I'm sorry I didn't sit back and let some Abercrombie model-wannabe molest you. Next time, I'll back off. Just, come on, I don't want to end the night like this. Come home with me."

At that, my eyes widen.

"Are you serious?" I ask, finally facing him again.

"Not like that," he clarifies quickly, his hands up like he comes in peace.

Yeah, right. That motherfucker came in like a hurricane.

"It's almost four in the morning and I know you've got to be hungry. Let me make us breakfast."

As if on cue, my stomach growls, reminding me that I didn't even eat before the auction because my nerves were so shot. Still, I haven't had time to digest the night, to digest the fact that my big plan of having Josh win me in the auction backfired, and now Erin's little game is in place — with me as the pawn.

I turn toward the window again, hoping he'll just drop it, but Kip scoots closer to me, instead. He sets his chin on my shoulder, his big, puppy dog eyes begging me through the reflection in the glass.

"I make killer chocolate chip waffles."

I try not to smile, but he's just so damn adorable, it's practically impossible.

"I'll strip down to my boxers and wear an apron for you," he adds, and I pinch my lips together, still trying to fight.

Kip leans in a little closer, his voice just a whisper in my ear with his next sentence.

"What if I told you I had bacon?"

I can't help it — I laugh. Kip knows he's won, but still, I shove him away, shaking my head. "You're the biggest nerd, you know that?"

"I've been called worse. So," he says, eyes hopeful. "Waffles and bacon? Please? I promise to keep my hands to myself and you can punch me if I start to annoy you."

I sigh, debating my options. I really *am* hungry, and as much as I want time to figure out what the hell to do with my feelings toward Kip, I'd also be lying if I said I didn't want to spend more time with him.

"Fine," I concede. "But only because I love bacon."

Legacy takes place during the same semester as *Black Number Four*. Whether you've read it before now or not, you'll get a wider view of what was happening at Palm South University (especially between Kip and Skyler) if you read *Black Number Four* as you read this season. I will help guide you, letting you know which chapters to read before moving on to the next episode.

FOR THE FULL READING EXPERIENCE FOR THIS EPISODE, **READ CHAPTERS 1-5** IN *BLACK NUMBER FOUR* BEFORE CONTINUING ON TO EPISODE TWO. (You'll get to see how Skyler felt when her and Kip met, experience the shot of tequila and first kiss from her point of view, read what happens at breakfast, and get an inside look into Kip's other motives for being at PSU. Hmmm... the plot thickens. ;))

EPISODE 2

Erin

"OKAY, WE HAVE A few visitors tonight before we end chapter," I announce to my sisters Sunday evening. They're all a bit cranky after a particularly long chapter, so I put on my best smile to help them get through the last half hour. It's been a hectic week since our date auction, and with Valentine's Day around the corner, every sister has more pressing things on their mind.

Like who will be bringing them roses.

"Please welcome the lovely ladies of Zeta Pi Alpha." I initiate the applause, which my sisters mirror as the ZPA girls make their way into our house. They're the first in a line of visitors who want our attention tonight. Now that the semester is in full swing, we're getting invited to participate in philanthropic events, dances, socials, and more.

Once the girls leave, the Omega Chi Beta brothers enter, and my stomach knots when I see Clinton for the first time.

He's dressed in his chapter best, donning charcoal gray dress slacks and a relaxed, cream button-down with the top button undone. The sleeves are pushed up his massive forearms, exposing the muscle there, and I can't help but notice he's been bulking up since the last time I saw him.

There's always a kind of magnetism I feel around Clinton, like no matter the time and place, I could always depend on him to be there when I need him. I can close my eyes and still see him in the soft light on the garden balcony at our semi-formal, feel his arms around me as I finally let out every tear I'd been holding back over what had happened.

He told me to go see someone, begged me to talk about it.

But it's not that simple.

His dark eyes are soft as he smiles and sings along with his brothers, but those eyes have seen darkness. They've seen horror, they've seen hardship, and yet he still finds a way to smile bright enough to light up an entire room.

I don't know how he does it, and I can't watch anyone but him as they make their way through the room, handing out roses as they sing.

They sound terrible, but they look nice — and that's all that matters when it comes to fraternity serenades.

I'm at the front of the room, so Clinton makes it to me last, and he pauses in front of me, offering me the very last rose from his bundle. He's still singing, though his eyes are different now — tinged with sadness at the corners instead of the joy I'd watched moments before.

I wonder if he'll ever be able to look at me without feeling sad, without experiencing some sort of pity.

After what I put him through, I can't imagine how he ever could.

I take the rose from his hands, my creamy fingers brushing the rough skin of his dark hand, and he finally offers me a soft smile as their song ends. Then, he turns to face the room with the rest of his brothers.

"Ladies of Kappa Kappa Beta," their president says. "I am pleased to inform you that our national chapter has granted us permission to attend Spring Break with you, thanks to our good behavior last semester."

All the brothers make lewd gestures at that, and everyone laughs.

"We can't wait to party with you like we always do, and until then, feel free to use our new pledges to do your homework or rub you down with tanning oil — whichever item is most pressing on your to-do list."

A few whistles ring out at that, and I shake my head, hurrying them along with a few snaps of my fingers. Once they make their way out of the room, it's Alpha Sigma's turn to come in, and if I thought the pull I felt to Clinton was strong, it's nothing compared to what I feel when Kip Jackson walks into the room.

Kip Jackson.

The only boy I've ever loved, the only boy I've ever wanted to save me.

The only chance at happiness I have left.

His blue eyes barely even skirt to mine before he's turned around, facing the rest of my sisters as his president introduces them, but just that tiny glance has me reeling back to the summer we were together. I can still see those eyes outlined by a black night sky, his smile bright and wide just before he kissed me.

I've seen him around campus a few times since I heard he was here, but we still haven't had the chance to speak. I'm not even sure if he knows I'm here, but being that he's in Greek life, I don't see how he could *not* have heard of me. I'm the president of the top sorority.

Still, whether he's heard of me being here or not, he hasn't searched me out, which confirms my suspicion that he probably doesn't really care to see me. After the way I acted at the end of our relationship, fueled by jealousy, I can't blame him.

All my money is on Skyler.

Just like I suspected, he outbid everyone at the date auction to "win" Skyler. But, to my knowledge, they haven't gone on the date yet. Once they do, the plan will be in motion, and my last-ditch effort to get Kip back in my arms will either do just that or blow up in my face entirely.

Am I crazy?

The thought passes my mind, just like it has several times since I asked Skyler for her help. I even gave her an out at the auction, right before she went on stage. But, she assured me she was fine, and she was all in to help me.

Sometimes I'm sure I don't deserve her.

Staring at the back of Kip's head doesn't make him turn around to look at me again, so I scan the faces of my sisters. When I spot Skyler, I see *her* eyes are fixed on Kip, too.

And I know without a doubt that he's looking right back at her.

"The brothers of Alpha Sigma would like to welcome back the lovely ladies of Kappa Kappa Beta to Palm South for spring semester," Adam says, gleaming at the new additions to his fraternity. They're all dressed in the same khaki pants, light blue button-ups and navy and white striped bow ties. "We proudly present our new pledges."

He reads off all their names before telling us that they've all prepared a little something to introduce themselves. The next ten minutes is pure laughter, with each pledge using poem, song, or stunt form to tell us their hobbies and interests — most of which include meeting girls.

Kip is the last pledge to perform, and when he steps forward, I feel all the oxygen available in the room pull toward him, like he's the only source of life.

"Hit it, boys!" he says, which cues his pledge brothers to break into a chorus of beatboxing. I have to stifle a laugh at their ridiculous movements, each of them acting like a B

Boy right out of the 90s as they circle my sisters and add to the rhythm, whether it be with bass, snaps, or some other sound.

And then, with his eyes on Skyler, Kip starts to rap.

Let me tell you a story about this girl I met,
She had the bluest eyes that were hard to forget.
She challenged me to a game of foosball,
Little did I know that I would lose all.

I scoff at that. *Lame.*

Cinderella stole a kiss and then she ran away,
So I gave her some space for a couple of days.
Then I took a thousand bucks and I played my cards
right,
I bought a date with the princess last Saturday night.

My stomach drops at the mention of that kiss. I knew he'd taken a shot off her body, and even though no one specifically *said* it, Jess had eluded to Skyler having her tongue down Kip's throat. Still, it stings to hear *him* say it, to hear him rap about it like it was the best kiss of his life.

I want to be the best kiss of his life.

And now here I am to collect my prize,
No more running and no more lies.
It's been over a week and now I'm ready for my date,
So what'ya say, Skyler Thorne, can I pick you up at
eight?

His brothers make the beat drop and the entire chapter room goes wild. I'm a little delayed, my eyes glued to the back of his head as everything around me morphs, the cheers muted, claps in slow motion. Shaking my head, I join in on the applause, my eyes finding Skyler along with everyone else.

She seems just as shocked as I am, her bottom lip pinned between her teeth as she watches Kip. I can't tell if she's pissed or swooning.

When Skyler's eyes find mine, I nod toward Kip, urging her to accept his date. As much as it makes my stomach curdle like an Irish Car Bomb not taken fast enough, it's the only way to get the plan in motion.

If I want Kip, this is part of it. Skyler will have him coming around us more, and then once she breaks things off, he'll be looking for someone to lean on, someone to confide in.

Enter: me.

"About time you did this the right way, pledge," Skyler finally says, appearing as confident as ever. "I guess you can take me out. Friday night. And seven, not eight."

She winks at him as everyone cheers, and I watch them staring at each other as Kip makes his way out the door with the rest of his brothers. His gaze never leaves her, and her eyes stay fixed on his, and I feel a little like celebrating and a little like throwing up all at once.

I adjourn chapter as soon as they're gone, rushing up the stairs after Skyler and the rest of the girls. Ashlei's pouring out of her room as soon as I make it upstairs, and we squeal together before bursting through the door to Jess and Skyler's room.

"This is so perfect, Little!" I say immediately as Ashlei pops up into Jess's bed with her. "I knew you would come through. I've been so busy getting everything situated for the semester that I haven't had time to check in and here you are outperforming what I could even imagine!"

My chest tightens, but I smile through the discomfort.

Pulling Skyler in for a hug, I assure myself again that this will work — this *will* be worth it.

"I knew there was a reason I picked you as my Little. You're a bad ass, just like me."

Skyler squeezes me back as the girls laugh, and I hold her a little tighter, thanking her as much as I can in that embrace for what she's doing for me. Even though I truly do believe Skyler *is* a bad ass, I know what I'm asking her to do isn't easy.

"Where do you think he'll take you on the date?" Ashlei asks, her eyes wide as I release Skyler.

"The better question is what are you going to *wear*?" Jess chimes in.

I launch into theories with them, the excitement and giddiness taking over me. When Skyler says she wants to get some sleep, Ashlei and I skip down to my room and rummage through my closet, trying to find the perfect outfit for Skyler to wear.

Sitting there on my bed, watching Ashlei pull out dress after dress, I finally let it hit me.

This is it.

In less than a week, they'll go on their first date, and it'll all start. I'll be one step closer to being with Kip again. My smile falters, brows pinching together as the reality of it sinks in. Kip will be on a date. With Skyler. And then, because of *me*, she'll pull him in, get him close enough to care about her, and then break his heart.

For me.

I should be happy. That giddiness I had before, that smile, it should be all I can register.

It's working, the plan is in place...

So then why do I feel like the scum of the Earth?

Jess

A GIRL HAS NEEDS.

The last time I had that one, steadfast thought on repeat in my dirty little pea brain, I met Jarrett. I never could have known what would come from that, but I'm pretty sure I know exactly what will come of tonight.

After chapter, I half-walked, half-skipped down Greek Row to the Omega Chi house. Greg asked me if I wanted to come by to "study" tonight, and I have a pretty good idea what that's code for.

"Study" equals "take our pants off and see what happens."

So, I decided not to wear pants at all, opting to stay in the same little black dress I wore to chapter. It's a little formal for the occasion, since we have to wear business casual for chapter, but it's also easier access.

Priorities.

Greg meets me at the door after I shoot out a text to let him know I'm walking up, and he leans against the frame, smirking as his eyes take in my legs.

"A little overdressed for studying," he muses. "And you didn't bring any textbooks."

"I don't really need them for the subject I'm studying tonight," I banter back, pausing in front of him. My eyes drink him in — the black sweat pants hanging on his hips, the large, heather gray Omega Chi t-shirt with the sleeves ripped off, arm holes gaping so far down I have full view of his glorious washboard abs.

"That so?"

"Mm-hmm," I assure him, tapping my temple. "All up here."

"And what subject is it that you're studying?"

"Anatomy."

He chokes out a laugh, shaking his head and holding the door wide for me as I slip under his arm and into the house. He tosses that same arm over my shoulder, guiding me through the hallway back to his room with my arm pressed against his bare ribcage — also exposed by that artfully shredded t-shirt.

"I really do have to study," he says. "I started my internship, and hatching season is coming up soon."

"That's right," I mused, snapping my fingers. "I forgot how much you nerd out over turtles."

"Don't act like it doesn't turn you on."

"Oh, it definitely does," I agree as he ushers me inside his room. "Which is exactly why I didn't bring anything to study, nor did I wear panties under this dress."

Greg groans, sitting on the edge of his bed with my hands still in his. He pulls me to stand right between his legs, his eyes roaming over my curves appreciatively.

"You just sit there and talk about turtles," I tell him, guiding his hand up my inner thigh. He bites his lip, shaking his head as he follows the movement with his eyes. "And I'll do my own kind of homework."

Standing over him, his hand inching closer and closer to my heated and severely underused treasure box, as Skyler would call it — I realize Greg is actually *insanely* hot. His features are all *so* dark — and delicious. From his caramel skin to his jet black, messy hair, he's like sin wrapped up in an ice cream cone. Add in his eyes, black and wide, like deep, bottomless pools of water, and his smirk, devilish enough to melt even the chastest of panties — and I can't figure out how I ever *didn't* notice his sex appeal.

I should have realized all of this the first night we met at Ralph's, but then again, my heart belonged to Jarrett that night. I couldn't think of any other guy in any kind of sexual way, not in the entire time I was dating Jarrett. I was literally broken when it came to having those thoughts.

And while my heart might still belong to Jarrett, it's different now, knowing he doesn't want it — knowing he's holding on firmly to another woman's heart now, and most likely holding on to a lot more than that at the present moment.

So, when Greg slides his hand up a little more, his fingers brushing my slick heat, I moan with him at the feel of it, closing my eyes and letting go.

Greg may not be Jarrett, but he *is* a sexy, fun, single male with his hand between my legs.

And right now, that's all I need, anyway.

As soon as he feels how wet I am, Greg stands, yanking my wrists over my head as he crashes his mouth to mine. He tastes like beer, like he's been drunk since noon, and I feel his kiss like an intoxicating shot of alcohol warming every single limb. His lips are firm but warm, his breaths coming harder now — which, coincidentally, leads to him growing harder in a completely different way, too. I lean forward, pressing my stomach into his erection, and he groans at the contact.

Running his rough hands down over my arms, he hooks them in the hem of my dress and yanks up, breaking our kiss long enough to strip me out of the black fabric and drop it to the floor. My bra comes off next, an easy snap of his fingers sending it down to the floor next to my dress.

I wait for it to hit, that shock of electricity I always felt when Jarrett touched me, but it never does. My heart is racing, my clit swollen and throbbing, just waiting for Greg to touch me. But it feels a little empty, a little detached — a little like every other guy felt *before* Jarrett.

Again, I'm reminded of how my life was severed by that man.

Shoving him out of my mind, I push my hands into Greg's chest until he's sitting on the bed again. I rip his shirt over his head, nodding to his sweat pants as I toss the shirt over the back of his desk chair. Greg just smirks, lifting his hips enough to take off his pants and briefs in one sweep of motion, and when his hard-on springs free, all I can do is lick my lips.

I drop to my knees, giving Greg a wicked grin as I take him in one hand and tease the tip of him with my tongue. He's not quite as big as Jarrett, and he leans a little to the left, but it's still a beautiful cock — and definitely a tool I can work with.

Greg leans back on his palms, watching me with rapt attention as I take him inside my mouth. My brows pinch together as I figure out how to fit him inside, working with his unique shape, and once I find the magic combo, he lets out a steely, "Fuckkk."

"Don't let me keep you from studying," I tease, releasing him from my lips with a pop. "Come on. Tell me about hatching season."

Something between a laugh and a curse escapes his lips as I take him inside my mouth again.

"I can't," he manages, his breaths labored.

Greg flexes his hips into my slick hand when I take my mouth off again, eyes meeting his.

"Come on. Talk turtle to me."

He spits out another laugh, but it dies quickly when I strengthen my grip, sliding down from his tip to his base. With a growl, he leans forward, hands wrapping around my upper arms as he tosses me onto the bed.

"We're done talking."

"Oh, are we?" I tease, spreading my legs wide open for him to see. He's on his knees above me, one hand stroking his cock as his eyes roam over my breasts, down my stomach, his pupils dilating when he takes in my wet pussy.

Greg bends forward, which gives me hope that he's going to spend some time downtown returning the favor I just paid, but instead, he grips my ass, yanking hard until my wet entrance is lined up with his ready member.

"Tell you what," he says, teasing the slick skin between my lips with his crown. "If you can say a word after this, you can talk about whatever the hell you want."

It's right on the tip of my tongue, the smart-ass remark to his challenge, but everything is wiped from rational thought when he slides all the way inside me — all at once, balls deep, not a single centimeter of space left between us as he groans in ecstasy and I try desperately to catch my next breath.

Before I can so much as moan, he's withdrawing, plummeting inside me again with just as much gusto. He feels even deeper somehow, and when he lifts my ankles up to rest on his shoulders, I finally cry out, the sensation too much — but in the *best* fucking way.

Greg works himself to a release within minutes, and I fake mine, just to give him credit for surprising me. The poor guy likely didn't stand a chance of getting me off, anyway — not tonight, at least. With Jarrett, it was easy to come. Hell, just looking into his eyes while he whispered that he loved me was enough to send me skyrocketing.

Still, when Greg rolls off of me, kissing my neck with a chuckle before retreating to the bathroom to clean up, I smile. And when he comes back with a hot wash cloth, wiping between my legs carefully, I smile a little wider. And when he hands me a pair of his boxers and an oversized sweater, when we crawl into bed — me with my phone, him with his textbook — I rest my head on his chest and revel in the comfortable silence between us.

Greg holds me while he studies, his fingers drawing circles on my shoulder, and I turn the page for him when he asks me to. Sometime after midnight, I pull the book from his sleeping hands, kiss his cheek, and slip out of the Omega Chi house.

He may not be Jarrett, but no one ever will be. And when I'm with Greg, I feel a little less shitty.

I'll take what I can get.

Adam

"WHAT HAPPENED TO GOING easy on the pledges?" Jeremy asks me, his voice low as we circle our new members. They're all standing huddled together in a kiddy pool full of ice water in the middle of our chapter room, teeth chattering as they silently pray not to be the next one I call on. "I mean, don't get me wrong," he adds with a chuckle. "This is priceless entertainment, but I thought you said you were going to run the pledge process differently when you were president."

"And I have been," I remind him. "But, some things are tradition — like the camping trip."

"And this particularly torturous brand of hazing."

"Exactly."

Jeremy smirks. "I will say, this might be the best pledge class we've ever had. Between Kade showing athletic promise and Kip already making such a big splash, we're on everyone's radar. Let's just hope they can keep their GPAs up."

Something twists in my stomach at the mention of Kip, a foreign feeling I can't fully digest.

"We shall see." I make my way toward Kip next, that same uncomfortable swell in my gut as I approach him.

"Go easy on him," Jeremy warns as I close in, but I brush him off.

"Pledge Jackson," I say, pausing to stand in front of him. His glasses slip down his nose a bit, and he pushes them back up, his eyes as confident as they can be as he shivers his ass off, waiting for my question. "Name the three founders of Alpha Sigma who helped the sisters of

Pi Gamma Zeta sneak out of their dorms when they were founding their sorority."

Kip forces a breath, and for some reason, I find myself silently wishing for him to screw up. Of course, that would earn him some groans and possibly a few punches from his fellow pledges. If they answer wrong, we start back over, and we go until they can answer ten questions in a row without missing one.

It seems cruel to anyone outside of the Greek system, but anyone who has had to earn their letters, to learn about how their organization was founded and discover a new kind of respect for the gentlemen who paved the way — they understand. These potential new members aren't getting hazed for fun. They're being tested, not just on their knowledge, but on their loyalty.

Alpha Sigma was quickly becoming a top fraternity on campus, and I would do whatever I could to ensure this next group of guys would add to that, that they would help us continue to build a legacy.

"Harry Winters, Edward Sanders, and..." Kip's voice fades, his eyes rolling up to the ceiling as he tries to grasp for the last name.

"Ten. Nine." I start a countdown, just to give him a little pressure, a little push. The rest of his pledge brothers groan, some of them cursing while others encourage Kip that he can do it. They're a small group, only eight of them, and they're already forming the bonds of brotherhood.

"Clarence Bell?" he finally says, the answer more of a question.

For a moment I just stand there, making him sweat his answer, but then I nod, moving down the line to the next pledge. Kip lets out a relieved breath, along with the rest of his brothers, but they still have one more question to answer correctly before they're out of the ice pool.

Jeremy suggests Christopher, our youngest pledge. He answers his question correctly, and all at once, the pledges tumble out of the water as our brothers toss them towels and bring them hot water to sip on. We push them to their limits, but we're still careful with them. The last thing we want is to end up like Omega Chi for not being smart with our pledging process.

"Can I ask you something?" Jeremy says, handing me two cups of hot water to deliver.

"You already did."

He smiles a little, rubbing the back of his neck. Jeremy is never nervous when it comes to talking to me. Hell, he's one of my best friends. So, the fact that he can't look me in the eyes when he asks his next question puts me on edge.

"What's your deal with Kip?"

I swallow, my eyes flicking over to where he and Kade are sitting on the couch, chatting and waiting for their water as they warm their feet.

"I don't have a deal with him."

"You're pretty hard on him," Jeremy argues. "Like, more so than the other pledges. Is it because he's got a thing going with Skyler?"

"No?" I say, but it doesn't come out confidently, and Jeremy cocks a brow. I sigh. "I don't know. Maybe. There's just something about him that irks me. I can't figure it out. I mean, I'm the one who wanted him to pledge, but he's just... he's so *showy*. And he's got all this attention on him already. He's not laying low, not working hard like the rest of the pledges. It's like he has this sense of entitlement or something."

"I think he's just confident," Jeremy says. "I mean... I hate to say it again, Adam, but..."

"If you say he reminds you of me again, I'll nut tap you."

Jeremy chuckles, tossing his hands up in surrender. "I'm just saying. He's a great pledge, and he's going to be a great brother, if he makes it through your tests, anyway." He lets his hands drop to his sides, tucking them in his pockets. "If it is about Skyler, just talk to him. Let him know whatever it is that you need to tell him. You're his president, man, and he wants to impress you. Don't make it harder on him than it already is."

I huff, aggravated both at the thought of talking to Kip and that Jeremy is right. I care about Skyler, she's one of my best friends, so maybe part of my annoyance toward Kip has to do with her. Then again, maybe it has to do with the fact that, like Jeremy said, he reminds me a little of myself.

Do I feel threatened?

I shake off the possibility of that. If jealousy has anything to do with my attitude toward him, I sure as hell wouldn't be admitting it to Jeremy — or even myself, for that matter.

With two cups of hot water in hand, I make my way toward where Kip and Kade are sitting, and their conversation comes to a grinding halt once I reach them.

"Kip, can I talk to you for a second?" I ask once they have their hot water.

Kade jumps up like my words were lava spilling on the floor at his feet, rushing to join the other pledges by the pool table. Kip follows him with his eyes like he wished he'd stayed, and I'm reminded of Jeremy's words as I take the seat next to him.

Don't be a dick, Adam. Don't be like Clay.

"Are you taking Skyler out tonight?" I ask, remembering from his little stunt at Kappa Kappa Beta's chapter that their date is supposed to be this evening.

Kip takes a drink of his hot water, simply nodding in lieu of an answer.

I sigh, running my hands back through my hair as I grasp for the right words to say. "Listen, I don't have claims on her or anything, but I still care about her," I say honestly. "And I swear to God, if you fuck her over, I will personally fuck you up."

So much for not being a dick.

The words fly out before I have the chance to run them through my head, to digest them and decipher a way to say them in a more respectful way. Still, I find myself watching Kip confidently, as if those words were exactly what I planned to say.

Kip swallows down his frustration, and I can't help but admire the way he's able to school his features and say his next words calmly and respectfully.

"You won't have to do that."

I search his eyes for a sign of a lie there, but find nothing. Satisfied, and frankly out of words to say, I just nod, standing and leaving him alone as I make my way back to Jeremy.

"Well, that looked like it went well," he says, his eyes on Kip behind me.

"I'm working on it, okay?"

Jeremy chuckles. "Okay. By the way, a cute little redhead just showed up asking for you."

I can't hide the smile that that news spreads on my face, and Jeremy waggles his eyebrows in response to it, as if he knows something no one else does.

"And on that note, I'm officially off duty," I say, walking backward toward the front door. "Can you handle wrapping all this up?"

"I got it, El Presidente. Go have fun."

I roll my eyes, turning away from him, but he calls out again.

"No. Seriously. Please, for the love of God and for all our sakes, have some fun."

I flip him off over my shoulder, tucking that little finger away as soon as I round the corner and see Cassie standing in the foyer.

Her back is to me, her unruly red hair pulled over one shoulder of her emerald green hoodie as she mindlessly twists the strands into a braid. She scans the picture of our founders hanging on the wall, her Keds turned inward a little, legs covered by a pair of dark jeans.

Sliding my hands into my pockets, I slip up behind her, my lips close to her neck as I eye the picture over her head.

"Back then, they were told not to smile when they took pictures," I say, and she jumps a little, but then a small smile spreads on her lips. "What's my excuse going to be when all the pledges from this semester look just as miserable in their photograph?"

Cassie turns, one eyebrow climbing toward her hairline. "I guess the rumors about you being a dictator president to the new guys are true, then, huh?"

"Hey, can't make it easy on them," I say with a shrug.

Her green eyes twinkle as she smiles wider, the gold flecks in those green irises even more pronounced thanks to the deep shade of her hoodie. "Can't make it anything less than brutal, from what I've heard."

"Yeah, yeah," I say, exasperated. I pull her under my arm for a hug, inhaling the scent of her strawberry shampoo. "Jeremy's already on my ass, okay? I'll ease up."

"Do whatever you want," she says when we pull away, my hand finding hers. "You're a great president, Adam. Whatever you think is best, I believe it."

A warm surge of pride tickles my ribcage as I tug her back toward my room.

"Alright, enough of that. I didn't ask you over to talk about Greek stuff."

"What *did* you invite me over for?"

"Mind-blowing sex."

She balks at my attempt at dry humor, coming to a complete stop inside my bedroom. A deep blush shades her cheeks, crawling quickly down her neck as she opens her mouth to respond and closes it again without a single peep coming out.

I chuckle, shutting the door behind us and plopping down on my bed, patting the spot next to me.

"Kidding. Come here."

She lets out a breath, but her body is still tense as she sits next to me.

"I got you something. Close your eyes."

Cassie watches me curiously, her nervousness easing as confusion takes its place.

"Close your eyes," I say again, leaning in to peck her lips.

She giggles, finally letting her lids flutter closed as I grab her wrists, turning her palms up toward the ceiling. Once I'm sure she's not looking, I reach behind my headboard for the gift, laying it in her lap where her hands are waiting.

Cassie's brows pull together once the board touches her palms. "It's kind of heavy. What is it?"

"Open your eyes and find out."

When she does, the little smile on her face fades instantly, her lips parting as her eyes sweep over the wood in her hand.

"Adam..." she says, my name just a breath on her lips. She pulls her hands from under the gift — a long board — and runs her fingertips over the designs splashed over the bottom of it. "Did you... did you make this?"

"I did. Well," I clarify quickly, one hand finding the back of my neck. "I mean, I didn't make the long board, of course, but I did the design. It's decoupage, or whatever it's called."

She smiles a little as I butcher the word, her eyes still glued to the board as she trails her fingers over each design.

"I did the Palm South University crest, of course," I say, pointing to it. "And then your letters — KKB — and I tried to make the whole thing in your colors. Lots of blues and golds. And I put some doctor stuff on there, see the stethoscope?"

She pauses when her fingers touch the bottom of the board — the Key West section.

"Dolphins," she muses, her eyes flicking up to meet mine. "Like the ones we saw when we did the boat trip."

"Yeah," I admit, heat tingeing my neck. "I put a little of us on there. Not too much, I wanted it to be mostly you, but I added the dolphins. And pizza from Moon Pie." I point to the oversized slice of Hawaiian. "Just a few things."

There are pictures of her with her sisters, the largest being one of her and Skyler last Spring Break, and she eyes each one of them before landing on a small one of us near the middle of the board. It's from one of the intramural football games she came to watch, right after I tackle hugged her in my dirty gear as she tried unsuccessfully to shove me away.

Cassie laughs, though tears flood her eyes. "It's so... perfect. I can't believe you did this." She looks at me then, swallowing. "Thank you, Adam."

"You're welcome. I hope you like it."

"I love it," she says quickly, running her hand over the board again. Then, she slips it carefully down to the floor, the nerves back on her face as she faces me again.

"What?" I ask, searching the unspoken questions in her eyes.

"I was just thinking..." she says, her voice a whisper as she scoots closer to me on the bed. One hand reaches forward, playing with the hem of my polo. "That first thing you said, about why you brought me here... you said you were kidding... but... maybe, it doesn't have to be a joke."

Her eyes flick up to mine then, wide and hopeful, and her cool hand slips under the fabric of my shirt, her fingertips brushing against my abdomen as I suck in a breath.

"Cassie..."

"We don't have to go all the way," she says hurriedly, but she slips her fingertips between the band of my jeans and my boxers, making every thought in my brain turn to fuzz. "I just... Adam, I can't go another second without you touching me. I mean," she clarifies, scooting even closer, one of her ankles crossing over mine. "*Really* touching me."

I growl out my next breath, my hand covering hers. I wrap my fingers around her wrist, pulling her forward, and she climbs into my lap without another word. When her thighs straddle mine, she rolls her hips hard, and I press my forehead to hers.

"Wait."

She pauses, her hands fisting in my hair as her eyes find mine.

"I just, before we go any further, I want you to know that every single chance I get to touch you, every chance I get to put my hands where you don't let any other hands go, it means... everything to me."

She swallows, the corners of her mouth turning up a bit.

"Does that mean you'll touch me where you haven't before?"

The question is just a whisper, but it pains me like it was blown through an air horn. I wince, gripping the thick fabric of her hoodie as I pull her flush against me.

"If you'll let me, yes."

"Please," she whispers immediately, rolling her hips again. Then, her lips land on mine, soft and inviting, and I know there's nothing else I can do but give her what she needs.

It's all I can manage to repeat my conversation with my aunt in my head, to remind myself *why* I'm waiting, why I'm going slow, as Cassie intensifies our kiss. She's all hands and moans, breaths and touches. Her hands rip at my clothes, my hair, my skin, her lips devouring mine. But I keep my pace, forcing her to slow down, asking her to trust me.

We've waited so long, had so many years — so many *people* between us — but I'd wait twice as long, and suffer through twice as much, if it meant I got to have her in the long run.

That's why I take my time, and that's why I promise myself again that I can make her feel good without hurting her, that I can give without taking, that I can go slow and make every moment with her count.

At the end of it all, when Cassie McBee looks back on her life, she will never forget the moments of us. She'll remember every word, every touch, every kiss — and in those moments, she'll find no pain — only the brightest joy.

That's the promise I vow to keep.

Cassie strips my shirt over my head, and I roll us until she's beneath me, her red hair splayed out against the light blue cotton of my pillowcases. I don't realize I'm trembling until I reach for the hem of her hoodie, helping her ease out of it. She lays back again, her chest heaving under the simple white tank top covering her bra.

For a moment, I just stare at her, eyes slowly climbing over every curve of her. When I make it back to her eyes, they're underlined by bright red cheeks and a shy smile.

"No one looks at me the way you do," she whispers.

"I'd kill them if they did."

She laughs, helping me as I work the button and zipper on her jeans. I pull the stiff fabric down over her hips, her thighs, until I can peel the denim off her calves and let it fall to the floor. A soft, mint green pair of cotton panties is the only barrier now between my eyes and the place I ache to touch Cassie most, and the weight of that is like a bag of bricks on my chest.

I force a shaky breath, dragging one finger over the cotton before dipping it just a centimeter underneath, brushing the soft, bare skin of her that rests underneath. Cassie arches into the touch, her eyes fluttering closed as both fists twist in my comforter.

I'm still trembling as I slip my thumbs under each strap of her panties, stripping them down slowly. I don't even know where I drop them, because my eyes are too busy devouring the newly exposed view — one I've never seen before. Cassie blushes deeper as my eyes greedily take her in — every inch, every freckle, every single centimeter of pale, white skin.

She still has her tank top and bra on, and as much as I want to see all of her exposed, I don't move to dispose of those last two articles. They're all that keep me from feasting on all of her, and I know if I had her completely naked in my bed, I wouldn't have the strength to stop until I was so deep inside her that I became a permanent mark.

Instead, I kiss my way slowly down her arms, shoving her tank top up enough to lick a line down her stomach, and then I settle between her legs. Her emerald pools never leave me as I hoist her thighs up, the backs of them resting on my shoulders, and I hold her gaze as my tongue flicks out, just marginally, just enough for the first taste.

We both moan, the sounds mixing together in a symphony of pleasure and pain.

I close my eyes, steeling a breath before I lower my mouth again, this time running my tongue long and flat against her. From her slick opening all the way up to her tender, swollen bud, I taste her, the heat from my next breath making goosebumps explode over her legs.

She whimpers, writhing under my hands pinned at her waist. I just hold her steady, lips closing over her clit as I suck gently. Cassie's legs quiver more, her fists twisting in my comforter more until they fly into my hair with the same pressure.

It would be a bold-face lie if I said I never imagined what Cassie would taste like, what she'd look like if I ever got the chance to throw her down on my bed and ravage her the way I wanted to. But everything I'd ever imagined, every wet dream I'd ever had was so wrong, so far off, I almost laugh.

She's so much sweeter than I imagined, and the vision of her in my bed is enough to make *me* come, even without her touching me. Her cheeks had started as a dusty pink, but they grow a deeper shade by the second, with each and every touch of my tongue adding another drop of crimson under her freckles. Her eyes, closed tight, hypnotize me every time they fly open, finding me there between her legs with my mouth fastened on her. Her hands, weaved into my hair, tug and grip, and I feel every movement like a direct electric spark to my dick.

My hands slide from her hips to grip the tops of her thighs as I pull her closer, swirling my tongue over her clit before I lick her with a flat tongue from bottom to top again. I moan with the motion, causing a new wave of goosebumps as she writhes beneath me.

"Adam," she whispers, my name such a sweet, torturous plea on her lips that I groan again, sucking her clit with more force between my teeth.

I could taste her forever like this — devouring her like she's my last meal, or maybe my first, or maybe both all in one. But she's close. I can tell by the way she moves under my touch, but the heat in her cheeks, by the way her eyes squeeze shut, the muscles in her legs tensing as she reaches for the finish line in sight.

And I want her to detonate under my touch.

Slowly, I run the fingertips of my right hand down over her inner thigh, my tongue still working her clit as my fingers find her slick entrance. My middle finger dances there, soaking up her sweet wetness, with just enough pressure for the tip of it to dip inside her.

Cassie moans louder, her fingers tangling in my hair with her plea. She wants more, she wants me inside her, and even though I know it will practically kill me — I answer her request like it's all I've wanted to do in my entire life.

With as much composure as I can manage, I slip that middle finger inside her.

We both moan when my first knuckle disappears, and when she squeezes around the full finger, coating my second knuckle with her desire, I curse out loud at the tight feel of her.

"Fuck, Cassie," I breathe, withdrawing my finger slowly just to slide it back inside her. I curl the tip of it, brushing her sensitive G-spot as she arches off the bed. "I thought I knew... I thought I was ready to feel you like this, but *God*, it's killing me." I kiss her mound. "You're fucking perfect."

She moans at my words, fingers flying from my hair back to the comforter as she grasps for something to hold onto. But it's too late. With a few more curls of my finger and a gentle suck of her clit between my teeth, she comes for me, flying into oblivion with only my hands to root her back to Earth.

Cassie doesn't scream like a porn star, or fake moan with the sole purpose of putting on a show. Instead, all the blood in her cheeks rushes down to her clit, swelling in my mouth as she whimpers through her almost-silent release. She calls my name under the soft, hushed groans of pleasure, her breaths shallow and heated, and when she's done, her entire body collapses into a satiated heap in my hands.

And I feel like I've just run a marathon in the desert heat.

I smile, kissing her tender clit softly as I withdraw my finger and crawl up to kiss her parted lips. Her breaths even out slowly, her mouth seeking mine between exhales.

Every time her tongue swirls in a dance with mine, she smiles a little more, like tasting herself on me is too good to be true.

I nuzzle into her neck as I roll her to one side, her back to me as she faces my wall and I wrap myself around her. We fit together so easily, so perfectly, my knees tucking into the backs of hers in an immaculate seam. I sigh into the back of her neck, kissing it softly before tugging her more into my chest.

Cassie rolls her hips, her bottom brushing against the swollen head of my cock as I inhale a stiff groan.

"Your turn," she whispers, hand reaching back, but I wrap my fingers around her wrist to stop her.

"Not tonight. Tonight, it's about you."

She rolls in my arms, looking up at me with a pout that I *know* got her whatever she wanted growing up.

"But I want to touch you, too. I want to taste you, too."

My eyes nearly cross at the thought of that, of her lips around me, her mouth taking me inside her. I groan, adjusting my throbbing hard-on under my jeans as I kiss her forehead.

"You will. But not tonight, okay?" Pulling back, I brush her hair out of her face, running the pad of my thumb over her blushed cheeks. "I meant what I said about going slow. We have all the time in the world to touch each other, to explore each other. But right now, I just want to hold you. I just want to make you feel safe."

Tears well in her eyes, and she shakes her head, burying her face into my chest.

We don't say another word, but her fingertips circle the skin on my back as I run my own through her unruly curls. I'm not sure how long she's in my arms before her breaths even out, her chest rising and falling in a slow rhythm as she falls asleep. I don't dare move, not even when my left arm screams at me before becoming numb altogether.

I hold that girl all night long like she's my entire world.

And that's when I realize she is.

Skyler

THIS MOTHERFUCKER IS CRAZY.

That's the first thing that pops into my head when I descend the stairs and see Kip waiting for me at the bottom of them — in his pajamas.

Here I am in high heels that already make my arches ache, and a black dress so tight I won't be able to eat more than a piece of cheese without busting out of it, and this motherfucker is in flannel sleep pants.

Flannel sleep pants that hang on his hips in a way that shouldn't even be legal, but that's beside the point.

I should have said no to this date. I didn't really have a choice — not with Erin giving me the death eye when he asked me in front of our entire chapter — but I should have found a way. Because I knew, I *knew* after last weekend that I was in trouble.

After the tournament, I went back to Kip's house and let him make me breakfast. Okay, fine. No big deal. It's just pancakes and bacon, right?

Wrong. *So* wrong.

Blame it on the high from winning the tournament, or maybe on the late-night hour, but something shifted during that breakfast-slash-dinner. Kip watched me in a different way, a mixture of respect and longing, and I tried desperately to keep my feelings at bay.

He's just a boy, I'd tried to tell myself. *There are plenty of others like him.*

But that's where I'd had to laugh at myself, because I knew it wasn't true. I've dated around PSU. Hell, I've even dipped my toes into other university's fishing pool, thanks to Spring Break ventures. And one thing I knew for sure, *especially* after he made me breakfast and walked on the beach with me as the sun rose, was that there were not plenty of others out there like Kip.

I'm pretty sure there aren't any. Period.

I watch his face as I make my way down the stairs, eyes tracing over the slight stubble on his chin, fixating on those damn glasses that make my knees do wobbly things. He looked so different in the morning light as the sun rose over the coast, and even though I was *sure* he wanted to take me home to try to get some, he didn't.

We talked.

About our family, our background, our goals. And, for the first time ever, I found someone other than my parents and Bear who seemed genuinely interested in my poker life.

He offered to help me, to get me prepped for the tournament, and that little offer did fluttery things to my stomach, the same way his stupid glasses do wobbly things to my knees. Not even my sisters had ever offered to help me with poker. Sure, they've supported me from afar, but even that has been slim.

Kip saw what I wanted, what I desired, and he wanted to help me achieve it.

This motherfucker is breaking down my body — more importantly, my mind — and it is *not* okay.

"Um, hi?" I ask, one eyebrow cocking up at his appearance when I hit the last step.

His blond hair is ruffled more than usual, a lazy, sleepy smirk resting on his face. It's that same face he had when he propositioned me for a date in front of my entire sorority. It's also the same stupid face keeping me awake late at night when I should be sleeping and *not* thinking about Kip motherfucking Jackson.

"Did I wake you?"

"I told you to stay in your sweats," he says easily, referring to my half-ass attempt to bail on our date earlier. I tried to avoid it at all costs — especially after the week of torture I'd had since the last time we'd hung out. Class, I could survive. Seeing him around Greek Row? No big deal. But knowing it would be just the two of us tonight? Doing very date-like things?

Nope. SOS. Cannot deal.

My original plan was to just avoid giving him the little date he'd "won" altogether. I thought maybe he'd drop it, maybe he'd forget. I thought maybe Erin would forget, too, with how much she has on her plate this semester.

But then, Kip showed up at our chapter and rapped — yes, *rapped* his plea to take me out. In front of everyone. In front of Erin.

I had no choice but to say yes, and I've been dreading this night ever since I agreed to it. I even completely ditched last night, but he wouldn't let it go.

We rescheduled for tonight, and even still, I tried to bail earlier, to reschedule. I said I was tired. I said I wanted to stay in my sweats, and he told me that was fine. He told me to stay in my PJs.

Of course, I was kidding.

But this. Mother. Fucker.

"Go change," he instructs.

"What? But we're going on a date."

"Your point? Go change, damnit, or we're going to be late."

"For what, a slumber party?"

Kip's eyes narrow, though a playful smirk plays at the corner of his lips. He steps toward me, and before I even register that I should take a step back, his hands find the small of my back.

"You know I like it when you're feisty," he husks. "So unless you want me to do very non-friend-zone things to you, I suggest you go change. And quickly."

All the blood drains from my cheeks. I feel it like cold, icy water slicking down my spine.

This. This is what I knew I couldn't handle, what I knew I needed to avoid. I can't handle him looking at me like this — like he wants to lick every inch of skin I have exposed in the little black dress I'm wearing, and then some.

"You said hands to yourself," I remind him, referring to our texts, to the promise he made me that even though this was a date, he wouldn't try to be more than friends. I tried to set up boundaries between us, to give us some sort of line to stay behind when it came to being around one another. I had to try *something,* anything not to test the little resistance I had when it came to him. "You promised."

"Then don't make me break my word," he muses, releasing me.

Fire.

Hot, burning, dangerous fire — *that's* what Kip Jackson is.

Erin wants me to lure him in, to get him to fall for me so she can pick up the pieces when I break him. I'm trying to save him. I'm trying to warn him, to keep my distance so we can stay just friends, so I can prove to Erin that her plan has no merit.

I can't break someone's heart if they don't give it to me, right?

But standing at the bottom of those stairs, all I see is fire. Fire I'm about to jump into like it's a deep pool of water, instead. He wants me, and I want him, and there is no fucking way any of this will end well.

For a moment, I debate my options. Could I fake a stroke? Run upstairs and lock myself inside my room for the entire semester? Nothing sticks as I grasp for straws, and Kip just waits, that stupid smirk on his face as I have a complete panic attack under a cool façade.

Finally, I huff, frustrated as I climb back up the stairs and change into sweats. I throw my hair up in a messy bun, too, before trotting back downstairs to join Kip.

Then, we're in a cab on our way to whatever place he has planned for our date, and all I can think about is Erin.

"If you want to be president, you have to make sacrifices."

I love her, and I *do* want to be president — but can I really do this? Can I really get close to Kip — close enough to hurt him — without also hurting myself in the process?

I know the answer to that question, and I feel more uncertainty bubbling up like acid in my stomach with each mile we drive away from campus as more questions pop in to take its place.

Erin has a plan, and once she has her heart set on something, there's no deterring her. There's no reasoning with her, either.

But... what if I can't follow through with my end of the deal?

Something tells me I'll find out the answer to *that* question soon enough.

And I probably won't like what I find.

As we wait for our check at Bella's, the cute little Italian place off campus, my knee bounces. To Kip, it probably looks like I'm nervous, like I'm still concerned with the fact that we're in our pajamas at a nice restaurant, like I'm scared we might run into someone I know.

But really, I'm wishing he would just stop talking.

Not because I don't love the sound of his voice, the smooth baritone of it, or because what he's saying is stupid or immature or rude. No, quite the opposite, actually.

Every time he opens that beautiful mouth of his, I want to listen. I want to believe the words he's saying, like that he thinks I look exquisite with no makeup on and my hair up in a bird's nest of a bun. Or that he sees me as a girl meant to stand out when all I've ever wanted to do at PSU is blend in.

Bella's is quaint, half indoors and half out, close enough to the beach to smell the salt on the breeze. I trace the hanging white lights twinkling against the night sky as Kip continues staring at me.

"Why are you watching me like that?" I ask him after a moment, noticing his gaze on my skin.

"I can't look at you?"

"Not like that, you can't."

He just grins, finishing off the last of the wine in his glass before standing and smoothing his hands over his wrinkled tank top. My eyes flick to his flannel pants again, to the delicious way they hug his hips, but then my eyes shoot up to his.

"What are you doing?"

This isn't good. This is *not* good. Kip has that look, that same mischievous look he had before he jumped on the bar and won me at the auction. The same look he had before he rapped to my entire sorority.

"Ella Mae," he says, his voice deep with a fake southern drawl.

Or is that midwestern?

Honestly, I have no fucking clue and I can't really think straight enough to figure it out because in the next instant, his hand grabs mine, and all I can do is stare at that point of contact.

"I know we've only been together for 'bout a year now, but I feel like you're my whole world."

I don't know how he's not laughing — especially with what I'm sure is a quite hysterical expression on my face. I'm watching him like he just sprouted a second head, or like he's talking in some fake accent super loudly while everyone around us watches.

Oh, wait, that's actually happening.

"I wanna drive our RV all over 'Merica and see everything with you. I can't imagine sharin' my pork rinds with anyone else. And, well, I guess what I'm sayin' is..."

Kip drops down to one knee, fishing a piece of trash out of his pocket. When he presents it to me like a prized pig, I realize he's twisted a piece of straw wrapper into a sort of ring.

Oh, my God.

I'll kill him.

"Will you marry me?"

The entire restaurant is wrapped around that little finger of his, some of them squealing or gasping or offering a collective chorus of "*awww*" that makes my skin crawl. Me? I'm too busy trying to figure out if I can somehow strangle Kip with my eyes somehow.

"I know it's just a straw wrapper," he continues. "Heck, I never have been able to give you the finer things in life.

But I promise to buy you a real nice ring when we can afford it. I'll buy you whatever ring you want! Just please, make me the happiest man this side of the Mississippi River and say yes."

It's hard to say how long I sit there, staring at his stupid, adorable face while everyone around me encourages me to say yes. I think very seriously about throwing something at him, or standing up and just walking right out, leaving him to sit there on his knee like a dumb ass alone in a room of strangers.

But then, I realize something that makes my stomach curl in on itself like a snake.

I want to laugh.

This is fun. It's fun-*ny*. And what's worse? I haven't had fun since Erin told me about her little plan, since my semester got flipped upside down in an instant.

The last time I smiled — *truly* smiled — and felt giddy like this was when I realized Kip and I were in the same class, right before Erin's emergency meeting.

I blink, and a flash of Kip grinning down at me before he licked a line of salt up my abdomen hits me out of nowhere.

All I can do is smile.

I slap a hand over my mouth, forcing fake tears in my eyes as I throw all the warnings out the window. "Oh, gosh, Tommy. I wouldn't spend my life with anyone else. Yes, a thousand times, yes!"

I bolt out of my chair, flinging myself into his lap as I throw my arms around his neck and pull him close. The restaurant erupts into applause and whistles, and Kip smirks, his lips brushing my shoulder as we hold each other.

"Nicely played, Ella Mae," he whispers.

I dig my knuckle into his rib before he yanks me to stand with him, facing the restaurant with a cocky grin.

"Kiss! Kiss!"

The chant starts somewhere in the back, but soon enough, it's all I hear as everyone in the restaurant joins in. I feel the blush on my cheeks before I even turn to Kip, sure that he'll wave everyone off and we'll gracefully exit. But when his aqua eyes find mine, they drink me in like a healing elixir, and his smile is genuine as he reaches for me, dipping me back in a dramatic fashion to more cheers.

His lips seek mine without a moment of hesitation, both of us caught up in the fake proposal. But the moment we connect, the *second* we kiss, every ounce of fakeness, or pretending, fades away in a flash, leaving us submerged in the thick, cool grips of reality.

One of Kip's hands is splayed across my lower back, holding me flush against him as our lips fuse together as one. I breathe him in deep, chills racing from the point where our mouths meet all the way down to my ankles. It's just like before, like our kiss the first night we met, except this time, the electricity is amplified like it's designed to kill.

Perhaps, I think as Kip grips me a little tighter, it is.

I nearly pass out, not another breath passing through me until Kip tilts me up again, the world coming back into focus. Someone snaps a picture, and that flash blinds me as much as the kiss. I just stand there, watching Kip with flushed cheeks as he pays our bill and grabs my hand, pulling me through the crowd and back into the Florida night.

The air is a little chilled when it touches my hot cheeks, and it's like that pinch of cold yanks me back to reality with enough force to knock my next breath out of reach. I don't say a word as we wait for the cab Kip called for us, and once we're inside it, I go off on him, fighting against every urge I have to laugh and feigning annoyance, instead.

I have to be annoyed, because otherwise, I'll be forced to acknowledge the other feelings resting below that pretense.

Like want.

And need.

And the cold realization that I'm in big, *big* trouble.

Erin

FOR THE FIRST TIME since I was raped, I'm drunk.

I've avoided alcohol like most college students avoid homework, knowing all too well what can happen when I lose control of my body, of my mind. I've had absolutely no desire to even have *a* drink, let alone several.

Until tonight.

I knew I shouldn't have followed Kip and Skyler. I knew I shouldn't have creeped on their date like some kind of psycho. But, then again, I've known since the moment this harebrained scheme formed in my head that I was tiptoeing on the line between *I'm okay* and *I'm completely insane*, but it didn't stop me.

Maybe I really am going crazy, but I can't find the will to care — let alone stop.

And so, I'd broken my dry spell, no longer able to survive the night sober after I watched them fake kiss at Bella's Italian Restaurant.

If I told my mom what I was doing, she'd likely pull me out of school and drag me kicking and screaming back home. But it was her who told me to channel my emotions, to put them to use, to find what makes me happy and cling onto that.

Well, Kip makes me happy. At least, he *did*, when we were younger, and I know he will again.

I just have to get to him.

And Skyler is supposed to be helping me do that.

I shift on the couch in our sorority common room, my stomach rolling as I finish off the last of the tequila I poured in a small tea cup, just in case anyone walked in. My thoughts swim in my intoxicated mind, fuzzy and unclear, and I try to pick them out of the murky water as they pass.

It's after two now, and Skyler should be rolling in any minute.

I know, because I watched them from afar as she and Kip said goodnight. I listened to him ask her to stay, to her saying she couldn't, all the while fighting off the urge to upchuck my dinner on the beach.

Sighing, I run the tip of my index finger along the lip of my tea cup, eyes on the small bit of liquid left in a ring around the bottom. Skyler was trying to keep her distance from Kip — that much I could tell with how she responded to his fake proposal at dinner. It was adorable, absolutely swoon-worthy for any girl trying to resist his charm. But Skyler had played it like a pro, only joining in at the very end to join his charade.

That hadn't been hard to watch.

In fact, not even that first kiss had been. I watched him dip her back in a dramatic fashion, watched his hands grip the small of her back as they kissed for the crowd, and though it stung, I knew it was all part of the show.

But then, I followed them to the beach, to the pier, and everything from that point on became a torturous affair.

I never would have labeled myself as a masochist before tonight, but that's the only word suitable for what I'd inflicted. I'd followed them around, watching from afar as Kip tried unsuccessfully to win Skyler a giant teddy bear before *she* finally became the one to pull it off. I tried to breathe normally as I watched them float up to the sky in a bucket on the Ferris wheel, tried to ignore the jealousy flaring in me as they laughed at the top, and I tried not to pass out altogether when I saw their lips still locked together as they floated toward the bottom again. Skyler had broken their kiss first, jumping off Kip's lap and running her hands through her messy hair, but I knew as much as she did in that moment that she was in trouble.

She was falling for him. He was falling for her.

And my plan was quickly getting sidelined.

A very small, very quiet voice in my head told me I should stop the charade altogether. I should tell Skyler she's off the hook, free to do whatever she wanted with Kip. I should move on, leaving my past in the past.

But that voice was like a quiet whisper compared to the other one, the one screaming like a freight train for me to hold onto this one, small sliver of possible happiness.

It's been such a long year, filled with so much pain, and all I want is to feel whole again.

I hear my mom's voice in my head again as I ask myself how many people I'll have to hurt in the process, and I can't find it in myself to care.

I steel my emotions as the front door creaks open, Skyler sneaking through it as quietly as she can. I deposit the empty tea cup on the table beside the couch, reaffirming my plan to pull her head back in the game. She had a fun night. She's distracted. She's possibly thinking of all the ways she can ask me to call everything off.

This is my chance to get us back on track.

Just before she hits the stairs, I find my voice, the sound of it almost foreign as I call after her.

"Good night?"

I can't disguise the touch of bitterness in my words, but Skyler doesn't seem to catch it as she clutches her heart and lets out a sigh of relief when she sees me on the couch.

"Holy shit, Big. You scared the living hell out of me."

"Sorry," I say with a smile, willing all the calmness I can from my inner pool of strength. "I was waiting up, wanted to know how it went tonight."

Skyler eyes me like she doesn't believe that for a second. My Little is smart, and she's careful with her word choice as she falls down into the cushions next to me, her pink cheeks framed by the long hair now falling out of her messy bun.

Effortlessly beautiful, that's what Skyler is. She doesn't need makeup, or a dress, or a strand of pearls. She's the kind of girl who can roll out of bed and have a man falling to his knees with want.

Kip was proof of that.

"It was nice," she says, her eyes soft on mine. "We went to dinner and to the pier, nothing special."

Liar.

The thought screams through me, but I force a smile, swallowing past the sandpaper knot in my throat.

"Good."

Skyler watches me for a long moment, like she's trying to decipher the thoughts in my head. If only she knew how difficult that was, how long I'd tried to untangle the sticky web of them.

There's a touch of something behind her blue irises... pity, maybe? But I don't let it sink in, don't let my heart soften at the sight of it. And when she moves to stand, saying she wants to turn in for the night, I drop that hard shield over my heart again.

"Wait."

Skyler turns, waiting for my next words.

"Has he asked you to the A Sig Valentine's Day dance yet?"

"No," she answers, her voice hesitant. "And I doubt he will."

"No, he definitely will," I assure her, a hint of bitterness back in my words. I cross my arms tight over my chest, testing my next words before I say them aloud. "When he does, you'll say yes. And that's the night you blow him off. I'll be there with Chance Griffins. It'll be perfect. Chance is a dog and will surely do *something* to piss me off," I think out loud, the plan forming as the words tumble out. "Kip will be heartbroken, and by the end of the night, we'll be consoling each other between the sheets."

Skyler's calm expression cracks a little at that, and I can't help but cringe with her.

Did those words really just come out of my mouth?

I'm distantly aware of how far I've fallen from the girl I used to know as I watch Skyler, looking for any sign of defiance, all the while wondering how the hell I got here.

"Okay, sounds like a plan," she says after a moment.

I nod, something between a smile and a grimace finding my lips as I lean back into the couch again. I wait for Skyler to make her way up the stairs, but she just watches me instead.

Then, slowly, she sits back down beside me and pulls me in for a hug.

I stiffen in her arms, warning bells going off at her proximity. But then her warmth transfers into me, and I break, leaning into her as I rest my head on her chest.

The urge to cry washes over me like a tsunami, but I swallow it down.

"You okay, Big?" Skyler whispers.

I sigh, one word slipping through my lips easily. "No."

After that, I'm not sure what to say.

I was raped.

I thought I was okay, but I'm not.

No one knows except Bear, and he can't help me. No one can. No one but me. But I don't know how to help me.

I'm scared.

I feel used. I feel broken. I feel ruined.

I don't know who I am anymore.

I hate myself for what I'm doing to you.

I don't know how to stop.

Each thought flicks in and out of range like low-flying birds, close enough to see but too far away to touch, to catch and hold onto.

So, I lie, instead.

Seems to be the only thing I'm good at doing, anymore.

"I'm stressed the fuck out," I say. "Being president is amazing, but it's a lot of work. I'm falling behind in class already and I feel like my social life is consumed with meetings and philanthropy work."

And stalking you and Kip.

"I'm happy," I whisper, the lie coming from my lips so effortlessly I surprise myself. "But, I don't know…"

"Can you take a break?" Skyler asks, her *Mrs. Fix-It* brain already kicking into high gear. "Let J-Love and Lei handle some of the weight for a while? I know you like to be in control, but maybe just let a few of the smaller things go so you have more time."

"Yeah, I guess I could," I say, my heart aching a little as she holds me tighter.

Here I am using her for my own agenda, and she can't help herself but to try to help *me* feel better.

The world doesn't deserve Skyler Thorne.

"You know how I am, though," I continue "I just feel like if I don't do everything, it'll all get messed up."

"I know, Big," she says with a laugh. "But trust me, the girls know what they're doing. Your G-Little is pretty smart, too. You should ask her for help."

I should probably also jump off a cliff because I'm quite possibly the worst human being to ever walk the Earth.

"Really?" I ask distantly.

"Seriously. She's amazing. I really hope you two can get to know each other more."

"I do, too," I say, this time genuine. Cassie and I used to spend more time together, studying and talking, sharing our mutual love for our majors. But after what happened last semester, I shut everyone out — her included.

Another wave of tequila rushes through me as my eyes find focus on my toes, and I finally let myself ask something real, bridging the gap between me and Skyler in a rare moment of vulnerability.

"Do you hate me for what I'm making you do?" I ask, my voice just a whisper. "Be honest."

Skyler tenses, one hand still rubbing my back as her eyes fall to the floor with mine. "No," she says on a long breath. "I mean, I'd be lying if I said it didn't bother me to play him this way, but I want to be president. I want to keep our Greek line tradition. And I know that you would do the same thing for me."

Her admission warms my heart, and I smile — because it's true. I would do the same for her. There's something special about the bond between sisters, and I know what she means by wanting to keep our Greek traditions alive. I know how much that want can grow deep within a heart, how deep the roots can be.

"It's about sacrifice sometimes," Skyler continues. "And I'm pretty selfish all the time, so it's a good lesson."

I want to argue with her, because in my opinion, Skyler is the least selfish person I know. But my words stick in my throat, and before I can fight back again, the tears I've been holding back pool in my eyes.

I wipe away the first tear before it can fall past the apple of my cheek. "Ugh, sorry. I'm such an emotional wreck right now." I watch her, forcing a smile. "You just make me so proud, Little. You're going to be an awesome president." I swallow, knowing that if nothing else I've said tonight is true, that definitely is. "I love you."

"I love you, too," she says, wrapping me in another hug.

When we pull back, I eye her sweat pants, my curiosity from the entire night getting the best of me. I was horrified when I saw them both dressed in pajamas in public.

"What are you wearing?"

A laugh bursts out of her, and she shakes her head. "It's a long story."

But she tells it, filling me in on the night as carefully as she can. And though it burns to hear her talk about Kip, I feel a touch of comfort at the fact that the plan has been solidified again.

We know the next steps. And with the Valentine's Day dance being just around the corner, I allow hope to bloom in my chest again, small and feeble, but blooming nonetheless.

Kip Jackson will be back in my life soon enough.

And then, hopefully, I'll find happiness again, too.

Skyler

THE NEXT MORNING, I somehow manage to peel myself out of bed just before sunrise. I'd like to say it's paddle boarding that made it possible to survive on less than four hours of sleep, but it'd be a lie if I didn't also include the blond-haired, blue-eyed boy waiting for me at the edge of the water.

The sun is still painting bright colors across the sky as I make my way toward Kip on the beach, paddle board in tow. It was a sick form of compromise that we agreed to — in exchange for me not staying with him last night, I agreed to show him how to paddle board today.

Stupid.

I knew I was in trouble after our kiss at Bella's, but then the pier had happened. We walked around laughing and playing games like a couple of high schoolers, and then, with no one watching, with no fake proposal as an excuse, Kip had kissed me at the top of the Ferris wheel.

My heart flutters at the thought of it, though I try my best to hold its wings down to keep it from taking flight. It's nearly impossible, especially now, staring at his back as he watches the sun rise over the waves. His hands are tucked easily into the pockets of his board shorts, his white t-shirt blowing in the breeze, bronze skin shining in the morning light, a brand new paddle board in the sand by his feet. The man is too beautiful for his own good, too sexy for me to even try to resist.

And I *had* tried.

But with him opening me up the way he is, asking me questions no one else ever has, breaking through walls no one else even knew existed... I'm helpless.

And at the top of that wheel, with his eyes on me and the lights casting him in a soft glow, it all seemed very simple.

I couldn't *not* kiss him.

That's just all there was to it.

Of course, I'd realized my mistake in the cab back to the sorority house, chastising myself for letting it go too far. And to top it all off, Erin had been waiting for me after our date, and she had the next part of her little plan in place. All I needed was one conversation with her to be brought back to reality, to be sobered up to what I was actually doing.

I have less than two weeks until the Valentine's Day dance, until the night when everything with Kip will end.

Thirteen days.

So, maybe it's a sick kind of self-flagellation, but I choose to ignore that ominous date when I should have it in the forefront of my mind. I choose to shove it down, bury it under the sand, and live in my fantasy a little while longer.

At least for today, I'm just going to enjoy the time I have with Kip. I'm going to pretend like we're just a boy and a girl, enjoying the sunrise on a couple of paddle boards. It'll all be fine.

Sure.

"Sorry I'm late," I say when I'm close enough for Kip to hear.

He turns at the sound of my voice, his blue eyes widening a little at the sight of me as he scans me from head to toe.

"Yeah, you better be sorry," he says with a grin, his gaze sweeping over the sunrise again as I sidle up beside him. "It's half past early as fuck and we agreed to meet at the ass crack of dawn. Way to make me wait."

I smile at his joke, dropping my board into the sand beside his. Without another word, and without a warning I probably should have given him, I strip my light blue tank top over my head and pop the button on my jean shorts, shimmying them down over my hips.

Kip watches my every move.

I know before I meet his eyes. I feel the heat of his gaze on my skin more than I do the rising sun, and when I finally look his way, I can't stop my grin at his dumbfounded expression.

"You just going to stand there and ogle my boobs all day or are we doing this?"

"Can't I do both?" he quips back quickly, and I shake my head with a laugh, making my way toward the water without checking to see if he's following.

It's been so long since I've been able to spend time on my board, I audibly sigh once we're out past the easy waves and gliding on the smooth water as the sun rises over the beach. I start out on my knees, showing Kip how to catch his balance and maneuver the waves before we both stand. Surprisingly, Kip catches on pretty quickly, and doesn't fall even once as we paddle parallel to the shoreline.

We're both quiet for the most part, enjoying the sounds of the beach waking up — the soft crash of the water on the shore, the high chirp of the birds, the distant sounds of the ships coming to life. When I notice a thin sheen of sweat gathering on Kip's defined abdomen, I nod toward a sand bar not too far away and we make our way toward it, both popping off our boards once the water is shallow enough.

We hydrate with the water I brought for us, both of us watching as more and more people make their way onto the sandy beach in the distance. Kip is quiet, but I feel him watching me, that same heat sparking on my skin like it did before when I stripped out of my shorts. Only this time, I hear questions he's not asking, and it makes me more curious about him.

I try to talk myself out of more conversation. *Just enjoy being close to him and keep that distance in place,* I silently warn myself. But the more we stand there, the more I want to know. And when I cast a casual glance his way as I tuck my water bottle away again, I can't help myself.

"So, what's your story, Kip?" I ask as he leans his elbows over his board.

"What do you mean? My story?"

I shrug, wiggling my toes in the sand. The sand bar is a little mushier than the sand that lines the beach, but the water is crystal clear, and I can see all the way down to my pink toe nail polish.

"I mean, why did you move out here? Why did you transfer to Palm South of all places? Where are you from? What do you like to do? You know, besides lick tequila off strange girls."

"Hey," he defends quickly. "That was not my fault. And who's worse off here — me or the strange girl?"

My throat warms, remembering the way it felt to have his wet tongue tracing lines on my stomach. "I think I got the better end of the deal."

"And I tend to disagree."

Kip's eyes fall to my stomach, half of it covered by the water, and my cheeks flush. But I just watch him, waiting for his response to my question.

"Let's see," he finally says, looking up at the white, whispy clouds floating by us. "I transferred to Palm South because I wanted to get out of the Midwest. And because Palm South has a pretty decent screenwriting program, which is what I want to do with my life. It's not the last stop by any means, but it's a good transition."

I smile, thinking about how Kip is in our Writing for Television class. It's only been a few weeks and I already know I won't be changing my major to anything related to writing, but it has been fun to read his pieces, to listen to him talk about his passion with Dr. O'Neal.

"It also helps that I could get away from my dad," he adds, his voice a little softer.

"Uh-oh, Daddy drama?"

Kip snorts. "Well, he's an Army Major General, if that gives you any idea."

"Yeesh," I say, raising both eyebrows at that. "Sounds fun."

"Yeah, real fun. I mean, I love him and everything," he says quickly. "He's my dad, he's a *good* dad in the sense of the word, but he just wants to live his dream through me and I'm over trying to be what he wants. It's nice to be out here away from his constant glare of disapproval."

My stomach twists at that as I try to imagine being in his shoes. My family and I may not have had much, but we had love. My mom and dad have always been supportive of me, and though I help them with their bills, they've tried everything they can to get me *not* to do that. They want me to live my own life, to do what makes me happy. But helping them is part of what makes me happy.

"What dream?" I ask after a moment.

"Huh?"

"His dream?" I ask, cocking a brow. "That he wants to live through you? What is it?"

"Uh..."

Kip's eyes widen, and I watch with curiosity as he scans the water with his breath coming a little harder, like he said something he wasn't supposed to. Playing poker lets me pick up on peoples' quirks easy, read when they're uncomfortable or, worse, when they're lying.

And something tells me there's a thin veil of dishonesty over his next words.

"Being in a fraternity," he says. "College, the whole thing. He went straight into the service after high school and I guess he always wanted to go. So he's had this big dream for me ever since I was little. Perfect school, perfect fraternity, you know."

He shrugs, his eyes still on the water as I watch him, trying to decipher the truth. It makes sense, what he said about his dad wanting that experience. Still... he's hiding something.

I pop back up on my paddle board, stretching until my back is pressed against the warmth of it. I breathe in a deep sigh, letting one leg hang in the water as I reach out toward Kip with the opposite hand.

"Hold me so I won't float away?"

Kip swallows, a smirk finding his lips as his hand wraps around mine. And just like every time the boy touches me, my skin sparks to life under his fingertips, a constant rush of energy flowing through me and cycling back toward him.

"So," I say, letting my eyes fall up to the sky. I stare at the white clouds through the safety of my sunglasses, bringing the conversation back around. "If it were up to you, would you be in a fraternity?"

"Maybe. I guess I don't really know. It's just always been ingrained in me that I would go to college and be in a fraternity. I've never really had the chance to think if I'd actually like it. But, at least being here, I can do what he wants and still do what I want, too. I don't have to live under his scrutiny, his constant judging of whether I'm doing the right thing or not."

I smile, holding his hand a little tighter. "I think you've got life figured out, Kip Jackson. At least, you seem like you do. You know what you want to do in life, you're not afraid to be who you want to be — I think your dad should be proud of you."

The words slip out before I realize the magnitude of them, and I feel the moment they hit Kip. His hand stiffens in mine, just a pause, and then his thumb rubs against my palm.

"You know, I liked the you that came out last night," he says, switching gears. "The care-free, I-don't-give-a-shit Skyler."

I shake my head, thinking of how he had me screaming — yes, literally *screaming* — at the top of the Ferris wheel. I can't remember the last time I let loose like that, that I let go of caring what other people thought of me.

"I still can't believe I let you take me around town in my freaking sweat pants."

"You looked hot in those sweat pants. And I dare you to tell me you didn't have fun."

I let my head fall toward him at that, my cheek resting on the paddle board. "I did have fun."

It's honest, and Kip raises his brows like he knew that all along. Then, he props himself up on his board, mirroring me as he lays the opposite way, his feet toward the end where my head is. We're still linked together, our hands wrapped around one another, eyes focused on the sky above.

We talk for a while longer, Kip telling me more about the kind of shows he'd like to write in the future. When the sun is higher in the sky, making me sweat even with my leg in the water, I suggest we head back to shore.

But before I have the chance to even stand fully on my board, Kip tackles me into the water.

"What the hell, Kip?!" I say on a laugh, splashing him when my head is above water again. "You're such a jerk."

He's chuckling, but the laughter dies in both of our throats when he steps into me, one hand finding the small of my back as he pulls me into him. My chest brushes his, my heart hammering so hard at his proximity that I'm sure he feels every beat.

Kip watches me, his eyes halfway hidden under his sunglasses, but I catch the exact moment when he moves a centimeter closer, his mouth on a track for mine. I close my eyes, screaming at myself internally that I should pull away, I should get back on my board, I should get away from him.

His lips brush mine, so softly I almost convince myself I didn't feel them at all...

And then, that motherfucker snaps my top off with a tug of the string.

I jerk back, hands flying to my chest just before the triangle-shaped fabric slips off. Kip laughs, already retreating toward his board.

"Oh my God! Kip!"

"Race you back!" he yells over his shoulder, and then he's on his board and half-ass paddling away.

I want to scream, but all I can do is laugh as I hastily re-tie my top and jump on my own board, catching up to him not even a full twenty-yards later. I beat him back to shore without breaking a sweat, and I stand on the beach where the water breaks over the sand, shaking my head at him as he walks his board up.

"You work pretty well with your clothes off," he teases. Water drips off his chest and down his abdomen, soaking his board shorts. A few droplets sneak under the band of his briefs beneath them, and I've never been more jealous of water in my entire life.

"You know you'll pay for that, right?"

He shrugs. "We'll see."

My eyes find the edge of his shorts again, noting the deep V that points down to an area of Kip I can only imagine is as impressive as the rest of him. And though I shouldn't, I find myself genuinely hoping I *do* get the chance to pay him back.

There are worse things I could see than Kip Jackson naked.

It's after noon when Kip clears the dishes from the turkey sandwiches he made us, and I'm back in the kitchen where he fed me pancakes and bacon at four in the morning thinking the exact same thing I thought last time I was here.

I should go.

Truthfully, the words were in my mind when I agreed to come back to his place after we rinsed off our paddle boards. I should have just gone back to the sorority house. But he'd begged me, saying his place is closer, that he wanted to feed me, that it was Sunday and I had nothing better to do, anyway.

Which was true.

So, I agreed, but now that I'm here, fed and sleepy from the sun and from a lack of rest last night, I hear the voice even louder.

I should go.

"Why don't we take a shower and watch a movie?" Kip suggests.

"I don't have any clothes here besides the ones I have on now," I say, my excuse weak. "And they're all sandy."

"You can borrow a pair of boxers and a shirt of mine."

I chew my lip, trying to listen to that little voice inside me when the other, louder one is telling me that a movie with Kip sounds pretty perfect.

"I don't know, I'm pretty tired," I finally say, adding a yawn for emphasis.

"So am I," he says, standing. He reaches for my hands and tugs me up with him. "So maybe we watch a movie and maybe we take a nap." He shrugs, as if it's simple. His blue eyes twinkle a little, a mischievous tell as they search mine. "Don't leave yet. I barely see you during the week and I know there's not many weekends where you don't have sorority stuff going on."

God, if looks could kill. Not that he's looking at me like he wants to kill me. No, it's more like he wants to hold me, and kiss me, and get to know me more. But *that* look kills me more right now. It's like a rusty, jagged knife straight to the throat. If he knew what I was doing to him, what Erin had planned, he'd hate us.

Both of us.

"I actually have a sisterhood event tonight," I admit.

"See?" He tugs my wrist, leading me toward his bedroom as alarms go off in my mind like a fucking pinball machine.

His apartment is small — a little studio close to the beach, with nothing but a curtain separating his "bedroom" from his small living area and kitchen. But it's cozy, and with a keyboard in one corner and various albums spread out on the shelf opposite his bed, it's very him. Simple, masculine, artsy.

Kip.

Kip drops my hand long enough to rummage through his dresser, pulling free a clean shirt and pair of boxers that he tosses to me without giving me another chance to argue.

He points to the bathroom behind me. "Towels are above the toilet in the cabinet, shampoo and shit's in there."

But I can't move. I'm still trying to convince myself to leave, to *run*, but I just stand there, instead.

"Come on," he says, moving toward me until he's close enough to touch. His fingers reach out, pushing a few strands of my salty hair out of my eyes. "Just for a few hours. You'll feel better once you shower and I know you're tired. You're not going to get any sleep if you go home to your sorority house."

At that, I let out a long breath and nod. "You're probably right about that."

Kip's smile is that of a winner, and he nudges me toward the bathroom again.

"Fine," I finally concede, the little voice inside me throwing her hands up in surrender. "But just for a little while. And no trying to ambush me in the shower, either," I warn.

"I promise," he says, hands held up high. "You can shower in peace."

I narrow my eyes at him. "Mm-hmm."

He's still smiling when I finally step inside the bathroom and close the door between us, his eyes disappearing on the other side.

I strip out of my clothes quickly, turning the water all the way hot in his shower before standing in front of the mirror over his bathroom cabinet. I stare at my hollow, tired eyes as the steam fills up the room, sighing with a shake of my head.

"This is not smart," I whisper, almost in a mocking voice.

Still, I step inside the shower, convincing myself everything will be fine. I'll rinse off, get dressed in *his* boxers, in a shirt that smells like *him*, and then we'll just lie around. I'll catch a nap, maybe watch a movie. No harm, no foul.

But before I can even realize how stupid I am for thinking any of that is possible, my entire body freezes at the sound of a soft knock on the door.

I haven't even pulled his shower curtain closed yet. I'm just standing there, the water hitting my stomach and running down my bare thighs as I turn my head — slowly, carefully — like I'm scared of what I'll find.

And I should have been scared.

Two bright, turquoise eyes stare at me through a barely-cracked door, and I swallow, not moving to cover myself like I should.

Kip pushes the door open a little farther, but his eyes don't skate down my naked body. He keeps his gaze locked on my own eyes, swallowing, and I watch his Adam's apple bob in his throat as I wait. For what, I'm not sure — an explanation? An invitation? A demand to get the fuck out of here before we both do something we can't take back?

Erin's voice pops into my head briefly, just long enough to make my stomach roll before it disappears along with every other rational thought at his next words.

"I suck at keeping promises," he admits, his voice low, mixing with the sound of the water raining down around me in the shower.

My breath catches, the lump in my throat too hard to swallow past when I admit my own secret to him.

"And I suck at pretending like I don't want you."

Kip's eyelids flutter a little, his jaw ticking under the skin as he moves toward me — slowly, cautiously, like I might bolt if he takes even one step too far.

"You want me?"

I should feel exposed, embarrassed, standing here naked in front of him. But I don't. I feel wanted, desired, and powerful as hell.

Still, I tremble as I let out something between a laugh and a whimper at the truth. "Kip, I've wanted you since the first time I felt your mouth on my skin. Maybe even a little before that." I press my lips together, knowing I should stop, knowing I should grab the towel hanging on the rack beside Kip and get the hell out of his apartment.

But I can't.

Not now.

"I hate pretending like I don't want you," I whisper. "But I don't know how to do this. It's dangerous, you and me. Being together. Like this." I tell him, wishing I could tell him exactly *why* it's dangerous.

But if he knew, if he *really* knew, he'd hate me.

I already do.

Kip is so close now, his hands reaching forward slowly until they cradle my face between them. I want to sigh, to lean into that touch, but I keep my eyes trained on his.

"This is about Erin, isn't it?"

At that, my chest deflates like a popped balloon, my knees nearly giving in under the weight.

Shit. He knows. He fucking knows. Oh, God.

Kip shakes his head, his eyes still hard on mine. "Listen, Erin is in the past for me. I'm sure she's telling you and everyone else to stay away from me, staking her claim — but she doesn't have a claim over me. I am not hers."

Another sickening wave washes over me the more he talks. *I wish* it was that simple, that it was just that she told me to stay away from him. I thought he knew, I thought he somehow figured out her plan, but he has no idea.

He has no idea how important my sorority is to me — my sisters, my line, my Big and my Little, my legacy as future president. He has no idea how much power Erin holds, or how much I love her, how much I would do anything for her — even this. Even as much as it hurts. Because she's one of my best friends.

They've always said, *sisters before misters*. And it's been easy, up until now, to follow that rule.

But staring at Kip, feeling his hands on me, I don't know how *not* to break that rule now.

"You don't understand," I say, my voice shaking. How do I even *begin* to explain it to him?

"I do," he interrupts, lifting my chin. "Are you going to let her dictate who you like? Who you touch? Just because she's your Big, because she's president of your sorority?"

"It's so much more than that," I try, ripping my gaze from his. "It would be easier if you just let me go, if we just stopped this right now. We could save a lot of hurt, a lot of pain."

"Skyler," he says on a huff. He lifts my chin again, forcing me to look at him when I'm trying to do anything but. "I want you. If what you said is true just now, then you want me, too. I don't care about Erin, I don't care about your sorority or my fraternity — not right now. Right now, I care about the fact that you're here, with me, in my shower, and I want you."

The hand not holding my chin in place slips down, down, over my arm to hold my naked waist.

"Now," he breathes. "Tell me you don't want me. Tell me you want me to stop."

His hand drops a little lower, his fingertip brushing over my clit so softly, so lightly, I inhale a warm, steamy breath and don't let it go.

"Tell me to let you go. Tell me to stop, Skyler."

I can't stop shaking, my eyes watching his as I try to find the right words to get me out of the hell I'm currently burning in. Erin will be devastated if she even finds out this much has happened, let alone anything else. I knew her well before Kip, before he came in and flipped my entire world upside down.

I owe it to my Big to stop. Right now.

But the truth slips from my mouth in a whisper, and I know I'll have to suffer the consequences.

"I can't."

Kip shakes his head. "You have to tell me to stop, Skyler, or I won't be able to. Once I feel you, once I taste you, I won't be able to stop then. If you don't want this, you have to tell me now."

But I do want this.

And that's all I hold onto, that simple truth, no matter how fucked up and selfish it is.

"I want this. I want you."

And just like that, with those six, simple, unapologetic words, all bets are off between me and Kip Jackson.

My hands are in his hair before I can register that I told them to go there, pulling and tugging, his lips hard on mine as Kip pushes me against the shower wall. He's inside the shower with me in the next second, still in his board shorts, not taking the time to strip them off before letting the water crash down on him, too. Steam swirls around us, our breaths making it heavier — hands touching, lips kissing, tongues licking. We're a mess of sighs and moans, the kiss without a doubt the most passionate one of my life.

I've never been a believer in love at first sight. It sounds crazy to even consider that I could be in love with Kip. But the way I feel with his lips on mine, the foreign, never-before-felt electricity that buzzes through me *every single time* we touch — it has to be a sign. It's not just because he's forbidden, because he's technically off limits to me — if it was, I wouldn't have felt it that first night he sucked tequila off my stomach. And it's not just because he's quite possibly the sexiest man I've ever known, with his icy blue eyes, his perfectly mussed hair, his strong, stubble-lined jaw. No, it's something more — something unexplainable, something I'm sure I'll never quite figure out.

Kip feels like forever, and I can't even call him mine.

Pinning my wrists above my head, Kip slides two fingers inside me quickly, the movement easy and fluid as he fills me to the hilt. I suck in a breath, the rush of blood heavy in my head before it all rushes straight back to where his fingers are buried deep inside. His cock strains against the wet fabric of his shorts into my stomach as his fingers work, steady and smooth, his mouth sucking and biting up and down my neck.

Thoughts are fleeting, all sense of time and rationality lost the more Kip touches me. I can't even touch him *back,* not with my wrists pinned above my head, so I just wrap my hands into fists and hold on, letting everything I feel escape in breathy moans through my parted lips.

Kip moans his approval as his kisses fall lower, and his eyes find mine just as he sucks one tender, puckered nipple between his teeth. My back arches off the wet wall, into the hot stream of water, and the new angle of Kip's hand has his palm giving my clit just the friction it needs.

"Oh, fuck," I breathe, almost a whimper, maybe a plea. "*Kip.* Yes. More."

The moment the word leaves my mouth, I realize that's exactly what I want. What I need.

More.

Ripping my wrists free, I immediately grab the strings on Kip's board shorts, untying them in an instant before I tug the shorts over his hips. The deep V I admired from above the hem of his shorts shoots down farther, the lean muscle framing where I want to see him most. And when the shorts fall into a wet heap at his feet, his hard-on springs forward, granting my wish with more enthusiasm than I could have imagined.

I've seen enough cocks to know a good one when it's in front of me, and Kip's is so hard, so long and thick, the head of it glistening with just a drop of pre-cum, that I nearly lose my mind with the want to drop to my knees and take him inside my mouth. I want to taste every inch of it, feel that perfectly mushroomed head hitting the back of my throat, lick up the thick vein lining the top.

When I reach forward, wrapping one hand around him with a firm grip, Kip's hand stills inside me, his fingers immobilized.

"Oh, fuck," he groans. His hips flex forward as I roll my hand from his tip to his base, slow at first before picking up rhythm as the water helps lubricate each pump.

Kip's fingers start moving again, this time with more fervor, the heel of his hand pressing more into my clit. He kisses me hard, sucking my bottom lip between his teeth and holding it there. Each time he works harder with his hand, so do I, each of us rushing closer to the edge.

My breaths are shallow, hollow, not a single one of them deep enough to provide enough oxygen. I feel the fire of my orgasm threatening to catch, each new rub of his palm on my clit another spark, another flick of the match. I feel my grip on him loosening, my focus lost, and Kip kisses my neck before growling out his next words against the slick skin.

"This is about you. I want you to come. Come on my fingers so I can taste you."

"Oh, God."

His words are so dirty, so unfiltered, they make my knees quiver under the pressure of them. I finally let my hand drop from his rigid cock, my fingers pressing into the slick wall behind me, instead, as I try to find something to hold onto before I fly over the edge of my release.

Suddenly, Kip pulls me up into his arms, bending so I'm cradled inside them before he steps out of the shower, carrying me into his bedroom with my body dripping water and marking a trail along the way. He drops me into the ruffled sheets, his mouth finding my skin in the next instant as he kisses down my stomach, biting the inside of my thighs before his tongue circles around my clit.

Oh. My. God.

If I thought the man knew how to work his hand, it's nothing compared to how he is with his tongue. It's like he knows every move to make, every spot to hit, like I drew up a personal map for him and he's writing the instruction manual. My legs tremble, thighs shaking on either side of his face as his blue eyes watch me like they're just *daring* me to come.

I've never been one to back down from a dare.

He plunges two fingers back inside me, and just a few curls of them combined with his tongue on my clit sends me spiraling. My toes spread, numb as all the blood in my body rushes to where Kip touches me. My vision grows black, and I have no idea if I'm screaming his name or if I'm completely silent. I feel myself pulsing around him, and my vision comes back just in time to see his grin turn wicked as he keeps his tongue working, his fingers in perfect rhythm, pushing and pushing until every ounce of my orgasm is spilled onto his fingers.

My tense muscles all let loose at once, my legs falling limp, and Kip carefully removes his fingers, causing another tremble. He softly kisses his way back up my body, and when he's balanced on one elbow above me, his blue eyes hard on mine, he smiles, slipping his still-soaked fingers inside his lips and licking them clean.

Goddamn.

I close my eyes, savoring the feel of that moment, of being desired *that* much. Kip's lips are on mine, pushing and eager, his tongue slipping in so I can taste myself there. And it feels a little like an hour, a little like only a second before his warmth leaves me as he moves to grab the towel I'd laid out in the bathroom.

As soon as he's gone, as soon as his hands are no longer on me, the spell is broken.

My heart ticks up a notch, the thumps hitting harder against my ribcage as the reality of what I've done settles in like a slow, cold flood. I watch the water rise higher, knowing it will suffocate me soon, and yet I still can't move.

I've betrayed Erin. I've betrayed Kip. I've put my *own* heart at risk. Because now that he's touched me, now that I know what it feels like to have a piece of him, I want all of him.

I *need* all of him.

But I can't have him.

In the moment, I convinced myself that I could. I told myself it would be fine, just let go, just exist with him now — here — in this moment. But here I am, sitting in the cold, merciless flood waters of the truth.

I'm royally fucked.

Kip is still smiling when he emerges from the bathroom, helping me dry off in a warm, fuzzy towel before helping me get dressed in his boxers and a t-shirt. He pulls me into the bed with him, tucking me close with his body in a perfect seam with mine. His knees fold into the space behind mine, his chest hot on my back, his arms wrapped around me like a body pillow.

I still my movements, closing my eyes and holding back the hot tears pooling behind my eyes. I've never felt more safe, more at home, than I do in his arms right now.

But he's not my home.

When he thinks I'm asleep, Kip lets himself drift off, too. I wait until I can say his name without him stirring, and then I peel myself out of his grip, slipping into the living area to redress. I leave his clothes folded on the bed next to him, watching his chest rise and fall as he sleeps for a long moment before I sigh, biting my lip against the urge to cry and crawl back into bed with him.

Then, I leave.

Because I'm Skyler Thorne. And like I've told every guy I've been with at PSU, Skyler Thorne doesn't sex and sleep.

Though for the first time, I want to.

And *that's* the worst part.

Cassie

"YOU LOOK LIKE YOU'RE on Cloud Mystery Man."

Erin's voice jars me from where I'm working on separating and stapling the packets for this week's Panhellenic meeting, and I pause, eyes meeting hers. My brows pull inward as I try to decipher what she means.

"What?"

Erin smirks, tucking her dark blonde hair behind one ear. She's typing away on her laptop, working on her agenda for the meeting, but her eyes hold mine for a moment before they return to the screen.

"You've got that look. That one that says there's a boy."

My eyes pop open wider, and Erin doesn't even look at me when she chuckles at the response.

"Don't worry," she says quickly. "I'm not going to press you on telling me who it is. I'm just saying, you had your heart broken by Grayson at semi-formal, and you popped back so quickly." One of her neatly manicured eyebrows lifts. "That doesn't happen unless there's someone else helping speed the healing process."

Heat sparks on my neck, crawling up to my cheeks as I let my eyes fall back to the packet I'm assembling. Flashes of Adam hit me hard, my stomach fluttering at the memory of his hands on me last night. We're in Erin's room now, but I know that just down the hall, the long board Adam made me sits propped beside my bed.

She's right.

I am on a cloud, floating high and free, intoxicated by what it feels like to be with Adam. He touched me last night like no one ever has — patiently, adoringly, like all he'd ever wanted in his life was to have that pleasure, and now that he was experiencing it, he would take his time memorizing every minute, every second.

My eyes flutter close, a soft smile spreading on my lips as I remember how he looked staring up at me, his mouth on the most sensitive part of me. I wanted to return the favor. I wanted to taste him so badly it *hurt,* like the lady version of blue balls. But, Adam's taking his time with me. He's moving slow, and not with the same, false intentions that Grayson had said he wanted to move slow with. *He'd* been getting some on the side.

No, Adam is mine, even if we aren't official yet.

... right?

I swallow at the possibility that he might be fooling around with someone else, though I know in my heart that it couldn't be true. Still, if he *is* only faithful to me... then *why* can't we just be together?

I've asked myself that a hundred times.

I believe him when he says he wants to move slow, when he wants me to focus on me, but then he goes and makes me a personalized long board. He holds my hand, he calls me every single night and texts me all through the day.

He's my boyfriend by all accounts... except the public admission.

"I think I just saw every single possible girly emotion cross over your face in a span of twenty seconds."

I snap my head toward Erin, forgetting she was even in the room until the moment she speaks.

She smirks, shaking her head. "If you want to talk about it, I'm here."

I let out a breath, returning her smile. Erin and I haven't hung out in a long time — not like this. I was surprised when she texted me this morning — or rather, *very* late last night — asking me if I had some time to help her prepare for the meeting this week. She wanted to catch up, she said, and I was excited to get some time alone with my Grand Big.

Still, what can I even say? If I tell her about me and Adam, she'll be the first one. And she's Skyler's Big. Will she understand, will she question when Adam and I started to feel this way? He never cheated on Skyler with me... but then again, he did kiss me less than a week after they broke up.

My stomach turns.

"Have you ever been in love?" I ask Erin instead of divulging my situation.

She pauses, her fingers hovering over her keys for a moment before she starts typing again.

"Once."

"Kip?"

Erin nods, her eyes softer now, tinged with a hint of sorrow.

"He was the first boy I ever loved... the only one. But, I messed it up."

I watch her with a sympathetic gaze, though I can't say I agree with her plan to get him back. Tangling Skyler up in her mess doesn't seem fair to me. But, Skyler is a big girl, and she agreed to it on her own free will. I keep telling her I'm here if she wants to talk about it, encouraging her to call it off if she needs to. That's all I can do — be there. I can't make the decision for her.

And watching Erin now, noting the sadness in her features, I know she must feel like this is the only way. I try to put myself in her shoes. If Adam slipped out of my grasp, would I ever do something as crazy to try to get him back?

I know that answer without even asking the question aloud. I would. In a heartbeat.

I'd do whatever it took.

"Do you think your plan will work?"

She shrugs. "I don't know. I hope, of course. I think it will. But it's hard to say. Until I have him alone, until I see what it feels like to be with him, I can't be sure."

"What do you mean?"

Erin presses her lips together, thinking. "Well, if there's anything I've learned in my dating experience, it's that if a guy wants to be with you — *really* wants to be with you — then he will be. So, if after Skyler pulls this off, Kip doesn't show interest? Well, then I'll know."

Though I hear what Erin says about Kip, I can't help but think about Adam.

He says he wants to be with me, that I mean everything to him... but he also says we should wait. He says I need to focus on myself.

Is that really what he means?

Or is it that he doesn't want to be with me at all?

I swallow, mind racing.

What if he just doesn't want to hurt me?

The thought grows from nothing, but sprouts to life like Jack's magic bean stalk, flying high into the sky and past the clouds with its realness. It's something Adam would do — keep me at a distance, do everything he could to be there for me and help me heal. He cares about me, that much is easy to see... but does he really want to be with me?

If he does, wouldn't he already *be* with me?

"Do you really think it's that simple?" I ask Erin. "I mean, what if you knew Kip cared about you. What if you were hanging out and he was telling you everything you needed to hear, but he wanted to wait a while before making things official. Would you wait?"

Erin scoffs. "Hell no. I mean we'd date, of course. But once the feelings were there for me? I'd ask him if he felt the same. And if he did, we'd be together. It's that simple. I'm not down to play that *what are we* bullshit. Been there, done that, bought the t-shirt." She chuckles, shaking her head. "I'm too grown to play those games."

My tongue is thick and sticky in my mouth, impossible to swallow past.

Erin's eyes flick to me, her brows pinching together when she notes my expression.

"He's toying with you, isn't he? Your Mystery Man."

I don't respond.

Erin sighs, closing the lid on her laptop to face me completely. "Look. Here's the truth. You want it?"

I just look at her, still unable to speak.

She dips until her eyes are at the same level as mine, a mixture of sympathy and hard-hitting realness reflected in her gaze. "The truth is, if you're not sure what you are to him, then you're nothing. A man who wants to be with you will be with you. Period. He won't be able to stomach the thought of anyone else being with you, therefore, he'll make you his. If it doesn't make him sick not to call you his girlfriend, if he doesn't feel some kind of sense of urgency to claim you, to mark you as his own, then he doesn't really want you. He's waiting for someone better to come along. He's getting what he can out of you because you're there, and he knows he can, but in the end?" She shakes her head. "Men are quite simple to figure out. And trust me when I say if he loved you, or even liked you — you'd know. There wouldn't be anything to question." She sits back, shrugging simply, as if it was all common sense. "A real man would never make you question what you mean to him."

Her last sentence hits me like a hot, deadly bullet to the chest. I lose my next breath at the impact of it, simply staring at her without a word to offer in response.

Because she's right.

It makes sense. Adam wants me to take time to "find myself" again, or whatever. But I can do that *with* him. I can be his girlfriend and still take time to heal. In fact, why wouldn't he want to be a bigger part of that?

He has the power to heal me, and yet he's only using part of it.

It's not that I don't see the value in being alone, in taking time to reconnect with myself... but the thing is, I'm *not* alone. We text all the time, call every night, hang out alone, and do very girlfriend-slash-boyfriend things.

Like stick our tongues down each other's throats.

And lick places not seen by the sun.

He's with me, in practically every sense of the word, and I'm not going to let him play this game.

As soon as I realize it, as soon as I make the decision, I'm up off the floor, shaking out my achy legs from sitting crosslegged for so long.

"I need to run an errand real quick," I say to Erin, casting a quick glance in the mirror at my hair. It's messy, my cheeks flushed, but I don't take time to fix it. "You okay for a little bit? I'll be back."

Erin smirks, like she knows, and opens her laptop again. "I'll be here, Grand Little. Just going to stop by Skyler's room here in a bit and see how her morning with Kip went."

"Okay," I say, not even really hearing her over the rushing rapids in my ears. "I'll be back."

Then, I'm flying down the stairs, out the door, and down Greek Row. My eyes are hot on the Alpha Sigma house, the words I'll say forming in my head so quickly that they disappear before I can practice them and get them on my tongue, ready to throw at Adam. But it doesn't matter. No matter how I say it, I will demand answers — and I won't leave until I get them.

I knock hard on the door, annoyed when it doesn't just open at the push of my hand. It's a fraternity house, for God's sake. They *never* lock their door. Beating my fist harder, I keep knocking and knocking, still to no avail.

The sun is setting off in the distance, the air growing cooler with its descent as Greek Row is cast in a low, orange light. Walking around to the backyard gate, I peek through one of the slits in the wooden planks, finding no bodies there, either.

Weird.

When I knock directly on his bedroom window without an answer, I give up, huffing as I rip my phone from my pocket.

- Hey. We need to talk. Where are you? -

But he doesn't answer.

Not that minute, not that night, not even that week.

And with each passing day, with each minute that goes by with him ignoring me, acting like what happened between us Friday night was *nothing*, I get the answer to my unasked question — louder than I wanted, with a harsher reality than I could have imagined.

He got into my pants, and just like Clay, he disappeared.

Without a word.

Without so much as an *I'm sorry, I can't do this.* Without an explanation. Without a care that he would break my heart in the process, just like every boy to touch it before him.

And suddenly, all the bullshit he served me on his shiny, golden platter rolls in my stomach, threatening to come back up.

I thought, when I was ready, I could fall into his arms and trust that he'd be there to catch me. But the truth is much harder to swallow.

The truth is, I fell a long time ago.

And Adam was never really there.

Legacy takes place during the same semester as *Black Number Four*. Whether you've read it before now or not, you'll get a wider view of what was happening at Palm South University (especially between Kip and Skyler) if you read *Black Number Four* as you read this season. I will help guide you, letting you know which chapters to read before moving on to the next episode.

FOR THE FULL READING EXPERIENCE FOR THIS EPISODE, **READ CHAPTERS 6-8** IN *BLACK NUMBER FOUR* BEFORE CONTINUING ON TO EPISODE THREE. (You'll get to see how Skyler felt when Kip asked her for the date, experience the first date from Kip's point of view, and get inside his head for their first sexual encounter. Ow oww. ;))

EPISODE 3

Cassie

TWO-HUNDRED AND SIXTEEN.

That's how many hours have passed since I went to the Alpha Sigma house, seeking Adam, needing answers. That's how many hours have passed since I sent him a text, telling him we needed to talk. That's how many hours have passed, and I haven't heard a single word from him — not a date, not a phone call, not a text, not even a stupid smoke signal.

Nothing.

And now, on the precipice of a holiday centered around love, all I feel in my heart is bitter, icky resentment.

"I hate Valentine's Day," I say to Skyler, for probably the fifth time this week, as another romantic comedy starts on her television.

It's a Monday — a rainy one, at that — and after my two morning classes were done, I slipped into Skyler's room and crawled into bed with her, taking solace in watching other romances play out on the screen.

"I mean seriously, whose bright idea was it to make a day to single out the already miserably single?" I pout.

"Oh, stop," Skyler says quickly. "Last year, Valentine's Day was the best day ever to you."

"Yeah, well," I say, reaching for our half-eaten bowl of popcorn. "That was because I had not one, but *two* guys fighting for my attention."

The words slip out before I have the chance to stop them, and I freeze, eyes wide with the realization of my admission. Skyler knows about Grayson, obviously. She knows he won me in the bid auction right before

Valentine's Day last year. But what she *doesn't* know is that her boyfriend at the time had also given me a pep talk backstage before the auction. I was nervous as hell, and Adam made me feel like the most wanted girl on campus.

He always has made me feel like that — wanted, desired — and not just for my looks.

I sigh, something between longing and frustration washing through me in a tumbling wave.

If Skyler catches on to me mentioning two guys, she doesn't say anything. So, I continue talking, hoping to keep her from asking who the other one was.

"How is it that Valentine's Day is in four days and I don't have a single option?"

I don't know why I'm even complaining about not having a Valentine's Day date. Maybe it's because I know the Alpha Sigma boys are having a dance, and maybe I assumed I'd be at that dance with Adam.

Then again, I never would have thought he could touch me the way he did and then disappear on me.

That longing twists harder toward anger, and I toss a kernel of popcorn in my mouth to keep from growling.

I should be focusing on me. That's what Adam said, right?

But maybe *that's* exactly why I want a date for Valentine's Day. Because I don't want to do what Adam thinks is right, not after he made me call his name with his head between my thighs and then hasn't talked to me for a week.

A *week*.

It's petty, I realize, that I want to get his attention, to make him angry, to make him talk to me out of jealousy if nothing more. But I can't help it.

Adam brings out the worst in me, just as he does the best. It's a dangerous, messed up kind of tango.

Skyler starts in on how she's not surprised I don't have a date, considering how crazy my schedule is with my major. But before we can get too deep into the conversation and figure out a solution to my dateless problem, the door swings open, and Jess flies in like the Tasmanian Devil in a tornado of rage.

"OH MY FUCKING GOD I'M GOING TO KILL SOMEONE!"

My instinct is to shield the popcorn from her, like she might come after it next since she's already thrown her hoodie across the room. "What the hell?"

Jess paces, her face pink, hair mussed. "Greg. Fucking *Greg*."

"What did he do?"

"It's what he *didn't* do," Jess says, flopping back onto her bed.

Skyler and I just exchange glances, waiting for her to continue. When she doesn't, Skyler clears her throat.

"Uh, care to divulge, J-Love?"

"I've got a really bad case of the Blue Bean, ladies. A major Violet Vulva."

I just blink, thinking maybe it's just me who doesn't understand. When I chance a glance at Skyler, her brows are pinched together tight, her expression just as confused as mine.

Jess peeks over her boobs at us, sighing and throwing herself up to sit when we don't immediately react.

"Blue balls!" she screams. "I have blue balls. Like, fucking bruised, swollen, black and blue balls."

I suck my lips between my teeth, fighting back the laugh that wants to break free. Usually, it would be no problem to laugh with Jess, but she looks more than a little frustrated right now.

Skyler peeks at me, and then holding back her own laugh, she squeaks out, "Would you like me to rub them for you?"

I break down, laughing so loud I'm a little embarrassed at the sound of it. Skyler cracks up when I do, tears streaking down her face as Jess tosses pillows across the room at us. One of them whacks Skyler in the head, which makes me laugh harder.

"Witches!" she yells as we burst into another fit of laughter.

"Sorry," Skyler says first, clearing her throat. I'm still trying to gain composure. "Sorry, Jess. Tell us what happened."

"No. Fuck you."

"Wait," I say when Jess covers her face with her sheets. "Does it really hurt?"

"Yes, fuckhead, it really hearts. I'm so worked up I'm pretty sure putting on sweat pants is going to make me orgasm."

"Well shit, let me at least put on *Magic Mike* or something," Skyler says, flipping through the channels.

Another pillow flies toward us.

"I hate you," Jess wallows. "What am I going to do? Like seriously, I'm going to kill him. *Murder* him. Hang him from the Omega Chi Beta roof."

When I ask her to explain what happened, Skyler and I both sit and listen attentively — half because we want to be there for her, and half because I personally find it fascinating as hell. Jess is a man killer. The fact that a guy left *her* hanging without an orgasm? It seems impossible.

And yet, he did.

Her frustration grows into a whine as she explains that he was finger banging her when his roommate walked in, and instead of telling him to get out, Greg stopped messing around with Jess and started playing video games with his roommate, talking about getting a pizza and this week's intramural game.

With her still there.

Ouch.

"Ugh!" Jess says, punching her pillow just as Erin and Ashlei walk into the room. "My pussy is so swollen right now I'm pretty sure it's hanging out the side of my thong."

"Ew! What the fuck, J-Love?" Erin asks, grimacing. That causes another roar of laughter from me and Skyler.

"Apparently we missed something," Ashlei muses.

"You don't even want to know, Lei," Skyler says.

Erin and Ashlei make themselves comfortable, Ashlei climbing into bed with Jess to play with her hair, and then the conversation switches with just one question to the most dreaded topic of conversation this semester.

Kip.

"Has Kip asked you to the dance yet?"

Erin stares at Skyler, the question silencing all of our laughter like a splash of water to a match flame.

I watch my Big, my heart twisting at the sight of her white face. I've tried to get her to talk about the whole situation, to tell Erin she needs out, but Skyler has always been good at shutting down when she's hurting.

If she doesn't talk about it, the pain doesn't exist, right?

"Uh, no..." Skyler finally answers, swallowing.

"What about your date last Sunday? He didn't ask then?"

"That wasn't a date. I taught him how to paddle board, that's all. And no, he didn't ask. And I haven't talked to him since." Skyler answers atomically, like a robot set to respond to demands.

"Why not?"

Skyler's eyes skirt to mine, and I smile, trying to give her comfort.

"I don't know. I may or may not have left his place without saying anything. And then he texted me and I didn't answer. And then he didn't show up for class Thursday, so I tried texting him and acting like everything was cool, but he didn't answer me. I think he's pissed. I don't blame him."

"What the hell?!" Erin asks, clearly upset, but Ashlei speaks over her, asking, "When was this?"

Skyler's eyes flick from Erin's to Ashlei's, and she seems to decide Ashlei is the safer one to answer.

"Last Sunday is when I saw him. I texted him Thursday after class."

"Aren't the A Sigs on their retreat thingy?" Ashlei asks. "You know, how they disappear every spring semester with the new pledges?"

"Holy crap, I didn't even think of that," Skyler says, and my stomach drops as the same thought passes through me.

Could it be *that's* why I haven't heard from Adam?

Every year, the Alpha Sigs disappear with their new pledges, finishing their initiation process. They return after about a week or so, throwing the New Member Bonfire to celebrate the new brothers.

It makes sense...

He's the president. If they're on that retreat, he would be leading them. And if they all had to surrender their phones, I imagine he would stay off his, just to set the example.

But could he not have told me before he left?

"I haven't seen Adam since last weekend now that I think about it..." I murmur, and Skyler nods, but then she snaps her head in my direction, one brow quirking up.

Shit.

She's probably wondering why the hell I would care that I hadn't talked to Adam in a week. We're just friends in her eyes, after all, and she doesn't even know the *half* of how deep our "friendship" runs.

"See?" Erin says, taking the attention off me. "I bet he's not mad at you. He probably disappeared not too long after you left that day."

"Maybe. Ex, I don't know about this anymore," Skyler breathes, and I perk up, hopeful that she'll tell Erin what's really been on her heart.

Tell *all* of us, really.

"I feel like he's going to get too caught up... I'm really starting to learn a lot about him and he's asking a lot about me. It's getting serious — and fast."

"Good," Erin says quickly. She stands, and with that motion, it's like all the power shifts in the room again — right back into the palm of her hands. "That's exactly what we want, isn't it? The faster and harder he falls, the more devastated he will be and the more he'll want what we had back. What we had was simple, true, uncomplicated," Erin says, her eyes lighting up, a small smile reaching her lips. It falls quickly as she shakes her head, as if she's afraid to submit to the feeling. "After the mess you leave him in, he'll be begging for that back."

Fuck.

I wince, and for the first time, the respect I've always had for my Grand Big wanes.

It's not fair what she's asking Skyler to do, and I reach under the covers, squeezing my Big's hand to let her know

I'm there. I can't get her out of this mess, but I can at least be there for her, let her know she's not alone.

"Okay," Skyler manages, her voice strained.

Erin goes on, talking to Skyler about the importance of the presidency and knowing how hard it is to make sacrifices along the way. I think it's all complete bullshit, especially since *I'm* supposed to fill that role one day and have absolutely no desire — at least, not now.

So, of course, my thoughts drift to Adam.

My stomach flips with the first thought of him, the realization that he maybe *wasn't* being a complete asshole and ignoring me all week. Half of me can't wait to see him, to see if he texts me as soon as they're back, if I see him at the bonfire. The other half of me can't stop replaying what Erin said last week.

"A real man would never make you question what you mean to him."

I wish I could talk to Skyler, take her mind off Kip and Erin and ask for her advice. She has been through so much with guys, and she knows how Adam is in a relationship. If anyone could help me untangle the knots in my stomach, it's her.

But even as the thought passes through me, I know it's selfish — and the timing couldn't be worse.

I can't talk to Skyler about him, about *us* — not now. With the Kip and Erin drama surrounding her like an Army set to attack, the last thing she needs is to hear that I'm in love with her ex-boyfriend.

And that I was even when he was hers.

With that realization, I button my lips, holding my tongue with the resolve to just wait. Wait to see what he says, to see when he comes back, to see why he didn't tell me he was leaving in the first place.

It's all I can do.
Sit and wait.
I hate this game.

Ashlei

GROWING UP AS THE middle child, competitiveness has always been a part of who I am. I was always working to stand out, to not be ignored or forgotten. It was easy for my parents to forget about me, with having an incredibly smart oldest daughter and an incredibly athletic youngest one. I was still there, excelling at nearly everything I did, but it was nothing my parents cared about.

So, when my internship was extended, my parents beamed like it was the first solid thing I'd ever accomplished in my life. Dad bragged about me at the country club over winter break, saying I would be the best event planner in south Florida, and Mom took me shopping for more amazing outfits to help me feel as great on the outside as I did on the inside when I walked into *Okay, Cool*.

But if they could see me today, I know they'd be disappointed.

It's Wednesday, which usually means everyone is in great spirits. We're halfway to the weekend, the hardest meetings of the week are done, and for all intents and purposes, it's a good day of the week. But today? Well, today feels a hell of a lot like a Monday.

"Do you have that report on Kiki Kween's athletic apparel line yet?" Kimberly asks, swinging into my cube like an unwanted, buzzing gnat.

I sigh, still tapping away on my keyboard and not even glancing up at her. "Working on it now."

"It was due to me EOD yesterday," she says, using the acronym for *end of day* like it makes her more powerful. She checks her watch. "And it's already three."

"I'll get it to you."

There's no use in telling her that Holly assigned me two other, more pressing tasks since we last divvied up the responsibilities for the Kiki Kween account. Or that I'm on my period, cramping like a sonofabitch and trying not to die. None of it would matter to Kimberly, and the last thing I'd ever do is admit any kind of weakness to her.

Instead, I aim for indifference, like I don't really care that I missed a deadline that *she* made after we were assigned the account.

"When?"

"Soon."

Kimberly rolls her eyes, a frustrated huff leaving her bright pink lips as she stomps away. When she's gone, I let out my own sigh, slumping back in my chair before closing my eyes and rubbing my temples.

It's been a hell of a week.

Between my classes and the internship, I've barely had time to eat. Add in the fact that Erin has been *extra* demanding since she became president, expecting more of me as her right-hand woman, and you could say that I might be in six feet of water with no heels to get me high enough to breathe. But this is who I am, and this is what women like me do — we push, we work hard, and we don't make excuses.

Even when we really, *really* want to.

I let my hands fall from my temples, palms smacking my skirt-covered thighs before I reach into my purse for two more Midol. I pop them in my mouth, chasing them with a swish of water, and then I nearly spit it out when I glance up at the source of the new shadow over my desk.

Brandon.

I somehow manage to swallow the pills, though they feel dry in my throat despite the water. Brandon's brows are pulled low over his fierce eyes, one hand clutching a stack of papers as the other rests calmly in the loose pocket of his robin's egg blue slacks. Those slacks hang *way* too deliciously on his hips, his all-white dress shirt buttoned up to his neck, the top button left undone, sleeves rolled up to his elbows.

I'm checking him out. Blatantly, unapologetically. I can't help it. His dark skin contrasts with the light colors in his outfit choice, and the way he's looking at me is a cross between anger and desire. Anger wins out, the tiny flash of want slipping from behind them as he drops the papers to my desk with a *thwap*.

"Good afternoon, Mr. Church."

"Do you know what these are?" he asks, ignoring my greeting.

Immediately, all the blood drains from my face, another cramp rolling through me. I'm pretty sure it's not the crimson tide's fault this time.

"I..." I stammer, picking up the papers and flipping through them. I recognize some of the reports, ones I'd worked on with Kimberly, including our first assessment of the athletic line. There are also countless emails from her to him, all with my name as the subject. I furrow my brows. "Well, sir, it looks like some of my reports from—"

"From the accounts you've been assigned to this semester? Yes. There are also countless emails from Kimberly to me, with explicit, color-coded mistakes you've made. From typos in a report to missing deadlines and everything in-between." My stomach drops as his eyes grow colder. "I've received at least three every single week."

My jaw pops open, but I clamp it shut again, swallowing down the urge to curse her name and rip her greasy hair from her skull.

"Sir, I apologize if Kimberly has been bothering you with this. Holly has had me working on a lot of different projects, outside of the ones Kimberly and I have been assigned to work together on, and I—"

"I don't want excuses, Miss Daniels. What I want is to not have to open an email with your name as the subject line from her ever again. I don't care what that takes on your end, just make sure it happens. I'm the CEO of a Fortune 500 company. I don't have time to read emails about an intern not doing her job."

Heat climbs up my neck, tingeing my cheeks as I press my lips into a thin line. "Yes, sir."

Brandon's jaw ticks at that, but if it affects him the way I mean for it to, he doesn't show it. Instead, he turns on the heels of his designer, leather shoes, and I watch his muscular back until it disappears around the corner.

My stomach rolls again, this time with a new kind of sickness, and I let out a long, pained sigh. I'm not sure if it's because of my period, or if it's because every possible chance I'd held onto that Brandon *might* come back to me, that he might let his wall down and let me back in, just disappeared into a cloud of smoke, but I'm done.

With Kimberly, with Brandon, with the whole fucking day.

I set up an out-of-office early email and pack up my bag, not even bothering to stop by Kimberly's desk on my way out. The only people I do say anything to is Holly, who takes one look at me and believes me when I say I'm not feeling well, and Mykayla, who offers to kick Kimberly in the twat for me.

I almost take her up on it.

When I regretfully decline, she gives me a hug, and I ride the elevator down to the lobby in silence, fighting back the urge to cry.

I consider myself a strong woman. A fierce storm. A force to be reckoned with.

But today? Right now?

I'm just a girl.

A sad, hormonal girl who needs three things and three things only: a bed, a movie, and a two-pound bag of gummy bears.

And I give myself all three.

I call out of work the next day.

I know I shouldn't, that technically speaking, my cramps are gone and I should get my ass to work. But the truth is, my ego hurts worse than my uterus ever did.

Brandon treated me like the gum on the bottom of his shoe, and I'm not ready to face him again. Not yet.

So, I ditch work, and Jess and I spend the morning hanging out, rummaging through her closet and Skyler's to find Sky the perfect outfit for tonight's New Member bonfire.

"I tried talking Erin out of all of this," Jess says, pulling another hoodie option from Skyler's closet. "This whole Kip thing."

"Yeah?"

She nods. "Yeah. I mean, I don't even think she heard a word I said, or if she did, she chose to carefully ignore all my questions and warnings." Jess sighs. "She's really set on this."

"I know. I tried talking to her, too — after Monday's little scene with Sky. I mean, we *all* knew she was uncomfortable, and Erin was unusually cold that night."

"She was. She *has* been, with this whole plan. It's like she's possessed."

"The things we do for boys," I said with a sigh, plucking two pairs of ripped jeans from Jess's closet. "We can't get her to see reason, not until she at least tries this crazy shit. All we can do is be there for Skyler and Erin *both* when this all goes up in flames."

"It will go up in flames, won't it?"

I nod. "I don't see any other possible ending. I sure as shit don't see it ending the way Erin thinks it will."

Jess frowns, pausing where her hands are hovering over a long maxi skirt Skyler wore last Spring Break. "This sucks."

"Indeed."

As if her ears were burning, Skyler walks through the door, and Jess and I exchange a *let's do this* power glance before I straighten my shoulders and toss her a handful of the hoodies we picked out. "Oh good, you're home. Try these on."

Skyler blinks as the hoodies hit her arms, a few of them falling to the floor. For a moment she just stares at them, then her blue eyes roll up to the ceiling.

"Are you seriously dressing me up for the bonfire? It's a bonfire... like, outside, in the dirt."

"And?" Jess says. "You need to look fucking hot, Sky. Try these on so we can see which one flatters you more and then we can pick accessories. And you're lucky it's in the dirt. We'll settle for cute boots, though wedges would look much better."

"You're not freezing my toes off to look cute at a New Member bonfire."

"I *said* we'll settle for boots, grumpy pants," Jess repeats. "Did you forget that Kip is going to be there and you haven't talked to him or seen him in over a week?"

I cringe, opening my mouth to smooth over Jess's hasty words and let Skyler know we're here for *her*, to help, but it's too late.

Skyler blinks, the movement more aggressive than it should be allowed to be before she claps her hands together. "Oh! Kip is going to be there? Well I'll be damned. Must have slipped my mind."

She pulls the first hoodie option over her head, and immediately Jess and I shake our heads, knowing it isn't the one.

"We're just trying to help," I offer as she strips it off again, moving to the next. It's a light blue zip up with hot pink KKB letters over the chest. When she zips it up, it frames her rack perfectly, and I try my best to bring some positivity back in the room. "Oh, I love that one! Brings out the blue in your eyes and you could show some cleavage. Put that one in the maybe pile."

"I know you're trying to help," Skyler admits on a sigh, tossing the blue zip up where I told her to. "I appreciate it, I do. I'm just..."

"Nervous? Scared?" Jess probes.

"Yes."

Jess and I exchange sad looks as Skyler's eyes fall to the floor. She's the most confident out of all of us — at least, it's always seemed that way. Whether it was kissing a boy from another university on Spring Break or answering a dare to jump on stage and do karaoke in nothing but a swim suit, Skyler made it all look easy.

But now, standing in the room with her hair a mess from ripping another hoodie off, I can see her true colors.

Skyler is scared. She's hurting. And she hates it.

"I just really need to push him away tonight while also making him think I'm still completely into him. It's a mess... *I'm* a mess."

Jess swallows, nodding to me to let me know she'll take the lead. "Hey, you got this, Sky. Who has the best poker face in the game? Who can bluff their way out of a speeding ticket? Who can play every single boy for a complete fool and leave them begging for more?"

Skyler is silent, so I move toward her, handing her another hoodie option. "You, that's who. I've never seen a girl who can play the dating game as well as you do. You get to have the fun you want without all the drama because somehow you keep every guy at just the right distance." I smile. "Don't let this kid get under your skin. You're so close to being done with this stupid game and then you can focus on the tournament in May and more importantly, Spring Break."

We all chuckle at that, and I rub Skyler's back encouragingly.

"You girls are right," she says, a little color returning to her cheeks. "I do this all the time, I don't know why I'm letting him get to me."

"Just brush him off. Pick out a pair of ripped, tight-as-fuck jeans and a hot sweater and we'll do your hair and makeup. You'll look and feel sexy and invincible, and before you know it, you'll be breaking his heart and moving on. End of story, next book."

Jess tries to make it sound easy, though all three of us feel the weight of the impending task. Skyler has a lot on her shoulders, and I know we all just want it to be over with.

Skyler still looks a little sick, and for the first time, the thought crosses my mind — does she *really* like Kip?

I mean, I heard about the night they met, about the tequila shot. I heard about their first date, about the paddle boarding. But from a distance, it all just seemed like part of the plan.

Staring at her now, at the slump in her shoulders, the bags under her eyes, I can't help but wonder if there's more to her side than she's telling us.

If I were in her shoes, if I liked a boy whom Erin liked first, one she'd laid claim to... could I walk away so easily?

I knew the answer before I even asked the question in my mind. The thought of her saying she wanted Brandon, even if it was after I'd first met him, it made me want to punch her in the tit and throw up all at once.

And she doesn't even *know* Brandon.

Skyler sighs, bringing me back to the current moment. "Okay, let's do this. Make me pretty."

I shake my head, swallowing back the urge to cry with her out of solidarity.

Stupid period.

"You're already pretty," I tell her. "We're just going to make you *feel* it."

And we do. After a tight hug and a couple hours of primping, Skyler is hot enough to spark that bisexual side of me and make *me* want to kiss her. I know without a doubt that Kip will be putty in her hands tonight, especially after she sets her game face in place.

None of us can help her out of the particularly sticky situation she's in, but we *can* be there to help her survive along the way. So, I hold her hand and Jess rubs her shoulders, giving her our final pep talks before setting her loose.

Skyler Thorne, set to win her next big game.

At least, we hope.

Skyler

MY STOMACH SHOULD BE in knots.

I should be shaking, the way I was when I left Kip's apartment last Sunday after what transpired between us. I should be staring at him across the flames of this fire right now and remembering what it felt like to have his hand between my thighs.

But my poker face is on.

Jess and Ashlei gave me a little pep talk before the fire, and it was exactly what I needed to hear. I've been in my head all week about Kip, wondering where he'd gone, wondering what he'd been thinking. *I* was the one who walked out on him, who left him guessing, and for a while, I was thankful that he hadn't pursued me. I thought maybe I got my point across, that we could end this little game early.

But then he didn't show up to class on Thursday.

That made me worry. It wasn't until Ashlei reminded us about the Alpha Sigma initiation camping trip that I was able to rest a little easier. Of course, that was also the night that Erin hammered home that she had *not* forgotten about Kip, or the game, and I was still very much a pawn.

Until I walked through my bedroom door and found Ashlei and Jess waiting for me, my day had been shit. I couldn't stop thinking about Kip, about what I was expected to do. I didn't know how to separate my heart from my bond with Erin, the promise I'd made her.

But the girls were right.

They reminded me who I am, how good I am at playing the game when I need to. I may have let myself get a little too caught up with Kip, let myself fall a little too far into the trenches, but now, tonight, I have control again.

Now, I just need to keep it.

Ever since the girls and I showed up to the bonfire — fashionably late, of course — Kip's eyes have been glued to me. He's trying so hard to pretend like he's not fazed by me being here, like he doesn't care that I didn't come up to him immediately, or that I've been talking to Adam and Cassie for the past forty-five minutes instead of him. But I see what he doesn't think I do.

I see him crush his plastic red cup when he sees Adam's hand touch my knee, splashing beer all over his friend. Adam and I are friends, nothing more, but to anyone who doesn't know us, I could easily see why it may be perceived as flirting.

So, being the power holder, I play right into that hand.

I nudge Adam when he teases me and Cassie, reminding us of the "Slip N Slide Sisters" days. I let the wind blow my hair over my face, dramatically blowing at it so Adam will shove it out of my eyes and make fun of me. And everything is working exactly how I want it to.

Just when I think he'll spontaneously combust, Kip's eyes lock on mine across the fire again as Adam gets up, telling me and Cassie he'll be back. He heads for the portable bathrooms on the other end of the fire, and as soon as his ass is up off the bench, Kip drains the last of his beer and storms toward me.

Here we go.

I remain calm, sipping on my beer and turning to face Cassie. "He's walking over here."

"Who?" Cassie asks.

Erin takes Adam's seat, and she leans in to catch the conversation.

"Kip," I answer.

Cassie's eyes widen, and Erin freezes before she's searching the crowd. She finds him quickly — I imagine because he's currently racing toward us like a pissed off bull.

"He's been here this whole time?" Cassie asks.

I almost snort. "Oh yeah."

She glances at him, then her eyes widen more, her voice lowering. "Oh my God, he's like Hulk raging his way over here."

"Shhh." I cut her off just as he reaches us, my eyes slowly making their way up to him, as if I'm surprised to see him, even though we've been trading glances across the party all night.

His lean chest is heaving under his new hoodie, the double-stitched Alpha Sigma letters rising and falling with every heated breath. His icy blue eyes watch mine from behind his glasses, the frames of them just as thick and strangely irresistible as I remember. He pinches his brows together, opening his mouth and closing it again like he's not sure what to say, or like he knows *exactly* what he wants to say but is trying to talk himself out of it.

I see it written all over him, question after question, the most confused expression I've ever seen him wear. It reminds me of my male opponents after I show my cards and they realize they've lost to a girl.

He has no idea who he's tangoing with.

One of Kip's brothers ask him if he's okay, but he doesn't so much as flick his eyes away from mine. He keeps those hypnotizing irises locked in on me, and Erin and Cassie watch him like they expect he'll explode at any minute.

I just smile.

I expect him to ask to talk to me, to perhaps grab my hand and pull me away from the crowd.

What I *don't* expect is for him to make a scene.

"I know I'm probably supposed to say I'm sorry right now, but I'm not going to. I'm not sorry about what happened between us last Sunday, Skyler."

My eyes threaten to bulge out of my head, but I school my expression, calming my racing heart. I feel Erin's heated eyes on mine, imploring me to look her way so she can ask me what the hell Kip's referring to, but I'm locked into the game now.

"I am sorry that I had to leave, that I couldn't talk to you afterward, but you left me first. Remember that. I woke up and you weren't there."

Erin is going to kill me.

"I'm sorry for that," Kip continues, his jaw ticking. "I'm sorry that I didn't chase after you or call you or make sure you were okay, but I'm not sorry about what happened. I don't regret it. I want to do it again. Right now, actually."

My cheeks flame at that, some of the students around us giggling at that, drawing their own conclusions. A few of his brothers hoot out their approvals, too.

I need to stop this soon. I need to take back control.

"I don't care about what people think, Skyler. I know you do, but I don't."

His words sting a little — both with the truth of them and his public delivery. It's one thing I envy about Kip — the way he seems to give absolutely zero fucks about what anyone else thinks.

And already, with just a few sentences, he's got my game face slipping.

"I'm not sorry. I want you. I want—"

Before he can finish his sentence, I shove my cup of beer into Cassie's hands and stand, taking a fistful of his hoodie and pulling him down until his mouth crashes into mine. There's a mixture of cheering and laughing around us, whistles ringing out, and in the back of my mind I know it must kill Erin to see me kissing him.

But this is all part of *her* game. If I'm going to shut him up, if I'm going to keep the control I somehow managed to get tonight, I have to act now.

I thread my arms around Kip's neck, his own hands pulling me tighter against him. When I pull back, both of us a little breathless, I run my hands through his hair with a smile.

"I've missed you," I say, which is more true than I care to admit. "Take me to the dance tomorrow."

I don't ask — I demand. That's where Erin wants this all to end? Fine. I'm more ready than she is at this point.

Kip watches me, his eyes lighting up and smile brightening at my request. But as I try to hold my poker face steady, his brows bend together slightly, his eyes searching mine like he senses that something is off, something is different.

So, I force an even bigger smile.

Play it off, Skyler. Don't let him see how you really feel.

"Like that was even an option," he answers, kissing me again.

I lean into the kiss, letting myself revel in the feel of his hands on my waist, his tongue dancing over mine. Someone yells for us to get a room, and I laugh, Kip tugging on my hand to pull me away from the fire. I glance over my shoulder as he pulls me away, and it's just in time to see Erin storming off in the opposite direction.

Shit.

"Don't worry about that," Kip says, his knuckle finding my chin and tilting it up once we're away from the fire. "She'll be okay."

A sigh leaves my lips as I watch Erin disappear across the crowd, the sound of the party muted now that Kip and I have migrated away from the action. I want to run to her, to explain, to see if she's okay. But in the end, what she *really* wants from me right now is for me to follow through on what I promised.

So, I throw on my best fake smile, turning back to Kip.

"Yeah, she'll be fine," I say, slipping my hands into the front pocket of my hoodie. Away from the fire, the chill of the night creeps in stronger. "So, you're officially a brother huh?"

Kip watches me curiously, his eyes searching mine.

He can tell.

He's reading me like an all-caps word on a giant billboard sign. I don't know what it is about my poker face that's slipping, but something is giving me away. It takes every ounce of willpower I have to try again, to solidify that smile, to force the joy into my eyes. It must work, because though Kip doesn't seem completely convinced everything is okay, he finally mirrors my smile.

"Nah, I stole this sweater from Goodwill. Don't tell."

I lift a finger to my lips in a *shhh* symbol. "Your secret is safe with me."

It's a deliberate move, one I know will take his attention to my lips, to the way they felt on his skin last Sunday — and it works. Kip swallows, his Adam's apple bobbing hard in his throat before he leans forward, taking my face between his hands. He pulls me into him, his soft lips pressing into mine, and when he slides his tongue between them, I moan, leaning into him more.

This is fake. This is not real. You don't really feel that tingling, it doesn't really feel that good, you don't really want him to take you home right now. It's a game. It's a game.

"Come home with me," he murmurs between kisses, and all I can do is kiss him harder.

Yes. Take me.

Pressing my hands to his chest, I pause for air, for clarity. I can't think with his lips on me like that, with his hands pulling, his mouth demanding.

"I can't."

He sighs. "Stop overthinking it and do what you want to do."

"It's not that easy."

My game plan slips, and suddenly I want to tell him everything. I want to tell him that there's more to this than he could ever understand, that he needs to walk away — no, he needs to *run.*

But before I can process the thought, a bright, assaulting flash strikes us both like a bolt of lightning.

Kip grabs me protectively, his arms surrounding me, both of our hearts ticking up a notch.

"You two are so cute together."

The voice is distant, unfamiliar, and with the bright flash still blinding me, I can't make out who it belongs to. Slowly, the fire behind their silhouette brings their frame into view, and I swallow hard.

"New boyfriend again, Skyler? Will he be with you in Vegas?"

"Shit," I murmur, my hand blindly reaching for Kip's. I yank it hard, steering him toward Greek Row. As soon as we catch our bearings, I start running, and Kip follows, still glancing over his shoulder as more flashes ring out.

The photographer follows for a short while, shooting out more questions, but we lose him once I take us through the Omega Chi Beta back yard. I keep running, just in case, not stopping until we're tucked away safely in the family bathroom of Hawthorne Hall.

We stand there, quietly, save for our breathing. Kip asks me what's going on but I cut him off quickly, pressing a hand over his mouth. Once I'm sure we've lost him, we let ourselves back out into the cool night, and I keep my eyes away from Kip's.

Great.

As if the night wasn't already bad enough, *of course* a reporter would show up. Dad told me I should be on the lookout for them, that they'd be seeking me out again now that it was public knowledge that I'm in the tournament this May. Still, I thought after they were banned from campus, I wouldn't have anything to worry about.

Then again, *technically*, the bonfire was right off campus.

I sigh.

"What the fuck was that?" Kip asks, his breathing still evening out as we make our way toward the sorority house.

"Probably a reporter," I answer, voice flat. "Or a freelance photographer low on funds. Or maybe there's another *Hottest Poker Players* issue coming out from some played-out magazine. I always seem to end up on those shitty lists."

The words flow out freely, my poker face temporarily stunned as the real pain in my heart slips through.

I'm entered in one of the biggest tournaments in the world. I've proven that I can handle my own, that I can be competition for even the top players in the industry.

And yet still, all they care about is what I look like and who I'm dating.

"What are you talking about?" Kip asks.

"This happened last year before I played a pretty massive tournament in Atlantic City," I say with a sigh. "My parents told me it would probably happen again and maybe be even worse with this one in Vegas, but I guess I didn't think they would find me here. They're not supposed to be allowed on campus, but technically the bonfire isn't on campus, is it? Fuck."

I repeat the words I'd thought silently aloud, and the more I think about it, the more upset I am.

I just want to be left alone. I don't want to be their pawn, or Erin's, or anyone else's.

How did I end up here?

Thoughts are hitting me faster than I can process them, and suddenly, Kip traps my wrist in his hand, pulling me back until I'm crushed into his chest, both of his arms around me. He holds me tight, rocking me gently, his lips finding my hair as he presses a soft kiss there.

And I let him hold me.

I'm tempted to cry, but I use every last bit of mental strength I have left not to. Instead, I focus on my breathing, letting it even out as Kip holds me, his warmth surrounding me as we stand in the yard of the sorority house. Everyone is at the bonfire, so I'm not worried about anyone seeing.

But I *am* worried about what I'm feeling.

Because I feel safe.

And I've never felt that with a boy before.

"It's all good," he says after a moment, pulling me back to look at me. "They're gone now and we can talk to the Dean tomorrow about this. Or President Whittington. They'll take care of it."

I nod, though my wheels are still spinning. "Okay."

Kip doesn't seem convinced by my verbal agreement. His eyes search mine, the light from the front porch just barely illuminating his eyes.

"Hey, look at me."

I suck in a deep breath, holding it in my chest before I let my gaze find his.

"The only thing you need to worry about right now is picking out a dress for tomorrow night, okay? I'll handle talking to the president." He smiles, so confident in the fact that he can take care of me.

And I so desperately want to let him.

"Pick you up at seven?"

I let myself study him for a moment, my eyes sweeping over his mussed hair, his high cheek bones, his strong jaw. I hover over his lips, still tasting them on my own.

And then, I force a smile, putting my poker face back on.

"Actually, Adam and some of your brothers are coming in a limo to pick a lot of my sisters up. Could we ride with them? It would be so fun!"

I can tell Kip hates the idea of sharing me with anyone, especially a car full of people, but he nods. "Okay, yeah. I'll talk to Adam."

"Okay."

I smile again, lifting up on my toes to peck his lips before turning for the door. I need to get inside. I need to put distance between us, to put my resolve back in place.

Thankfully, Kip doesn't follow me. He doesn't tug my wrist and pull me back, deepen the kiss, ask me again to come home with him. *Thank God,* I think, because I doubt I could decline again.

I don't feel the weight on my chest recede until I'm inside the house, the door closed behind me, serving as a barrier between me and Kip. And even then, the weight only lifts a little, just enough to let me breathe.

I don't even bother taking a shower.

As soon as I'm up the stairs, I strip out of my hoodie, kick off my boots, and face plant on my bed. When my cheek hits the cool cotton of my pillow, I know the truth. It screams at me, taking over every other thought now that I'm alone, and it won't let me rest until I look it in the eye — until I acknowledge it.

I can't do this.

I can't play this game anymore. I can't pretend I don't have feelings for Kip, and I can't lure him in just to hurt him. I have to tell Erin that I need out.

I have to tell her I like him.

Taking a deep breath, I let the weight of *that* settle in on me.

And only then, in a dark room without a single other sister in the house, I finally let myself cry.

Adam

"YOU DID GOOD," JEREMY says, slapping me on the back before giving my shoulder a squeeze.

He scans the bonfire with me, hundreds of Greek students gathered to celebrate our new members. It's my first New Member bonfire as president, and the pride I feel swelling in my chest is almost too much to bear. I can't help the goofy grin on my face, the warm, fuzzy cloud floating through me — though that might be the alcohol.

"Thank you. And it wasn't just me. *We* did good."

"We did, didn't we?" Jeremy smiles wider, shaking his head. "I think this is our best pledge class yet. This is *definitely* the best turnout for the fire, that's for sure."

I nod in agreement, taking another drink from the red Solo cup in my hand. The night is still going strong, the kegs slowly tapping out one by one as the hours stretch into early morning. And as proud as I am of Jeremy and myself, of our leaders, I'm even more proud of our pledges.

It wasn't easy, what we asked of them.

Dropping your cell phone for more than an hour is hard for our generation to do, let alone giving it up for over a week. Add in the fact that we put them through a little hell, a little bonding, and a *lot* of brotherhood testing out at the cabin, and it's no wonder they're all wearing their new letters like a badge of honor tonight.

My eyes skirt to where Cassie is, where I left her moments ago with Skyler. I'd sat and talked with them for almost an hour, loving the way Cassie seemed to be letting herself have a little fun, but I knew from the moment I sat down that she wanted to talk to me — and I couldn't blame her. I had some explaining to do.

I wanted to tell her I was leaving after we hooked up last week. The last thing I wanted her thinking was that I would do that and then stop returning her texts — and I had turned on my phone to one from her saying we needed to talk. My stomach had dropped at that, but I knew she'd understand once I explained.

I was the president, and I had to lead by example. If the pledges couldn't be on their phones, I wouldn't be on mine, either.

Still, I feel her eyes from across the fire, hear the plea behind them. She needs answers, and when Kip and Skyler disappear, Erin heading off in the other direction, it leaves her all alone on the bench we were just sitting at together.

I take another drink, hoping the beer will somehow give me the right words to say.

"I'm going to go see about a girl," I say to Jeremy.

His brows knit together, but when his gaze follows mine to Cassie, he smirks. "Have fun, El Presidente. You deserve it."

I hold up my cup toward him with a little nod, and then one hand slips into my jeans pocket as I make my way to Cassie.

Her eyes widen a little when she notices me moving across the lot, and she looks around for someone to talk to, someone to save her from having to stare at me while I walk her way. I can't help but smile at how easily she wears her nerves, her cheeks flushing the closer I get, fingers brushing her hair behind her ear. She takes a sip from her cup, balancing it on one shaking knee as she looks anywhere but at me until I'm right in front of her.

"Hey, you," I say, plopping down beside her where Skyler sat before. She'd been between us then, a barrier, but with nothing between us now, that same familiar buzz surges to life as soon as her eyes find mine.

"Hey."

I sigh, hating the way she's looking at me, like I can't be trusted, like I'm not the person she thought I was. It's everything I've been trying to avoid. I want to be a man of my word with her, want to be different from the others, and yet I know without asking that I've hurt her.

"I'm sorry," I say immediately.

Her eyes widen, the emerald flecks of them flickering in the fire light. "You are?"

"Yes, I am," I say, smirking. "I know the week must have been hard for you, with me not responding to your text. You had no idea where I went, and I didn't tell you I was leaving. But, I want you to understand that Alpha Sigma and my brothers are important to me. I wanted to tell you, but I had told everyone else in leadership that they were explicitly forbidden from telling *anyone* what the date was for us to leave for the trip. I wanted to lead by example." I shrug, scratching at my neck. "Although, saying that out loud sounds a little silly. I know I could have told you and you wouldn't have told anyone else."

"I wouldn't have."

I search her eyes, wanting so desperately to reach for her. "I really am sorry, Cassie. I wanted to tell you, but I was trying to do right by my fraternity. And I hope you know now that I'm back, that you know where I was, that everything is okay between us. I meant what I said to you last week," I promise, and then I lower my voice, leaning in closer. "And I meant every single touch, too."

Cassie inhales a shallow breath, her bottom lip trembling slightly. Her knees clench together, but then her eyes rip away from mine, hands slipping under the backs of her thighs as she stares down at her Keds.

"Talk to me," I beg her, scooting closer. Our legs brush, the energy transferring between us.

"You said everything is okay between us," she whispers. "But... is it really?"

"Of course, it is."

I shake my head, finally giving into the urge to reach for her. I grab her wrist, pulling one hand from under her leg and into my grip, but she slides it away immediately, tucking her hair behind her ear before sitting on the hand again.

"Cassie... what's wrong?"

She rolls her eyes, letting out an exhausted huff. "How can you even ask me that when you know the answer?" Her eyes land hard on mine, the pain ridden in them. "Why aren't we together, Adam? Why don't you want me to be your girlfriend?"

"I do," I assure her. "When the time is right."

"What does that even mean?" She throws her hands up, letting them smack her thighs when they fall. "You know, Erin said something to me last week that really hit me hard. She said, if a guy wants to be with you, then he will be. And a real man won't make you wonder what you mean to him."

Her words are like a slap to the face, and I flinch back at the sting of them.

"You don't know what you mean to me?"

"Not anymore," she answers quickly, and then her hands are tucked under her thighs again, her little shoulders shrugging as she looks down at the dirt. "Maybe not ever, really."

I drag a hand over my jaw, closing my eyes as I search for the right thing to say, to make her understand. Right now, it feels like everything she just said stole my breath, my will to speak along with it.

How can I make her understand?

To tell her I don't want to just be another Grayson or Clay would insult her. She knows I'm not them, and it's like me telling her that she needs to have better judgment, that she needs to take a step back and evaluate before jumping in. But I don't mean it that way. I only want her to be happy — *truly* happy — with herself, and with me.

I can't tell her I'm doing this for her, because I know as much as she does that she's a strong, resilient girl. She can make her own decisions, and I *honor* those choices.

I just want her to take a moment for herself.

I want her to know that I will wait, that there's no rush.

Sitting next to her now, her bottom lip sucked between her teeth, I have to remind myself again exactly *why* I want to wait.

"I don't know how to explain this in words," I say softly, resting my hand on her knee. I don't reach for her hand again, but I crave the connection, the need to let her feel me when I speak. "And I may not ever be able to fully explain it. But, my grandfather taught me that actions speak louder than words. And you've heard a *lot* of talk, Cassie."

She sniffs, eyes still on the dirt.

"You heard Clay tell you you could trust him, that he wouldn't hurt you — but his actions proved you wrong. You heard Grayson when he said he loved you, that he would take care of you, that you were safe — but then *his* actions proved you wrong again. And now here I am," I say modestly, shaking my head as I swallow past the knot in my throat. "Just another boy completely fascinated with you, who has loved you for *so* long — longer than I should have. And I'm telling you all those same things."

Cassie slowly pulls her gaze to mine, her shiny green eyes shielded under bent brows.

"You can trust me," I say, repeating what I know those other boys said. "I won't hurt you. I love you, I want to take care of you, and you're safe with me." I swallow again, harder this time. "I mean every word, Cassie. But give me the chance to prove it to you. Let me show you I mean it, while you take the time to heal those scars the other guys left. Do I want to help? Absolutely. But I know your strength, and I know the girl who existed *before* those scars were left. She's different now — stronger, smarter, even more beautiful, somehow." I smile at that, and the corner of her own mouth twitches up. "And I want her to remember that. I want *you* to spend some well-deserved time on yourself because I care about you. *That's* the first step for me in my actions speaking louder than my words. Because as much as I want to wrap you up in my arms and tell everyone that you're my girl, what I want *more* is for you to be happy, to be free, to be *you*."

Cassie smiles then, her eyes glossing over so much that one tear leaks free.

"You're not just mine," I tell her, wiping the tear away with the pad of my thumb. "You belong to *you*. Take this time, just heal a little, and know I'm always here. I'm not going anywhere. Those guys lied when they said you were their girl, when they said you were the only one they wanted. When I say it, when we make it official, you'll know in your heart that there's no possible way it could be a lie." I shrug. "You'll know, because even without saying it, without anyone else knowing, it's already true."

It's as if my words break her, because Cassie's face warps, and then she buries it in her palms, her shoulders shaking a little. I pull her into me, not worried about the eyes around us now. Most of her sisters are gone, and anyone who's still partying is too far gone to care what's happening around them, anyway.

Cassie's hands grip at my hoodie, pulling me closer as she rests her face in the crook of my neck.

"I'm sorry," she says with a sniff. "I'm such a mess."

"No, you're not."

"I am," she insists, pulling back to look at me. "I've been going crazy, convincing myself that you didn't really care about me, that it was all a lie. And why? Because that's what I've been conditioned to do. That's what those other guys taught me. So I was so quick to just assume that you would do the same." She shakes her head. "I'm so sorry. I assumed the worst of you, when all you've done is prove to me that you care."

"That's not true."

She sniffs again, watching me.

"Cassie, I've hurt you, too. When I was with Skyler, when you were with Grayson, and so many times between. What we have? It hasn't come easy." I chuckle. "Not even close. And it's okay that you feel the way you do. That's why I want to prove to you with my actions what I mean with my words."

She lets out a long, exasperated sigh, nodding. "I do, too."

"Hey," I say, rubbing my hands on her sweater-covered arms. "Why don't you come to the dance tomorrow night? Take my extra ticket. We don't have to tell anyone that you're my date. You can just come and hang out with your sisters, and maybe save me a few dances."

Cassie smiles. "Really? I was hoping I could go, but wasn't sure if you'd ask."

"Really. And you know what else?"

She shakes her head.

"I'm going to book you a spa day for this weekend. Go get your shoulders rubbed, a little face mask action." She shakes her head, eyes wide like I can't possibly spend my money on her. "Don't even try to argue, I'm doing it. And you're going."

She laughs, still sniffling. "You're impossible."

"I know. But, it's Valentine's Day. As much as I want to take you out on a date and then take you back and do *very* not-safe-for-work things to you, I think this year it should be a little different. This year, maybe you spend the holiday of love loving yourself a little."

Cassie shakes her head, a bright smile breaking through as she slips her hand into mine. "I like that idea."

"Yeah?"

She nods. "Yeah."

"Good. It's settled then. We have a big limo picking up some other sisters from your house tomorrow. I'll save you a seat."

"Okay," she says, smiling. And then, she just watches me, her big green eyes nearly doubling in size as she searches me. It's like she's checking to see if I'm real, or memorizing the moment to hold onto forever.

Maybe both.

And it's the first time I feel like maybe my plan is working. Maybe I really can show her with my actions what she means to me, instead of just telling her. Maybe I really can treat her like the woman she's always deserved to be treated like.

Cassie McBee has never been loved the right way, and I vow to be the one to break that streak.

I vow to be the first one to really love her, to really *be* loved by her.

And, hopefully, the last one, too.

Erin

THE SUN HASN'T COMPLETELY shed its light over the university, hasn't spilled in through our large kitchen window, but yet still I stand at the counter, eyes on my phone, two names fighting for attention.

I didn't try to sleep last night — not after seeing Skyler pull Kip in for a kiss, or hearing him talk about how he isn't sorry for what they did. Whatever it was, he wanted to do it again, and as much as I know it's all part of the plan *I* set up, I couldn't stomach it.

So, I did what I do best. I fled.

Drinking hadn't helped last time I'd felt that ickiness settling in my stomach after their date at the pier, so I tried running, instead. Stopping by the sorority house long enough to change into long pants and a light long-sleeve shirt, I set out across campus, running along the dimly lit paths until my muscles were screaming at me to stop. Every step took a tiny bit of the pain, every sharp breath through my lungs gave a little bit of strength. When I hit the reflection pond on campus, I stopped, collapsing in a heap on the grassy hill that overlooked it.

I close my eyes, one hand wrapped around my steaming mug of hot chocolate as I go back to that moment, to the stars spread above me, the cool, wet grass on my neck, my breaths shallow but sure.

It was then that I realized it wasn't the kiss that hurt me the most. It was the *way* they kissed — the way Skyler tried to fake it, but gave into Kip with every second that passed, melting into his arms. It's the way Kip spilled his heart out to her before she shut him up with her mouth on his, and the relief that spilled off of him when she was pressed against him.

Sobs racked through me on that hill, every fear and damning emotion surging over me like a tidal wave. I had no choice but to succumb to it, to let it roll me under its powerful waves before it spit me out. And when it did, I sniffed, wiping my eyes dry and staring up at the unblinking stars in the sky as I realized the truth.

I was stupid to think this was ever a game.

He likes her. And she likes him.

And now, I have to figure out what to do about it.

My eyes flutter open again, the first bit of sunlight slipping inside our small sorority kitchen. I stare at my phone again, debating my options.

The first person I want to call is Clinton.

We haven't talked since the semester started, but he always said he'd be there for me if I needed him. And I need him. *Bad*. He'd know what to say, how to help me see sanity, to make the right decision.

But that's the problem.

As much as I need him, as much as I should pick up the phone and call him or storm down Greek Row and right into his bedroom, I don't want to. *Because* he would tell me the right thing to do.

And right now, I don't want to be right.

Right now, I want Kip Jackson to be mine again. I want to find happiness with him, the kind of naïve, untouched happiness we had before. I want to remember what it feels like to be held by a man and not flinch away from his touch, to be kissed because I asked for it, not have my lips taken greedily and without mercy.

I want to be taken to bed, softly and gently, and cherished. I want to feel Kip's hands on me, his lips, his eyes...

Clinton would talk me out of the whole thing, and although that might be what I *should* do, I don't.

Instead, I pick up my phone and dial person number two.

Mom.

"It's early, Erin," she answers gruffly.

"I need you."

There's shuffling on the other end, and I hear my father's voice murmur something before my mom covers the phone to answer. A door clicks, and I imagine her retreating into her master bathroom, perching on the edge of her deep bath tub.

"Okay, I'm here. What happened?"

She still sounds slightly annoyed by me waking her, but the fact that she's still on the line brings me comfort. I sigh, feeling stronger already just by hearing her voice. She was the only one I could lean on after what happened, the only one who knew how to take what I felt and turn it into something I could control, something I could manage.

As sick as it sounds, that horrifying day brought me closer to my mom, and for that, I'm thankful.

"It's nothing big," I say quickly, to ease her mind. "There's something I want, something I feel like might really help me find some happiness again."

"Okay," she says softly. "Well, you know you can do anything you put your mind to. If there's something you want, take it. Make it yours. Make it happen."

"I know, I know, and I have been trying. I have a plan in place, a way to get what I want, but..." My voice fades, my eyes losing focus on the marshmallows floating in my hot chocolate. "I'm hurting someone I care about in the process. And I'm afraid that the more I use her, the more she'll hate me in the end."

"A sister?"

I sigh. "Yes. A very close sister."

"Oh, Erin," Mom says, the annoyance back in her voice. "Listen to me. College is such a small, temporary part of your life. I know these girls feel like they're everything to you right now, but one day, you won't even talk to ninety percent of them. Don't let your emotions and feelings stand in the way of your goals. What does that get you? Where has it ever landed you before?"

Every word she says is like a little prick of a needle, like motherly acupuncture, a mixture of discomfort, pain, and relief.

Maybe I want to hear someone tell me what I'm doing is okay.

Maybe I knew she'd be the one to say it.

"I think it's really hard on her," I say, not sure if I want my mom to hear it or myself. "But we're so close, and what I want is within reach. I'm just not sure if, ethically, the way I've gone about it is okay."

"Well, ethics aren't everything," Mom answers matter-of-factly. "Listen to me. You've had things taken from you, Erin. You've given when you didn't want to. This is karma, the balance of the universe. Now, it's your turn to take a little, to get back what you desire to make yourself happy again. And that doesn't always happen without a few fires along the way — fires that burn people you care about."

"That doesn't sound right to me."

"It's not always about being right. Sometimes, it's about the end game. Let me ask you this. When you close your eyes and think about reaching that goal, about getting what you want, how do you feel?"

I do as she says, an overwhelming wave of warmth and joy washing over me when I picture myself back in Kip's arms, his blue eyes looking into mine, his lips kissing the soft skin of my neck.

"I feel…" I shake my head, eyes opening with a new resolve. "I feel perfect. I feel whole again."

"Then you have your answer."

I swallow. "I think she wants out of the plan. I'm not sure how to get her to see it through."

"Well, you got her to agree somehow, didn't you? Think about what motivates her, what her weaknesses are, and play into them. Remind her why she agreed, why this is important not just for you, but for her, too." Mom pauses. "You're smarter than you think you are, Erin. You're just a little soft. Don't let what happened to you play into that softness. Let it harden you — your heart, your resolve — and take what you want from this world."

In the back of my mind, I realize the twisted, questionable morals that my mother's advice is laced with, but in this moment, I can't find it in me to dissect it. She said exactly what I needed to hear — what I *wanted* to hear.

She gave me permission, encouragement, and any thought of backing out is long gone.

When I end the call with Mom, I make another mug of hot chocolate, leaning one hip against the counter and watching the sun rise through the kitchen window as I formulate a new plan. I know Skyler's weaknesses — her desire to fit in, her need to fulfill our Greek line's legacy of being the next president. Before she came to Palm South University, she was a no one. Here, she's everything.

But a reputation is a futile thing.

And a delicate, self-conscience girl is easy to prey on.

I almost shutter at that thought as it rolls through me, at how easily I think it, but I don't have time to digest it before the universe hands me my first test.

Skyler shuffles into the kitchen, hair a rats nest on top of her head as her eyes widen when they land on me. It's early, the rest of the house sleeping, and she likely imagined she'd find the kitchen empty.

It's now or never.

"Hot chocolate?" I ask her, lifting my mug a little.

Skyler smiles, but it falls quickly as she props herself on the counter beside me. "I think I need something stronger."

It should scare me, how quickly I shove my emotions down into a box, slamming the lid shut and taping the edges for good measure. I can see it all over Skyler's face, her desire to talk to me, to tell me she wants out. It's in the knit of her brows, in the way she chews on her bottom lip. This is it — my last chance to get her to seal the deal.

So, I set a plan into place, not questioning a single step in it as it forms.

First, I have to break her down, tap into *her* emotions. Skyler is perhaps the most caring human being I know, soft at the heart no matter how she tries to hide it. And, unlike me, she doesn't possess the will to box her emotions away. Sure, she may be able to disguise them with a poker face now and then, but in the end? They always overwhelm her.

"It's funny, you know," I say, grabbing another mug from the cupboard and starting a cup of coffee for her on our Keurig. "Parents. Kids. The whole relationship that exists there."

"I'm not sure I'm following, Big."

I sigh, debating my next words before I say them as I detangle my hair with a wave of my hand through it. It's a delicate balance, what I'm about to do. I need to tap into her sympathy for me while also relaying my warning, my threat — or rather, my promise.

She's not getting out of this.

"I mean, we grow up looking up to our parents. We envy them, build our dreams and our goals around who they are and who they aren't. But do we ever really make them happy? Or proud? They say we do, but would they really tell us if we failed them?"

I turn again, pulling the fresh cup of coffee from the Keurig and handing it to Skyler. She holds it in her hands, the steam wafting up as she thinks.

"I don't think we can fail them," she finally says. "I think just by existing, we make them proud. They see themselves in us."

I see my in, my way to tap into her sympathy for me, to get her putting me above her own wants and needs.

And as selfish as it is, as fucked up as I've become, I take it.

Scoffing, I take another sip of my hot chocolate. "All my parents see when they look at me is a blurred, imperfect reflection of what they wish I was. I feel it. They don't say it, but their eyes do. They're ashamed of me."

And that was true, this time last year. My parents were only concerned with me finding a husband in college, nothing more. But after what happened to me, my mom finally understood, finally got behind me and supported me getting a degree I loved and forging my own path.

Still, Skyler is close with her parents. She's helped them in times of need, and she understands family obligation and pride. So, I continue.

"I know, right? It doesn't make sense, does it? Most parents would be proud of me, I guess. But then again, most parents didn't dream of their baby girl growing up and getting a MRS degree and banging a rich lawyer or doctor or whatever. You would think I shot a puppy by telling them I'd rather *be* a lawyer than marry one."

It's silent a moment, and I hear Skyler's wheels turning. Her initial worry that was laden on her features when she walked into the kitchen is gone, and I've successfully pushed those thoughts aside long enough to get her to think of how to help me. She wants to make me feel better.

Time to reel her in.

"Ex, you have nothing to be ashamed of and your parents are crazy if they don't see the amazing things you're doing for this campus, this sorority, and for yourself. They come from old money, they're not used to a world where a woman wants to be educated simply because she can be. You're too smart and too damn talented to get married and sit at home. Not that there's anything wrong with that, but it's not your style. Could you imagine that? You would go bat shit crazy. You can't even sit in your pajamas for a full day!

I giggle at that, heart warming a little at her words. Because as much as I may be putting on a show for her, Skyler is being nothing but real with me. She really thinks those things, and that stubborn voice inside me tries to pipe up again, the box rattling, everything threatening to break loose and remind me why I should let Skyler call everything off.

I shove it all back down.

"You have to say that," I say to Skyler, sniffling a little like I might cry at any moment. "You're my little nugget of sunshine."

Skyler watches me a moment, a strange smile on her face. And in that moment, we're just Big and Little, two sisters brought together by circumstance, staying together by choice.

But would she choose to keep that relationship in the end, after this... after Kip?

I could never be sure. And though I should have, I couldn't find it in me to care.

"I don't *have* to say anything," Skyler argues. "Except the truth. And I mean it when I say you are the bomb dot com and your parents are insane if they don't see that. They'll come around and realize that your dreams are just a little different than what they had in mind but that it actually makes you even better than they could have ever imagined. Just wait until family weekend. When they come up here and see everything you've done for Kappa Kappa Beta and for Palm South as a whole, they're going to lose their shit. And your grades are off the charts. You're going to get first pick of law schools and they're going to brag to all their friends at the country club about their amazing daughter who's not only drop dead gorgeous, but a lawyer, to boot."

And with that, I've got her right where I want her.

Step one: complete.

I smile, eyes watering a little as I cross the kitchen and wrap Skyler in a hug. "I love you, Little. Thank you."

"I'll always be honest with you," she says, pulling back and taking a deep breath. "And I'm sorry about last night."

My façade falters, a coldness sweeping over me at the mention of the bonfire.

"It's okay. I know it's part of it, it's part of the game. It's hard to watch, but I get it. You did good last night."

Positive reinforcement. Make her feel like what she's doing is good, that it will lead to something she wants.

"Thanks," Skyler mumbles. "But, I wanted to talk to you about it."

I swallow, alarms ringing in my head as I grasp for how to steer the conversation away from what I know she wants to say. Even after sucking her in with the sympathy card, she still wants to call it off.

Time for the threat.

"I—"

"You know," I say quickly, cutting her off. "I knew this was a crazy plan when it first slipped out of my mouth that night in my room. In fact, that night I stayed up all night thinking about how crazy I was being," I say, and that part is the truth. "But then I realized that I couldn't have had any better luck. I mean, how ironic that my Little just so happened to meet my first love and develop a connection with him?" I ask, reminding her who had him first, who he is to me. "It was almost too perfect."

Skyler watches me carefully, her face neutral.

"And being that you're the best damn poker player around," I say, feeding into her ego, tapping on that most important part of her life. "There literally is no better person for the job."

She swallows. "Ex, that's just the thing. I'm not sure—"

"And you know what else?" I say, not letting her finish. I drop my mug into the sink, turning to lean against the counter again with my eyes hard on Skyler. "I know it's not just about the presidency for you. I know it's because you care about me, because you know what I'm going through right now and you genuinely want to see me happy."

Skyler fumbles her mug a little, just enough to spill a drop of coffee on her sweater, and I know it's sunk in.

I'm reminding her what's at stake.

Not just the presidency, which she wants not only for herself, but for our family, too, but also our friendship. I asked her to do something for me, for girl code, and she agreed.

And I see it all set in as she schools her features, her resolve to tell me she wants out extinguished like a match under a bucket of water.

Handing her a napkin for the spilt coffee, I smile. "I'm so lucky to have you in my life, Little. You know, for a second last night I thought you were actually into him. It was so convincing!" I sigh, letting out a short laugh as I make my way toward the kitchen exit. "But of course, that would be silly," I say at the door, turning to face her again. "I mean, what kind of relationship could you possibly have with him now? If he ever found out about the game, about the set up... I can't even imagine what he'd think, how he'd *feel*." I smile a little, the intention clear as day. "He'd probably never talk to you again."

I watch as Skyler tries to swallow, though I can feel that same tightness in my throat.

I'm being an absolute bitch, the worst I've ever been to Skyler or anyone else in my entire life... and the worst part is...

I like it.

The power surges through me, the overwhelming rush of knowing what I want and taking it, no mercy, no excuses.

"Anyway," I say, still smiling. "I'm so excited for tonight. It's going to be perfect! Come up to my room around four and we can all get ready together. And, Little?"

Skyler looks back up at me from where her eyes had fallen to her lap, face a little white.

"Thank you, for talking to me. You really are one of the best friends I have."

I smile a little wider, knocking once on the door frame before I leave her in the kitchen alone, making my way upstairs.

And just like that, I'm back in control.

Right where I belong.

I'M GOING TO FUCKING kill him.

He's my Little, one of my best friends, my brother and my mentee. But none of that matters. Because he made me sign up for this stupid motherfucking dating app, and I am going to *kill* him.

"*Gosh*, this was just so fun," Kimona says, smiling big enough to show me the piece of pepper she's had lodged between her two front teeth all night again. "We have to get together again soon."

"Definitely," I grind out, holding my breath as she leans in for a goodbye hug. This girl has no concept of personal space, which *normally* wouldn't be a big deal. But when she smells like our fraternity house after an intramural game and a keg party, it's an issue.

"Walk me to my car?" she asks when she pulls back.

For a moment, I just let myself stare at her, convincing myself that it's not my fault she bottled all that crazy up in that hot, tight little package and put it on a dating app for me to swipe right on. Her abdomen is lean, all of it showing under her tiny crop top. The ripped-up jeans she's wearing hug her hips, rounding over her firm ass in the perfect way, and her hair is straight as a pin, flowing down behind her shoulders to touch the top of her belt. She's got style, her kicks matching the floral designs on her crop top, and her makeup flawlessly applied.

But that's the thing about online dating — no matter how hot the girl looks, and how well she sells herself in her bio, and how funny she is in text messages — you never really know what you're getting into until you meet her in person.

And boy, did I get myself into a big, steaming pile of horse shit with this one.

Kimona, though cute as hell, is fucking insane.

I'm talking Mike Tyson taking a chunk out of Holyfield's ear crazy.

If her *starting* off our "casual" Friday night date of bowling by bringing me a stuffed bear wearing a t-shirt with her name on it and box of *her* favorite chocolates — because she "just knew I'd share" — for Valentine's Day wasn't weird enough, the fact that she was so genuinely appalled that I didn't buy *her* a gift that she made me buy enough tokens in the arcade to *win* her a teddy bear pretty much sealed the deal.

And this was in the first fifteen minutes.

Forget about the entire two hours of bowling, listening to her talk about her Instagram followers and her crazy fucking friends, who, by the way, ended up *video chatting us* after the first game. One of them drilled me about my background, and the other made me lift up my shirt to show her my abs, to which the third friend, a slender kid with his makeup done better than Kimona, celebrated with a *"Yes, daddy."*

"Um, I actually think I left my jacket inside, so I'm going to run back in. But I'll call you," I told her, offering a hand in a wave.

She started to pout, opening her mouth to ask something else, and then she paused, brows pinching together like she was trying to remember what jacket I'd worn.

The answer was that I *hadn't* worn a jacket. I needed a drink, which they conveniently had at the bar inside the bowling alley.

Before she could say anything else, I turned, booking it toward the bar. I checked over my shoulder to make sure she left, and when she had, I slid into the first barstool at the edge of the bar, running my hands over my fade with a groan.

I'm going to kill him.

It would be one thing if this had been the *first* horrific, nightmare-inducing date from this stupid app. But no, this was now the fifth one in a row. And, sadly, Kimona, as crazy as she is, was the best of those five. Between the girl who neglected to put in her profile her obsession with vampires and desire to have her blood sucked, to the girl who cried about her ex the entire time we were at the nauseating romantic comedy screening — that *she* chose — well, you could say I'm over it.

There *was* a little promise in the date I had last Saturday with a girl who, oddly, reminded me a lot of Shawna — only her hair was pink instead of purple and she didn't wear those sexy glasses I loved so much. But, after two hours of a pretty decent date, I rode home with her in a taxi only for her to tell me it was going to cost me five-hundred dollars to go past that point.

Sighing, I thumb out an angry text to Josh warning him to guard his loins next time I'm around him. Then, I text Skyler, telling her I hope her night at the Alpha Sigma dance is less of a disaster than my fifth and final blind date. She doesn't answer, which doesn't surprise me — she's been *more* than a little occupied with the new transfer since she sank her teeth into him the night they met at rush. We have plans to meet up for breakfast next week, so I decide to fill her in on my dates then, and toss my phone on the bar face down with another long sigh.

"You know, I want so badly to tease you about all that huffing and sighing, but I had a front row viewing of that train wreck and I can't say I blame you. Here," a commanding, yet melodic voice says. "This one's on me."

A tall glass filled to the top with a light, amber-colored beer appears in front of me, and I follow the hand hooked to it.

To a girl so beautiful that I have to actively think about keeping my jaw clamped shut.

Wow.

It's been a long time since a girl has stunned me with her beauty alone. In fact, I can't think of the last time it happened. Perhaps when I met Skyler? As much as I was into Shawna, it wasn't the same kind of beauty. Shawna was different, unique. She stuck out with her purple hair, her glasses, her pierced nipples.

But this girl? This girl is a classic, timeless kind of pretty.

She looks like she walked straight out of a 1970's issue of *Ebony* magazine, her skin dark and smooth, hair just a couple inches longer than mine, framing her face with natural, easily styled curls. She's dressed in the aqua blue bowling alley tank top that all the other girls working there are wearing, paired with a short pair of white shorts, but she adds her own flair with an aqua and orange bandana tied at the front edge of her hair. Large, gold hoop earrings adorn her ears, her makeup natural and slight, but what catches me most is the combination of her smile and her eyes.

That smile, not a bright, blinding one, but a comfortable smirk, like she knows something the rest of the world doesn't. Her plump bottom lip is nude, giving her a natural pout, and the way those lips complement her bright, golden eyes is enough to make me blink to be sure I'm seeing it all as it really is, and not as a dream.

Because she *must* be a dream.

I'm not sure how long I stare at her before my ability to find words comes back, but she's just waiting, watching, that beautiful smile in place as she hangs one hand on her hip.

"You mean you saw that whole thing and didn't send help? What kind of monster are you?"

She chuckles, tossing her hands up to reveal her smooth, light palms. "Hey, it's not my business to get involved in the affairs of customers — even if they are poor sonofabitches dating quite possibly the worst kind of girl."

"We're not dating," I clarified quickly. Then, I tilted my head with a cock of one eyebrow. "Well, *technically*, this was a date. But it was our first one. And our last."

"Bit off more than you could chew, huh?"

"Let's just say I've quickly discovered that online dating is *not* for me."

I take my first drink as she laughs, savoring the cool, refreshing bubbles as much as the sound of her delicate voice.

"Oh God, don't tell me your friends suckered you into downloading one of those atrocious apps."

I point one finger at her like a gun. "Bingo."

"Poor thing. Tell you what, the second one is on me, too," she says, nodding to my already half-empty glass.

Cocking one brow, I take another small sip. "Buying me two beers within the first five minutes of talking to me, huh? Is this what it feels like to be a chick at a bar?"

"Don't get used to it. You're buying on our next date."

I have to swallow slowly not to choke on my beer at that. "I didn't realize we were having a first."

"Well, now you do." She winks, nodding at a customer down the bar to let him know she's on her way over. Then, before she makes her way toward him, she extends her hand for mine. Her nails are nude, just like her lips, but each delicate finger is covered with gold and silver rings. "It's Becca, by the way."

I take her hand in mine, not fighting the smile she brings to the surface after such a shitty night. "Bear. Er—" I pause. "Clinton."

"Which one is it?"

"Both. Clinton is my real name, but my friends call me Bear."

Becca smirks, that same confident, sexy-as-hell one she had when I first laid eyes on her. "Well, let's start with Clinton then." Then she knocks a knuckle on the bar. "Be right back."

She sashays down to the other end of the bar, and I don't dare tear my eyes away from her plump ass, even though I should. Nope, I shamelessly watch her for the rest of the night, whether she's tending to other customers or hanging out in front of me. We talk as much as her busy bar allows, and at the end of the night, she puts her number in my phone — and a kissy face emoji right next to her name.

The next thing I do is delete that fucking app.

Cassie

IN HINDSIGHT, PERHAPS USING Kade as a secret way to talk about Adam with the girls wasn't my smartest plan.

It started earlier in the week, when I was feeling particularly bummed out *before* my talk with Adam at the bonfire last night. Skyler asked me what was wrong, and in an effort to get her fabulous boy advice, I told her about my flip-flop emotional feelings toward Adam.

Except, I said it was Kade I was feeling them for.

It seemed smart at the time. If I used a code name, then I could talk about my feelings and get them out of my head. I could get advice from my sisters. And Kade is such a flirt, he's already had three "girlfriends" in his short time since joining Alpha Sigma. It would work, I told myself. No one would question it.

And they haven't.

But now, it's a little harder to hold the façade as I carefully craft my words before I say them to Skyler in the bathroom at the Alpha Sig Valentine's Day dance.

To say that I'm frustrated would be a drastic understatement. I huff again, sliding my lip gloss over my lip for the thirteenth time. My lips are shiny. I should put it away, but it's giving me something to do.

Adam sat next to me in the limo on the way to the dance, but other than our conversation there, he hasn't said a word to me.

And he hasn't asked me to dance.

I *know* it's his duty as president to make sure everything is going smoothly, and I know his brothers are here, and his new members, and he's got his hands full. I know all that. But here he is, less than twenty-four hours after preaching all this *actions are louder than words* shit, and in my eyes, he's failing. His words might have said that he thinks I'm beautiful tonight and he can't wait to spin me around the dance floor, but his actions are saying I'm the last thing on his mind.

I should be calm, I should know he'll ask me to dance soon. I should still be comforted by all the wonderful, perfect, amazing things he said to me as he held me by the bonfire last night.

But my anxiety is a nasty, wild beast, and right now, I can't fight against it with an animal as weak as logic.

"So, do you see what I'm saying?" I ask Skyler, continuing our conversation about Adam — AKA, Kade — not asking me to dance yet. I slip my lip gloss back in my purse, turning to watch her finish touching up her mascara. "He's more difficult to read than my fucking biology books."

At least *that* part was true.

"Take control, Little," Skyler says, as if it's easy. As if every girl in the world has the same bad ass, cocky style that she does. "Kade is young. Hot, but young. If you want him, make a move."

Things I want to say:

I *have* made a move, but he wants to take it slow. What's up with that shit?

I understand his motives for wanting to move slow. It's the most amazing, most respectful way I've ever been treated. But I simultaneously hate it.

I feel completely out of control of my emotions and have no idea what is happening.

Oh and PS, it's actually Adam I'm talking about.

Instead, what I *actually* say is, "Ugh. I'm not you, Big. I can't just make a move."

And again, at least that part is true. At this point in our story, I am not asking Adam to dance. He should be asking me.

"I'm confident," I tell Skyler, believing it only about sixty percent in my heart. "But, I'm also traditional. I want him to ask *me*."

I watch her slick the mascara over her lashes one last time, chewing my lip with a question I've been burning to ask her since last night at the bonfire. I know she and Adam are just friends, that they have a close relationship — definitely not a traditional one for exes to have. Still... the way she looked at him, the way she flirted with him...

Does she still like him?

Because I'm almost entirely sure that if the answer to that is yes, I will literally die. And not a cute, movie kind of death. I'm talking the gruesome kind that they can't show on the news.

Kappa Kappa Beta Sister Dies of Heartbreak, Explodes Into Mess of Guts and Feelings.

"Ask me whatever it is you want to ask me before you chew off your bottom lip," Skyler says, grinning at me in the mirror.

I sigh, leaning a hip against the bathroom counter. I debate my next words carefully. I haven't talked to Skyler about Adam in... well, ever. Our entire friendship, or whatever you call it, has been kept away from Skyler — mostly because I was a little ashamed of having feelings for someone who used to be her boyfriend.

But I can't go any longer without knowing.

"Are you and Adam still a thing?" I ask, trying to sound naïve. I aim for somewhere between idle curiosity and bored concern. "Like, when this thing is over with Kip... are you going to date him again?"

A friend would ask another friend that, right? That's normal, right?

Skyler's face warps into confusion as she tucks her mascara away. "What?" she almost scoffs. "No, not even close. Adam was fun last year and we're still good friends, but he's president and doesn't have time for a girlfriend."

Tell me about it.

"And even if he did," Skyler continues. "It wouldn't be me."

"Why?" I say quickly, almost too quickly.

"I don't know," she says with a shrug. "I'm just not into him like that anymore." Suddenly, Skyler turns on me, one brow popped up in curiosity. "Why do you ask?"

I have to focus not to blanch, not to blush, and I'm sure my cheeks shade pink, anyway. But I keep my voice steady, convincing her as much as I can that this is a normal conversation.

"I don't know," I say, shrugging and facing the mirror again. "I was just curious. Just wondering if you'd have someone to fall back on, I guess."

Yeah, that sounds legit.

Blessedly, Erin, Ashlei, and Jess pour into the bathroom, saving me from having to answer any other questions about my sudden interest in Skyler and Adam. Ashlei gets to us first, and she slides right between us, one arm hanging on each of our shoulders.

"J-Love is D-Runk," she announces.

"I am not!" is the immediate argument from Jess, but the words slur a little as she says them. "I'm just having fun. You should try it."

"No Violet Vulva tonight, J-Love?" Skyler asks.

"Nope." Jess holds one finger up, waving it side to side. "Let's just say there's a little garden that's not so innocent anymore."

We all laugh out a mixture of *ew* and *gross*, and through the spew of laughter, Skyler says, "Kip gave me a gift in that garden, you skank. You ruined my Valentine's Day."

"Oh hush, I didn't fuck on your precious glasses, you prude," Jess retorts, referencing the new pair of Ray-Bans Kip gave Skyler as a gift. They're actually perfect for her, and one of the most thoughtful gifts I've ever seen her receive. I eye her as Jess keeps talking, noting the tinge of sadness in her eyes.

She likes him.

It's as clear as day, and we all know it.

My stomach knots, thinking about how this is all going to end.

"Just on the bench where he *gave* them to you," Jess continues, which earns another round of laughter and a playful shove from Skyler.

Jess escapes into one of the stalls to pee as Ashlei leans up agains the wall, taking pressure off her feet in the sky-high heels she's wearing. "Speaking of Kip, how's it going?"

Erin has been surprisingly quiet, just laughing along with everything until that exact moment. She watches Skyler carefully, as if she's ready to catch her should she try to run away — like a lioness hunting a gazelle.

"It's fine. We're having fun, everything is going according to plan."

The words roll off Skyler's tongue easy enough, but we all know it's a lie.

Even Erin.

Which is why I can't contain my reaction to what she says next.

"The dance is almost over. I think you should do it soon. Use Adam."

The room tilts, the laughter of other girls around us suddenly too loud, the lights too bright. I'm sure my knees will buckle at any moment, and I grab the counter to hold myself up.

"What?!"

That's the word out of my mouth — and it's the same one out of Skyler's. She turns to look at me, as if it's strange for *me* to react in that way, and with her now knowing about me and Adam, I guess it kind of is.

But I can't look at her.

All I can do is gape at Erin, silently begging her with my gaze to reconsider what she's asking, to come up with a new plan.

"Why would I use Adam?" Skyler asks Erin, though she's still watching me.

"It's believable," Erin answers easily. "It's obvious Adam still has a thing for you, so tell Kip you have feelings for him, too. Tell him you were using him to make Adam jealous and it worked."

That tilt turns into a full spin, warping my reality like a washing machine set to high speed. I grip the counter more firmly, my only assurance that I'm not actually tumbling to the floor of the bathroom. Every breath comes shallower, every blink invades my vision with more blackness that doesn't recede when my eyes are open again. I tell myself to calm down, to breathe, but I can't do either.

This cannot be happening.

I think I tell the girls I need air. I think I tell Skyler good luck. I think I tell Erin to go fuck herself. Maybe I say nothing at all. I don't know anything for sure, not until I'm outside, in the garden, away from the noise and the reality of what's about to happen.

It'll be fine. Adam cares about you, he wants to be with you. He's not going to be with Skyler just because she says she wants him back.

I say the words in my head, even risking it and speaking a few of them out loud. But they do nothing to soothe my racing heart, because the truth of the matter is I don't know any of those things for sure.

Do I trust him? Yes. Do I believe that he feels what he says he does for me? Without a doubt.

But things between us have been muddled enough without any interference. What will happen when Adam hears Skyler say she wants him again? Will it stir something inside him, wake him up to a feeling he thought was gone that has always existed?

Will he want her, too?

My mouth waters, almost as if its sweating, and heat rushes away from my face, leaving it clammy and cool. I'm sick. I'm absolutely sick at the thought, at the possibility of losing Adam again — losing him before I've even had him at all. I force a breath, closing my eyes for five long seconds to try to find calmness, to find assurance, to find peace.

But what I actually find is the nearest bush, just in time to pull my hair back and forfeit my dinner.

Adam

I SIGH AS THE first drink I've had all evening is handed to me over the bar, and when I take that first sip, I close my eyes and savor the taste. It's just a Bud Light, but after a long night of running around making sure everything was going according to plan, it tastes like heaven.

I'm not sure why I thought it was a good idea to have our Valentine's Day dance the day after our New Member bonfire, but I feel the ramifications of that choice as I take another, longer pull of my beer. It feels like I haven't caught a breath since I sat on the bench with Cassie last night. Between the catering for dinner being all wrong, the bars only being half stocked and us having to figure out how to get them *fully* stocked, and watching the under-age new members to make sure they weren't doing anything stupid — like trying to give a fake ID to one of these bartenders — and you could say I'm more than a little stressed.

But, Jeremy has stepped in, taking over the last of our night's worries, and I'm on strict orders to enjoy myself — even if it is just for the last couple of hours.

So, beer in hand, I make my way through the room on a hunt for the one girl I've been thinking about all night.

When the limo pulled up in front of the KKB house earlier, there were way too many pretty girls on the lawn waiting for us. I mean, between Skyler in her killer red sequin number and Ashlei in her jet black, slinky thing, it was all I could do to get my brothers to stop drooling and howling like a bunch of animals when we piled out of the limo to let them get in.

Part of me was glad Skyler was dressed to kill, because while most of my brothers' eyes were on her, mine were stuck like lasers on Cassie.

I had to laugh a little when I first saw her, because just like the first dance I'd seen her at, the one where Skyler had been my date, she was wearing white while Skyler wore red. Only this time, her dress wasn't quite so conservative. The front neckline dipped dramatically between her small breasts, showing freckles I didn't yet know existed, ones I wasn't sure I wanted anyone else to know about, either. The white fabric hugged her slim waist, rouching around her hips before it flowed down to her slender ankles strapped into nude heels.

She was an angel, just like she had been at that first dance.

I'd kept my promise to her, giving her space to enjoy the dance with her sisters and not worry about me. Honestly, I had my hands full anyway, so it was a little easier to do than I had thought it would be once I saw her in that dress. But now that I finally have a second to breathe, she's the only thing I can think about.

I don't care if I promised I'd give her the night with her sisters, with herself. I have to get her in my arms.

I have to get her on that dance floor.

A slow song comes on as I search for her, trying to spot her bright red hair in the sea of blondes and brunettes. I seek that white dress, hands aching to hold her, but the entire song plays through and I still don't see her. I look outside in the garden, check the bars, even ask a girl to yell out her name in the bathroom.

Nothing.

I'm just about to double check the garden when I notice a small crowd gathering around the bar across the dance floor. Curious, I make my way toward the commotion, and when I notice Skyler and Kip in the center of it, my throat tightens.

Skyler's face is cold as she says something to Kip, something that makes everyone around them start whispering to each other, trying to appear like they're not eavesdropping. He reaches for her, but she steps back, and my stomach sinks again.

What did this motherfucker do?

My jaw is set, lips pressed together as I get close enough to hear what's going on. But it's a blessing and a curse when I reach my destination. My curiosity is cured, and I finally know what's going on, but at her next words, everything I thought I knew goes up in flames.

"It's done, Kip," Skyler says, her voice shaky, emotion threatening to overtake her. "I don't need you anymore. I just wanted to get back at Adam. I wanted to make him jealous. And it worked. And now I don't need you."

My beer slips in my hands, and I grip it just in time to save it from crashing to the floor.

What the actual fuck did she just say?

My knee-jerk reaction is to laugh, because she clearly has to be joking. Skyler and I haven't had more than a late night, drunken hookup since we broke up last year. We're friends, sure, but I know without a doubt that she doesn't have feelings for me.

"Is this a joke?" Kip asks, his thoughts mirroring mine.

"No, it's not a fucking joke, Kip," Skyler says, her voice louder.

The crowd thickens, and the president side of me says I need to shut this down. *Now.* But I'm rooted to where I stand, only capable of hanging on to her next words, waiting for an explanation as much as Kip is.

"I don't feel anything for you. I never have, okay?" She says, and though her words are convincing to the entire room, I note the way her voice shakes, the way her hands tremble.

What's going on?

She looks on the verge of tears, and I watch for more signs as she continues.

"I've been in love with Adam since last year and that hasn't changed. Now that I have his attention again, I don't need you. It was fun, but it's over."

A slew of heads turn in my direction then, and I swallow, heat rising up my neck like a bug.

First, she says she's made me jealous — which is entirely false. Now, she says she has my attention, that she's been in *love* with me since last year?

Something is up.

In the back of my mind, I wonder if maybe she's telling the truth. Have I been so blind to not see that she still likes me? Sure, we've hooked up, and yes, we still flirt with each other. But that's just who we are. That's just how our relationship is.

Right?

Dread seeps through me at the possibility that I may have been reading it all wrong, that I may have been leading Skyler on without even knowing it. She thrusts a box into Kip's hand, telling him to take whatever it is back, that she doesn't want it anymore. And then, as Kip stares down at that box, Skyler pushes through the crowd and out the front doors.

Fuck.

My wheels turn faster than I can keep up with, turning over words and thoughts that can't find traction before another one knocks them out of the way. I'm still watching those doors when Kip lets out a frustrated growl, and he goes barreling toward them, too. I follow without thinking, without having a plan, the only driving motivator being my need to know what the hell is going on.

By the time I make it outside, Kip and Skyler are standing at the far end of the car loop, Kip's hand cradling Skyler's face. She's crying, yet leaning into his touch, as if he's the source of the pain and yet the only way to heal it all at once.

I swallow, watching them from a distance, but when she pulls back again, when more tears slip from her blue eyes, I can't watch any longer.

"Hey, man," I say, grabbing Kip by the shoulders to guide him toward the venue. "I think you need to go back inside."

I'm just trying to dissolve the tension, but I realize my mistake as soon as its made when Kip shrugs me off forcefully, turning on me like I'm the dog that shit in his yard.

"Don't fucking touch me."

My defenses kick in automatically, chest broadening as I set my jaw. "You don't want to do this, Kip. Don't lose your head right now."

I try that gentle reminder of whom he's talking to, of where he is, but it only adds fuel to the fire.

"Fuck you."

The words barely meet my ears before I'm shoved back hard. Skyler screams out for Kip to stop, and I'm not in control of my body anymore as I spring back toward him, shoving just as hard.

His eyes are menacing as some of our brothers step between us, Kade holding Kip back as Jeremy does the same with me.

"Calm down," he whispers.

I thrust a hand toward Kip. "I'm calm! It's this motherfucker raging out, not me."

Jeremy gives me a warning look, and I concede, throwing my hands up to let them all know I'm fine as they work on cooling Kip off. The only person I care about right now is the girl crying behind me, anyway.

Turning, I find her with her hands over her mouth, tears streaking her black mascara over her cheeks. I have no idea what's going on, why she's so upset, why she's calling things off with Kip when it's clear she still cares about him. And I *definitely* have no idea how I got pulled into this mess.

But what I do know is that Skyler needs to go home, to get away from Kip and this dance, and I make it my mission to do just that.

"Come on," I tell her softly, offering her my arm. "Let's get out of here."

She takes it as Kip surges toward me again, our brothers holding him back, and she casts one last glance over her shoulder before I open the door to one of the waiting cabs, ushering her inside. She slides across the seat, making room for me to dip in with her, and as soon as the door shuts behind us, she breaks.

I grit my teeth against the sound of her tears, pulling her into me immediately and rocking her as one hand smooths over her back. She's practically sweating, her skin hot to the touch, and she fists my dress shirt as her tears stain my shoulder.

"I'm sorry, I'm so sorry. I'm sorry. I'm sorry."

She says it over and over, and I'm almost positive it's not me she's apologizing to.

So, I just hold her, rocking her, letting her know that whatever it is, it's going to be okay. I don't pry, don't question what happened, or why my name was brought up as an excuse to break up with Kip. Who knows, maybe she just didn't want to be with him anymore and didn't have an excuse to break up.

But even as I think it, I know it's a lie. If that were the case, Skyler would be partying still, not crying on my shoulder.

Sighing, I tuck her a little closer, knowing I won't get answers for a while.

But one thing I know for sure is that Skyler is my friend — nothing more — and she needs me right now. So, if she needs me, I'll be here. Just like I told Cassie, I want to be a man of my word, I want my actions to speak louder than any promise I've ever made.

When Skyler is back at the sorority house and safely tucked away in her bed, I pull out my phone to call Cassie. There's no answer, so I leave a voicemail.

"Hey, it's me," I say on a sigh, tucking my free hand in my pocket as I make my way down Greek Row toward the A Sig house. I open my mouth to say something else, but for some reason, no words come.

Where were you tonight?

Are you okay?

Are we *okay?*

I consider telling her that I got Skyler home safely, but for some reason, it almost feels as if that would make things worse.

But I can't figure out why.

After too many seconds pass, I settle on asking her to call me back, and then I hang up.

And I wait.

Ashlei

"SHIT," I MURMUR UNDER my breath the morning after the Alpha Sigma dance, clenching the pole as hard as I can with my thighs. But it's too late. I'm already slipping out of the spin I attempted, and I throw my hand out in time to catch myself before I face plant on the mat.

When my entire body reaches the floor, I flop out on my back, letting hot air through my flat lips like a balloon deflating after a birthday party. Pretty much sums up how I feel about everything right now.

Karen chuckles, bending down to pat my stomach twice before standing tall and hanging her hands on her hips. "You're not going to be able to just jump back up on here and do everything you were doing a year ago," she says, the ring on her left eyebrow lifting.

"I know, but I didn't think I'd be *this* out of shape."

"You're not out of shape. You're in fantastic shape, honestly," she says, eyes scanning my exposed body. In pole, I never wear more than tiny dance shorts and a strappy sports bra. "But you haven't had to lift all of your body weight and then invert and spin and make it look pretty in over a year. It's going to take some time. And some *practice*."

I sigh again, scrubbing my hands down my face before reaching one hand up. Karen takes it, tugging me up to stand again.

"Twenty more minutes and then call it quits for today. You can come back tomorrow, okay?"

I nod, thanking her again for letting me come to her studio for an open pole session on such late notice. I was thankful to find another pole studio near school — one *not* connected to the awful memories of what happened at my last one — and the fact that she could get me in this morning was everything I needed after the Valentine's dance.

Last year, I spent Valentine's Day with Bo.

And last night, she called me.

The same feeling moves through me when I think about the call as did when it came through — like a little bug crawling down my neck and venturing all the way down my spine. I rub down the pole with a rag and alcohol, then I climb up again, this time working on tucks and other strength-building poses as I try to process.

Just seeing her name light up my phone screen was panic-inducing enough, but when I connected the call and the video came in clear, showing a face that seemed almost like a ghost to me after a year, I couldn't breathe. Literally, I stood there with my mouth hanging open and didn't take a single breath for a full minute.

Bo had smiled, reminding me with just that simple notion how much I'd loved her, and then I had to try not to throw up as she told me how happy she was. She told me she's up in New York City now, enrolled in a fashion school, and I marveled at how she looked almost nothing like the Bo I knew before. Her hair was a bright, almost neon pink, cut short and shaved on one side, and she had a piercing in the little dip at the bottom of her lip.

Just about the time I figured out how to breathe normally again, she told me she has a girlfriend.

My hands slip a little as that same feeling rolls through me, but I grip the pole tighter, using my shoulders and lower abs to swing myself up and around the pole until my feet land gracefully on the mat. I walk slowly around it, feeling out my new grip before launching myself back up.

It's not that I'm not happy for Bo, that I don't feel a little better knowing she's alive and happy, but I think I realized when she called me that *I'm* not happy — not the way I should be, anyway. Between Kimberly and the drama at work, trying to put fires out in sorority land, and not having anything to fuel me in my spare time — like pole used to — I feel a little aimless.

And, underneath all those shallow reasons for my unhappiness lies the real truth.

I miss Brandon.

I still want him, which is absolutely ridiculous after the way he's given me the cold shoulder at work. The memory of his biting remarks earlier this week make me grunt as I release my hands from the pole, inverting backward and holding myself with the strength of my legs and core alone. And it's there, hanging upside down doing something I used to love so much, something that feels so challenging an unfamiliar to me now, that I realize I've lost myself.

For the next fifteen minutes, I try to clear my head, focusing only on using my body to practice old spins and climbs. After a quick cool down, I pay Karen for the drop-in session and we set up a training schedule.

"You know, we're looking at going to competition later this year," Karen says, handing me my credit card back. "Think you'd be interested? You're already better rusty than half the girls on our team."

I smile, swallowing down the memories of my last competition. "Thank you, that's very flattering, but this time around I'm just doing pole for me. No competitions."

Karen watches me curiously, her almost gray eyes searching mine. "Okay, I can respect that. But let me know if you ever change your mind."

"I will. And hey, thank you again for today. I really needed it."

She chuckles, eyeing the new bruises already showing on my arms and legs. "Well, now you'll probably need an ice bath and some Arnica."

"No shit," I agree with a laugh of my own as I tug on my loose-fitting travel pants over my tiny shorts. Adjusting the strap of my gym bag over my shoulder, I give her a little wave and make my way through the studio hall and back out into the Florida heat.

It's a beautiful morning, just past nine now, and I plug in my headphones to start the walk back to campus. The studio was only a little over a mile away, so I took the walk this morning to warm up.

This one, I need to clear my head.

I scan the windows of the little shops I pass as I weave through downtown, enjoying the cool breeze mixing with the sunshine hitting my shoulders. I work through my plan for the week, starting with a beach day with the girls tomorrow and then back on the grind early Monday morning. Pulling out my phone, I jot down when I'll go to pole between work and class. My chest feels lighter with every step, and the more my plan falls into place, the easier my breaths come. I know pole isn't the answer to everything, but it's the first step to getting a little of the old me back.

I drop my phone back into my pocket, hooking one thumb on the strap of my gym bag as I go back to scanning the shops. My mind drifts from Bo back to Brandon, and my stomach turns.

I miss him.

My hand itches to grab my phone again, to call him and ask to see him. What's the worst that could happen? He says no and I feel just as annoyed and hurt as I do now? The possibility that he might say yes is enough to shove that fear down, but when I ask myself if I can truly handle another rejection from him right now, I know the answer without saying it out loud.

Taking that roll of my stomach as a sign from the universe, I decide to wait, to talk to him on Monday in the office, instead. At least there, I can't break down crying asking him if he ever thinks of me anymore. Maybe I'll have a small chance of keeping my shit together.

The decision is made, but when my eyes flit through the next shop, I wonder if I was reading the sign from the universe all wrong.

Because there he is.

As if he's a mirage, or as if my soul called to him without asking permission first, I spot Brandon standing inside a suit store, his beautiful, chiseled jaw casting a shadow down his neck as he appraises himself in a mirror.

My feet stop working.

I just stand there and gape from the sidewalk, watching Brandon eyeing himself in the full-length mirror as a shorter, slightly chubby man takes measurements along his inseam and then jots down notes in a little notebook. Brandon's eyes are hard, the irises scrutinizing as he scans the new suit. It's a creamy beige, complementing the caramel tones of his complexion, and even now — before it's been tailored — it fits him in a way that should be illegal.

I lick my lips, remembering how hard the body is underneath all that fabric, and it's as if that little spark I taste on my lips shocks him, too. He pauses, flattening a palm over his abdomen before lifting his eyes to the window beyond the mirror he's staring into, the window where I stand.

His gaze hits me like a wave of fire, burning me from the inside out.

I pluck the neck of my tank top away from my skin, a bead of sweat dripping down the back of my neck. I swallow, wrapping both hands around the front strap of my bag to keep them from nervously fidgeting. Somehow, I manage a smile, but Brandon doesn't smile back. Instead, he says something to the man working on his suit, and then he steps down from the platform, his feet moving him quickly toward the door.

Toward me.

I steal a breath before he opens the glass door, and when we're face to face on the sidewalk, I smile, squinting a little at the sun streaming in behind him.

"Fancy meeting you here."

Brandon tucks his hands easily into the pockets of his slacks, ones that hang on his hips a little now but I know will fit like a glove once he's done. It's the way all his suits fit — tailored to perfection, hugging every asset.

"Fancy, indeed," he says, his voice smooth and steady as his eyes rake over me. I catch a slight tick in his jaw then, especially when he takes in my tiny sports bra. "You're dressed... interestingly."

I glance down at the bra, my abdomen still exposed, but I at least took the time to throw on travel pants over my skimpy shorts.

"Ah, yeah. I just got done with a pole session, actually."

Brandon lifts a brow. "Pole? You went back?"

"I went back," I say, voice soft. Then, I shrug, running a hand over my high pony tail. "It's just been a really stressful couple of weeks, and I needed to blow off some steam. I suck, though," I say quickly. "My body is out of shape. I have a lot of work to do to get back to where I was."

"You are not out of shape."

"You didn't see me try to climb a pole."

"I'd like to."

I clench my teeth together to keep my mouth from gaping open again, and Brandon just watches me, his gaze smoldering.

"What's wrong?" he asks after a moment.

Um, besides the fact that you just said you'd like to see me climb a pole?

"You said you went to clear your head," he clarifies when I don't respond. "What's wrong, what's been going on?"

I sigh, turning so I don't have to look at him when I lie. "Nothing. I'm fine. Just a little stressed from work and stuff."

"Just because you're not looking at me doesn't mean I don't know when you're lying."

His voice is lower, and when he takes a step closer, my façade breaks. Tears prick my eyes, everything I haven't been facing welling up at the absolute worst time possible. I sniff, holding it all in, trying my damnedest to pull myself together even as my vision floods.

"Really, I'm fine," I say, but my voice is weak — pathetic.

Brandon reaches for me, but stops himself short, tucking his hands back in his pockets as he watches me. My eyes stay focused on the sidewalk, and I sniff again.

"What are you doing today?"

I glance at him then, but then my gaze is right back on the ground. "I don't know, I have some homework."

"Can it wait?" he asks, almost hopeful. "I want to show you something."

And when I pull my eyes back to his, watching him through my wet lashes, I know there isn't a chance in hell I could say no. The way those dark pools swallow me is just all kinds of wrong. I feel like a tiny little guppy trying to swim upstream in white water rapids — completely helpless.

"What do you want to show me?"

"Oh, my God. You're kidding, right?"

I gape at the monstrous boat in front of us, taking in the crisp white build of it, contrasted by large, dark, tinted windows. The railing spans the top deck, silver and shiny, complementing the wood flooring and accents. It's the kind of boat I've only seen in movies, the kind I've only dreamed about ever being this close to — let alone being *on*.

Brandon hands his bag to one of the crew members who just met us at the bottom of the ramp, ignoring my question. My eyes widen even more when he says something to the woman in Spanish, and she nods with a bright smile, taking the bag and greeting me with a shy smile before she heads back up the ramp.

Brandon smirks when he sees my mouth hanging open. "What?"

"Don't *what* me," I chastise. "Usually when someone says they want to show you something, it's an old family photograph, or a cool, limited edition comic book, or maybe even a secret place where they go to think. They literally never mean, 'Let me show you my *yacht*.'"

He chuckles, rolling up the sleeve of his loose, white, button-up shirt and revealing a dark, toned forearm. That button-up shirt is paired casually with a pair of baby blue shorts that end just above his knee, his boat shoes pulling off the sailor look he has going. It was the outfit he changed back into after leaving the suit for the tailor, and I wonder if he had plans to come out here before he saw me or if he was just dressed and ready.

"Are you just going to stare at me or can we get on board now?"

"I think I'll just stay here and stare."

He smiles at that, showing me his perfect teeth as he gestures one hand toward the ramp.

"Seriously, I don't have a swim suit or anything. I wasn't prepared for a boat day."

"We have everything on board."

I scoff, crossing my arms over my chest. "Oh, so you've just got swim suits waiting in every size so you can entertain whatever lady you have with you, huh?"

"Maybe."

Anger flares deep in my belly, boiling my skin. "That's disgusting."

He laughs, stepping into my space as his eyes descend on mine. "I called ahead and asked Marietta to go down the street and grab you one from one of the tourist shops, okay? Now, stop being such an adorable pain in my ass and get on the boat."

I chew my lip, which makes his gaze fall to my mouth.

And if the sun was hot before, it's absolute fire now.

Brandon keeps his eyes fixed on my lips as he swallows, stepping back and gesturing toward the ramp again. This time, I step onto it, making my way toward the boat with him following close behind.

I can't take everything in, it all happens so quickly. My eyes try to take in every accent, every luxurious corner of the yacht as the captain and crew greet us. They each shake Brandon's hand first, and then mine, and the next thing I know I've got a glass of champagne in my hand, a beach towel laid over one arm, and directions to a room inside that has a swim suit waiting for me.

Well, this day turned around quickly.

"Why don't you go get changed," Brandon says, nodding inside. "I'm going to speak with the captain, and then I'll meet you on the top deck?"

I shake my head, still looking around. "This isn't a boat, this is like a... home. A *mansion*." My eyes widen when I glance over his shoulder. "Oh my God, is that a pool? A pool, on a boat." I press a hand to my forehead. "What even."

Brandon watches my little meltdown with amusement, standing just as confidently and casually as he had on the sidewalk outside the tailor.

"Trust me, it's a lot more exciting once we get out on the water. Go, change, then meet me up top."

I think I nod, though I can't be sure. I just let my feet guide me inside, following Marietta's instructions until I find a beautiful bedroom. It's like the master bed and bath of a mansion, a grand California king bed sprawled out in the middle of the room with gorgeous views out the large tinted window. A tiny, white bikini is laid out on the deep burgundy comforter, and I hold up the top with one eyebrow quirked.

"Nice," I murmur, realizing how much my tits are going to spill out of the fabric. I may not be a super curvy girl, but I'm blessed enough for my athletic figure.

When I hold up the bottoms — which might as well have been just a thong — I laugh.

But once I'm dressed in the suit, staring at my reflection in the full-length mirror fixed to the wall opposite the foot of the bed, I smirk.

"Damn, girl," I say, turning to see my tan backside

before taking in the full-frontal view again. Thank goodness Erin has been obsessed with getting sun lately. The suit reveals a little bit of my tan lines from my other suit, but it fits perfectly, almost as if it was tailored for me.

Thanks, Marietta.

Tossing the towel back over my arm, I take a sip of my champagne and carry it with me as I make my way up to the top deck.

Of course, I can't get to the top deck without first passing the massive dining area, the living area — complete with the biggest flat-screen TV I've seen in my entire life — and that damn pool. There are chairs lining the edge of it, but I find Brandon casually reclining on a couch on the very top deck, his bare feet kicked up on the table in front of him and his arms lining the back cushions as he stares out at the water.

I didn't even realize we were moving, but up here on the top deck, it's easy to see the water spreading for the nose of the yacht. The blue is reflected in the lenses of Brandon's dark sunglasses, and I watch him for longer than I should before finally dropping my towel next to him.

He glances up, and when he does, I swear I see his eyes widen even through his dark shades. But he doesn't let his neck move, doesn't give away whether his gaze is roaming my body or staying fixed on my face. My cheeks warm regardless, and I cross my arms over my middle with a shrug.

"Thank you for the suit, Mr. Church."

He just stares for a solid thirty seconds more, and then he clears his throat, patting the cushion next to him.

"It's no problem. Here, sit." When I do, he holds up his glass of champagne toward mine. "And you can call me Brandon, Miss Daniels."

My heart leaps into my throat, but I hold my glass just a little away from his. "Is that only for today?"

His smile falls a little at that, and in lieu of answering, he just clinks his glass to mine.

"To secret getaways."

I swallow, holding his gaze as we both take a sip of the crisp bubbles.

And for the next hour, not another word is said.

Brandon asks Marietta to put on his playlist, which includes everything from Chance the Rapper and Kendrick Lamar to The Dirty Heads and Sublime. He sings along to every song that comes on, tapping his feet on the table, and I sprawl out on the circular couch next to his. As the sun warms my skin, and the champagne warms my blood, I let out a content sigh and soak in the day.

Sometime after I flip onto my stomach, I doze off, and Brandon wakes me with a gentle sweep of my hair off my slick forehead.

"How do you feel about some lunch?" he asks, the sun serving as a halo around his silhouetted frame.

My stomach grumbles before I have the chance to respond, and we both chuckle.

"There's my answer," he says, holding out a hand to help me up off the couch. When I slide my fingers into his palm, he tugs me up, catching me in his arms once I'm standing. His Adam's apple bobs hard in his throat, and he lets me go slowly, stepping back with a hand gesture to the lower deck. "After you."

I debate wrapping my towel around me, but leave it behind, saying a little prayer to the cellulite gods that my ass looks good as I strut inside. Brandon follows behind me, and when I stop at the sight of our lunch spread with a gasp, he runs right into my backside with an *oof*.

"Sorry," I murmur, but I still can't move. "You said lunch. I thought, like, sandwiches."

My eyes scan the massive spread, complete with what looks like a full raw bar of oysters and crab legs. There is more champagne waiting where our plates are set up, and a bowl of fruit large enough to feed ten easily makes my mouth water. I eye the juicy watermelon, the bright strawberries, the crisp grapes.

"I love how surprised you are by all of this," he says, moving past me to the table. He pulls one chair out, holding out a hand to help me sit. "Sometimes I feel like I take it for granted."

"I don't think I ever could," I say, still amazed as I take my seat, eyeing the rest of the table.

"You think that, but even when you come from humble beginnings, it's easy to get used to this kind of life. If you don't take the time to appreciate it, that is." Brandon sits across from me, unfolding his napkin onto his lap. "I'm glad you came out here with me. Makes me slow down and really take it all in, the way I used to."

"What was it like the first time you set foot on this monster?" I ask.

I go to lay my own napkin out, but it feels strange setting it across my bare thighs. Marietta seems to pick up on my discomfort, and she exits her post at the far corner of the dining area, returning quickly with a plush, beige robe.

"Oh, thank you," I tell her as she helps me put the robe on. Brandon watches every move of my body with a tense jaw, not speaking until I'm seated again.

"The first time I set foot on this, I was twenty-seven," he says. "Single, on top of the world — at least, it felt like it."

"Did you have a big yacht party with all your friends?"

He smirks, plucking a grape from the bowl between us. "Not really my style."

"You're telling me you came out on this thing all by yourself?"

He nods. "I did. We took it to… Bimini, I want to say?"

"The Bahamas," Marietta corrects from her corner. "Bimini was our second trip."

"Ah, that's right."

I shake my head, using the tongs to fish out a collection of fruit onto my own plate. I pop a strawberry between my lips, trying to imagine his life.

"Do you ever have anyone else out here?"

Brandon shifts. "I have. Clients, mostly. But, there have been friends, too."

"Female friends?" I pry.

He doesn't answer, just sips his champagne as if he knows better than I do that I don't want to hear his response to that.

My cheeks flame, and I follow his guide, sipping from my own glass. "Well, thank you for inviting me out today. This is… incredible."

And it is. I truly am thankful to be spending the day with him, especially after the week I've had. But as we talk through lunch and make our way back out to the top deck, I can't help but wonder what changed. Why the sudden friendliness, the sudden olive branch? And does it only exist here, or will he be friendly in the office, too?

More than that, can I handle being *only* friends with Brandon?

This, the laughter and stories on a beautiful yacht, it almost hurts worse than him shrugging me off in the office. At least there, I can put him in a box. The Mr. Church box.

My boss, my CEO — *not* my friend, and certainly nothing more.

But now?

My mind is spinning with the confusion of it a few hours after lunch when Brandon asks if I'd like a tour.

"We're heading back toward shore, but it will take a while. We'll probably get to see the sun set over Miami before we dock," he explains as I wrap my robe around me again, following him inside the yacht. "I guess I should have started with this tour, huh?"

"It's okay, I've enjoyed just lounging on the deck."

"Me, too."

He slides his sunglasses up onto his head with those words, his dark eyes finding mine as we cross the threshold inside. I tuck a strand of hair behind my ear, trying to hold his gaze but finding it impossible to do so without leaning up to kiss him.

God, I want to kiss him.

I can feel his lips on mine like they were just there, only seconds ago. I remember the firm, yet soft press of them against mine. I remember the way he smells after sex, the way a thin sheen of sweat always gathers on his chest and abdomen after we finish. I remember the way he feels inside me, when he stretches me open.

Clenching my thighs, I tear my eyes away from his, blinking away the very not-safe-for-work thoughts.

"So, where do we start?"

Brandon takes his time, weaving us in and out of the yacht. He takes me through the entertainment areas — both dining and gaming — and out to each of the two decks I hadn't visited yet. One of them hosts the pool, while the other is a mostly-shaded bar and lounging area similar to the top deck, but with more seating.

Inside, we tour the back kitchen, the captain's post, and the crew quarters. Then, Brandon takes me through the meeting space he had designed for clients, the various bedrooms and bathrooms, and then, at the end of the tour, we're back in the first room I entered when we boarded.

The master bedroom.

Brandon pauses at the door as I wander the room, really taking it in this time around. I note the gold and burgundy accents, the way the setting sun casts a soft, orange glow over the entire room. The master bath is visible from the bed, the two rooms joined, no walls between them. I eye the large tub, wondering what it'd be like to soak in it, wondering if he's ever had another woman in it before me.

I spot a picture frame on a small dresser to the left of the bed, and I carefully pick it up, my fingers brushing over the photo inside it.

"Is this Darnell?" I ask, eyes flicking back and forth between a younger Brandon and a tall, strikingly handsome man with his arm around Brandon's shoulders. I remember Darnell from his speech at the award banquet in Atlanta, the man who took Brandon under his wing as a young kid.

They look like brothers, their smiles wide, both of them dressed in basketball shorts and loose-fitting t-shirts. Brandon holds a basketball under one arm, the street court laid out in the background behind them.

"Yes."

His voice is soft, and suddenly the vibe in the room changes. The air is sucked out with that word, leaving us in a hot, sticky vacuum where breaths are limited.

Gently placing the frame back on the dresser, I turn, pulling my robe tighter around me. There's an entire room between us, yet I feel the warmth of Brandon's breath like he's only inches away.

"Why did you bring me out here today?" I finally ask, my voice barely a whisper.

"Because you were sad. Because you needed to get away."

"Since when is my emotional state any of your concern?" I bite back, though my voice is still subdued. I shrug before adding, "It certainly hasn't been since I came back to *Okay, Cool.*"

Brandon stands taller, his eyes never leaving mine, hands still casually tucked in his pockets. "I want you to be happy, Ashlei."

I shiver at the sound of my name on his tongue, but close my eyes against the feel of it.

"That's not true."

"It is," he implores, taking one step. It's such a small movement, I almost question he took it at all. "I've always wanted that, from the moment I met you."

"No." I shake my head, opening my eyes again to find his boring into me from across the room. "If that were true, you wouldn't ignore me. You wouldn't treat me the way you do." I swallow. "You reprimanded me like... like..."

"Like one of my employees who didn't do her job correctly?"

I clench my jaw to keep it from popping open.

"I—"

"Don't you understand?" he asks, cutting me off as he walks purposefully toward me. "I *have* to do that, treat you like you're just another employee. It's the only thing I can control. That office," he says, pointing one hand back toward shore, "is the only goddamn place where I have any semblance of power over you." He takes a larger step, and then another, until he's only a few feet away. "In every other place," he says, chest heaving. "In every other time — you consume me. You *own* me."

I swallow, back hitting the curved glass of the window. My hands press into it for stability, but the next step Brandon takes puts us chest to chest. Breathing is impossible, and my knees are so weak they tremble under the weight of my body, ready to collapse.

"When I'm in my car, you're in my head. When I'm at the gym, trying to sweat you out of my system, your eyes are all I see. When I'm in my bed, I imagine your hair splayed over my pillows the way it fell over the pillows in Atlanta. And when I give in? When I finally fuck myself, and let out all the tension you cause, it's *you* I think of when I come. Your mouth," he says, reaching out to touch my lips with his fingers. I gasp, opening them just enough to taste his skin. "Your body, your tight, always-wet, always-ready pussy. It's you I think of, Ashlei. Always. Ever since I met you, and ever since I touched you, it's only been worse."

He pulls his fingers away, running his hands down my shoulders until they hook behind my elbows. Pressing off the glass, I lean into him, pushing onto my toes so my whisper reaches his ear.

"Touch me again."

He groans, letting his forehead drop to mine, our breaths heavy and heated between us. "This is dangerous. You know that. We talked about it — what people would say about you, if anyone found out."

"Who said anyone has to know?" I ask, sliding my hands over his chest. I hook my fingertips in the band of his shorts, tugging him forward, our lips nearly touching as he groans again. "That toast earlier, it was to secret getaways, right?"

Brandon blows out a breath. "It can only be here. It can only be when we're not at the office. We can't have a relationship, Ashlei."

He pulls back enough to look me in the eyes when he delivers his next blow.

"You won't be mine," he says. "And I can never be yours."

I swallow those words like knives, letting them shred permanent marks into my throat on the way down. But, despite how they hurt, despite how hard I know it will be, there's only one thought on my mind. Only one thing matters.

So, I lean in again, my lips touching his as I repeat my plea.

"Touch. Me. Again."

Then, I bite his thick lower lip, pulling it between my teeth and sucking before I release it with a pop.

Brandon full on growls, bending just enough to palm the back of my thighs and lift me. My back hits the glass, my throbbing middle presses against his solid bulge, my ankles clasp behind him, and his lips finally claim me — all of me — regardless of what he said.

I'm already his.

The burst of want that surges through me with his lips on mine is palpable, like the hot lick of a flame held only inches from my skin. I feel it crawl over every centimeter of my body, leaving goosebumps in its wake. Everything I remembered — the feel of him, the taste, the smell — it all crashes back over me like the sweetest burn.

Brandon pulls his lips away long enough to rip the tie loose from my robe. I tug it off my shoulders, letting it fall to the floor before my arms are back around his neck, pulling him closer, needing his mouth on mine again. He kisses me for just a second before his lips travel down, down, over my neck, my collarbone, to the gentle swell of my breast. One finger pulls the top away, his tongue flicking in to brush my nipple as I arch into him, and then his arms are around me again.

He lifts me, tossing me to the bed as if I weigh nothing, and with his eyes still on me, he slowly unbuttons his shirt.

"Take that off," he says, glancing at my top.

I sit on the bed, knees clenched together to fight the release already building as I watch him undo his shirt. Each button reveals a new sliver of his hard abdomen, and I keep my eyes there as I reach back for the clasp of my top. Once it's unsnapped, I pull the tie around my neck, and my breasts spring free just as Brandon tugs his shirt down off his shoulders.

He inhales deep, his tongue sneaking out to lick his lower lip as he stares unabashedly at my exposed chest. His hard-on twitches under his shorts, and his hands immediately move there next, flicking the button and pulling the zipper down in one fluid motion.

"That, too," he says, nodding to the bottom half of my bikini.

He lets his shorts fall to his ankles, tugging his briefs off next before kicking them both to the side.

And then, Mr. Church is gloriously naked, and gloriously hard — all for me.

I bite my lip, lying back on the bed and lifting my hips enough to slowly strip my bottoms down my legs. Then, I peel them off one ankle, letting them hang on the other as I lean back on my elbows and spread my legs for him.

Brandon lets out a pained breath, one hand stroking his impossibly hard erection as he stares at the wet pool between my thighs. I watch his hand roll over his shaft, his fist tightening over his mushroom tip before pushing down again.

"This is such a bad idea," he rasps.

"The worst," I moan in return, shifting my weight to one elbow. I use my free hand to spread my lips, letting my head fall back as I slip one finger inside me.

"We should stop."

My head pops up at that. "Damn it, Mr. Church, touch me. *Now*."

And it's then that I see the power he was talking about, like I hold the handle to a leash tied around his neck. He jolts forward, one hand lifting me from the small of my back until he's between my legs, balancing on his elbows over me, my lips kissing down his shoulders.

There's no warning, no foreplay, no fingers or mouths on either of us. Just one slip of his hand between us, lining him up with my entrance, and then he thrusts inside me — hard and greedy and relentless.

"Fuuuuck," he groans, stopping once he's filled me all the way. My legs tighten around him, my nails scratching down his back to give him some of my pain. "I thought I had just imagined how tight you were."

He withdraws, flexing in again and finding new depth somehow. Each new flex of his hips has our breaths coming harder, his arms trembling around me, my legs mirroring the same pleasure as I squeeze him tight.

Maybe the fact that it's so bad to be with him is what makes it so fucking hot. He's my boss. I'm his intern. I shouldn't be on his yacht. He shouldn't have his mouth around my nipple. I shouldn't have his cock buried deep inside me.

But the things we shouldn't do were everything we wanted to do, and neither of us was used to hearing the word no.

Brandon's tongue is just as expert as I remember — the way he rolls it over each of my nipples, the thick warmth of it dragging up my breasts to claim my mouth again. He kisses me like I'm his only possession, the last thing he has left in this world — like he'll never let me go.

Pressing my hands into his chest, I lean up off the bed, giving him the signal to roll us. And when I'm on top, sitting on my throne, I glare down at him with a wicked grin before lifting off him and lowering back down. It's so slow, the pace I take, the way he stretches me open even more in the new position. Brandon's fingers dig into my hips, sure to leave bruises just like the pole did this morning, but I don't care.

"Always a tease," he whispers, his eyes rolling back.

"You love it."

Brandon spanks my ass, thrusting his hips up to meet my slow torture. The new depth elicits a loud, crying moan from me, but he doesn't stop his assault. Faster and faster his hips move, and when his thumb finds my clit, circling with just the slightest pressure, I come apart from the inside.

And I don't see stars, I don't feel numbness. No, it's like I float above my body in that moment. I see the water, the sun setting over the shore, Brandon splayed beneath me, a satisfied smirk on his lips as I call out his name with every new wave.

I am floating, so high I could never truly come back down to Earth. I'll forever exist in this new purgatory — a sweet kind of heavenly hell with Mr. Church as the only god.

Like a snap of a rubber band, my universe warps, and I'm catching my breath at the end of my orgasm, shaking as my hands reach for stability on Brandon's chest. He smirks wider, biting his lower lip, and then all the control I had is ripped away again.

He flips me, rolling me onto my stomach with one smooth motion, his legs straddling mine. Brandon palms my ass, appreciating the firmness of it with another smack before he spreads my cheeks apart. My own legs are sealed together under him, making it even tighter when he presses into me from behind, filling me to the hilt. I'm so wet from my own release that he slides right in, but I'm swollen, sated, and every inch of him feels like a mile.

"Oh, God. Please. Come for me," I plead, a mixture of pain and ecstasy ringing through me as he thrusts inside again.

He groans, balancing on his fists as his hips work. "Fuck, you feel so incredible like this. So tight. So fucking wet."

"Please," I repeat, just as he hits a new depth. "Oh, *God.*"

He picks up his pace, hips working as his breaths shallow out. A few grunts, his forearms tightening, and then one last, long thrust inside me as he finds his release. He spills into me, pressing so deep I'd surely have twins if I weren't on the pill. And when he's done, his arms cave, just a little, and he lowers himself down onto me as he softens inside.

The weight of his slick, hot body presses me into the comforter, and I sigh, a smile splitting my face as pleasure rolls through us.

"Whoops," I say.

Brandon chuckles, rolling off me and onto one elbow. He watches me as I stare back under a curtain of sex hair, still grinning.

"You're impossible."

I crawl toward him, pressing my lips to his in a long, slow kiss. "And you're insatiable."

"Also true."

When I pull back, Brandon runs his fingertips over my bare shoulder and down the curve of my back, tracing a circle on my hip before dragging them back up. He watches me, eyes searching mine before he asks the question we've been avoiding.

"So, now what?"

Now what, indeed.

Erin

I'VE NEVER HAD AN ulcer, but at just twenty-one years old, I might be experiencing my first.

There's a gnawing, intense pinch in my stomach as I eye Skyler in my right peripheral, watching the waves crash in the reflection of her aviator sunglasses. She's been staring out at the water, not saying a word to any of us since we got to the beach. We're all lined up in a row — me, Ashlei, Jess, Cassie, and at the far end, as far as she can be away from me — Skyler.

We haven't spoken since Friday, since the night my plan went up in the most catastrophic of fires. Not only did Skyler have to make a public scene, including making an early exit with Adam, but Kip *also* left — which was not part of the plan. I expected him to run to me, or at the very least, to stay at the dance. I could have found him later, comforted him as he got wasted, been there for him as he tried to make sense of what happened with Skyler. I expected it to be a slow transition, but a transition, nonetheless.

But, he'd just left. He'd left without so much as a glance in my direction. And I haven't heard from him since.

And Skyler isn't talking to me either.

Cool.

It's a beautiful Sunday, one of those days in Florida where I'm more than thankful I don't live anywhere else in the country. There's a blizzard up north, meanwhile it's sunny and in the seventies here in South Florida.

In February.

I sigh, tearing my eyes away from Skyler to take another drink as Jess continues her story.

"I don't know, he's fun, and the sex is good, but..." She pauses, chewing her lip. "It's just..."

"He's not Jarrett," Ashlei finishes for her.

Jess lets out a long exhale, sucking the vodka and pink lemonade mix up through the straw in her tumbler. "He's just not Jarrett."

I smile, reaching over Ashlei to swat Jess's knee playfully. "Hey, don't overthink it so much. Do you like this guy? Greg?"

"Yes," she says, circling the lid of her tumbler with her index finger.

"The sex is good, you like hanging out, he makes you laugh... right?"

She nods.

"Well," I continue with a shrug. "Then, maybe instead of trying to distract yourself from Jarrett with him, you actually try to let yourself *date* him — like, for real. I mean, have you guys talked about that at all?"

"We haven't. And it's weird because I thought we were just kind of hook-up buddies or whatever, but we talk every day. He calls me all the time, and we hang out almost every night. He talks to me about his internship, about his family. He's really been letting me in."

"And have you done the same?"

At that, Jess frowns. "No. To tell you the truth, I'm a little scared."

Cassie glances over at us, like that statement resonates with her, but she doesn't say a word. She's been just as quiet as Skyler since the dance on Friday, and we had to drag them both out today. She watches us for a moment before watching the water again, sitting in content silence with Skyler.

"It's okay to be scared," Ashlei says, the wind blowing her hair over her shades before it whips it back again. "Dating is scary. I mean, seriously, is there anything more terrifying than showing someone your heart and just hoping they'll stick around after they see the crazy shit inside it?"

We're all quiet at that.

Jess sighs after a moment. "He did ask me to go see a movie this week, one of the new superhero ones."

"Sounds date-ish," I assess. "You should go."

She nods, chewing her cheek as if she's giving herself a pep talk in her head. "Okay. I'll go. Why shouldn't I try to move on?" She pauses. "I mean, it clearly didn't take Jarrett long to."

Ashlei squeezes Jess's knee, and I just take a sip of my drink. Sometimes, there are no words to cool the sting of betrayal, especially from someone you loved as much as Jess loved Jarrett.

I reapply my tanning oil as Ashlei changes the subject, filling us in on the terror of a coworker she's interning with this semester. I'm forming my advice for her in my head, ready to relay some of what my mom taught me over the years, but everything washes away when a shadow crosses over us and we all turn to find the source.

Kip.

In nothing but a pair of red, white, and blue board shorts and his reflective aviators, I have a hard time not letting my jaw drop the way the rest of the girls did. His hair is mussed, being continually tussled by the wind, and he tucks his hands in his pockets easily as a cocky grin spreads over his face.

"Afternoon, ladies."

I swallow, the act strained against the lump forming in my throat. I trace the sexy stubble on his jaw, let my eyes crawl over the tan skin stretched over his abdomen muscles, and when my eyes find his again, I smile.

"Well, hello there, handsome," I say, hope blooming in my chest as I hold up one hand to shield the sun streaming in from behind him. I shouldn't have hope so easily, shouldn't assume anything. He could be here for Skyler. He could ask her if they can talk.

But I can't help it, because though those things might be a possibility, his eyes are locked on me right now.

Me.

Not Skyler.

And my fractured heart can't help but hold onto that.

"You girls need a drink?" he asks, thumbing over his shoulder to where his brothers are set up down the beach. "We've got a cooler up by the volleyball net."

"We're all set, thanks," Jess says quickly, but I don't take my eyes off Kip.

And he can't seem to take his eyes off me.

He smiles. "Well, if you run out, you know where to find us." He glances at Jess when he says that, but then his focus is right back on me. "Erin, are you free tonight?"

My heart leaps up into my throat, thumping an unsteady rhythm somewhere right under my tongue as I try not to squeal out loud.

"I was thinking maybe we could catch up. I haven't really had a chance to talk to you since I got here, and before that it had been at least two years since we had a conversation. What do you think? Wanna grab a bottle of Jack and reminisce on the good ol' days of harvest?"

That hope that had popped its head up before jumps out completely now, filling my chest with a new, lighter breath. I wonder if I have literal hearts in my eyes, and I'm thankful for the sunglasses covering them — just in case.

Holy shit. It worked. The plan actually worked.

"You bring the bottle and I'll make my grandma's famous sandwiches," I say, focusing on keeping my breaths steady. "They'll be the perfect ingredients to travel back in time."

Kip nods, a smirk curving up the right side of his beautiful lips. "I can hardly wait. Pick you up at seven?"

Seven!

I need to shower. I need to do my hair. I need to pick up new lipstick. Oh my *God,* what will I wear?

"It's a date," I say, my mind racing with everything I need to get done. It's still circling and circling as Kip holds up his hand in a slight wave, turning his back on us without another word to rejoin his brothers.

Oh. My. *God.*

I turn toward the girls, finally letting my mouth pop open. "Did that just happen?!"

Ashlei and Jess smile, Jess nodding as she removes her sunglasses and gazes down the beach where Kip just walked. "Uh, yeah. Holy shit."

"I can't believe it! It *worked*, girls. It actually worked!"

Cassie is still watching the waves, but she forces a smile, glancing over at me quickly before returning her gaze. "Congrats, G-Big. Mission accomplished."

I shake my head, mouth still open as I try to process it. "I can't believe it actually worked. And I couldn't have done any of this without you, Little," I say, tears springing in my eyes as I turn to face her. I take my sunglasses off, letting my emotion show. "I mean that. I know this was so hard, and that you had to do something that made you really uncomfortable. But I..." Words fail me, and I laugh, still shaking my head. "I can't ever tell you how much this means to me, how much I needed this. Thank you, Skyler. Thank you."

Ashlei squeezes my forearm as Jess smiles in my direction, and even Cassie gives me a little quirk of her lips, though she still seems lost in her own world.

Skyler just watches me for a moment, and I wonder if her eyes are on me or on where Kip just walked behind me.

"Of course," she says after a moment, her voice soft. She clears her throat, smiling for the first time since Friday. "It was hard, but it's over now. And you got what you wanted all along. I'm so happy for you."

I search for a hint of sarcasm, but find nothing. Skyler seems genuine, her smile true, her eyes kind as she takes off her own shades.

"Thank you."

She smiles a little wider, holding up her empty cup with a rattle of the ice. "I'm going to go refill. Be right back."

"I'll come, too," Jess says, popping up with her.

When they're gone, Ashlei and I talk excitedly about what I should wear, and my mind runs wild with possibilities of what the night might hold. Will we talk all night, reminiscing about old times? Will he tell me all about his life since I left, about how he missed me after that summer, about how he's thought about me so much since then? Will I tell him about the times I called, when I never said a word, or will I keep that to myself? Will he hold me and tell me everything's okay, that he's here now, that he's back in my life for good?

Oh God, will he *kiss* me?

I cover my mouth with one hand at that, touching my lips with my fingertips and not even fighting against my smile.

I'm going on a date with Kip Jackson.

I never thought I'd ever get to say those words again, let alone say them and they be true.

But I am.

And finally, after a year of suffering, a year of nothing but regret and painful reminders of all the scars PSU has given me, I see a soft light at the end of the long, dark tunnel.

Happiness.

And it's finally within reach.

Legacy takes place during the same semester as *Black Number Four*. Whether you've read it before now or not, you'll get a wider view of what was happening at Palm South University (especially between Kip and Skyler) if you read *Black Number Four* as you read this season. I will help guide you, letting you know which chapters to read before moving on to the next episode.

FOR THE FULL READING EXPERIENCE FOR THIS EPISODE, READ **CHAPTERS 9-12** IN *BLACK NUMBER FOUR* BEFORE CONTINUING ON TO EPISODE FOUR. (You'll get to see Kip's rage at the bonfire, get in Skyler's head the morning she and Erin talk, be there for the gift Kip gives Skyler before the dance, and experience the break up from Kip's point of view. You'll also get inside information on what Kip's "plan" is after the dance, and how Erin is involved.)

EPISODE 4

Erin

THE LAST TIME I went on an actual date, I was raped.

It's a blunt and sad truth, but a truth, nonetheless.

The last time I got dressed up for a boy, with the intention of having a good time and possibly growing in a relationship with him, he betrayed me in the absolute worst way — and changed my life forever.

When I put on my lipstick tonight, I could still feel how it had smeared across my jaw that night, when Landon's hand covered my mouth, forcing me to hold in screams that wouldn't come, anyway. When I slipped into my heels, I remembered how much the balls of my feet had hurt as they bent me over the table, thighs digging into the corners, their hands pinning me in place.

Those were memories I would never shake, nightmares I would never escape.

But tonight, almost a year later, I'm finally trying again. I'm finally putting on the lipstick, and the heels, and the smile — believing for the first time since that night that my heart may be able to bloom again, that those walls might be able to open.

I'm on a date — a *real* date — with a boy I know I can trust.

It's such a foreign feeling, walking with my arm looped in Kip's as we make our way toward the small paint store. It's our third time hanging out this week, though this is technically our first *date*. On Sunday night, after the day at the beach, we just hung out at his apartment, catching up, eating my grandmother's famous sandwiches while Kip sipped on whiskey. I listened to him recount the years we'd lost between us, and he seemed to hang on my every word as I caught him up on my life. It was nothing special — no fancy restaurants or expensive entertainment — just a boy and a girl laughing and existing together.

I walked home on cloud nine that night, head floaty and stomach flipping as I replayed every look, every word, every single moment. And when he texted me, asking to see me again, I clutched my phone to my chest like a love-sick teenager. Since then, we've texted all day and all night, every day since Sunday.

In some ways, reconnecting with Kip over the last few days has felt like no time has passed at all, like we're still those same kids spending the summer together and falling in love. But, in other ways, it feels like we're strangers now — like we've only scratched the surface of everything we need to know about one another.

I love that part the most.

The thought of re-discovering Kip excites me — and I can't remember the last time something truly made me giddy with hope and joy the way being with him does. It's a little naïve, I realize, as I tighten my grip on his arm. But isn't that where love is born — somewhere between hope, happiness, and blind trust?

I decide not to overthink it — for once in my life — and focus, instead, on how his hard bicep feels under my arms as we reach the door of the art boutique. There are canvases displayed along the windows, showing local talent as well as group party projects — the paintings of everything from hot air balloons and palm tree beach scenes to abstract shapes and realistic self-portraits. I smile a little, eyes roaming the mini masterpieces as Kip covers my small hand with his when we reach the door.

"Are you sure you're okay with getting a little messy?" he asks, eyeing my outfit again.

I knew pairing high, sexy heels with my bright pink, business casual shorts was a risk. I had no idea what we were doing, but the girls all assured me I looked hot, and I figured it was dressy, yet casual enough, to pass for whatever we did.

"I'm sure," I say, leaning into him a bit with the word. "I've never done this before. Have you?"

"Nope. It'll be a first for both of us." He grins, holding the door open to usher me inside first. "After you."

For a moment, I just stand there, staring at the boy holding the door for me. Maybe it's *him* that's the real masterpiece, here. Dressed simply in a dark pair of jeans, a black, v-neck t-shirt, and a backward white-on-white ball cap, he looks confident, sexy, and cool. Add in his classic, black-framed glasses and the little grin he's giving me as he waits for me to step over the threshold, and it's all I can do to not float away.

He's the same boy I fell for, and yet so much more — like a sketch that painted itself in my absence, showing me the colors I never would have thought to paint it with.

I wonder if he can paint me to life, too.

There are a few other couples already seated in the studio when we walk in, and a bright, cheery woman greets us before the door even shuts behind Kip.

"Hi! Welcome to *The Fuzzy Canvas!* I'm Regina," she says, waving at us with one paint-covered hand. Her hair is a bright auburn, her cheeks speckled with freckles and her eyes wide, endless pools of green. She reminds me a little of Ms. Frizzle off *The Magic School Bus*, her hair wild and smile a little too big. "Take a seat wherever you'd like, and go ahead and put on an apron. We have a few others joining us and then we'll get started."

Kip and I thank her before taking the back corner seats, and as I tie a paint-splattered apron around my waist, watching Kip do the same, I smile.

"I'm really excited," I say. "Thank you for asking me out tonight."

"Of course," he answers easily. "It's been nice reconnecting this week."

"It really has been," I agree, taking my seat first. Regina brings us each a full glass of red wine, but I slide mine behind my canvas and out of sight. "You know, I wasn't sure how you would feel about me... after the way everything went down."

"What do you mean?"

I shrug. "I just, I know I didn't handle our break-up in the most graceful way. I was young, Kip — jealous, insecure. And you were the first boy I loved. It was just... I was a mess."

"Hey," he says quickly, taking the seat next to me and pulling my hands into his. He levels his aqua eyes with mine, crooked smirk falling on his lips. "We were *both* young, and I'm sure there are things we both wish we had said, or done, or maybe *not* have said or done," he adds and we both laugh a little. "But, the past is the past. Tonight, we're older, we're a little wiser, and," he says, holding his glass up. "We can drink. Legally. So, let's cheers to that."

I smile, reaching for my glass behind the canvas. I tap it to his, but instead of taking a drink when he does, I place it back in its original place."

"Not a red wine fan?" Kip asks, one brow quirked as he sets his own glass down.

"I don't really drink."

"At all?" He presses his lips together, digesting that. "Huh. Don't take this the wrong way, but that's kind of impressive — especially considering you're in a sorority."

I chuckle. "Yeah, well, I *used* to drink, but I learned the hard way how alcohol can impair judgment and get you caught up in situations you don't want to be in."

Kip watches me curiously when those words slip out, and suddenly his eyes are too much for me to handle. I drop my gaze to the floor, shaking my head and turning toward my canvas.

"Anyway, speaking of Greek life, how do you like being an official brother of Alpha Sigma?"

Kip lets me change the subject, and the conversation flows like that all night — back and forth, the two of us swapping stories in-between taking painting instructions from Regina. We're working on painting a beautiful sunset scene, contrasted by the silhouette of a tree in the foreground. When we're finished and push the canvases together, our two tree shapes will make a heart, and the birds we painted on the limbs will join each other, too.

"This is fun," I say when we're almost finished, painting a little bow on my bird's head. "I needed it."

Kip sighs, his chest deflating long and slow as he drags his fat brush over his sunset, deepening the reds in his sky. "Tell me about it."

"Rough week for you, too, huh?"

He shrugs, eyes still on the canvas. "Rough semester, honestly."

Swallowing, I dip my paint brush into our jar of water, rinsing it off as my heart ticks up speed. "That have anything to do with Skyler?"

Kip's hand stills over the canvas, his jaw clenching, but he doesn't answer. Instead, he makes a broader swoop with his brush, pressing a little too hard and creasing the canvas as he works.

"It's okay," I assure him, wiping my hands on my apron. "We can talk about it, about her, if you want. I know that must have been hard."

My stomach rolls at the reminder of what I put him through — of what I put *Skyler* through. Now that it's all over, I should feel better about it all. I should feel like I've won. I mean, here I am, on a date with Kip, reliving old memories and making new ones, too. Still, I can't help but feel like there's a curtain between us, like he's putting on some kind of performance, not letting me in completely.

I know how hard that can be to do after you've been hurt.

"Nothing to talk about," Kip says, his words curt. "We weren't official or anything. She's into Adam, I guess. It's whatever."

His words sound blasé, but the way his brush strokes grow more aggressive give him away.

"Besides, her being out of the way leaves more time for me and you, doesn't it?"

He glances sideways at me then, his smirk sexy, eyes low, and my cheeks flame at his insinuation. For a split second, my heart feels whole again — my soul reconnected to my body — and before I even realize I'm thinking it, two words slip out in an almost-silent whisper.

"Fix me."

I balk when the words hang between us — both mortified that I spoke them out loud and confused as to why I thought them at all.

Kip frowns. "What?"

Clearing my throat, I pick a small brush back up, fixing the little leaves on my tree. "Nothing, just realized I didn't do these very well."

Kip looks at my tree. "I think it's perfect. And, look," he says, sliding his canvas over to mine. Our little trees align, making the heart complete, and our birds join each other at the bottom point. "We make a pretty good team."

"We do, don't we?" I ask.

Our noses are so close, his lips near enough to mine that I feel every hot breath he takes. I lean in, just a little, hoping he'll kiss me — hoping he'll seal in this happiness with his lips and never let that hole in my heart be empty again. His eyes flick to my lips, the irises dancing back and forth before they find my gaze again.

"Oh, this is *beautiful!*" Regina says, popping up between us.

Kip straightens, clearing his throat as he drops his paint brush in the water jar and smiles up at her. "Thank you. We had a great teacher."

"Oh, aren't you sweet!" she giggles the word, swatting at his shoulder with a wide, blushing smile before moving on to the next couple.

I glare at her as she passes, the moment gone, Kip's mouth too far away from mine now.

Kip holds my hand on the cab ride home, and just like a gentleman, he walks me to the door at the sorority house as a gaggle of my sisters stare at us out the various windows. But, he doesn't move to kiss me before he leaves, pulling me in for a long hug, instead.

"Thank you," I whisper into his chest. "For tonight. It was perfect."

"I'm glad you had fun," he says, pulling back with a grin. "I'll text you when I get home?"

I nod, biting my lip. "Please do."

He goes to pull away, but I hold his hand, tugging him back. When his eyes meet mine, I push past my nerves and lean in, pressing my lips to his before I have the chance to psyche myself out.

Kip stiffens, the kiss not really returned at first. But then, his lips soften, and his hands move up my arms, one sliding behind my neck as the other cradles my cheek. The kiss is soft, sweet, nothing too passionate or earth-shattering. But it's nice.

And it's a kiss I asked for, one I wanted.

When he pulls away, Kip smirks, nudging my chin with his knuckle gently. "Goodnight, Ex."

"'Night," I whisper back, my voice light and airy as I watch him trot down the steps of our front porch.

I'm not sure how long I stand there, or what I say to all the girls waiting inside when I finally make my way in. I'm not sure of anything, really, except how good it feels to kick my heels off and flop down into the plush comforter of my bed. When my back hits it, my eyes on the ceiling, a smile splits my face in two, my stomach light and giddy.

And it's then that I realize why I asked him to fix me.

It's because I know he can.

Jess

THIS SON-OF-A-BITCH.

This crooked-dick, turtle-loving, lying son-of-a-bitch.

Swiping another handful of nuts out of the bar bowl, I crunch them a little too aggressively, staring across Ralph's at Greg. Every time he laughs, flashing that ridiculously beautiful smile of his, I imagine what he'd look like if I slammed his face into the bar and he lost a few of those pretty teeth.

It may be borderline psycho bitch how long I've been here, at the other end of the bar, angrily eating bar nuts and drinking my beer and wondering when this son-of-a-bitch is going to look up and realize that the girl he bailed on is at the same place he is. This guy owes me a drink and a mind-blowing orgasm after leaving me with a serious case of the lady blue balls last week, and that was all supposed to be rectified tonight.

Except, he was "sick," and had to bail last minute.

I check for signs of illness as he pounds back another shot with a group of his fraternity brothers. He doesn't look sweaty, or clammy, and by the way he's drinking, I'd say there's no chance in hell that he has a stomachache. Nope, this son-of-a-bitch looks healthy as can be, and he also looks like he's not the least bit bothered that he lied to me less than an hour ago, or that he's left my vulva a throbbing violet for over a week now.

Bastard.

For the past five minutes, I've been trying to convince myself that it isn't worth saying anything. So what, he blew me off? Point taken. He's not interested. No big deal, moving forward, on to the next poor guy.

But for some reason, I can't let it go.

Maybe it's because I haven't been bailed on since I sprouted boobs sophomore year of high school, or maybe it's because I'm particularly sensitive after being dumped by Jarett, or hell — maybe it's just because I'm three days away from being visited by the crimson tide. Regardless, I can't seem to find the common sense or couth to keep my ass planted or get up only long enough to get the hell out of this bar.

Nope, instead, I swallow down a few more nuts, slam back the rest of my beer, and storm toward the group of Omega Chis.

They're all crowded together around a high-top table, playing various drinking games, and I have to shove a few of the smaller ones aside to reach Greg. When I do, I thrust my finger into his shoulder with a hard poke, hanging my hands on my hips as he turns around to face me.

His eyebrows are bent together at first, as if he doesn't realize who I am, and then he smiles, dimple and all. "Oh, hey, Jess."

Oh, hey, Jess?

This son-of-a-bitch.

"Didn't realize they had doctors at Ralph's now," I deadpan. "Looks like they work fast, too, because you don't seem sick at all. It's a miracle!"

I throw my hands up at that last part, not even bothering to hide my flair for the dramatic. Greg's brothers all watch me before giving each other wide-eyed looks. They go back to drinking their beers, albeit a bit uncomfortably, as Greg crosses his arms over his chest.

"What's your deal?"

"What's my *deal?*" I repeat incredulously. "We were supposed to go out tonight. We had a date. You literally told me less than an hour ago that you were sick, and then I find you here drinking like a frat boy."

"I am a frat boy."

I narrow my eyes.

"I don't get what the big deal is. I had a change of plans."

"You *lied* to me, asshole."

"And?" he asks, like I don't have a point. "Like you've never lied to get out of a date with a dude before? Come on, J-Love. I know about your reputation."

At that, a few of his brothers let out low *oooohs* and my jaw pops open. I clamp it shut quickly, face heating with rage.

Two can play this game, buddy.

"Oh, you've heard about my *reputation*, huh? Well, I wish I would have heard about yours. If I'd have known you have a dick that leans west and doesn't get the job done, I could have saved myself the trouble."

Greg's eyes widen, his hand reaching out to wrap around my wrist and drag me away from the table as his brothers burst into a fit of laughter. They're still cracking jokes when Greg pulls me into the corner near the DJ booth, his expression cold as stone.

"Not cool."

"Yeah? Well, neither is you bailing on me. What the fuck, Greg? You should have just told me you had other plans."

"Why are you acting like you're my girlfriend?"

His question stops me short, and I open my mouth to pop back at him but nothing leaves my lips.

"We met when you had a boyfriend, Jess," he says, twisting the knife more. "And we've never had that talk. Yeah, we hooked up a few times, we've had some fun, but honestly, I thought we were just friends." He shrugs. "Look, I'm sorry I lied to you about tonight or whatever, but I don't owe you anything, and I don't expect anything from you, either."

"We text every day," I finally say, though I know the argument is weak before I even give it. "And we talk about shit. And bang. How are we not in a relationship status where you at least owe me the truth if you bail on me?"

"That's not what I'm looking for," Greg says easily. "I thought it was a kind of *see ya when I see ya* thing. I have fun with you, don't get me wrong, but I don't want a relationship." He cocks one brow, lips pulling to the side. "And from the sounds of it, you *shouldn't* be in one — at least, not right now."

"What the hell is that supposed to mean?"

"Let's just cut the shit. I was a distraction for you, which I was fine with, since I'm not looking for anything, anyway. But somewhere along the way, you started lying to yourself, saying I was what you wanted when you know that's not true. We have fun, but we're not relationship material."

I swallow, crossing my arms.

"And you're not over Jarrett."

He says the words so easily, like they won't hit me like rusty scissors straight to the heart.

"Which is fine," he continues. "I'm not saying you all of a sudden should be. But, take the time to figure that shit out. If you did, I think you'd realize how crazy you're acting right now."

My nostrils flare, fists clenching as I open my mouth to show this son-of-a-bitch just how crazy I can be, but he holds up his hands quickly to calm me.

"I didn't mean that disrespectfully, okay? You're a cool girl, and that's the only reason I used that verbiage, because I know that if the *real* you — the you I met here last Thanksgiving — was here, she'd tell you the same thing. You're not yourself right now."

"Are you telling me to eat a fucking Snickers bar?"

He laughs, reaching out to pull me into a hug. I'm still stiff in his arms, my own crossed over my chest, but as he chuckles again, I soften.

"Just take a breath, okay?"

I sigh, groaning as I lean into him a little more. For a moment, he just holds me, and when he lets me go, my desire to punch him in the groin has decreased by at least forty percent.

"You're still a dick," I say, pointing at him with my index finger. "But, you're not entirely wrong. We never had any kind of talk about what we expected out of each other, and I shouldn't have assumed."

"You shouldn't have, but I also shouldn't have lied. So, for that, I'm sorry."

I nod, still grumpy as I wave him off. "Go take shots and be a frat boy."

Greg gives me another hug and ruffles my hair like a stupid older brother before he rejoins his brothers, and I pay my tab quietly, mood sinking by the second. When I'm finally in a cab heading back toward the sorority house, I sigh, staring out the window and digesting Greg's words.

That son-of-a-bitch was right.

And I hate it.

Thumbing through the pictures my phone, I hover over one of me and Jarrett, taken in bed at the hotel he booked when he came to visit last semester. I trace the lines of his smile, the stubble on his jaw, the ink splayed across his bicep where he cradles his head on the pillow. And then there's me — my smile genuine and wide, my eyes tired but sated. I miss that girl.

I miss that boy even more.

I click the side button on my phone when we pull up to the house, making the screen go dark as I pay the driver and climb out of the car. My mind is still racing as I climb the stairs, crawling into my bed as quietly as I can so as not to wake Skyler.

I thought using Greg as a distraction would help, that it would be part of my healing, but the truth is I wasn't using him to distract me — I was trying to use him to replace Jarrett.

And that's impossible to do.

I need to move on — *really* move on — and that starts with focusing on me.

So, starting tomorrow, that's exactly what I plan to do.

Bear

I CAN'T HELP BUT chuckle as Skyler barrels toward me, her entire face covered by a scarf wrapped at least eight times from her neck to her ears. Her arms are crossed tight, brows furrowed as I swing the door to the cafeteria open when she reaches me.

"Gah!" she huffs, still bouncing and rubbing her hands together once she's inside. "How is it that it was seventy-six degrees yesterday, and then this morning, it's forty-eight?! I can't handle this."

I take my spot in line behind her, savoring the smell of bacon as we shuffle along behind the other students. It's been a while since we've met for breakfast in the old university cafeteria, but I haven't spent one-on-one time with Skyler since the semester started, and this was the only time we could both make work this week.

"Psh, Floridian. You wouldn't last ten minutes in a Pennsylvania winter," I tease.

She sticks her tongue out at me, swiping a plate from the stack before handing one back to me. "You're damn right I wouldn't. Who wants to live in Pennsylvania, anyway?"

At that, I laugh. "Hell if I know. I got out of there as soon as I turned eighteen," I point out. And while it wasn't necessarily because of the weather, it is true that I couldn't wait to leave that state. Still, thinking about my little brother living back there makes me miss it. I wish I could be there for him while he grows up. But, he has Mac and his family. I'm grateful for that.

"My point, exactly." Skyler smiles, popping a blueberry muffin onto her tray before we split up, making our way down the buffet line.

Once our plates are piled high with more breakfast than either of us can actually eat, we settle into a small table by the window facing the library. I watch Skyler take her first bite — mostly because I can tell she hasn't been eating. Or sleeping, from the looks of it. Something has been off about her all semester, and after the shit show I heard happened at the Alpha Sigma dance, I knew she needed some Bear time.

Maybe a hug or two, too.

"So, how are you?" I ask once she's devoured half of her muffin. I keep my eyes on my plate, building a sandwich out of my eggs, bacon, and toast. "I'm still kind of pissed that we haven't hung out since Rush week."

Skyler cringes. "I know, I suck and I'm sorry. But I'm good. Counting down the days to Spring Break." She picks at the wrapper of her muffin, her long, dark hair falling in a curtain around her face. She's trying to force a smile — one she should know won't fool me. "You?"

"Cut the shit, Sky."

Her eyes grow wide, brows bending together like she doesn't know what I'm talking about.

"I know what happened Friday night... everyone on Greek Row is talking about it. So, are you going to tell me how you are — for real — or am I going to have to tickle it out of you?"

She smiles, making a joke about the last time I tickled her, which ended with her pissing herself. It was hilarious. And though the smile she wears now is smaller than her fake one — at least it's real.

Skyler chews her lip, and I just take a bite of my

sandwich, giving her time to think through what she wants to say.

"Bear, honestly, I'm okay," she says on a sigh, picking at her muffin wrapper again. "I'm not good and I'm not bad, I'm just okay. That's all I can really say right now. I love you, and I know you're here for me, but I just really don't want to talk about it."

I've heard those words before.

A flash of Erin comes to mind, but I push her away, focusing on Skyler.

"I got involved in something I never should have agreed to, and now I'm paying for it," she continues, a slight shrug finding her shoulders. "It's my fault, so it would be stupid to ask for sympathy from anyone. Even you."

My chest squeezes, my next breath a sort of sigh as I lean back in my seat and force a smile. Skyler is my best friend, and hearing that she's hurting and feels like nothing can be done about it kills me — especially since she does everything she can to help her friends when they're in the same position.

Me included.

"I'm sorry, Sky," I say after a beat. "I don't know what you got yourself into, but I know you don't look like someone who just blew off a guy after using him to get back at an ex," I say, repeating what I heard happened at the dance with Adam and Kip. "You look like someone who was on the *other* end of the break-up, actually."

She shrugs, her eyes empty. "Well, there's a lot behind the situation that nobody knows."

The way her shoulders slump, the gloss of her eyes, the pain creasing her every feature — it's enough to make me want to convince her to skip school and just let me hold her all day.

Because she's lying, and we both know it.

"You like him, don't you?"

She closes her eyes, forcing a swallow.

"All that shit about Adam was bull crap. I know you, and you were over Adam the week after you broke things off."

Skyler crosses her arms over her chest, sinking down in her seat. "Yeah," she whispers. "I do like him."

I sigh. The transfer didn't seem like a big deal to me — hell, I didn't want him in Omega Chi at all. But, after getting to know him at some of the Greek events, I can see why Skyler is into him. He's cool, a good balance of both nerd and jock that we don't see around PSU very much. And, from what I could tell, he was treating Skyler like she should be treated. He liked her — a lot.

So, if she liked him, too, then what the hell is going on?

"But it doesn't matter," Skyler continues, answering my question. "Because Ex is into him and they have a past. And now they're talking, which was what she wanted from the start. So, whatever, my part is done, I guess."

I cock a brow, everything clicking into place as she talks.

"So, you were playing him for your Big?" I ask. "Shit, I should have known."

Erin is desperate for something — *anything* — to make her feel happy again. It doesn't surprise me that she would go for a guy from her past, one who made her feel good. And using Skyler? That's a no-brainer. The girl plays poker for a living. If anyone is going to be a part of an Erin scheme and pull it off, it's her.

"No one has a better poker face than you," I muse aloud.

Skyler chuckles, though there's no humor in the situation. "Yeah, well, my poker face pretty much goes to shit when I'm around him." She shakes her head. "I'm pretty sure he knows I fed him a lie, but he doesn't know the truth so he won't call me out completely. But, then again, he moved on to her pretty quickly," she points out, her expression turning sour. "So, maybe that was his plan all along, too."

Bullshit.

I know dudes, and I know the games they play when they want a chick to want them back. The biggest, easiest target to hit with any girl is her jealousy button.

"I don't think it's like that," I say, washing down another bite of food with a swig of OJ. "I mean, I don't know the kid, but I saw him at the auction and the bonfire. He put himself out there for you and, to me, it seemed like he didn't give two fucks about what anyone else thought. Including Erin." I shrug. "I think he's just trying to get to you by talking to her now. Does he know about their past?"

Skyler nods, frowning as she considers my point.

"Well, then this is probably his way of calling you on your bluff. You said you wanted Adam all along, and maybe he knows that's bullshit, so he's pulling the oldest trick in the book to see if you get jealous."

She's still nodding, and I can hear the wheels turning in her head from across the table. "You might be onto something, Bear."

"I mean, I *am* a genius," I tease. "You should know that by now."

Skyler doesn't eat much more the rest of breakfast, and I keep the conversation light by talking about my brothers — mostly about how we can't wait for Spring Break, since we've been starved from fun on probation. I leave out the details of my horrific dating app encounters, knowing I can save those for another time, and though Skyler still seems lost in her own little world when we begin to make our way outside, it doesn't bother me.

She's been there for me when I needed her most, and I'm just glad I can return the favor.

"Thanks for asking me to meet this morning, Bear," she says when we drop our trays by the door. She wraps her scarf around her again, smiling up at me. "I've missed you."

"You know I had to check on my baby sister," I say. "Just stay away from pledges and maybe we can hang out more. I couldn't have you cramping my style before."

She punches me in the shoulder as we push through the doors outside, and even I shiver a little against the cold whip of wind. Florida winters — gotta love the inconsistency.

"Trust me," she says. "I'm staying away from boys for a while."

"Yeah, good luck with that," I say, laughing. "I have a feeling you and Nerd Boy aren't done causing drama in Greek world just yet."

"What's college without a little drama?"

I smirk, tugging on her wrist until she's wrapped in my arms. "Just be careful with that heart of yours, okay?"

"I'll try."

I squeeze her hard, and she sighs.

"Your hugs are the best."

"You're biased."

"Doesn't mean I'm not right."

I chuckle, releasing my grip. "Get to class, and text me later. Let me know how everything works out."

"I will. Love you," she says, and then she's pulling her phone out, typing out a text as she bolts across campus.

Tucking my hands in the pockets of my coat, I veer off in the opposite direction, making my way toward my Digital Imaging Fundamentals class. I only make it a few steps before I stop dead in my tracks, just a few feet away from a smirking Becca.

One hand hangs on her hip as she cocks a brow up at me, her eyes playful and wide. I can't help but return her smile, and my eyes flick to her lips as her first words ride out on a cloud of breath.

"So," she says. "Did you lose your phone, break it, or just forget how to use it? Because I *know* you haven't texted me yet because you haven't wanted to."

She's still smiling, though her neck weaves a little with each word, adding sass to her appraisal of me.

I laugh, holding up my hands in mock surrender. "It's only been a few days, I didn't want to seem eager."

"Mm-hmm," she muses, brow climbing higher on her forehead. "That was Friday, it's been five days — almost a week."

Touché.

She's right, I have wanted to text her — since the very moment she put her number in my phone next to a little kissy emoji, actually. Still, something warned me to wait, to give it time, to remember what happened last time I rushed into something without thinking it through. Sure, Becca is gorgeous — stunning, even — but Shawna was just as hot.

And that girl nearly killed me.

"You're right," I say. "I'm—"

"What was that?" she asks, stepping closer with the most adorable little grin. "Could you say it again, a little louder for the people in the back, please?"

For a moment I just stare down at her, a stupid smile locked on my face, and then I laugh, rolling my eyes and repeating my sentiment. "You're right."

"Ahh," she says, inhaling deep like my words are a delicious meal she's about to devour. "I could get used to that."

"I'm sure you could," I muse, smiling. "I'm sorry I didn't call yet, I just wasn't sure what to say."

"How about, 'Gee, Becca. I sure had a good time the other night. How about you let me take you out on a proper date this weekend?'"

"Since when am I a cowboy from an old western?"

"Just let me live out my fantasy here."

I laugh, and Becca nudges me, crossing her arms over her chest.

"I'm serious. Take me on a date. A real one, not one where you use my bar to lick your wounds from a date gone wrong and I foot the tab."

"Hey, you didn't even let me try to pay for those."

"And I told you you could pay me back," she reminds me. "On a *date*."

I nod, hands sliding into my pockets as I smile down at her. I'm pretty sure my face is going to break any second now, my cheeks hurt so much, but I can't help it. Becca is different — bold and witty, sexy yet classy. On the surface, she's everything I want in a girl.

So why am I being such a pussy about getting to know her better?

"Okay," I say after a moment. "Gee, Becca. I sure had a good time the other night."

She cracks out a laugh at my imitation of her.

"How about you let me take you out on a proper date this weekend?"

"That's better."

"How's my accent?"

"Terrible, but luckily your biceps make up for what you lack in acting skills."

I laugh again, shaking my head.

"Pick me up at eight on Saturday. There's this coffee shop by my place that has open mic night."

"Wow," I say. "A girl who not only tells me what time to pick her up, but where to take her, too. You make it too easy on me."

"Apparently, I have to, otherwise I'll be old and gray by the time you figure out how to use a phone again." She rolls her eyes, but winks at me playfully. "Now, text me, so I can text back with my address."

"I will," I say. "Looking forward to Saturday."

But she doesn't move.

"No, I mean, text me *right now*," she says, motioning to my pocket. "Because I don't trust that you actually will."

I smirk, biting my lower lip as I take out my phone and hold it up for her to see. Then, I slide it open with one thumb, text her a bear emoji, and drop my phone back in my pocket as hers pings with a notification.

Satisfied at the text, she smiles, nodding and adjusting her bag on her shoulder. "Alright, then. See you on Saturday, cowboy."

I watch her walk away, her hips swinging in a natural rhythm. Once she's around the corner of the library, I finally shake my head, making my way across campus again. I'm going to be late, but I don't give a fuck — because I have a date. A *real* date, with a girl who isn't a psycho off a dating app.

My phone lights up with two back-to-back texts from her a few moments later — one with her address, and the other with one last subtle hint for our date.

- I hate flowers, but I love donuts. Don't fuck up. -
A girl after my own heart.

Ashlei

"SO, ARE YOU ACTUALLY going to come to happy hour tonight, or are you just saying that so I'll leave you alone?" Mykayla cocks a brow, tossing her lipstick in her purse before slugging it over her shoulder. "Because this is like the eighteenth time I've asked you, and you've always said no, and I feel like you're lying now that you've said yes because it's just too good to be true."

I roll my eyes. "Stop being dramatic. I'll be there, okay? Promise." I move a hand over the stack of files on my desk. "I'm just reviewing a few things for the meeting Monday morning with our new client and then I'll be right down."

"Just come now. It's almost seven, everyone else is gone. It's *Friday*, for Christ's sake."

"I'll just be twenty minutes or so. I promise."

"Mm-hmm," she muses. "If you're not down there in an hour, I'm coming up to drag you down myself."

I laugh. "Permission granted to do so, but you won't have to."

Mykayla smiles, waving a hand over her shoulder as she rounds the cubicles and swings through the front office door. When she's gone, I sigh, kicking my heels off and stretching my sore arches out as I filter through the files.

It's been a long week, and with Kimberly still on my heels and doing everything she can to outshine me, my competitiveness is in high gear. Last week, I was slipping, falling behind on projects and just not feeling like myself. But after my run in with Brandon on Sunday and a few more pole sessions, I'm feeling back to the old me — powerful, ready to take on anything.

Including a snobby, bitchy intern.

I feel her watching my every move, especially when I'm around Brandon. After Sunday, I was hoping to steal a few glances in our meetings, or maybe pass sexy notes between the folders of our reports we passed back and forth. But with Kimberly around, it's impossible. Any time I talk to Brandon in a meeting or pass him in the hallway, I'm guaranteed to find her eyes staring back at me in the next instant. She's like a hawk, trained on me as her prey, and she's just waiting for one false step to attack.

A normal mouse might be a little weaker, a little quicker to relent. But not me.

I take notes on our new clients, making speaking points I want to be sure to remember for when we speak on Monday. It's more than I need to do right now, but if I give myself the weekend to think, I'll be ready to shine on Monday, to grab their attention in a fresh, new way. It's my hope that they'll want me as their event coordinator, the same way *Bare•ly* did last semester. If there's a full-time job opening up in the near future at *Okay, Cool,* it has my name on it.

I'll make sure of it.

"Sore?"

My heart leaps into my throat, hair standing on end as I jump in my seat at the sound of Brandon's voice. I don't register that it's him until after I've spun around in my chair, one hand pressed to my chest and eyes wide as I try to catch my breath.

He just smirks, amused.

Pushing out my breath in one long exhale, I drop my head on a laugh. "Jesus Christ. How about a little warning next time?"

"All I did was speak."

"Yeah, but," I argue, hand motioning to the otherwise empty office. "I'm supposed to be the only one here."

"Actually, *no one* is supposed to be here — you included," he points out, leaning against the side of my cubicle. His burnt orange dress shirt is unbuttoned at the top, his sleeves rolled to his elbows like usual, bottom him tucked into a pair of cream dress slacks.

So much for casual Friday.

"Well, looks like I'm not the only one breaking the rule."

Brandon drags his gaze down my neck, following the line of my necklace to where it dips between my breasts in the loose blouse I'm sporting with tight, ripped-up jeans. "We do have a knack for doing that, don't we?"

I bite my lip, ready to spout off a sassy retort when he drops to his knees, wrapping his strong fingers around one of my delicate ankles and tugging until my chair rolls toward him.

And then, he touches my foot.

I rip it back, but his grip is firm, and he eyes me from where he's bent on the floor. It shouldn't feel so right, seeing a man of that power kneeling beneath me, but *damn* does it turn me on.

"What are you doing? I've been sweating in these heels all day. Don't touch." I swat at his hand for good measure.

"Exactly. You've been in heels all day. Let me help."

Brandon presses his thumb into the bottom arch, and I moan, eyes rolling up before I try to pull away again. "Seriously, don't. They're dirty. They probably smell."

He chuckles. "They're fine. Now, sit still and let me make you feel good."

Our eyes catch, and he holds my gaze as his hands move to my foot again, this time digging deep into the arch before smoothing down over the aching ball. I moan, sliding lower into my chair and relenting.

"Good girl."

"Shut up," I murmur, but another roll of his thumbs has me groaning again, each new pressure massaging away the aches. "This might be better than sex."

"Liar."

I cock one brow. "Okay, I said *might*, don't get so huffy. Besides, if you were on the other end of this foot massage, you'd understand."

Brandon is quiet, though he smiles at that, his eyes focused on where his hands are working. I watch him, remembering what those hands felt like on Sunday, the way they lit me on fire with every touch. Just like he promised, he was all business again when we walked through the office doors Monday morning. Still, the energy between us has shifted.

Before, I wasn't sure if he was still into me, if he still wanted me. Now, there was no denying. I knew when we sat in the same room together that it was torture for him not to look at me. And I knew when I wore a skirt that was a little shorter than business appropriate on Wednesday that he was going mad not being able to touch me. And more than anything, I knew the next time we were alone — *truly* alone — he wouldn't be able to resist me.

Power is a dangerous addiction.

"So..." I say when he carefully drops my left foot to the floor, cradling my right in his lap next. The first touch on that foot makes me groan again, the ecstasy renewed. "You taking the boat out this weekend?"

Brandon glances at me from under his brows, smiling as he turns his attention back to my heel. "I've thought about it. Why, you interested?"

"Oh, me?" I ask. "I could never go on my CEO's yacht with him. I mean, that would just be inappropriate, to wear only a bikini around you, and get all *wet*."

He pauses, his hands just cradling my foot as I continue.

"I mean, even if it has been a *long, hard* week... I couldn't possibly *ride* my CEO..." I pause long enough to make him look up at me, his eyes darker, before I continue. "... 's yacht."

"I'll give you something to ride," he murmurs, but I don't even have the chance to laugh before he grabs both ankles in his hands, tugging me to the floor with him and catching me when I tumble down. His lips are on mine in the next second, one hand in my hair, the other palming my ass in my impossibly tight jeans.

"Oh, my," I gasp the words between kisses as Brandon tugs my blouse over one shoulder, licking the skin stretched over the bone. "Mr. Church, we shouldn't. We *can't*. I'm the intern, this is wrong."

"I know you're making a joke right now," he says, nipping my jaw before claiming my mouth again. "But if you haven't noticed, there are consequences for every word you're rasping out between those pretty, strawberry lips of yours."

He thrusts his hips up, letting me feel his firm cock against the seam of my jeans, and I grin, crashing my mouth back on his.

"So, you're saying these consequences are my punishment?"

Brandon growls, smacking my ass and lifting me off of him before he stands and pulls me up to join him. "I'm going to bend you over this desk and show you punishment."

"Wait!"

"Oh, no, you asked for it now," he says, smile wicked as he presses me against the edge of the desk. The pain of it shoots through me, mixing with want and desire in the best concoction.

"No, really," I pant, pressing my hands into his chest. "Not my desk. There's too much shit on it and we're going to have to pick it all up after."

Brandon pauses just long enough to let that sink in before he nods, grabbing my hand and pulling me through the office. We swing into the first empty conference room, not even bothering to shut the door behind us before he does exactly what he promised.

One of his hands grips my hair, the other hooking at the crease of my waist, and then I'm bent over, cheek to the cool, black metal of the long conference table. His hard on presses against my ass, his chest hot on my back as he sucks my ear lobe between his teeth.

"You're going to pay for that little skirt you wore Wednesday," he says. "Among other things."

"Promises, promises," I tease, but all laughter fades from my voice when one hand reaches around, flicks open the button of my jeans, and in the next instant, he pulls them down by the back loop, just enough to expose my ass. He smacks it hard, and I bite my lip against the sting of pleasure, arching my back up into him. "*Yes*," I breathe. "More."

Brandon rears back, smacking the skin again before tugging my jeans down farther. One hand crawls between my thighs, the other pinning my wrists to the table as he slips just the tip of one finger between my wet, throbbing lips.

I gasp at the feel, my knees trapped by my jeans. I can't open wider for him, can't give him better access, and he just teases me more — not fully entering, not filling the depth I ache for him to fill. Instead, that fingertip just tickles my skin, building my desire, the feather-light touch not enough.

"It's maddening, isn't it?" he rasps, leaning down to bite my neck. His finger presses just a centimeter deeper, and I moan, arching my back more as if that will force him all the way inside. "Being so close to something you want, something you desire, and yet not being able to have it?"

Oh, he's good.

That power I thought I held over him is instantly reverted back to the original owner, and Brandon claims it proudly, as if it never left his hands in the first place.

Maybe it never did.

He's the cat, I'm the mouse.

I like when he reminds me.

"Please," I whisper, squirming. "You made your point. Let me touch you. Get inside me."

"Which one first?"

"Both."

He smirks, the curve of his smile on the skin of my neck as he pulls back from the table. In an instant, I'm standing, ripping my jeans and panties down my legs in one fell swoop. I don't bother with my top, reaching for Brandon, instead. He backs me up to the table, lifting me and spreading my legs wide.

"I'll touch you," he promises, his fingertips teasing my throbbing middle again. He pulls them away too quickly, running them up my arm until one hooks between my lips. "But I'm not done punishing you yet. Lie down."

I do as he says, my ass still at the edge of the table as my head hits the other. He walks around the edge of it slowly, unzipping his dress pants and pulling them down to his knees. He stands wide once he's above me at the other end, his erection posed above me, and then he leans forward, gently grabbing my hips and pulling until my head is hanging off the table.

My instinct is to clasp my legs together but he stops me, pressing one hand onto each knee to keep me spread eagle. Then, he stands again, smile wicked as he gazes down at my mouth.

"Open."

Oh.

I swallow, heat pooling between my legs as I do as he demands, opening my mouth slowly with my eyes locked on his. But when he steps forward, the tip of him touching my tongue, all I can see is his glorious shaft, his smooth balls, his slacks stretched around his knees, his designer shoes. I take a breath and hold it as he slides all the way in, slowly, coating himself with my saliva before he hits the back of my throat.

"God*damn*," he groans, withdrawing before flexing his hips into me again. He fills my mouth, pressing into my gag reflex as I gag, my back arching off the table. "Stick your tongue out, hold your breath."

I do as he says, sticking my tongue out as far as I can and holding it there as he drives in again. He's slower this time, careful, and with the new lubrication and angle, he slides even deeper — deeper than I even knew I could fit him.

"Yes," he whispers, his voice heated. "Good girl."

Why does it turn me on so much when he says that?

I've never been dominated like this, and yet I feel no desire to pull the power back into my own hands. I want him to own me, to use me, to find his pleasure in *only* me.

"Do it again," he says, withdrawing to give me a breath. "And hold on, because this might be rough."

I nod, inhaling and pressing my fingertips into the cool metal of the table for grip as I stick my tongue out again. He cradles my neck, sliding in slow and easy, somehow deeper than before, and then he lets out a long, animalistic groan of approval.

"Fuck yes, Ashlei. God, that's incredible."

He holds me there, one of his hands tracing my throat as if he can feel himself inside it. And then, slowly, carefully, he pumps.

In and out, just marginally, his shaft stretching my throat as I hold my breath and ride out his thrusts. It's uncomfortable, yet the powerful feeling of being so desired by him, and so sexually satisfying, has me fighting against the urge to push him away. It's only when my body reacts, when a gag heaves through me that I press one hand into his thigh and he backs off, stroking my hair.

"Are you okay?"

I nod, wiping my mouth. "Yes. More."

He smiles, tracing my lips with his thumb. "That's my girl. Open."

This time when I open, his hard cock slides inside my mouth at the same time as he leans forward and slides two fingers inside my soaked pussy. I moan around him at the feel, the ache inside me growing stronger. He leans forward even more, his cock deeper in my throat, but then his mouth is on my clit.

Another moan surges through me, muffled around the fill of him as he carefully thrusts. I find a breathing pattern, slowly and deliberately pulling oxygen through my nose so as not to gag again. It's hard to do when all I want is to focus on what he's doing between my thighs. His fingers work in and out effortlessly, his tongue circling in perfect rhythm, and when I reach forward to cup his balls in my hand, his guttural groan sends a wave of want through me.

"Oh, fuck, yes, I'm coming," he grunts, and then he thrusts in one last, hard time, and I can't fight the gag as he spills inside me.

His release is warm in my throat, but I swallow it down, and the god that he is — he never stops working me. He sucks my clit between his teeth, sucking and letting me go with a pop as his fingers dive in deeper. He's still coming, his ass flexing, balls throbbing in my hand as he empties. And it's that reaction to what I do to him that makes me come, too.

I can't scream, can't say his name the way I want to as I fall apart under his touch, his cock still in my throat. I just swallow as I can, eyes closed before they burst open with the incredible ecstasy surging through me. My knees shake on the table, my glutes on fire as I squeeze, chasing my release until the very last vibration.

And when we're both sated, when the final wave subsides, Brandon carefully removes his fingers first and stares down at me one last time with his softening cock in my mouth. When he pulls it out, I gag a little, but not a drop of his release is left.

"Damn, girl," he says, holding out one hand. He helps me sit up and spin on the table before my feet find the ground, and he pulls me into him, hugging me tight before his lips press against my forehead. "You are phenomenal."

I smile, inhaling the scent of his cologne on his collar as I blush. "And you are a sadist. That wasn't just punishment, that was downright torture."

"You loved it."

I can't even argue that.

When both of our pants are back on and the conference table wiped down, Brandon walks me back to my desk, watching me pack up my purse.

"Come stay with me this weekend."

I smile. "On your yacht?"

"If you want. Or my apartment, or a hotel, or a fucking hotel in Paris. Where do you want to go?" he asks. "Just say it, and I'll take you there."

My eyes find his, flicking between the golden hue of them, trying my damnedest not to fall in love. Because that's what I feel, I recognize, every time I'm with him. I feel desired, and wanted, and safe, and cared for. And if I'm not careful, I'll make more of this than I should.

"Anywhere?"

"Anywhere."

I smile, shaking my head as I toss my purse strap over my shoulder. "Happy Hour."

He balks.

"You said anywhere," I remind him, one finger extended. "And Mykayla is literally going to burst through that door in five minutes to drag me down if I don't show up."

"I can't go with you."

"Sure you can," I say. "Stay up here another half hour and then casually show up. They'll love it, getting to spend time with you outside of the office."

"Sounds like more work. It's the weekend."

"It'll be *fun*," I promise him, leaning up on my tiptoes to plant a kiss on his lips. "And I'll be there."

He groans, conceding though he makes it seem like I'm twisting his arm. "Fine. And after? Will you come home with me then?"

At that, I press another kiss to his lips, sauntering off with him still standing at my cube.

"If you behave."

I throw him a wink over my shoulder, blowing a kiss before I push through the glass door.

Bear

JUST AS PROMISED, I show up at Becca's dorm at eight on the dot Saturday night — box of donuts in hand. She smiles when she opens the door to greet me, tapping the lid of the box with one nude fingernail.

"You remembered."

"I already screwed up once, figured I wasn't ready for strike two yet," I say, and she smiles wider, taking the box from my hands and depositing it on a small table near the door behind her.

As she says goodbye to her roommate, I shamelessly check her out, starting with the ample curve of her ass highlighted in a pair of high-waisted, bell-bottom pants. They're a thin fabric, flowy at the bottom and too tight for church at her hips. When she swings around, joining me in the hallway, I step back enough to let her out, but don't stop my visual assault.

I'm blatantly staring at the way her simple white crop top hugs her rack when she crosses her arms, pushing them up a little more.

"Either you haven't been laid in a long time, or you're not used to a girl with curves like me," she muses.

My eyes flash to hers, meeting her cocky smirk with my own.

"Both. Definitely both."

She laughs, threading her arm through mine as we make our way down the hall and out into the fresh, cool night. Her earrings jingle a little as we walk, and she watches me from her peripheral as I take in her natural hair, styled in a beautiful afro and framed by a unique headband.

"The coffee shop is just a few blocks down and around the corner," she says, smiling and keeping her eyes forward. "Unless you'd rather just stare at me all night instead of watching the open mic."

"Sorry," I say, but it's an insincere apology. I'm not sorry at all. "It's just, you're unlike any other girl I've seen. That sounds lame and cliché, but I don't really know how else to say it. You're just... strikingly beautiful, Becca."

"Oh, stop it," she says, swatting at my arm playfully. Then, she leans in and whispers, "Tell me more."

We both laugh.

"So, no working at the bowling alley tonight, huh?"

"My one Saturday off in the past three months," she says. "Hence why I was so adamant about you taking me on a date."

I chuckle. "Yeah, definitely can't say that you're subtle."

"Never promised to be." She winks, tightening her grip on my bicep a little. "So, Bear-er-Clinton, why the hell were you on a dating app?"

I smile at her reference to me telling her what my name was the night we met.

"Honestly, I have no fucking idea. My fraternity brother suckered me into it, said I've been grumpy lately due to my lack of..." I almost say pussy, catching myself at the last second. "*Dating.*"

"He said you needed to get laid."

"He did," I admit on a laugh.

"And why haven't you had a lady friend in your bed in a while?"

I scratch the back of my neck, a little uncomfortable at how fast the conversation has gone toward my lack of sex in the past year. "Let's just say I was getting it on a regular basis, but then circumstances changed."

"You were dumped."

"Technically, I did the dumping, but yeah... same shit."

I feel Becca watching me as we round the corner, and I shift to the other side of her so I'm walking on the edge closest to the street. That earns me a smile.

"Ah, I see," she says after a moment. "So, you had a girl break your heart, decided *fuck that shit*, and swore off every other girl."

I clear my throat. "Kind of. I was hooking up with this one girl, not exclusively or anything, but it didn't last long."

"Probably because you were still hung up on the other girl, huh?"

I stop, turning to face her as we reach the coffee shop. "It's like you've read the book on my love life."

Becca snorts, both eyebrows raising. "Well, let's just say I could have wrote it."

"Someone break your heart, too?"

Her face falls then, and she shrugs. "We've all had our hearts broken, and probably done some breaking, ourselves. But, I'm not focusing on what the past has held for me anymore," she says, decidedly, her chin lifting and her eyes finding mine. "I like how the future looks better."

I smile, eyes washing over the beautiful angles of her face highlighted under the neon buzz of the coffee shop logo.

"Me, too."

I gently guide Becca inside the shop with a hand at the small of her back, keeping it there until we find an empty table near the front corner of the stage. There's a young guy with long, blond, almost dreaded hair playing a set of bongos as we find our seat, his raspy voice fitting in the cool vibe of the shop. Our waitress stops by to take our order with a smile, and once coffee is on the way, I take the time to look around.

It's like a psychic and a hippie got married and made this place their love baby.

The menu is filled with tea and coffee of all different flavors, each with its unique, "star-given" name. The wall is covered with photography from around the world, mostly in shaded hues of sepia, and behind those photos hang large, yoga-inspired tapestry sheets. The ceiling is dotted with tiny, luminescent lights that give the appearance of us being under the stars, and with the lights dimmed low other than the spotlight on stage, Becca's face glows in a mixture of warmth and shadows.

"You come here a lot?" I ask, still taking in the décor. There's a faint scent of burning wood and essential oil, likely from the incense lining the bar.

"At least a couple times a week," she answers, waving to one of the bartenders. "It has a great vibe, doesn't it?"

I shift in my chair. "It's... interesting."

Becca chuckles. "I take it you're not really connected with spirit and the universe, huh?"

"Not particularly."

"Well, don't be scared. I won't force you to get a tarot card reading or anything."

I smile, leaning back a little in my cushioned chair as our waitress drops off our orders. I opted for coffee, but Becca chose tea, and she pours the steaming hot water from the little tea pot they brought her as I consider my next words.

"I'm surprised you haven't asked me my sign yet."

"Oh, I don't have to. I already know."

I balk at that, watching as she dunks the little bag of herbs into the hot water. "Bullshit. How?"

She smiles, eyes on her tea. "It's in the way you carry yourself. You're practical, very grounded. You seem to think before you speak or act, and you're aware of how your actions affect those around you. You're not necessarily an *overly* caring person, because you watch your own back, but you also don't intend to run people over in your path. It's not that you don't have emotions — because you do — but you're not ruled by them, you don't let them deter you from your main focus."

I shift.

So far, she isn't wrong.

"You're a bit shy, a little reserved, but at the same time, open to the possibilities around you." She continues, chuckling. "Like going on horrendous dating app dates, or meeting a weird girl in a hippie coffee shop."

I smile. "Hmm," I muse, thinking over her assessment. "So you think you have me all figured out, then?"

"No, not even close," she says quickly, slipping her fingers around the handle of her mug. "But, I know enough to hope I get to discover more."

Well, that was adorable.

"You never did say what you think my sign is."

"Capricorn."

I blanch, lifting my coffee for the first sip. "That's pretty impressive. And what's yours?"

"Pisces."

"I'll have to research the sign to figure you out."

She lifts her tea, taking the first light sip. "Or, you could just get to know me yourself. It's way more fun than reading astrology books, I promise."

"Oh, that I don't doubt."

We both pause our conversation to clap as our friend on the bongos finishes up, and a soft music fills the shop as they prep the mic for the next performer.

"Tarot card reading, huh?" I ask, taking another drink of coffee. It's warm and nutty, with just a touch of cinnamon. "You must do that all the time."

"I do. Tarot cards are fun, they help you when you're navigating through trying times, when you have a question or are unsure about a path to take. But, my favorite, personally, is palm reading."

"That so?"

She nods, sipping her tea. "I had mine read at a young age, and I've had follow-up readings. I loved it so much I actually studied it so I can do it on my own."

"Wait," I say, holding out my hand in a pausing motion. "You're telling me you read palms?"

"I do."

I raise my brows, setting my coffee down and propping one elbow on the table before handing her my right palm. "Do me."

She cocks a brow back. "Right here? Now? I think we might get kicked out, but I mean, I'm not opposed."

I smirk, shaking my head at her joke, though I can't deny that my dick hardens at the thought of her mounting me right here and now. "My palm. Read my palm."

"I don't know if you're ready for that," she says.

"Humor me."

She narrows her eyes, taking one more sip of her tea before sliding it to the side and grabbing my hand in hers. "Okay, but don't say I didn't warn you."

I watch Becca as she studies my palm, taking any excuse I can get to study *her*. As much as I wouldn't mind having her ankles hanging over my shoulders as I plow into her, I oddly find myself wanting to just stay up all night *talking* to her, instead. What makes her mind tick? What was she like as a kid, what does she want to be as an adult, who broke her heart, and where does he live so I can break his fucking face?

Or thank him, because now, she's sitting here with me.

I don't believe in love at first sight.

To me, that's ludicrous. I barely believe in *love*, period, let alone in falling into it without knowing someone.

But, something inside me shifted the night I met Becca, and I feel that same stirring now as I watch her brow crease in concentration, her eyes flying over the different lines on my palm. It's like a cold pool of water in the depths of my chest, coming to life as hot water mixes in, warming me from the inside out. It's like finding something I never knew I lost, something I forgot about, or maybe never even realized existed.

It's like a strange recognition, an unfamiliar thing I knew all along.

"So," she says after a moment, scooting forward in her seat. "The first thing I notice is that you have an earth shape to your hand, which makes sense, considering how you're an earth sign. With palm reading, it signifies to me that you've been shaped a lot by what has happened to you — more so than anything you've learned from, say, reading, or school. You've learned by living."

I nod, the truth of that sinking in deeper than she could ever know.

She goes on to assess three different lines on my hand — the "head" line, the "life" line, and the "heart" line. And while I walk into the reading skeptical, I find myself leaning more and more into her as she traces the lines on my hand, telling me what they speak to her. She points out how the shortness in my head line tells me that I prefer more physically demanding tasks, and that I throw myself into physical work when I have difficult decisions to make or when I'm hurting. That wakes me up, the truth of it so real it sends a tingle down my back.

On and on she goes, pointing out how my life line tells her that I keep distance and caution in my relationships, and also that my heart line indicates that I have difficulty expressing my feelings, even when I'm aware of them. Each new word from her lips has me reeling, my wheels spinning as I conjure up example after example of how her assessment is true. Am I reaching for this stuff, or is she actually onto something? I can't be sure, but all I know by the time she grins up at me, watching the different shades of confusion on my face, is that she's an incredible girl.

Weird, but incredible.

"So, what do you think?" she asks as they announce the next performer — a young girl who will read slam poetry.

"I think that's some crazy shit."

She laughs. "It is. There are more lines, too, but I'll go easy on you for this first one." She furrows her brows, pulling my hand back to her. "Wait. There is one other thing here... it's kind of troubling."

"What is it?" I ask, leaning forward.

"Well, see the way this line curves?" she asks.

I nod, focusing on that line as she continues.

"It's troubling, because that tells me that there's someone in your life you've wanted to kiss, but haven't. Someone you want to touch, to feel, but you've refrained. It's a terrible, pent-up energy, and it should be rectified immediately."

I let out a soft laugh, shaking my head at my embarrassing eagerness, which only makes her teasing funnier. When my eyes find hers, she smirks, the light glossing off her irises.

"Real smooth."

She shrugs, waiting, and I lean across the table, lifting my palm from her hands. My thumb finds her chin, tipping it up just a bit, and then I close the distance between us, pressing my lips to hers.

There's a curve in her mouth during our first kiss, a sweet smile that permeates into my own lips like honey. She giggles when I break away, just marginally, enough to lick my lips and dive back in for more. It's a kiss I never could have had with Shawna, or Lacy, or any other girl. It's a kiss reserved for books and movies, for sappy, romantic guys who don't refer to girls as bitches and fantasize about banging them the first time they meet.

What's happening to me?

I vaguely recognize that I should care, I should give a damn that my chest is light, my heart kicking as her hands wrap around my neck. She pulls me in closer, nipping at my bottom lip, and suddenly that ravaging beast inside me is awake again. He kicks the sappy bastard who preceded him out in a flash, and I slide my tongue along the crease of Becca's lips until she lets me inside. Our tongues swirl, a soft moan leaving her mouth for mine, and as the performer begins her first poem, we back away, our breaths heavy between us.

"What does my palm say now?" I ask, offering her the same hand.

She blushes, tracing one finger down the middle of it before tapping it twice. "It says you need another coffee, because it's going to be a *long* night."

Now *that's* a future I can get on board with.

Skyler

MY MOTHER TOLD ME about Murphy's Law when I was seventeen.

I still remember that day — how I'd woken up late, missed the bus to my field trip and had to stay back while the rest of my classmates went to a local museum, then I'd broken my sandal, having to use duct tape to temporarily fix it for the day. When I got home, thinking that the bad day was over, I discovered that I had lost my wallet somewhere between school and home — and it had all my babysitting money in it. The final straw was when Mom brought me my laundry later, showing me one of my favorite shirts with a rip in the side from the washing machine.

That's when I'd lost it.

Mom held me as I cried, soothing me as she told me about Murphy's Law, about when you just have a day where nothing can go right. But, she said the best thing about it was that I would go to bed, and the day would end, and I'd wake up to a fresh new start tomorrow.

I'd thought that was the worst day ever, thought I knew how bad Murphy's Law could get.

But today proved me wrong.

Kip is on my heels as I storm toward a waiting cab outside the downtown casino, and I slide in without a word or a glance in his direction. My eyes focus somewhere beyond the glass, on nothing in particular, as I try and fail repeatedly to calm my racing heart.

I blew it.

I blew a tournament that I should have easily won, not only missing out on the opportunity to stack up my savings for the entry fee in Vegas, but also giving the tabloids plenty to write about. I can already see the headlines.

Skyler Thorne on Tilt at Local Tournament — Pressure Too Much?

I sigh, leaning my head against the back of the seat. It bounces a little as Kip climbs in next to me, and I'm reminded that now I have to share a ride home with him, with the guy I want to blame for everything tonight, even though I know it's my fault.

I can't look at him when he shuts the door behind him. I can't do anything but sit there and wonder how the hell this all happened.

Last week after my breakfast with Clinton, I'd gone straight to class to find Kip waiting for me in our usual spot — with a coffee for me in hand. It had become a running joke between us, him trying to guess what kind of coffee I drink — which is ironic, considering I only drink hot chocolate. But after the dance, I figured that would stop. Hell, I figured he wouldn't even *look* at me, let alone invite me to sit next to him.

But he'd been there, and he'd acted like nothing was wrong. In fact, *he'd* apologized, told me he understood my feelings for Adam and respected them, and asked if we could be friends.

Friends.

I laugh a little, my breath hitting the cool glass at the fog. How naïve I was to believe I could go back to being Kip Jackson's *friend* after having his tongue down my throat.

But for some idiotic reason, I'd agreed — and not just to being friends. He'd also asked me to do the tournament tonight, telling me it would be good practice, and a great way to make some cash for the entry fee. He wasn't wrong, but honestly, this tournament wasn't even on my radar until he suggested it.

I'd said yes as if I had nothing to lose.

Maybe it was because I didn't want to lose *him*.

Selfishly, I wanted to hold onto him — however I could, even if it wasn't the way I wanted to. I told myself this was better than nothing, that being with him in any capacity was better than not having him at all.

Wrong.

So, so wrong.

If I hadn't figured it out when my stomach rolled every time he came to the house for Erin over the past week, or how I felt like throwing up when I saw her name pop up as a text message on his phone, then I definitely got my reality slap to the face earlier today at the gym.

There I was, just minding my business on my way to spin class when I saw Kip in the weight room. He was already dripping sweat, his arms and chest bulging as he did reps, and for a while, I just stared. That's when I first realized it. I felt a rolling wave of something unfamiliar, yet something I placed immediately.

Mine.

The thought had crossed my mind unashamedly, and I didn't even take the time to process it before I jogged over to him, ripping his headphones out of his ears and making light conversation. That's what we'd been doing since we had our truce. The conversation stayed surface level, nothing deep, nothing too emotional.

But he'd flirted with me.

His eyes couldn't stay off my cleavage in my workout tank, and I'd felt that heat of his gaze all the way to my core. Trying my best to shift the conversation into safe territory, I'd asked him if he wanted to take spin with me to get in some cardio. He'd smiled, that same sexy smirk I'd come to love, but his words were delivered like a bullet to the chest.

"I got in plenty of cardio earlier, trust me."

It was a casual enough response, but the implication behind it was murderous. He'd been with Erin this morning. I knew because she'd come in from seeing him high as a kite and giddy as a lottery winner. If he'd gotten in cardio, I was pretty sure I knew exactly how he'd done so.

And that was it.

That stupid, ridiculous scene was what threw me for the rest of the day. I bailed on spin class early, dodged across campus, and let myself stew. Then, when it was time for the tournament, I'd dressed in my classic jeans and black hoodie and I'd settled into my pre-tournament rituals like I had a shot in hell of getting out of my head and into the game.

Fat chance in hell of that.

Kip didn't even glance at me in the cab as he told the driver the address, and I couldn't blame him. I'd been nothing short of sassy to him all night long. From him trying to coach me before the tournament to him slipping up and saying my name in the bar, getting me roped into an interview with a reporter who overheard him, I made it clear that Kip wasn't welcome in my head that night.

Or in my heart.

It's only when I close my eyes and take a deep breath, trying to reconcile with the fact that the tournament is over and there's nothing I can do about it, that I realize *which* address Kip gave the driver.

My eyes pop open.

"Wait," I say, turning to Kip. "She needs to take me home first. It's on the way."

"You're coming home with me tonight."

My cheeks betray me in a blush, but I use the heat to fuel my anger. "What? Um, no," I correct him. "Not happening."

I lean forward, ready to spout off my address to the driver when Kip's hand reaches for my elbow.

"Damnit, Skyler, you're coming home with me or I'm going to call that reporter and tell her I was the guy from the bonfire."

My eyes widen, stomach sinking at the headlines that would run with that. Lacy, the reporter from earlier, had asked if Kip was the guy I'd been caught kissing at the bonfire. We'd played it off, me making a joke about it being cute that she thought I was only kissing one guy. I told her I didn't even remember his name, and Kip played along.

If only that were actually true, maybe I wouldn't be in this mess.

"And I can tell her way more fun stories about you than what she got earlier," Kip finishes, his threat clear.

My mouth pops open, something between disbelief and intense hurt passing through me. He wouldn't do that to me, would he? I mean, I knew I hurt him at the dance, but he wouldn't put my career on the line...

Right?

"You wouldn't do that," I challenge.

Without so much as a second of hesitation, Kip pulls Lacy's business card from his pocket, holding it like a weapon between his fingertips.

I just stare at that little card, wishing I could set it on fire with my gaze, and then I throw myself against the seat like a child throwing a tantrum.

"You're a Class A douche right now."

"You can insult me all you want, but you're still coming home with me."

"Why do you want me to come home with you, anyway?" I argue, crossing my arms over my chest. And before I can stop myself from the pettiness, the next words slip out. "Wouldn't you rather call *Erin?*"

Kip isn't phased in the slightest.

"I'm not asking you to come home with me for sex, Skyler," he chastises, like I truly am a child throwing a fit. "I'm your friend, and whether you want to let me or not, I'm helping you get ready for May and we need to talk about tonight."

I barely register the last of his explanation, because I'm too busy focusing on the first blip that came out of his mouth. I gave him a chance to prove me wrong, to ask me what the hell I was talking about when I referenced how Erin should be the one he's calling for a late-night booty call. Instead, he'd only proven my suspicions right.

He's had sex with Erin.

That bullet from before is lodged somewhere in my throat, making it impossible to swallow. Bile rises anyway, my stomach churning. But as much as I want to break down and sob, my poker face is in full effect.

We pull up to Kip's apartment, and I whip around to face him fully as the driver brings us to a stop.

"You aren't *asking* me anything," I remind him. "You're blackmailing me."

I throw open my door, the weight of it bouncing off the hinges before I stand and slam it shut again. Leaning down to glare at him through the window, I steady my voice as much as I can to deliver my final blow.

"And it's so nice to know that if it were Erin here, it would be for sex. Sorry I'm cock-blocking your *cardio* plans."

Then, I storm off toward his apartment, realizing I've just cornered myself and admitted I'm affected by who he has sex with.

Fuck.

So much for my poker face.

Kip is hot on my heels when I reach his apartment door. I try but fail to open it, huffing like my flagrant annoyance and anger will save me from the fact that I just put my foot in my big, stupid mouth.

Before that moment, Kip had no idea why I wasn't on my game tonight. It could have been anything — a sorority event, my family, school. But no, I just lit up a bright neon sign that said *he* is the one on my mind, the reason I'm so off, the reason I couldn't keep my shit together and win the tournament.

I'm supposed to be into Adam — *that* was the role I agreed to play. That's what Kip is supposed to think. And if that was the case, then there is absolutely no reason I should be upset about him being with Erin.

I'm not supposed to care about him.

I *told* him I didn't care.

And now, I've fucked everything up.

"Skyler," Kip says my name again, out of breath as he jogs up the last of the steps after me.

I cross my arms over my chest defiantly. "Just open the damn door."

He huffs, shoving the key in the lock and swinging the door open. "What the fuck, Skyler?" he yells when we're inside, tossing his keys on the table by the door. His hands run through his hair next, pulling a little like I'm driving him mad. "Why are you mad at me?"

My eyes skirt to the bedroom, to the bed where Kip put his hands on me.

The same one he fucked Erin in.

Ugh.

"You wanted this, didn't you?" he presses when I don't answer. "We're friends. You have Adam, and I've moved on. I haven't made this weird. I didn't hold what happened against you and I didn't make shit awkward. I moved on and you got what you wanted, because clearly Adam wants you."

His voice cracks a little at that.

"I see him texting you every fucking day, and he's always talking about you. This is it." He tosses his hands up, letting them slap against his thighs when they land again. "You asked for this. So, why does it matter who I'm fucking?"

And there it is.

I assumed before, and after his admission in the car, I may have been reaching. But with those words, I know with absolute certainty.

I'm not allowed to care that he's fucked Erin. That was the plan, that was what I signed up for.

I'm not allowed to care.

But that doesn't change the fact that I do.

"Let's just drop it, okay, Kip?" I beg, crossing my arms over my middle to try to suffocate my urge to vomit.

One quick glance at Kip has me wishing I could sink into the floor and disappear. He's just standing there across the room, arms outstretched, chest heaving as he watches me under bent brows. He's sporting a light green t-shirt, one that sets his icy eyes ablaze in the low light of his apartment.

He's absolutely beautiful.

And absolutely off-limits.

"Let's just talk about the tournament," I try. "And then we can both go to sleep and clear our heads."

"No." The word is more of a growl, his jaw tense when it leaves his lips. "Fuck that."

He takes a few steps toward me and I instinctively back up, finding the wall with my back and then my palms.

"I don't know what fucking game you're playing," he spits. "But I'm calling it tonight. Why do you care about me and Erin?"

"Kip, please..."

"You broke me that night, Skyler."

My chest tightens at the rasp in his voice, the earnest honesty. He moves closer, and I pin my bottom lip between my teeth, willing it not to quiver. I roll my eyes up toward the ceiling, fighting against the urge to cry, to break and tell him everything.

Kip taps his fist on his chest. "Everything I felt between us," he says, voice thick with emotion. "Everything I *know* is here, you told me it didn't exist. And you know what? I knew it was bullshit. I *knew* it. The words were coming from your lips, and it was your eyes I was looking into as each one slammed into me, but it wasn't *you* I was hearing. So," he says. One step closer. "Now's your chance to tell me — why do you care?"

I shake my head as tears blur my vision. Kip takes another step, the warmth from his chest warming my own.

"Was it Erin?"

All I can do is focus on each breath. In and out, inhale and exhale.

Do not cry.

Do. Not. Break.

But one tear breaks loose, scarring my cheek with its wet betrayal. It might be an invisible scar, but I'll feel this tear forever. And that's the thing about scars. They're like skid marks on the highway. No one slows down enough to see the painful proof that something happened. But the road? The road will always remember. The road can't forget, no matter how many times it's repaved.

"Was it?" Kip repeats. "Or was it that you were starting to feel something, too?"

I swallow, my eyes on his, trying and failing to meet his challenging stare with my own.

"I know you, Skyler," he whispers. "I know who you pretend to be in front of all these people." He sweeps his hand behind him, toward campus. "And I know who you *really* are."

His eyes soften a little then, and he leans forward, the electricity sparking between us. I focus on his eyes, willing myself not to notice the thick bulge of his neck, the tightness in his biceps, the heaving of his chest.

"I know the you who doesn't fit in because you were never meant to. You were *born* to stand out. You want to pretend like you're untouchable and nothing can phase you with those people? Play around with a few frat boys, dress up in frilly dresses and keep your reputation? Fine," he says. "But don't sit here and feed *me* that bullshit. I see you, Skyler. I. See. You."

His hands find my arms, tenderly, but I jump anyway. His cool palms slide up, slowly, covering me with goosebumps as he runs them over my shoulders, my neck, until my face is cradled between them. More tears fall, landing between us as I keep my chin high and my eyes on his.

"Why do you care?" he asks again, his voice low.

"I don't."

"Liar."

My entire body trembles as I lick my lip and pull my eyes to the ceiling again. My next confession slips out in a whisper, a solemn admission I wish I didn't have to make.

"I don't want to."

"But you do."

I can't answer. I just swallow, closing my eyes and setting two new tears free.

"This is a no-limit game, Skyler," Kip says. "Neither of us went into it thinking we would be here, but now we've got everything on the table because we're both too stubborn to give in. I raise, you call. You raise, I call." He shakes his head. "Back and forth, always in this fucking game. You want to win? Fine. Take it. Take everything I have, but I'm not the one who's going to walk away the real loser."

I can't breathe. My chest squeezes, my breaths like fire instead of oxygen in my lungs.

"If you don't wake up and realize what you're feeling — what *we're* feeling — is real, then it's you I feel sorry for," he says, taking a tentative step back. His eyes never leave mine. "It's *you* who loses."

His words are an ice bucket of water, poured over an already trembling me, the truth of them permeating my skin like they'll forever be a part of me now.

Kip turns, throwing his hands up and letting them rest on his head as he faces the door. For a moment, I just watch his back, the ebbs and flows of the muscles as he breathes. I feel sick as I squeeze my eyes shut, holding back the sob stuck tight in my throat. My next move isn't clear — not even close. It's like staring into murky, black water and trying to find the one and only shiny penny on the bottom.

He's right.

We are in a game, and if he knew everything I've done to play this hand, if he knew about Erin, about the deal, he would hate me.

Which is why I can't tell him.

And though my stomach sinks at that, at a truth I have to bury away and never let him see, my hands stop trembling. My breaths come more even as I open my eyes, lifting my gaze, and the endless flow of tears halt.

Because I'm done playing the game.

I can't imagine it, moving on without him, walking away like I don't give a damn. I can't imagine a world where his hands don't touch me, where his eyes don't light up at the sight of me, where I'm not the one responsible for that sexy smirk.

Kip is mine. He has been since the moment we met.

And I can't just walk away.

Not even for Erin.

"I care," I say quietly, weakly, like a prized fighter tapping out in a choke hold. "I've cared about you for *so* long."

Kip doesn't face me, but his shoulders pull back, his stance straightening.

"I care that I hurt you, I care that even though I did, you still stuck around, and yes," I admit, pushing away from the wall until I'm standing straight, too. "I care that Erin was here, that she was in your bed, because I don't want anyone else in your bed but me."

The dam doesn't just crack — it crumbles, the once solid walls tumbling down and letting everything out that I'd fought to hold back.

"I don't want anyone else in your *arms* but me," I continue. "I want to be the only girl in your head when you wake up and I... I was petrified, okay?" My stomach twists. "I thought if I told you I wanted Adam, you would leave me alone. I thought you'd be pissed off and you'd be out of my life completely and I wouldn't have to worry about feeling this. And on the beach?" I shake my head. "I actually *wanted* you to be with Erin. It made sense. I figured it was your plan all along."

Kip scoffs at that, still not facing me.

"No, I'm serious. It makes sense." My insecurities float to the surface, and for once, I don't cover them with a cocky façade. "Compared to her, I'm nothing. And I was happy for you. At least, that's what I told myself. But I don't know what to do, Kip, because I *do* care about you." I swallow. "But I can't."

"Why?" He finally faces me, and his aqua eyes are still wild, their intensity locked in on me.

"It's complicated."

What more can I say without telling him the truth?

Kip watches me for a beat, and then a long, frustrated sigh breaks through his flat lips. He takes one step toward me, then another, shaking his head as he descends. "I didn't have sex with Erin, Skyler."

My heart skips.

"I don't *want* Erin," he says, his strides more purposeful. He's so close, and he isn't stopping this time. "It's *you* I want."

My back hits the wall, his chest meeting mine, hips pinning me where he wants me. Every breath that leaves my lungs threatens to never return.

"And less than three weeks ago, you stood in that shower and told me you wanted me, too. So stop being scared, stop caring what other people think, and for once in your life, take what you want."

My eyes flick to his lips, their demand still hot on my ears as I press forward, closing the distance between us and slamming my mouth on his. We both inhale a breath, long and sharp, our hands reaching, pushing, pulling, all the want and need pouring out of us in one passionate flood.

And I don't just fall into him — I leap.

I jump, head first, more sure than I've ever been that this is right, no matter how wrong it feels. I can't think of Erin, or of what I'll do tomorrow when I wake up and realize all that I've said that I can't think back.

All I can think, all I can see, all I can *feel* is him.

That electricity that sparked between us when we shared our first kiss roars back to life, its energy so powerfully overwhelming my knees buckle from the shock of it. Kip is there in an instant, leaning into me, his hands rounding over my hips until they cup my ass and lift. The force of him pinning me to the wall steals my breath, but I wrap my legs around him, pulling him closer, needing more.

My fingers claw at his shirt, the breaths heavy in my chest as the hunger builds to an impossible level. He pulls it over his head effortlessly and lets it fall to the ground before his eyes meet mine.

And we both stop.

I see the questions, the uncertainty, the wonder if he's going to wake up to an empty bed again. And right now, I can't promise him anything, so I don't speak. And he doesn't push.

We both know what this is and what it isn't, and that's enough.

I grab the bottom of my hoodie and pull it over my head, taking my small tank top with it. Kip's eyes fall to my chest and I feel his hard bulge between my hips. Moaning at his reaction to me, I grab his neck and pull his mouth to mine again. The first time Kip touched me, I was caught off guard. I was timid and afraid and overwhelmed with guilt. Now, I still know it's wrong, but I don't care. I don't feel ashamed. I don't feel guilty.

I just feel... alive.

Kip thrusts his hips into me, kissing his way down my neck. When he bites down, I hiss with the mixture of pleasure and pain.

"Fuck, Skyler," Kip growls, his scruff against my skin making me shiver. "If you keep making noises like that, this is going to be over before it even starts."

Our breaths are hard, our skin slick with sweat. Warning bells sound in my head — or are those church bells? I can't decipher if they're joyous or haunted with warnings of danger.

"Hang on, let me grab something," Kip says, starting to drop me to the floor.

I shake my head, wrapping my arms around his neck tighter. "I'm on the pill."

"Thank fuck," he groans, pulling me in his arms and moving us quickly to the couch. He throws me down, towering over me, lust rolling off him like steam.

I lean up and make quick work of the button on his jeans before tugging them down and over his hips. They fall to the floor, exposing Kip's more than ample bulge straining against his cotton boxers, and I groan with appreciation. Slowly, I run my hands up his thighs and palm him through the fabric, his head falling back as a deep groan escapes his throat.

Last time, it was him who pleasured me, who brought me to ecstasy with his hands alone.

Time to repay the favor.

Moving my fingertips to the band just below his waistline, I tug them down and his erection springs free, sending a warm pulse of need between my thighs. My eyes find his again as I move my lips to his head, slowly swirling my tongue around the tip before running it along his length.

"Fuck," he whispers, dragging out the word. I take it as my cue and suck harder.

Blow jobs have always been my gift, and it might as well be Kip's birthday tonight.

He curses again as I pull him all the way into my mouth, feeling myself grow wetter at the taste of him. I want to devour him completely, to banish every other woman from his memory with my mouth.

Grabbing his ass in both hands, I pull him into me forcefully, his dick hitting the back of my throat. He curses louder this time and pulls out quickly before lifting me to my feet, his eyes wide and wild like he was close to coming, like if he hadn't yanked me to my feet, this would have all been over already.

I smile up at him wickedly, licking my lips and wiping the corners with my fingers.

He runs the pad of his thumb along my bottom lip, shaking his head. "You know exactly what you can do with this mouth of yours, don't you?"

Slowly, he runs his hand down the front of my body before tucking his fingertips in the band of my jeans.

"Take these off."

I do as he says, kicking them to join the rest of our clothes piling up around us. Before I have the chance to look at him again, his mouth finds mine and his hand slips beneath the lacy fabric of my panties. He dips two fingers inside me quickly and I moan against his lips, my legs weakening at the touch.

"I've got some talents of my own, you know." He grins, working his fingers as his palm rubs against my clit. My breath is already labored, my body dangerously close to the edge of release.

Kip uses his free hand to unclasp my bra and sends it flying across the room, an expert move I didn't expect, and it only fuels my desire more. When one hot hand palms my breast as he continues his assault between my thighs, I moan.

"Goddamn, you are so fucking wet, Sky."

Desperate, my hands find his cock again and I move in time with his fingers inside me. Our breaths mingle together, both of us wide-eyed as the heat builds. So long I've wondered what this would feel like, what it would do to me if I just threw caution to the wind and gave in to my need for him.

Now that I know, I know there's no going back.

Kip removes his fingers without warning, spinning me around and using his palm to push my upper back down and bend me over the couch. His hands run down my hips and over my ass, hooking my panties with his fingers and pulling them down to just above my knees before letting them fall.

I look back at him, completely exposed in this position as he kisses the backs of my thighs, his eyes locked on mine with reverence. When he stands, he grips himself in one hand, using the other to slide a finger inside me again. I bite my lip and let my head fall back and he quickly withdraws and grabs my hair instead, tugging it with force.

When he positions himself at my entrance, my breath catches, every inch trembling with the need to feel all of him. I'm so far past what's right and wrong I can't even see the line anymore. I just breathe him in, the need to be under him, to be claimed. Arching my back, I push my ass against him, the tip of his dick just barely slipping inside me.

Kip groans at the feel of it, and I hiss as he tugs my hair again, gripping it in his fist.

"I'm going to take you, Skyler," he husks. "But I need you to know that once I do, I'm going to own you. You're going to be mine. This game between us? The rules are going to change."

"Take me," I whisper, the words leaving my lips before I have the chance to decide if I mean them or not.

"Is that what you want?" He tugs my hair a little more, his lips by my ear now. I feel his breath hot on my skin and chills race down my body.

"Take me, Kip. Now."

He growls, biting down on my neck before pushing inside me — not slowly, but all at once, like a man on a mission to take back what's his. I cry out as he fills me, again and again, my fists gripping the sofa as the pleasure pulses through me. Kip releases my hair, his hands trailing down my back before gripping my hips. He slams into me harder, pushing deeper as my orgasm builds.

"God, you're so beautiful, Skyler," he breathes, his breath strained. "So fucking sexy."

I don't even attempt to hide my moans now and they ring out in his apartment, the sounds echoing off the walls as we move. He leans down and palms my breasts in his hands, pulling me up and against him. Moving slower now, he kisses my neck as his hand falls to my clit. He applies just a little pressure but it shoots straight through me, my entire body igniting at the touch.

I moan louder, my breaths uneven until he finally pushes me over the edge I've been dancing on with him since the first moment we met. His mouth finds mine and I moan into his lips as I come, my legs shaking against him, all of my weight supported in his arms. Waves of heat roll through me and every sense is dulled, my orgasm owning me completely.

Just like him.

"That was so fucking hot," Kip says, kissing down my neck before flipping me over. He grabs my hips and lifts them to meet his before pushing into me again, before my orgasm has even fully resided. The intensity throttles me, every nerve jumping to life at the sensation of him stretching me open again. He's even deeper now, my hips elevated as he pounds into me.

His eyes cascade over every inch of my body as if he can't get enough of me, as if he's never seen anything he's wanted more. He's the musician, and I his muse — the one he's been chasing his entire life.

He palms my breasts, pushing into me once more before he finds his release with a groan and my name on his lips. His eyes roll back and I drag my nails down the muscles flexed in his arms as he comes inside me, our bodies trembling together.

And for one, blissful moment, we're sated and complete.

Then, my anxiety rears its ugly head like it never truly left at all, but just watched from the corner, waiting to pounce as soon as the pheromones were gone.

I reach up and pull Kip down on top of me, kissing him hard as we come down from the high, like those punishing kisses can band all other thoughts. But as our breaths begin to even out, the weight of the night folds in on us.

Kip wraps me tighter in his arms, pulling me into his chest as if he feels it, too. As if he's trying to protect us from the inevitable reality we have to return to.

My fingertips slowly run the length of his abs and chest, leaving a trail of goosebumps in their wake. He runs his fingers through my hair and we both submit to our thoughts, nervous to say anything out loud.

"Kip," I start, but he pulls me in tighter, shaking his head.

"Not tonight, Skyler. Just... let's not ruin tonight."

I nod, nuzzling into him more.

We know that when the sun rises, it'll shed light on everything the darkness consumed tonight. Silently, we consider what that means.

We both know what this is and what it isn't.

But the question remains – can we live with that, or is it time to change the rules?

"Wake up," a voice says.

I stir a bit, the soft sound of rain pattering against the window as I stretch. Soft lips touch my shoulder and my eyes flutter open. I smile as Kip kisses up my neck to just behind my ear, my entire body coming alive at the touch.

"Mornin'," he says, pulling back and resting on an elbow. The shadows from the rain on the window dance over his skin and I stare in awe, mesmerized by his effortless beauty.

Suddenly, it hits me.

Everything that corresponded between us last night flashes through my head and I blanch, eyes wide in horror as I bolt upright.

Kip frowns, sitting up with me, one hand reaching out to touch me. I pull the sheets higher, covering myself, my eyes darting around the room for my clothes.

"Don't do that," he says softly, shaking his head. "Don't look at me like you just made a mistake."

I try to make my face change, to relax my breathing, to find the calm that I had last night but I can't. Kip's expression looks pained as he rolls to the other side of the bed, his feet hitting the floor. He runs his hands through his hair.

"Fuck, Skyler."

"No, wait, just…" I lean up, relieved when I realize I'm wearing his shirt and I'm not naked like I thought. Slowly, I crawl over to Kip, tucking my hands under his arms to place them on his chest as I plant small kisses on his back. He stiffens at first, but each kiss unties the knots of tension just a little more. "I'm sorry. I don't regret last night. I don't."

It's true, I don't regret it, but I still know that I should. Erin is one-hundred percent into Kip and falling faster than the first time and I had sex with him. Worse than that, it wasn't a one-time thing. I knew it last night, Kip knew it, too – and we both know it right now.

Something changed last night.

The presidency aside, my relationship with all my sisters is at risk now. I broke girl code.

And I just wish I was sorry about it.

I pull away, sighing as I move to sit next to him. "I don't know what to do," I admit, glancing over at him.

He turns to me, worry still laden on his face as if he's battling with his own guilt. Maybe he does care about Erin? Or maybe there's something else behind those furrowed brows.

"If I told you I was an asshole, that I'm going to end up hurting you and this is all going to end just as fucked up as it started, would you hate me? Would you leave?"

I bite my lip, the bluntness of his words slamming into me like a club. *If only he knows.*

"Am I stupid if I tell you I don't think it's possible for me to hate you?"

He sighs, as if he knew I'd answer that way and it makes him hate himself even more.

I shrug, leaning down to look into his eyes again. "I already tried."

His hand finds mine and for a few moments we just sit there, staring ahead and letting the rain pour down outside. Finally, Kip speaks again. "I'm going to call things off with Erin."

I nod, feeling a mixture of guilt and relief. I don't want him to be with Erin. "We still need to keep this a secret for a while," I say, gently rubbing his fingers between mine. "I think after a while, Erin and my sisters and just everyone in general will be okay with us being together. But right now, it's going to be too obvious. Erin would know we hooked up when you were together. She would hate me. Everyone would hate *us*."

"I'm not with her, not the way you're putting it, anyway. I'm going to make that clear to her, too," Kip says quickly, turning to face me. "And why does it matter what everyone else thinks?" He's saying the words like he wants us to be together now, but there's still something in his eyes that tells me he's not sure that's what he wants, either.

"It's not that easy, Kip. They're my sisters and I'm in line to be the president next year. I can't lead a sorority of girls who don't trust me." My eyes fall to the floor. "Plus, Erin is my Big. We've had some issues this year but I love her, I don't want to hurt her."

Her face flashes in my mind, the girl who convinced me to rush Kappa Kappa Beta, who held my hand and helped me change everything I wanted to change about myself. I went from nobody to one of the most popular girls on our campus. She was instrumental in that transformation.

And I've betrayed her.

Kip nods, sighing as he reaches out and pulls me into him. "I know, I'm sorry. You're right. Laying low for a while is a good idea. I'm sure Adam would be pissed, too. You need to figure out what to say to him."

I roll my eyes. "Ugh, I don't know how he hasn't gotten the clue yet. I've barely spoken to him. He texts me every minute of the day, it feels like."

That's been the most surprising part of this, how eager Adam has been to talk to me, to get inside my head. He's been trying to get me to talk to him about what's really going on since the dance. Not that I can blame him, after what I said, but he and I *both* know that we could never be more than friends again. We tried, and it just doesn't work. Hooking up a few times? Sure. But past that, nothing exists.

I should have just told him I was drunk, that I didn't mean what I said about still being into him. But with Erin breathing down my neck and watching every little piece of her puzzle closely, there was no way.

I had a part to play, and up until last night, I'd played it perfectly.

Best poker face in the game.

A smile curls on Kip's face. "Is it bad that I kind of look forward to seeing his face when he realizes you're with me?"

I nudge him playfully and he pulls me in tighter, laughing.

"Just saying, he thinks you played me to get him back. It's going to be sweet revenge to prove that assumption incorrect."

I roll my eyes again and Kip pulls me back onto the bed quickly, wrapping his arms around me. I laugh and push at his shoulders but give in too easily, not really wanting to get away from him in the first place. His smile fades slowly and his eyes search mine as he moves a strand of fallen hair from my face.

There's a storm brewing in those blue eyes of his, but I can't figure out if I should be afraid or excited for the rain to pour.

"Stay with me today," he says, leaning up on one elbow.

I nod in response and he leans down again, pressing his lips to mine.

The rain sounds softer now, replaced by the internal buzz I feel when Kip kisses me. I've decided he's one of those kissers who really takes his time. He runs his hands through my hair and moves his lips slowly against mine, his tongue sweeping in at the perfect time to cause my breath to catch. He touches my face, my neck, my lower back. When it's natural, he catches my bottom lip between his teeth, tugging just enough to make my stomach flip.

Kip kisses me like I'm a goddess, like he's lucky to even be near me, let alone with his lips on mine.

And with Kip, I *feel* like a goddess.

Beautiful.

Invincible.

Immortal.

But the truth is, I'm not a goddess. I can break. I know that, and yet I'm still here, wrapped in the arms of the one who could shatter me into pieces.

I guess I should start praying now.

Erin

"ARE YOU OKAY?"

I blink, those words oozing over me like sick, poisonous slime.

How many times have I been asked that, if I'm okay, like that's the only way to be? To live? Do I not deserve to be happy, or elated, or glowing with indestructible joy?

The answer to that question, it appears, is no. I am forever destined to exist somewhere between okay and not okay, never surpassing, never able to exist in a state of being that surpasses that purgatory.

Okay, or not okay.

And right now, I am *not* okay.

Kip watches me, his brows furrowed, hands folded over mine between us. He just broke up with me — if you can even call it that, seeing as how according to *him*, we weren't even truly dating.

Since when is making out, going to dinners, seeing movies, hanging out and talking for *hours* not dating? Since when is holding my hand and walking me home not dating? Since when is texting me all day, every day, not dating?

My nose flares as a new wave of anger washes over me, but I hear my mother's cool, calm voice in my head.

Hold your power, baby girl.

I smile, though it's weak on the inside. "I'm okay," I lie. "And, I understand."

"You do?"

I nod, clearing my throat and pulling my hands from his. "It was all a little fast. Maybe we can start over, go slower. Start as friends."

Kip nods, but his face folds, like he already knows there's no way he'll ever be with me. My stomach turns.

"Yeah, friends. I like that plan."

I smile again, but it falls too quickly. "Well, I have to run. Panhellenic meeting soon. I'll see you around? Spring Break is just a few days away."

"Yeah, it'll be fun," Kip says, standing with me, but his brows are still pinched together in concern. "Thanks for being so cool about this, Erin. Are you sure you're okay?"

That fucking word.

"Mm-hmm." I pull my purse strap over one shoulder. "Bye, Kip."

I don't linger on his eyes, or his strong, square jaw as I turn and strut away from him, my kitten heels click-clacking across the tile floor of the coffee shop. He couldn't even "not-break-up" with me in private. No, he had to do it at Cup O' Joes, where everyone could see, where everyone could watch me do everything I can to hold it together when all I want is to fall apart.

If I broke, if I just gave in and slumped down into a pile of nothing on the floor, would anyone help me stand again? Would anyone pick up the pieces?

Clinton would.

The thought passes like a flash of lightning, strong and shocking and gone in an instant, leaving only the roll of thunder in its place. I swallow, shaking him from my thoughts as I make my way across campus, back to the sorority house.

"Okay, Erin," I whisper to myself, holding my chin high. "New plan. That's all you need, a new plan."

I think over everything Kip said, how he told me things didn't feel right, that he wasn't interested, and he thought we should just be friends. I scour our text messages, our dates, looking for some sign I missed — but I come up empty. He'd seemed interested, touching me when we were in public, kissing me when we were alone, rubbing my shoulders and losing afternoons with me as we watched movies and caught up. He even listened to me talk about sorority drama, which I knew was torture for any guy.

So, then, *what happened?*

I chew my cheek, the methodical click and clack of my heels soothing my thoughts.

Maybe he's just scared, freaked out by how much he's feeling. I've heard of guys backing out for that reason more times than I can count. Maybe he likes me so much, he doesn't know how to deal.

But when I round the corner onto Greek Row and see Skyler on the front lawn, I pause.

Of course.

I watch her throw back her head in a strong laugh, she and Jess soaking up sun rays on our front lawn. They clink their plastic tumblers together, sipping a light pink liquid, and I laugh out loud at my stupidity.

It's her.

It *has* to be her.

All of a sudden, out of nowhere, Kip breaks up with me. And all of a sudden, out of nowhere, Skyler is back to her happy-go-lucky self after weeks of sulking.

Something happened.

I can't believe I didn't see it, can't believe *they* were stupid enough to think I never would.

Skyler's laugh reaches my ear, and I clench my fists, forcing a smile as I straighten my back and find my pace again. Kip mentioned something about him helping Skyler with a tournament on Friday night, and my bet is *that* is where something happened — where something changed.

I smirk.

They think this is over? They think I'm going to just lie down, roll over and forget any of this happened? That I'm just going to move on, and maybe *one day* they can date, and I'll be just fine?

As if.

I'm Erin Xander, and I decided almost a year ago that for the rest of my life, I would take what I wanted — just as others had taken from me.

And I want Kip Jackson.

I'll get him back. There's no question, no doubt in my mind. They may think I've played all my cards, but I'm smarter than they give me credit for.

Kip loves me. He did when we were kids, and he still does now. Once Skyler is out of the way, he'll realize that.

Now, I just have to sit and wait for the perfect time to play my ace.

Game on.

Legacy takes place during the same semester as *Black Number Four*. Whether you've read it before now or not, you'll get a wider view of what was happening at Palm South University (especially between Kip and Skyler) if you read *Black Number Four* as you read this season. I will help guide you, letting you know which chapters to read before moving on to the next episode.

FOR THE FULL READING EXPERIENCE FOR THIS EPISODE, READ **CHAPTERS 13-15** IN *BLACK NUMBER FOUR* BEFORE CONTINUING ON TO EPISODE FIVE. (You'll get to see how Skyler was feeling when Erin was dating Kip, see inside Kip's plan to win Skyler back, experience the "make up scene" between them from Skyler's POV, and see the entire tournament from Kip's POV... not to mention, relive that couch sex scene. Ow oww. ;))

EPISODE 5

Ashlei

SPRING BREAK.

It's the Holy Grail of college, the one week every student looks forward to. For seven, blissful days, there are no exams, no homework, no fraternity or sorority events, and, though I haven't decided if it's a good thing or not yet — no internships.

So, it's no surprise to me that at the end of my last day in the office before break, I get called into Mr. Church's office.

I made sure I was the last one to leave again today, knowing it would be my last chance to see Brandon before I left. I also made sure to wear a skirt that's just a little too short, and a little too tight, and my hair up in a clip that I know he's dying to unfasten so he can see my hair spill over my shoulders.

After our last weekend together, I've got him under my spell.

And he's got me under his.

I tried to tell myself before that it was just our dynamite sex keeping us entwined, but after spending two days in his luxury downtown sky-rise condo, I couldn't lie to myself anymore. Brandon didn't just fuck me and then kick me out the door. No, he made me breakfast, and took me out on his boat, and rubbed my feet after a long night of dancing in the VIP section of one of his favorite clubs. He drove me to pole practice Sunday evening, kissing me in the car where the tinted windows hid us before watching me leave, knowing we wouldn't touch again for a while.

But this is what we signed up for, this cat and mouse game, this hiding in the shadows romance. For now, at least while I'm his intern, it's the safest bet. Not that he would lose his career, but his reputation might suffer for a while if he were discovered. And me?

Well, I'd be fucked. As in, all up in the booty hole, no lube, kind of fucked.

That should be the loudest thought in my head as I walk quickly and purposefully across the office toward his door.

I should be thinking of someone catching us, of what would happen if we had to pull footage off these cameras for some reason, what I would do if everything I've worked for at *Okay, Cool* came crashing to the ground — all because of my sex life.

But I can't.

All I can think about is his white dress shirt, top three buttons unfastened, sleeves rolled like they always are at the end of the day. All I can see is his dark, wicked eyes watching me as I ride him in his office chair. Slowly, step by step, the closer I get to his office, the more he overtakes every sense.

He's poison dressed as a delicious apple, and I'm powerless to resist temptation.

I have to have a bite.

I smooth my skirt and brush my hair out of my face as I near his door, rapping my knuckles just twice on the frame when I reach it.

"Mr. Church?" I ask innocently, batting my lashes. "You wanted to see me?"

Brandon smirks, kicking back in his chair and letting his eyes roam me shamelessly.

"I did. Come in," he commands, and that's the way his voice always is — demanding, deep and powerful and impossible to disobey. "Have a seat."

I do as he says, making a show of crossing my legs, one stiletto hanging between us as I fold my hands in my lap. Brandon eyes that heel, tracing the arch of it before his eyes flow all the way up my legs to my skirt.

They snap to my eyes next.

"I know you've been focused on Spring Break," he says, "But it's come to my attention that you're past due on a very important task you were given." Brandon pauses, his eyes growing dark. "You know I'm not a fan of missed deadlines."

Immediately, I scan through everything I'd had on my to-do list for the week, knowing there was absolutely no way I left anything off. But as Brandon's grin grows wider the more I pinch my brows together, I realize his accusation is part of the game.

He does love to play boss.

"Oh, my," I breathe, feigning disappointment in myself. "I'm so sorry, Mr. Church. It's just been such a busy week, I couldn't get everything done. But I'll make sure to handle it first thing on my return."

Brandon rests his elbow on one arm rest, twirling a pen between his fingers as he watches me. "I'm afraid that won't be enough, Ms. Daniels."

Why does that work for me? Why does him using my last name, talking to me like I'm just the intern, and looking at me like a hot apple pie mix into the perfect concoction to get me wet? When we're alone, in his apartment or on the boat, the way he makes love to me is reverent. It's slow and romantic, calculated and pure, like a slow Sunday morning bang every single time.

But here? In his office? Or on his jet? He's Mr. Church, and I'm Ms. Daniels — and we both know which one holds the power.

"I'm sorry," I breathe again, biting my lower lip and leaning forward enough to show a hint of cleavage. I hold my eyes open wide, my head tilted down a little as I look up at him through my lashes. "Are you going to punish me, Mr. Church?"

When the word *punish* leaves my lips, Brandon's eyelids flutter a bit, his nose flaring. And when I use his favorite name, the one that holds that power, he shakes his head, a lustrous gaze fixed hard on my mouth.

"I'm afraid I have no other choice."

His hands shoot out, grabbing the armrests of my chair and tugging until my legs are between his. As soon as those hands move from the chair to my thighs, sliding up the sensitive skin to spread me open, I reach for the collar of his shirt and pull his mouth to mine.

We both exhale the moment our lips touch, Brandon's hands still steadfast on their mission to reach my center. His pinky finger brushes the lace of my thong and I moan, bucking my hips, ready for more.

Always ready for *so* much more of him.

And he delivers, slipping one finger under the lace when I lift my hips again, a ragged *please* escaping my lips. But before that finger can dip all the way inside me, before that void is filled, Brandon's eyes widen at something behind me. He yanks his hand back like he's touched fire, his face ashen, and when I glance over my shoulder, I regretfully understand why.

"Well, well, well," Kimberly says, tongue pressing into her cheek as she glares at us with a satisfied grin. I thought I hated seeing that spiky hair and messy lipstick every morning, but it's nothing compared to the sinking stone I feel in my gut looking at her now.

Shit.

She crosses her arms over her chest, casually leaning a hip against the door frame. "I would say I'm surprised, but I called this from day one."

"Ms. Marks, it's after hours. You shouldn't—"

"I shouldn't *what*, Mr. Church?" she asks defiantly, chin raised high. "Please, I'm *dying* to hear you tell me what *I* shouldn't be doing right now."

At first, I swear I see Brandon shrink in size, his shoulders deflating a little like he's ready to accept defeat. But I know this man, and I know he doesn't react to someone trying to exert power over him well.

Unless it's me. And I'm naked.

"You shouldn't assume things," he finishes, standing.

As soon as he does, the power shifts, like the wind switching directions mid-storm. He stands so tall, so straight, his eyes on Kimberly like she just interrupted a meeting instead of walked in on him with his hand up my skirt.

"It's late, it's been a long week, and it's Spring Break. You should go," he says calmly, and I pull energy from him, straightening my shoulders and smiling at Kimberly like she has nothing on us, even though we both know we're in deep shit. "And consider the consequences of your actions, or your words, should you choose to utilize either."

Kimberly swallows, her confident stance weakened for a split second before she shakes her head, that wry grin back in place. "Oh, I will. Trust me when I say I will." She snaps her menacing gaze to me next. "Your days are numbered, slut."

She turns on the heel of her suede pumps, and damn it if she doesn't keep the cocky swing in her walk all the way to the front office doors. When they close behind her, the relief I thought we'd find once she was gone isn't there. In fact, the air is thicker, coated with a hot, wet heat like the Florida humidity — sticky and heavy and uncomfortable.

I just close my eyes, finally letting out a long, weighted breath.

"I'll fire her."

Brandon speaks first, his words punctuated and sure.

"I'll fire her immediately, have her manager call her tomorrow and tell her not to come back after Spring Break."

"You can't fire her," I say with a sigh, kneading my temples.

"I can, and I will."

"No." My voice is louder, eyes hard when I tilt my chin up to find his gaze. "That's a law suit waiting to happen, Brandon. There are cameras, and logs of our key access into the building. She'd have too much against us, and then you'd really put your career — your business — in jeopardy."

He shakes his head, frown firm. "I don't care. She can't take me down."

"She could, if you fire her," I quickly correct. "But if you just wait and let me handle this—"

"I can't *wait,*" he says incredulously, dropping back into his chair with a huff. He reaches for my hands, pulling them into his own with his eyes locked on mine, brows bent. "Don't you understand what this means, Ashlei? This could... this *will* ruin you. If she talks, if she tells *anyone,* you're in danger. Me?" He shakes his head. "I'll be fine. Even if you left, even if I had to submit to a slew of rumors or whatever, this is my business. *I* make the rules. Sleeping with the intern wouldn't hurt me. Hell, the guys would high five me, and the women would probably ask where the line is to be next."

The truth in his assessment stings like a slap to the face, and I swallow, nodding in agreement.

"That's all true. You would be fine, but my name, my reputation would be damaged. I wouldn't be able to stay here," I say quickly. "And, if I left, I'd have to go somewhere far enough away that they don't know about *Okay, Cool...* or what happened... *is happening* between us."

"So, out of the southeastern United States," he says gruffly, a curt shake of his head. "No. Absolutely not. We have to do something. I can't let this... I can't let *her...*" his voice fades, and he swallows hard. For the first time since his speech in Atlanta, emotion strangles him — all because he can't bear the thought of me being hurt.

Am I allowed to swoon right now? Because... SWOON.

"I know," I say, squeezing his hands. "I know. But, I think I have a plan."

"You do?"

I nod, the thought still forming in my head, like a caterpillar wrapping itself in a cocoon.

"But, you have to trust me," I say, forcing him to meet my eyes again. "And you have to wait."

"*Wait,*" he says, already shaking his head again. "We can't wait. She could run out and tell someone tonight. She could be telling someone right *now.*"

"She could, but she won't. Kimberly is smart," I say, believing it more when I say it. "And she's calculated. She's been waiting for this, to get something on me, to prove what she's always suspected — and she's not going to waste it as soon as she has it by just telling anyone who will listen.

No, she's going to sit on it, and she's going to come up with the perfect time to take me down."

"And when would that be?"

I swallow, almost smiling at the obviousness of my enemy. "The staff meeting on Monday. That's when they're announcing who the event coordinator is for the project we've been splitting. If it goes to me, which we both know it will, she'll do it then."

"Fuck!" Brandon runs his hands over his head, kicking back in his chair. "I hate this. I fucking hate this. I'm so, *so* sorry, Ashlei. I shouldn't have—"

"Don't," I cut him off.

Brandon swallows, his eyes searching mine.

"Don't tell me you shouldn't have touched me, or kissed me, or made me feel the way you have. I've been happier in the past few months with you than I have the past few years before I knew you existed," I admit, voice rough. "And I'm not letting some *girl* set on taking down a fellow female co-worker because of her own insecurities ruin that."

For a moment he just watches me, his eyes softening as the left side of his mouth quirks up in a soft smile. He rolls closer to me, framing my cheeks in his hands and planting a long, sweet kiss on my lips.

"You're amazing, you know that?"

He rests his forehead against mine as I smile, the heaviness gone if even for just a moment.

"Okay, I won't fire her," he concedes, as if that was still an option on the table. "What's your plan?"

I don't have the full answer to that question yet, but as it forms slowly in my mind, I see it playing out the way I want it to more and more clearly. It will take patience, and courage, and the timing has to be perfect. With one wrong move, or one mistake on my assumption of my opponent, everything I've worked for could go up in a dumpster fire.

"Simple," I say, trying to convince myself of the same. "We beat her to the punch line."

Bear

"HOW DO YOU LOOK like this," I ask Becca, one hand sweeping over her ridiculous physique, "when you eat donuts like *that*."

She bites off another hunk of the maple bacon donut she's devouring, grinning at me as much as she can with her mouth still full. Her eyes are shielded by round sunglasses, straight out of the seventies just like everything else about her, as we people watch on a bench in front of the fountain. I leave for the Spring Break cruise tomorrow, and it's my last chance to see her before I go.

On a shrug, she licks the frosting off her fingers and swallows. "Donuts don't count as calories."

"Tell that to the gut you're going to give me if I continue eating them with you." I pat my stomach — still hard as stone under my t-shirt.

She laughs. "Whatever. Pretty sure you could eat twice as many donuts as I do and not workout for three weeks and you'd *still* have that six-pack."

"What makes you think I have a six-pack under here?" I lift a brow. "Not like you've seen."

"Not like I haven't *tried* to see," Becca counters with a sassy head swivel. She opens up wide for the last bite, wiping her hands together and sending dry glaze all over the cement beneath us.

I don't have anything to retort to that. The fact that I've been dating Becca for almost two weeks now and we haven't hooked up is a miracle. The fact that she's *wanted* to and I've insisted we wait is a goddamn oxymoron. I'm Clinton Pennington — fucking is one of my favorite hobbies. But, everything feels different with Becca, and after Shawna, I know how fast *different* can turn into *gut-wrenchingly painful.*

"You'll see it soon enough."

"Mm-hmm," she grumbles, clearly not convinced.

"You will," I promise. "Trust me, I want to do…" I shake my head, eyes roaming down her body and back up again. She's wearing a bright orange dress, modest at the top but so short I know just a few more inches would reveal everything I want to see. "*So* many inappropriate things to you. But, I've never done slow before," I confess. "And, honestly, you're the first girl I've wanted to try with."

At that, Becca smiles, nudging me with her shoulder. She doesn't lean away again, but stays close, her skin as warm against mine as the sunshine. "Don't think saying cute shit like that is going to get you out of banging me for very long."

A laugh bursts out of me.

"I mean it," she continues, poking me in the chest. "I want the goods."

"Oh, you'll get them."

She crinkles her nose, pressing up on the bench until her lips meet mine. That first touch is always overwhelming to every sense, and for a moment I'm paralyzed, just breathing and kissing the most beautiful girl in the world. Then, my hands find her hair, and I pull her closer, realizing again how much I don't want to let her go — not even for a short cruise.

When she pulls back, Becca's eyes catch on something behind me, and she cringes. "Damn, poor girl."

I turn, searching the courtyard until I spot a girl with a mess of shit at her feet — books, pens, highlighters, planners, a Diet Coke can — the contents of that sprayed all over everything else on the ground. She huffs, letting her head fall back before dropping to her hands and knees. And when she does, she pulls her hair over one shoulder, and my heart squeezes painfully in my chest.

Erin.

"I know her," I murmur, carefully maneuvering until my arm is out from behind Becca's shoulders. I hop up, jogging over to where Erin is still retrieving everything that fell from her bag.

"I'm fine, I've got it," she says before even looking up, but I bend down anyway, working on the pens and highlighters as she stacks the papers.

Erin huffs, grimacing a little as she falls from her knees to her hip, grimacing a little as her skin scrapes against the sidewalk.

"I said, I'm—"

She stops when she sees it's me, a glimmer of something passing over her as she takes me in. Her eyes graze my shoulders, my chest, before they land on my own eyes.

"Fine?" I finish for her. "I know. Erin Xanders is the queen of *fine*."

She narrows her eyes at first, but then she smirks, covering her face with her hands as I continue picking up her stuff. "Ugh," she groans. "Is it Spring Break yet?"

I laugh. "Almost. Here," I say, handing her everything I've gathered. She shoves it into her bag, picking up the last book and forcing it inside, too. When I'm standing again, I hold out a hand, helping her upright.

"Thank you."

I nod, tucking my hands in my pockets. And then we're just standing there — me staring at her, her staring at me, and all I want to do is ask every question she still hasn't answered. I want to know if she's gotten help, if she's okay, if she's even remotely close to the girl I once knew who looked like her and wore her name.

Something is wrong.

I know what Erin looks like when she's hiding something, when she's hurting — but this is different. This is something deeper, another scar, another permanent mark on her that she's trying to learn to wear with the same grace as she does her others. The longer I watch her — the bags under her eyes, her nails chewed down to the nub, skin pale and slick — the more questions I have.

And she feels them.

Her cheeks flush, eyes skirting to the ground as she tucks a strand of hair behind her ear. "I'm fine, Bear. Really. You can stop looking at me like a charity case."

"I'm looking at you like a friend," I correct her. "Don't expect me to ever stop doing that."

She peeks up at me through her lashes, her brows bent, but then her gaze draws to my left.

"Hey," Becca says, sliding up beside me. Her arm wraps under mine, hand folding over my bicep as she eyes Erin curiously. "Everything okay?"

"Actually, you might want to take a picture and mark the date and time," I say. "Not very often you catch Erin Xanders anywhere outside the lines of perfect, poised, on time, and put together."

Erin laughs, shaking her head before reaching her hand out for Becca. "Hi, I'm Erin."

"Becca," she answers, eyes finding me before resting back on Erin. "Did you guys used to date or something?"

"Oh, God, no," Erin says quickly, and my jaw tenses, though I can't place the discomfort.

We *didn't* date, but she doesn't have to say it so sure, like it's impossible to fathom.

"Erin is the president of Kappa Kappa Sigma," I explain. "We're friends."

"That's the sorority you're going on Spring Break with, right?"

"It is," I confirm, noting that Erin can't stop staring at Becca. Her eyes sweep over every inch, and she shifts, tucking the strap of her messenger bag back in place.

"Yep," she echoes. "And I'm late for my last final, so I better be going. I'll see you tomorrow, Bear." She won't meet my gaze, barely glancing at me before she's smiling back at Becca. "It was nice to meet you."

And then she turns, strutting off in the same hurried fashion she always has.

I watch her go, a frustrated sigh leaving my lips before I turn back to Becca. She has her weight balanced on one hip, arms crossed, and one brow cocked as she peers up at me.

"Just friends, huh?"

"It's complicated," I try. "I promise, we never dated. But, we did hook up. Once."

"Hmm."

But instead of diving more into whatever the hell Erin and I were — *are?* — I take the chance to tease Becca.

"Wait..." I stroke my chin with my fingers and thumb, grinning. "Are you *jealous*?"

She shoves me in lieu of an answer, already storming back to our bench, but I grab her from behind and lift, crushing her into me with a classic Bear hug from behind.

"Put me down!" She laughs, pounding her little fists on my forearms. "Ugh, you're so infuriating."

"But how turned on are you right now?" I whisper against the skin of her neck.

That just earns me another punch.

When we're back on the bench, Becca tells me about her plans for the week, and I kiss her goodbye just a short hour later, wishing she was going to be on the boat taking me to the islands tomorrow. But on my walk back to the house, it's another girl on my mind.

One who maybe never left it in the first place.

I'll have a whole week with Erin on this cruise, and one thing I know for sure is I'm done playing this *I'm fine, I promise* game. This week, I'll get her to talk. She's gone long enough shoving everyone away, and I won't stand back and watch her deteriorate any longer.

This time, she'll let me in.

I won't take no for an answer.

Cassie

I HATE HIM.

I absolutely, without a doubt, whole-heartedly hate him.

Just standing within fifty feet of him now makes my jaw ache, my teeth are clenched so tight. Adam is laughing and smiling and goofing off with his brothers like he doesn't have a care in the world. And maybe he doesn't. Maybe, to him, everything is fine. Because to his knowledge, I've been "working on me," and everything between us is just fine.

I laugh.

Sure, he's assured me that there's nothing between him and Skyler, that they're just friends and he has no idea why she would ever say she had feelings for him. He's assured me that he's just trying to be there for her — *as a friend* — and there's nothing to worry about.

Of course, *I* know the background behind why Skyler said what she did about still being in love with Adam. I know the real plan behind her actions, the real motive, fueled by Erin — but Adam doesn't. And the fact that he still cares about her enough to run out of his own dance for *her* without even spending one full minute with *me*? Well, call me petty, but that hurts.

And no matter what he says, it's not okay.

I've done all the "me" stuff I can stomach. I've done yoga, and spa days, and long evenings on my longboard cruising the campus. I've studied, aced my midterms, picked up meditation and even pinned more than thirty-five possibilities for cutting my hair this summer. I'm over it, the me time, and whether *he* thinks I'm ready or not — I want *us* time now.

If Adam wants me, if he cares about me the way he says he does, then time is up.

All the games end this week.

But first, I have to play my own.

My stomach churns a little as I watch him, playing over my sister's words in my head. I called her yesterday, needing to talk to someone about Adam and actually use his name. The other girls still don't know about me and Adam, but my sister? She's a safe place.

"For the record, before I tell you anything else, I think you're being stupid," my sister, Claire, had said.

"*Me*? It's *him* who's being stupid! He's texting my Big, who he *used to date*, Claire."

"I get that, but have you seen his texts to her? Is he sending dick pics and asking her to make out?" She didn't let me respond. "No, he's not. He's being a *friend* to her, just like he told you he was." Claire had clucked her tongue then. "Adam is being mature beyond his years, if you ask me. I can't think of one single guy who tried to date me in college and told me I should take some time to focus on myself, or held me in their arms and said anything even close to as sweet as everything he's told you. If anything, they wanted me to lose myself in them, to do whatever they wanted to do. I'm telling you, if you're still single when you're my age, you'll kill for a guy like Adam."

I'd huffed, staring at my pile of clothes on my bed, still trying to figure out what to pack for Spring Break.

"Just help me," I had begged, my voice soft. "Please."

And with that, Claire had cracked, giving me advice that I should have already known myself.

"It's the oldest trick in the book, but there's a reason that sucker is still in there. Men are simple creatures, and boys are even more so. It's simple, really — you just need to make him jealous. If you think he's sleeping on you, if you think he's too comfortable or not moving fast enough, show him that other people are noticing you and you've got options."

"But I don't," I'd quickly pointed out.

"Doesn't matter. It can be a friend or one of *his* friends — anyone. Doesn't matter what they look like or what kind of connection you have. If there's another guy even *talking* to you, trust me, Adam will notice."

And so, I'd stewed on that advice overnight, packing and repacking and staying up way too late to feel functional on my first day of Spring Break. I still hadn't had any idea of what I'd do, of when I'd make my move.

But now, staring across the deck at Adam, Kade, and their other brothers, I know the time is now.

The cruise ship is buzzing with the energy of Spring Break, so similar to my first one last year and yet heightened somehow. This isn't just a road trip to Key West — it's an all-inclusive *cruise*. For the next five days, our only obligation is to drink, party, and soak up the sun.

It's college bliss.

And I'm damn sure not spending it alone.

As soon as the safety drill ends, we all disperse, making our way to various parts of the ship. The girls and I are on a mission to snag prime real estate at the pool, and as soon as we make it to the top deck, I spy my first opportunity.

I grab Skyler's arm, tugging her toward Adam and his brothers before I can talk myself out of my next move. Without warning, I launch myself at Kade's back, wrapping my arms around his neck and my legs around his waist in a forced piggyback ride.

"It's Spring Break, bitches!" I yell, loud enough to cause several people to turn around and look — Adam included.

He smiles at first when he realizes it's me, but his eyes darken at the sight of my legs wrapped around Kade, of his hands holding my thighs in place as he adjusts me on his back. Kade laughs, smacking my butt playfully, and Adam's jaw clenching is the last thing I see before I pull my attention back to the task at hand.

"Where's our shots?" I ask.

I don't even realize it's Kip standing next to Kade, not until I glance over and see that's who Skyler jumped on, mirroring me. For a second, I see it — how good they would have been together, had it not been for Erin. And even though I know he's called things off with Erin, we all know there's no chance for Skyler now. It'd be against girl code, and I know my Big well enough to know she'd never break that.

"I've been on this boat for seven-and-a-half minutes now and I still don't have a frozen, fruity drink in my hand," Skyler chimes in.

Kip stares up at her over his shoulder, a wry grin on his face. "Well, that sounds like a problem I can solve."

The next thing I know, I'm hanging on for dear life as Kade and Kip take off sprinting toward the bar. I squeal extra loud as we pass Adam and his brothers, but I don't take my eyes off the bar, acting like I don't even realize we passed him.

"Okay, transportation complete," Kade says, dropping me to my feet once we make it to the pool bar. "Now the only question is — which shot?"

"Hmmm... something fruity."

The bartender overhears, holding up an "okay" sign with his fingers to let us know he's got just the thing. Kade and I chat while she makes our drinks, and anytime I can, I touch his arm, laugh at his jokes, stare into his eyes. I'm pleasantly aware of the other set of eyes locked on me at the present moment, and that only fuels my fire.

"To Spring Break," Kade says, holding up his shot glass to mine.

"May we survive it."

He laughs. "Hear, hear!"

We down the shot, Kade howling when his is down, and then he winks at me before trotting over to join his group of brothers. Skyler is preoccupied with Kip at the bar, so I sip my piña colada, waiting for her to finish up so we can make our way to the pool.

And just like always — I feel him before I see him.

I wonder if that will ever go away, the way my body reacts to Adam before I should even know he's nearby. Will he ever be able to surprise me, to catch me off guard, or will my hair always stand on end, my stomach always tighten, my heart always skip before picking up a notch?

"Happy Spring Break," he says, tapping his knuckles on the bar.

"Yep."

The word leaves my mouth with a pop, and I take another drink, not so much as glancing his way.

"You okay?"

"I'm great!" I force a smile, finally meeting his eyes. "How about you?"

Two lines form between his brows, like he can't figure out if he should believe me or not. And he shouldn't. He definitely shouldn't.

"I'm good... I saw you with Kade," he says, broaching

the subject like Mr. Subtle himself. "I didn't realize you two knew each other."

On the outside, I'm calm and cool, merely shrugging and taking another sip of my drink. But inside, I'm wearing the most satisfied grin.

"Oh, yeah, we met at rush," I say coolly. "I didn't really talk to him much until the Valentine's Day dance. We hung out a lot that night."

I practically shoot lasers at him with that last line, making my message clear. It's been almost a month since that dance, and I'm still not over the fact that he ran out with Skyler that night. Yes, he explained later. And yes, we've hung out since. But still, I know he's texting Skyler, and I know I'm tired of the *let's take this slow* bullshit.

"Oh," Adam answers.

He pauses a moment, sliding closer to me, his pinky finger brushing mine. And as much as I want to hold his hand, as much as I want to hear what he has to say next, I cut him off with his mouth still open.

"Well, have fun today."

I turn, linking my arm in Skyler's and guiding her toward the pool where Erin, Ashlei, and Jess are already set up. We dip our feet in the cool water, clinking our glasses together and celebrating the start of the best week of spring semester.

I don't have to glance over my shoulder to know Adam is still watching, and I hope like hell he's feeling even a margin of the kind of hurt he made me feel the night of the dance. I've never done anything like this before, never been about playing games, but if that's the way to get his attention, I'm damn sure not above it.

I served the ball, now it's his move.

He better choose it wisely.

Skyler

SPRING BREAK.

Every year, we count down the days until this magnificent week. Every year, we push our diets, tan as much as we can, and buy way too many clothes because we have "nothing to wear" — regardless of our closets being stuffed full of clothes.

But this year? I'd almost forgotten.

I've been so focused on Kip, on trying *not* to focus on him, that I forgot how much fun Spring Break is. I forgot that I'd have the week with my sisters, that I'd have the chance to earn my entry fee for the tournament by doing the small tournaments on board, that I'd have days in the sun and nights dancing the hours away with my favorite people in life.

But I could never forget that *he* would be here, too.

It's been a week since Kip and I hooked up, since the night of the tournament downtown, and ever since then, we've played our cards as carefully as we could. A few stolen glances here and there, a hot kiss in the Greek library, a few text messages — all disguised by putting different names on our phone numbers just in case. I feel like I'm cheating on someone, even though I'm single, but I don't want to hurt Erin.

I *can't* hurt her.

Until she gives me the sign that she's fully over Kip, this will have to do. I tell myself I can handle it, I can keep everything on the down low, can control myself around big groups of people and sneak around to touch him the way I want to. But when he slides up behind me as I place another bet at the roulette table, I know I'm walking a very thin, very dangerous line.

"Why black number four?" he asks over my shoulder.

His breath warms my neck, and I smile, keeping my composure as best I can and focusing on my chips laying on the table.

"It's a long story," I answer, taking a marginal step back — enough to touch him, just a little bit, our bodies sparking to life at the contact.

"I'm in no rush. I'm actually on vacation, believe it or not."

I roll my eyes, taking a sip of my drink as other players place their bets.

"My dad has this formula," I say, smiling at the mention of him. It's been a while since I've talked to either of my parents, and I miss them. They were my best friends before I had any at all. "He uses it to find out people's lucky numbers. He used to do it all the time, sort of like his party trick, I guess."

Kip is so warm behind me, so close, I nearly forget what I was saying. But I shake my head, brushing it off.

"Anyway, obviously he figured mine out the day I was born, and it's been drilled into my head ever since then that my lucky number is four." I shrug. "When I played little league sports, four was always my number. If anyone asks me to choose a number between one and ten, that's my go-to — always. I have a tattoo with it, I purposefully buy scratch-offs that are the fourth ones on the roll, I mean, literally anything involving numbers leads me straight to number four."

I smile, knowing how superstitious and, frankly, ridiculous I sound, but continuing regardless.

"And, honestly," I say. "It really is lucky for me. I've won a lot of money by betting horses racing with the number four and on the scratch-offs, too."

I pause, turning to face him to deliver the last of my story. His strikingly blue eyes meet mine with a glittering interest, and my knees shake, my hands reaching for his forearms to steady myself.

"Except, something weird happens in poker," I say, doing my best not to drop my focus from the story to how delicious he looks in his crisp white button-up and navy blue dress pants. "For whatever reason, anytime I'm dealt a black number four in poker, whether it's a spade or a club, I lose the hand. No shit," I say, holding up my hands. "Even if I have a pair of aces in the hole, if a four comes up — I know I'm going to lose." I chuckle. "Kind of ironic, isn't it? My lucky number screws me in the game I need it most."

Turning back toward the table, I gesture toward my bet. "So, because I'm superstitious and a little crazy, I play black number four on roulette. Every time. I guess I'm convinced that if a black four can hit for me here, it'll reverse my luck with the cards."

"Has it ever hit for you before?" Kip asks.

I scrunch my nose, half because I can't believe he's actually interested in this stupid, crazy story and half because I realize my theory about number four always being lucky except for poker is a little flawed.

"No, it hasn't," I finally concede. "So, I guess my lucky number is kind of cursed in this game, too."

Kip doesn't answer, but instead reaches into his pocket for his wallet. Before I can even register it, he flicks a crisp one-hundred-dollar bill on the table. The dealer exchanges it for one black chip, and Kip's eyes find mine as he plucks it from the green.

"Maybe you're just not betting enough," he muses, voice low. "Maybe your lucky number feels cheated."

And then, he slaps that one-hundred-dollar chip right on top of my measley one dollar one.

I'm already shaking my head when I turn to face him, my eyes wide with worry. "Kip! Don't do that, that's so much money." My heart races, knowing he's about to lose a hundred dollars all because of some stupid superstition of mine. "It won't hit, it never does, I don't want to be the reason you lose that!"

"No more bets," the dealer says behind us, and all eyes move to the ball spinning on the number wheel — except for mine.

"Too late now." Kip grins, and I just groan, covering my face with my hands.

"Oh, my God. I can't breathe."

Kip laughs, but I can't hear anything past the *click-click-clicking* of the ball on the wheel as it rolls over the wooden wheel. It'll drop any moment now.

"You have a tattoo?" Kip asks. "I don't know how I missed that."

I laugh at his stupid attempt to distract me, still covering my face with my hands. "If you're still talking to me after this, maybe I'll show you later."

Kip leans in closer, his voice a growling whisper. "Looking forward to it."

Heat creeps up my neck as I nudge him, but I still can't take my hands down. I know the ball is going to land anywhere but on the number we bet on, and it makes me sick to think about how Kip will look at me once he realizes I cost him a hundred bucks. The ball hits one of the silver knobs, the sound as distinct as my own mother's voice, and the bouncing begins.

My heart kicks up another notch, beating painfully hard in my chest.

"I seriously can't breathe," I whisper, and Kip's hand slides down to my hip. He squeezes it gently, but doesn't say a word.

And then, a gasp from the other players at the table as the dealer announces the winning bet.

"Black four."

Chaos. Complete and utter chaos.

Everyone at the table cheers, regardless of their own bets as I throw my hands up into the air and stare at the ball resting in the little black crevice of number four on the wheel. I still don't believe it, not when I wrap my arm around Kip, not when we jump up and down screaming like a couple of lunatics, and not when the dealer puts the little glass marker on top of our bets, sealing the deal.

"OH MY GOD! That did not just happen!" I stare at the marker, blinking over and over, the reality not sinking in. "Kip, that's like three thousand dollars," I whisper, turning back to him with my hands fisting his dress shirt. "Holy shit!"

The rest of the table laughs, my whisper anything but discreet. Even the dealer cracks a smile as she calls the pit boss over to check the pile of chips she's piled up for Kip.

"Well, I guess we better find a really awesome way to spend it tomorrow on the island, huh?" Kip says, spinning me around to face him again. "See?" His eyes zero in on me, that same flood of weakness consuming my knees. "You just needed to have a little more faith in your number. That's all."

I smile, throat tightening with emotion. There are so many things I want to say to him, so many places I want to take him, so many things I wish I could take back, and so much time lost I wish I could have again. How is it that my entire life was turned upside down by a transfer, a silly boy with blue eyes, blond hair, and glasses? He walked onto our campus and into my life and nothing was ever the same.

I know it never will be again.

"I think I just needed you," I argue. "Maybe you're my lucky charm."

His face falls a little, a shadow of something similar to guilt crossing over him before he grins. It happens so fast, I know I must have imagined it, but I wonder what was going through his mind.

"I'll take that title," he says. "Am I the kind of lucky charm you never take off? You know, the kind you shower with?"

Kip waggles his brows and I just roll my eyes, turning to collect chips from the dealer. There are a few more congratulations from the players at the table and then new bets are placed, our win forgotten.

When I face him again, my eyes trail his entire body, knowing that what lies underneath those clothes far outweighs the threads.

"Well, I did say I'd show you my tattoo," I tease.

Kip bites his lip, and just like that, we're racing to find our next hiding spot.

I can't wait to have his lips on me, to have his hands on me, to have his body on mine. And more than anything, I can't wait until Erin gives me even one small sign that she's over him.

Because I can't wait until he's mine — *truly* mine — for everyone to see.

Cassie

ON THE SECOND NIGHT of Spring Break, I press a cool hand to my cheek, sipping on my frozen daiquiri as I attempt to soothe my sunburn. It's not bad, just a light blush of pink over my face, arms, and legs, but it's enough for me to feel it. My cool hand only soothes it for a moment, a temporary fix before the burn singes through and leaves my hand just as hot.

Yesterday, I got so drunk I ended up turning in early after dinner. Then, today, we partied on the island, Kip blowing the money he won last night on a couple of cabanas for his brothers and our sisters. Again, I found myself drinking to forget about Adam, to try to avoid him *and* my feelings.

Now, sitting at the bar with my sisters as we try to turn our day drinking into a successful night, I feel silly.

No, I feel stupid.

Before I came to Palm South, I rarely ever drank. I'd had a few wine coolers, stolen from my mom's stash, but other than that, I'd never indulged. And while I love having a great time with my sisters, I've never used alcohol before as a way to avoid, as an attempt to feel better.

I found out quickly it doesn't work.

If anything, the more I drink, the worse I feel. The game I'm playing with Kade to make Adam jealous only adds to how shitty I feel, and I just want it all over with.

I just want to talk to Adam.

Sighing, I push past the sickening drop of my stomach as I finish off my drink and stand, searching the piano bar for the one guy I've been avoiding.

"You okay?" Ashlei asks, eying my empty glass. "Need another drink?"

My stomach rolls at the thought of it. "I think I just need some fresh air. I'll be back."

She frowns, but nods. "Okay, babe. Let me know if you need anything."

I somehow manage a smile, and then I'm shoving through the crowd of fraternity brothers and sorority sisters, making my way toward the deck. Adam comes into view once I cross the room, and at the sight of me, his face falls, brows bending together. He pushes off where he was leaning on the wall, meeting me in the middle of the room with his hands in his pockets.

The red polo he's wearing blazes against his tan biceps, and I watch the muscles flex and move as he makes his way toward me. His hair is mussed, as if he didn't even shower after spending a day on the island. He looks like he just threw on new clothes and embraced the salty waves, and somehow, he looks even sexier than if he were all dressed up, hair gelled back and bow tie in place. And I can't stop staring at his arms, wishing I was in them, wishing they were my place to call home.

"Hey," he says over the sound of a new song starting when he reaches me. The entire room erupts into cheers before I can answer, a drunken choir pouring out the first verse of "Tiny Dancer."

"Hi."

I cross one arm over my middle, holding onto my opposite elbow and staring down at my open-toed heels. I paired them with a pair of white, high-waisted shorts and an Easter yellow crop top. I wanted to stand out, to make him notice me.

Now I just want to hide.

I should say something, I realize as we stand there — starting with an apology. But all I can do is stand there, staring at my feet, and even that is a task. If I wasn't using every ounce of strength I have left, I'd be on my knees, or curled into the fetal position, begging him to leave me alone.

Begging him to never leave.

Adam doesn't say a word, just gently grabs my hand and guides me through the crowd, the same direction I was heading before I saw him. In a matter of moments, we're out of the bar and on the outside deck, the rambunctious sound of music and singing replaced with the soft crash of the waves against the ship.

My hands wrap around the railing, the cool metal soothing as much as it is shocking. And I can't look at him, can't bear to have him look at me — not after how I've acted.

"You okay?" he asks after a moment, sliding up to rest his elbows on the railing next to me.

I pinch my eyes shut, willing myself not to cry. "I think we both know the answer to that."

"Cassie…"

His hand moves for mine, but I rip it away as soon as our fingers brush.

"No," I say, voice firm. I lift my eyes to his, swallowing down my nerves. "No, I get to talk this time."

Adam doesn't argue, his face ridden with a mixture of apology and shame before I even start talking.

"I can't do this anymore, Adam. I can't."

My voice breaks, tears filling my eyes, though I don't blink to let them fall. Instead, I hold my shoulders back, standing straighter.

"I know you want me to focus on me, but I have. I've had months to myself, and I appreciate that you pushed me to do that, that you encouraged me to find myself again, to be happy *alone* — without a boyfriend." I sniff. "But I love you," I whisper, and that breaks me, two tears spilling down my hot cheeks as Adam's shoulders crumple. "And I don't want to be without you anymore."

Adam steps forward, his arms reaching out for me and pulling me into his chest. He wraps me in the tightest hug, one that tells me more than words that he doesn't want to be without me, either. And even though I'm still hurting, comfort sneaks in, warming me from the inside out.

"I don't want to play the games," I say through my tears. "I don't want to wonder what you're texting Skyler, or why you can touch me but not *be* with me. I don't want to do anymore yoga or meditation or post anymore stupid Facebook statuses about having my 'me time'."

Adam chuckles, and I can't help the smile that cracks through my tears.

"I don't want to flirt with other guys to make you mad."

He sighs, stroking my hair with one hand before planting a kiss to my forehead. "That worked very well, by the way."

"I'm sorry," I whisper, pulling back just enough to look up into his eyes. "I did that to hurt you, even when I know you would never do anything to hurt me. I wanted a reaction. I wanted you to care."

"I've always cared."

I watch him for a moment before softly shrugging. "I couldn't tell."

Adam sighs again, framing my face with his hands as his thumbs wipe away the tears from my cheeks.

"I'm so, so sorry, Cassie. For everything. I thought I knew what was best for you, thought I was doing the right thing by having you take some time for yourself. But all I did was hurt us both."

I swallow, leaning into his touch.

"I meant everything I said about you spending time on *you*, and I'm glad you have. But, I was wrong for chasing Skyler out of the dance, for putting her above you even though that was not my intention. I care about her, Cassie," he says, and the words are like ice picks through my heart. "I do. But as a *friend* only. I won't lie, her profession of love for me threw me. For a moment, I wondered if I'd read our entire relationship wrong. But, there's something going on between her and Kip, and I know I was just part of her game." He smirks. "Your Big is really good at playing those, too."

I scoff. "Don't I know it."

"But, I focused on making sure *she* was okay," he confesses. "When I should have been focusing on you. And I can't take that back, but I can apologize. I am truly sorry, and I don't ever want you to feel like you're anything but the most important girl in my life." His thumb swipes away a fresh tear, one corner of his mouth quirking into a soft smile. "Because you are, Cassie. You are everything to me."

"Then let me in," I whisper. "Please, Adam. Let me in. Be with me."

"Would you stop?" he says, laughing and wiping away more tears. "I'm trying to do the apologize and grovel thing and you're just being so damn adorable I can't focus."

I smile, but can't help crying even more as he pulls me into him. He hugs me tight, kissing my hair.

"I'm yours, Cassie McBee," he whispers. "I always have been. I always will be."

He lifts my chin with his knuckle, and when his lips touch mine, every game, every fight, every ounce of hurt that's ever existed between us melts into a puddle at our feet. I press onto my toes, strengthening our kiss, my arms wrapping around his shoulders and pulling him closer.

"I love you," he says softly, the words hot on my mouth. "I know I haven't shown you that, not in the right way, but I promise that from this moment on, I will do everything I can to prove it to you."

"You better."

We both laugh at that, and then he kisses me again, and for the first time since the semester started, I finally feel whole again.

I finally feel okay.

Erin

FOR THE FIRST TIME, I hate that my plan is falling into place.

Ever since Kip broke up with me, I have been scheming to get him back. I knew I would, it was just a matter of time.

And the first step in my plan? Prove myself right about Skyler.

I had to know she had betrayed me, that she was the reason he broke up with me. I knew it in my gut the moment he said we were done, but I had to play my cards right. I opened up to Skyler, told her I understood and I was sorry I ever put her through my stupid plan. And tonight, getting ready for our second night out on Spring Break, I mentioned being ready to move on — to bring a guy home. I put up the front that I was over Kip, and just like I knew she would, Skyler took the bait.

She's been staring at him all night.

At least for the past week, they've been *trying* to hide their relationship. Tonight, there might as well be a blinking neon heart hanging over them with arrows pointed at each of their heads.

And even though I know it's working, even though I know she'll reveal everything soon, it hurts. I thought it wouldn't, thought I could be strong enough to brush it off. But when I watch him watch her, I know they've touched. When I see her smile at him, I know they've laughed.

And in my heart, I know my own Little betrayed me.

It wasn't fair, what I asked of her, but I never imagined she'd go behind my back and be with Kip, anyway. What hurts the most is that she did it while I was still *with* him — before I even had the chance to see if we could make it

"

work. Kip is *mine,* he's supposed to be with me, but she just couldn't stand it.

I know I hurt her, and I know I'm not perfect — but what she did to me is worse.

I've been drinking too much. I realized that earlier on the island, but lost the ability to care. Instead, I kept drinking, and now, at almost midnight, everything is blurry. I can't even hide my glares toward Skyler, or my longing stares toward Kip. I can't hide the fact that I'm two seconds away from losing my shit. But I have to.

I have to hold it together.

The piano bar is packed to the brim, and after the third round of "Benny and the Jets", I'm about ready to throw in the towel for the night and head up to my room. But just when the thought crosses my mind, I see Kip being shoved toward the piano by his brothers, all of them chanting his name.

I blink through the fog in my head, leaning against the bar as I focus on Kip. He slides behind the piano with a wry grin as the cruise ship pianist stands, microphone in hand.

"Ladies and gentlemen, I'm told we have a pretty good piano player here on board from Palm South University," he says. The entire bar erupts into cheers — even the brothers of Omega Chi. Somehow, a sort of bond has been formed between the opposing fraternities, though I'm skeptical it will last past this week.

Kip seems almost shy at the piano, his cheeks reddening as everyone starts chanting his name. I open my mouth to join in, but can't be sure if I actually do.

I'm really, *really* drunk.

After a moment, his hands move over the keys, a soft melody filling the bar. "Go easy on me, guys," he says into the microphone, and every girl — including me — melts into a puddle on the floor.

How could we not?

Kip's wearing a hot pink button-up, the sleeves shoved up to his elbows, hair mussed, and of course, he's wearing his damn glasses — which apparently make every girl weak. But all I can stare at is the eyes *behind* those frames as he starts playing a familiar song, and as soon as he leans into the mic and sings the first line, the entire bar goes silent.

And his eyes lock onto Skyler.

My stomach rolls, every shot of alcohol threatening to make a reappearance as he belts out the ballad. He doesn't take his eyes of Skyler, and every smooth croon of his voice enhances my urge to vomit. I know I'll never hear this Michael Bublé song the same again, and I know I'll never want to.

I hate it. I hate him.

I hate *her*.

As it always does when I'm drinking, time passes in a morphed loop, the song seeming to replay over and over even when Kip finishes and stands from behind the piano. The bar is alive with cheers, everyone clapping and chanting his name again, but that's nothing compared to how loud they are when Skyler jumps behind the piano with him.

Then, time slows down.

Every cheer morphs, the sounds muted, and I watch in slow motion as Skyler grabs Kip by his collar and pulls his lips to hers. Somehow, I know the crowd is louder, but I only hear a ringing in my ears. I blink, trying to decipher what I feel, but everything is numb. Just like it was when I aborted my child. Just like it was when four men pushed inside of me without me saying they could.

It's defense mode, a method of survival.

I'm no longer a human with feelings and fears. I'm a machine — an unbreakable force.

Or maybe I'm nothing at all.

"Ex…" Jess starts, her hand reaching for my wrist. "You okay?"

I sniff, forcing a smile and blinking away the fog. "I'm good! I'm going to go find someone to fuck."

Ashlei's eyes widen at that. "Maybe you should just chill tonight, you've been drinking a lot."

"I'm fine."

"I don't know, Grand Big," Cassie chimes in. "Maybe we should just go back to the room."

"I said, I'm *fine,*" I say louder. "If you girls want to call it a night, be my guest. I'm going to the club."

I don't wait for them to answer before I'm pushing through the crowd, avoiding Kip and Skyler at all costs. A hand wraps around my wrist from behind, and I whip around, ready to unleash my anger on Jess and tell her to fuck off and leave me alone.

But it isn't Jess.

It's Clinton.

His grip on me softens, but he doesn't let me go, his brows bent into a hard line over his dark eyes.

"Let me go," I demand, but I don't rip away from him. I don't have the strength.

"Only if you talk to me."

I scoff. "What is there to talk about?"

"I don't know, maybe you should tell me. Because clearly you're not okay right now." He shakes his head. "What's going on? What's happening with you and Sky, with you and this new kid?"

I finally rip my wrist from his hands, tucking my arms over my chest. "Doesn't matter."

"It does to me."

My heart squeezes, façade dropping at his words. I trail my eyes up his broad chest to lock on his, and the sympathy I find there, the genuine care — it nearly kills me. I want to fall into him, to break in his arms, to let him fix me.

But he can't.

No one can.

"Please, Erin," he tries again, his hand reaching for mine.

I let him take it, let him thread his fingers with my own. Black and white, large and small, hard and soft. We don't make sense, and yet Clinton is the only one who can make me feel anything at all anymore.

"Talk to me. Let me help you. I..." He pauses, wetting his lips. "You're not alone, okay? Even when you feel like you are. I'm here."

My eyelids flutter, the threat of tears stinging my throat so strongly I nearly let them fall. But instead, I pull my hand from his, my mother's voice loud in my foggy mind as I steel myself.

"I am alone," I whisper. "And I prefer it that way."

His chest deflates. "Erin."

"Goodnight, Bear."

I turn and leave him behind, along with the rest of my morals. It's like I lost the very last piece of myself in that bar, in that moment, and now I'm just the black, charred shell of a woman who once was. I only want justice. I only want what's rightfully mine.

I only want revenge.

And I don't care who I hurt, or who I lose — I will get it.

Jess

"ANDDD SHE'S BACK, ladies and gents!" Ashlei announces, smacking my hand in a high five as I wipe leftover beer from my mouth.

I let out a loud belch, slamming down my empty cup on the pool bar. "Back and better than ever."

"Gross."

"You love me."

"Also true."

Ashlei taps the bar, and the bartender refills our cups before we make our way back to our lounge chairs at the edge of the pool. Ashlei slides into hers gracefully as I plop down on mine, crossing my ankles with a satisfied sigh.

"Spring Break fixes everything. It's science."

Ashlei chuckles. "It is a pretty great medicine. I'm glad you're feeling better, babe. I've missed you."

"I've been right here," I argue, poking out my bottom lip.

"I know, but you've been distracted. Heartbreak diet and all." Ashlei shrugs. "And then you were trying to use Greg as a distraction, which took up all your time. I'm just saying, I'm glad I have my feisty best friend back."

"Me, too."

We both smile, and I cheers her cup with mine before taking a swig.

"How's the internship going?" I ask as we both kick back.

Ashlei sprays her legs with tanning oil, rubbing it in as her lips pull to one side. "It's... good. A little challenging this semester, but nothing I can't handle."

"Damn straight. You're Ashlei Davison — Certified Bad Ass. But what's been going on?"

She sighs, tossing the tanning oil back in her beach bag and leaning back. "Just some drama with another intern. She was with me last semester, too. She has it out for me for some reason, just determined to take me down."

"Want me to cut her?"

Ashlei chokes on a laugh. "No, but thanks. With Kimberly, I've learned I have to fight dirty just like she does. Dirty, but gracefully, if that makes any sense."

"Of course. Brain fighting instead of fist fighting."

"You could say that."

"Well, I'm here if you need to talk out any plans. How's that hot ass CEO of yours? You let him bend you over a desk yet?"

Ashlei coughs on her beer, wiping foam from her lips as she faces me. "What? No, of course not."

I cock a brow. "I was kidding..." Then, I gasp. "WAIT! Have you *actually* let him bend you over a desk? Oh, my God, Ashlei, you better spill the juice. NOW."

"Shhhh," she spits, looking around us like anyone is at all interested in our conversation.

"Oh, stop. Everyone's drunk. And *you're* hiding something. Spill. Now."

She groans, setting her beer on the table between us before covering her face with her hands. "Fine. I'm banging him."

"YOU LITTLE OFFICE WHORE!" I scream, and she smacks me as I laugh. "Oh, my God. I'm so happy. And so proud. Tell me more! Tell me *everything*."

And though I have to pull every little detail out of her, Ashlei gives me the dirt, making me gasp over and over again the more she reveals. By the end of her story, when

I'm all caught up, I'm pretty sure I could catch flies with how big my mouth is hanging open.

"So, let me get this straight. You've been banging your fine ass CEO since last semester — on his private jets and his fucking *yacht*, AND in the office — and you never told me?"

Ashlei rolls her eyes. "That's what you're taking from all this?"

"Well, that's clearly what's most important, here."

"Oh, my bad. I thought what was most important was that Kimberly *saw us* and my entire career is in jeopardy. How silly of me."

I wave her off. "No way. Like you said, you've got a plan. Put that bitch on blast when you get back. If you own what you and Mr. Church have before she has the chance to throw you under the bus, *she's* the one who will look like an idiot."

"I hope so."

"I know so. Now," I say, draining my beer. "Go get us another round, and then I want details on the yacht sex because seriously what the fuck."

Ashlei laughs, shaking her head and taking my empty cup before prancing off toward the bar.

Stretching in my chair, I let my head drop back and tap my bare toes to the beat of the steel drum the band is playing on the pool deck. The sun warms my skin, blending with the heat from the alcohol, and I smile. Greg was a wake-up call, and ever since he handed me my ass at Ralph's, I've been on a mission to get back to the old me. It hasn't been easy, since most of my nights end with me thinking about Jarrett, no matter how hard I try not to. But, the more time passes, the easier it gets. And the more drinks I have, the more I remember what it felt like to be single — the *before Jarrett* era.

Spring Break? Well, it's exactly what I needed. Sunshine, booze, and quality time with my sisters. This is what college is about. This is what Jess Vonnegut does best.

This is my element.

At least, until I'm suddenly covered in shade.

I scowl, lifting my head and pulling my sunglasses down to peer at the shadow-inducing figure.

"Oh, God. Not you again."

Kade smirks, holding his arms open wide. "You know you missed me."

"Like I miss a yeast infection."

His arms drop, his face screwing up in confusion as he considers what I've said. Then, he points a finger at me. "That's gross. But you're still hot."

He plops down in Ashlei's seat, giving me my sun back in exchange for an annoying new neighbor.

An annoyingly *hot* neighbor, too — but annoying, nonetheless.

"What's shakin', sexy?"

"Ugh."

I reach for my drink, and then remember I don't have one, which leaves me groaning again. Kade just smiles, handing me his beer, and I take a large swig before handing it back to him.

I met Kade on the island yesterday, hanging out with Kip and his brothers in their cabanas. I'd seen him around, knew he was a new Alpha Sigma brother, but yesterday he was like a fly I couldn't get rid of. He hovered around me, playing drinking games and following me every time I went to the water. He even pulled me out to dance at the club last night, which apparently I was too intoxicated to say no to.

He's so young. And so annoying.

And yet for some reason, I'm intrigued by him.

Maybe it's his goofy, somehow sexy grin that is permanently plastered on his face. Maybe it's his ridiculously cheesy pick-up lines, or his blatant ogling of my tits when he thinks I'm not looking. He's like a little kid, one I want to take under my wing.

And simultaneously give a wedgie.

"I thought I got rid of you after yesterday."

"Nah," Kade answers, resting his hands behind his head. "After watching you do three beer bongs in a row in that skimpy little bikini you wore yesterday, you're stuck with me. Sorry, not sorry, princess."

I scan his built frame, which — in my opinion — doesn't match his personality. He looks like a beef head, tattoos sprawling down his left side and bicep, his dark hair cut short and gelled like a *Jersey Shore* cast member. But his goofy ass grin combats all of that hard muscle, the only evidence I need that he's still just a kid.

"Don't call me that."

"What should I call you, then? Please, tell me the dirty nicknames you love." He rolls over, resting his chin on one hand as he leans in. "I bet you want to call me Daddy, huh? I'm down for that, just so you know."

I try to roll my eyes again, but a laugh bursts out of me before I get the chance. "Who *are* you? Does that ever work for you? Like, ever?"

Kade shrugs. "Wouldn't you like to know."

"How old are you?"

"Twenty-one in September, gorgeous."

"You're a baby."

"Does that make you a cougar?"

I shake my head, ready to pop off a retort when Kade chuckles and holds his hands up, rolling over on his back again.

"I'm just kidding. But seriously, how are you today? Working on that tan, I see."

I'm so annoyed, and yet I smile.

Why do I smile?

"I'm fine," I answer, clipped. "Don't you have somewhere to be? Some brothers to annoy or something?"

"I do, but I'd rather sit here and stare at you."

I shake my head again, but can't help the blush that spreads on my cheeks. *God,* he's so young, and so fucking childish. Why is that somehow adorable and infuriating all at once?

Kade reaches out, his thumb brushing my cheek. "Was that a blush I saw?"

"Don't flatter yourself." I smack his hand away.

"God, I love when you get angry. That little scowl, those pursed lips." He groans. "I just want you to sit on my face."

My mouth pops open, body jolting off the back of my chair as I sit up straight and stare at him in shock. "Do you *hear* yourself? You're like an over-eager puppy dog."

"Mmm, want to put a leash on me and train me to be a good boy?"

"Jesus Christ." I cover my face with my hands, but can't help but laugh. I may or may not be covering another blush, too, because the thought of Kade on his hands and knees for me with a leash around his neck does tingly things to my nether regions.

What the fuck is wrong with me?

"That'll be ten dollars," Ashlei says, delivering me my new drink and a breath of relief.

"How about I pay you in ass smacks?"

"My favorite."

She hands me my beer, staring at Kade in her chair with a raised brow.

"Oh!" He jumps up, gesturing to the now-empty chair like it's a throne. "M'lady. I was just leaving. Your friend here wants to tie me up, and I'm just not ready for that."

"GO AWAY."

He laughs, and Ashlei watches me with a curious smile as Kade bows to me.

Brat.

"As you wish, my queen. See you in the dungeon of pain."

"I hate you."

"More like you wish you did."

And with that, he slides his aviators down his nose and winks before jogging back over to his brothers.

"What the hell was that?" Ashlei asks, taking her seat again.

"Nothing. That was nothing," I say quickly, cheersing her cup with mine. "Drink up, betch."

I chug before she can say anything else, and ignore the damn puppy dog eyes locked on me from across the pool.

Adam

"THIS IS THE LITERAL worst time to have to pee," Cassie says, bouncing a little as she watches Skyler shove all her chips in. It's the final table of the tournament onboard, and it's down to Skyler and one older guy from Germany.

I chuckle. "You better go now. He's going to take a moment to call, and then the cards will come quickly if he does. They'll both flip their hands over."

"I can hold it," she says, but as she does, her face goes ash white and she squeezes her knees together.

"Go pee, crazy girl." I shove her toward the bathrooms.

"Yeah, girl. Trust me when I say you do *not* want to deal with a UTI," Jess chimes in.

At that, Cassie's eyes widen and she bites her lip. Then, a soft curse under her breath.

"I'll be *right* back. Don't let them end this without me!"

She half runs, half wobbles off toward the bathroom as Jess and I chuckle before turning back toward the table. It's a fairly small crowd gathered for the final table, and the only ones from PSU are me, Kip, Clinton, Jess, Ashlei, Cassie, and Erin. We're the Skyler Thorne fan club, and we've been the most obnoxious of the night. Now that it's down to just two, I know we're about to go wild.

Because Skyler *will* win this thing. There's no doubt in my mind.

"God, she's got to be sweating so bad," Ashlei whispers, her hands over her lips. "I can't imagine the pressure. That's so much money on the line."

Clinton crosses his arms over his chest. "Nah, she's cool as a cucumber. That's part of what makes her game so incredible to watch — she never shows her tells."

"Oh, shit, he called." Jess points to the table as the guy from Germany shoves his chips in, and then both him and Skyler flip their cards over. When they do, everyone in the little crowd except for us laughs.

He has a queen, king suited.

Skyler has a pair of fours.

"Shit," I murmur, but Kip smiles, nodding like it's the best hand she's had.

"This is perfect," he says.

"How so? There's a queen and king on the table. That's *two pair* — and she has one," Jess argues.

Kip just smiles wider. "I have faith."

A hush falls over all of us as the dealer burns one card before turning the next. Nine of hearts. No help for either of them. One more card is burned, and Skyler can't even look. She watches Kip instead, and I can't help but grin. I'm glad they've finally figured their shit out, and now that they've made it public that they're a thing, they both seem happier.

I wonder if the same will happen for me and Cassie.

I check over my shoulder for her, but there's no movement from the bathroom.

"Come on, babe. Get back out here," I whisper under my breath.

But, it's too late. The dealer burns and turns, and then, the entire room gasps.

Four of spades.

Three of a kind for Skyler.

Everyone claps in a polite manner, but I can't help letting out a whistle. Clinton follows up with a classic "Bear howl" until one of the ushers quiets us down.

She did it. I knew she would.

Skyler stands and shakes hands with her opponent, and I turn to Kip, wanting to tell him he better take that girl to celebrate. But when I do, he's already talking to someone else.

Erin.

"You think you know her, but you don't," she says, her voice low, but just loud enough for me to overhear.

I furrow my brows, moving closer as my eyes flick to Skyler and back. She's still shaking hands with other people at the table, oblivious to her Big standing so close to her boyfriend.

"You think she really likes you, but she only hooked up with you because I told her to. For me. I wanted you back, Kip, and I used her as bait to get you around more. I told her to date you. And I told her to kiss you. And I told her to invite you to the dance and to break up with you there, too. It was all a game."

My stomach sinks, and when I look back at Skyler, there's no denying she's feeling the same thing. Her eyes are wide, locked on Erin, her face pale white.

"No," Kip tries, shaking his head. "What we have is real. Skyler wouldn't..."

"She wouldn't?" Erin interrupts. Then, she gestures to Skyler. "Go ahead. Ask her."

And when Skyler and Kip's eyes lock, the guilt written all over her face, Kip shuts down. His eyes harden, his mouth flattening to a thin line, and without another word, he turns, pushing through the crowd.

"Kip! Wait!"

Skyler tries to run after him, but he's already gone by the time she reaches us, and tears flood her eyes as she grabs Erin.

"What did you do?! What did you tell him?!"

Erin is stoic, her jaw set. "I told him about our deal,

about everything. He needed to know, Little. It wasn't fair for him to think what you have is real."

"Damn, Ex," Jess murmurs, stepping back. "That's fucked up."

I doubt Erin hears her. I doubt Skyler does, either. They just stare at each other, while the rest of us stare at them. I always knew Erin was tough, that she was uptight, and some would even say she's a bit bitchy. But I never, *never* thought she would do anything to hurt Skyler.

"What the hell is wrong with you?!" Skyler yells, tears streaming down her cheeks. "Why would you do this to me?! What we have *is* real, Erin. I've never felt anything more real in my life. It was real before I knew you dated him that summer and it was real the whole time I was trying to play your stupid game."

Erin just stands straighter, unaffected. "He needed to know," she repeats, but this time, her voice is softer — just a whisper.

Skyler backs away, her eyes like lasers. "I *hate* you," she spits. "How dare you call yourself my Big. A Big is someone who loves their Little, sets an example for them, cares for them, guides them." She shakes her head. "All you did was use me."

Ashlei covers her mouth, tears in her own eyes as Jess grabs her other hand.

"Don't ever talk to me again," Skyler finishes, sniffing and wiping her cheek with the back of her wrist. Then, she turns, racing toward the elevators.

My eyes shoot to Clinton, sure he'd be the first to take off after her, but to my surprise, he's pulling Erin away, consoling her under one arm as Ashlei holds Jess back.

"Just let her go. She needs to be alone."

And that may be true, but I can't let her. I can't let her think she's alone in this.

With one last glance toward the bathroom, Cassie still not emerging, I curse under my breath and take off sprinting.

Skyler is pushing the elevator button wildly when I reach her, and I wrap my arms around her from behind, shushing her as I try to soothe her cries.

"Shh, it's okay. It's okay, Sky. I'm here."

When she hears my voice, she relaxes, and I hold her until the elevator door opens before ushering her inside.

She's like a wild animal, her eyes rimmed in mascara as she tucks into the corner of the elevator. I just watch her, wondering what to say, wondering what the hell happened between her, Kip, and Erin. It's apparent that what Erin said isn't wrong, but it can't be right. There has to be more to it, a side yet to be seen.

When we reach the floor for Skyler's room, she bolts off and I follow, slipping inside her room behind her. She immediately flops onto the bed, tucking her legs up and burying her face in her arms as more tears rack through her.

It's hard to see Skyler Thorne broken. She's the toughest girl I know, and nothing can get to her — least of all a guy. If I told anyone who wasn't there tonight that a boy made her cry, made her lose her shit, no one would believe me. She's untouchable, unstoppable, and unbreakable.

At least, she was.

Until tonight.

Until Kip Jackson.

I sigh, carefully sitting on the bed next to her and gently resting my hand on her back. "Are you okay?"

As soon as the words are out of my mouth, I curse, shaking my head as she cries harder.

Of course, she's not okay, genius.

"I know, stupid question. I'm here, Skyler. I'm right here. I'm not going anywhere."

Skyler sniffs, turning until her wet cheek is resting on her knees. Our eyes meet for just a split second before there's a soft click at the door. It swings open, and I expect to see Kip, or possibly Erin, but it's neither.

It's Cassie.

Her eyes are on Skyler first, her brows bent in worry, but when those emerald eyes float to me, they harden, all worry fading into anger.

"What are you doing here?"

Shit.

I swallow, taking my hand from Skyler's back and holding them both up. "I just came to check on her."

It's the truth, and I shouldn't feel guilty for that, but the way Cassie's glaring at me tells me it's a statement I'll regret.

"Of course, you did."

Her words are menacing, and my shoulders slump. I plead with her with my eyes, begging her to understand, to see that Skyler needed someone. I didn't do anything inappropriate, nothing that a friend wouldn't do.

I open my mouth to explain when Cassie cuts me off.

"Can you leave us alone, please?"

My throat tightens, but I nod, standing and offering Skyler one last look to let her know it'll all be okay. That earns me an eye roll from Cassie and a stiff shove toward the door.

"Stay here," she whispers to me when I'm outside the door, low enough that Skyler can't hear. Her eyes are still shooting venom at me. "I have words for my Big, but you're next."

"Can—" I try, but the door slams shut, cutting my plea short.

Shit.

I sigh, running my hands back through my hair as my back hits the wall next to their door. I slide down, elbows meeting my knees, eyes on my shoes.

I fucked up.

Again.

No, I shouldn't be sorry for making sure Skyler is okay, but the problem with that scenario is that, once again, I didn't think of how my actions would affect Cassie before I made my move. I ran after Skyler, wanting to make sure she was okay, when I could have easily waited a few more minutes for Cassie. I could have ran to the bathroom, beat on the door or had someone go in after her. We could have gone after Skyler *together*.

But none of that occurred to me in that moment.

I think it was my grandfather who always said hindsight is twenty-twenty, and it's always easier to see our mistakes after they've already been made.

I've never wished for a time machine more.

I begged Cassie to trust me, to let me show her I loved her with my actions instead of my words. And just last night, I promised her I'd prove to her how much she meant to me.

I didn't even make it twenty-four hours before fucking it all up.

I groan, knocking my head back against the wall. "Idiot."

What are only minutes feel like hours as I wait for Cassie. I can't hear what's happening inside, but when the door does open, it swings back against their wall inside and Skyler takes off sprinting down the hall, not so much as a glance in my direction before she's gone.

Cassie emerges next, her eyes on where Skyler just disappeared before they fall to me. I jump up, brushing my jeans off and moving toward her instinctively.

"Cassie, I—"

She just holds up her hand, eyes squeezed shut as she looks away from me. "No."

"Please, just let me—"

"Explain?" She finishes, her eyes snapping back to me. "Why should I? Once again, you picked her over me, Adam. You left *me* behind to make sure she was okay."

God. When she says it like that, it makes my stomach curdle like sour milk.

"I know," I confess, swallowing. "I know, and I'm so sorry. I wasn't thinking, I just saw how hurt she was and no one went after her and—"

"And so you did."

My jaw clenches, and I shove my hands in my pockets, eyes dropping to the floor like the sad, guilty dog that I am.

"You told me to let actions speak louder than words," she whispers. "Well, your actions have been screaming for months. I just haven't listened."

My chest splits open with her words, the truth of them cutting me like a knife. I shake my head, eyes watering as I find hers again. "Cassie, please. I'm sorry. Just give me—"

"I'm not *giving* you anything," she spits, her own eyes flooding. "Not anymore. From this moment on, you have to earn it. You have to earn *me*." Then, she turns, waving one hand behind her without another look in my direction. "Don't follow me."

And she doesn't run. She doesn't jog. She just walks, slowly and purposefully with her head held high — away. Away from me. Away from us.

All I can do is watch, falling more in love with every step she takes, my heart aching and reaching for her, begging my feet to move, my mouth to work. But I do as she asked. I don't follow her. I just stand there, knowing in my heart the one and only gut-wrenching truth.

I blew it.

LIFE IS A FUNNY thing.

The way it shifts, changes, flowing easily from complete bliss to complete and utter chaos. One day there are kisses, and laughter, and long nights spent between the sheets, and little love notes left on napkins. The very next, there are tears, and promises broken, and two chests aching with the pain of lies.

It happens so fast, and yet in slow motion, it seems.

But I can't change what's happened. I can't go back to yesterday, to Kip's arms around me, to his lips on mine. And I can't take back what I've done, the lies I've told, the deal I agreed to just to appease Erin. All I can do is take my Little's advice.

"Stop running from this secret, from this stupid game. Make him understand. Show him how you really feel. Don't give up on him. Have faith."

Those words cycle through my head on repeat, over and over, each time growing louder as my feet carry me across the ship. Clinton calls out for me as I run past, but I keep going, my heart pounding hard and fast in my ears.

I can't lose him.

I *won't* lose him.

When I round the corner toward the stairs, I slam right into Kade, knocking us both off balance before he catches me at the elbows. His eyes watch me under bent brows, taking in my erratic breathing, and he doesn't even ask. He just points.

"He went up to the top deck," he says, but then his face breaks. "He's a mess, Skyler. He wouldn't listen to anything I said."

I swallow, nodding before taking off again. My legs are weak, the tears still drying on my face as I sprint through the ship and up the stairs four decks to the top.

When I reach the top floor, I run even harder, my ribs aching, chest heaving as my legs pump faster and faster. The wind whips my hair around wildly, the moonlight casting an eerie glow over the water as I scan the deck for Kip. I have no idea what I'm going to say when I reach him, words won't form in my head as I run. All I know is that I have to find him. I have to explain.

I can't lose him.

I *won't* lose him.

This game ends tonight.

My chest is burning when I finally spot him, his back hunched, arms resting on the railing as he stares at the light cast over the waves by the moon. I push harder, sprinting through the pain, but it's even harder to breathe when he turns to face me.

Kip's eyes are wide, searching, and when recognition hits him — when he realizes it's me — the hardness that falls over his features is enough to knock what little breath I had right out of my chest. He shakes his head, turning to face the water again as my run slows to a walk, and then to nothing.

I stand there and watch him.

He stands there and watches the water.

And now I need to speak, and I have no idea where to start.

Kip won't turn to face me, like even *looking* at me makes him sick — and I can't blame him. I'm still trying to catch my breath, bending at the waist for a moment before standing as tall as I can.

"Kip, please," I start, breath still ragged. "Let me explain."

Even as the words leave my mouth, I know how pathetic they are. And as he should, Kip just laughs.

"Don't bother, Skyler," he says, voice low but firm. "You played your game, and you played it really fucking well."

I cringe.

"Are you sure you're sold on the poker world?" he continues. "Because with the performance you gave, I think you might want to move to Hollywood."

Ouch.

His words are harsh, and even though I deserve them, it doesn't lessen the sting. I want to retreat into myself, to throw my hands up in surrender and crawl back to my room with my tail between my legs to cry the night away.

But that's not me.

That's not what Skyler Fucking Thorne does.

So, instead, I reach for his arm and whip him around to face me.

"Okay, you're mad," I say. "And you deserve to be. But don't you dare treat me like that. You're going to let me explain myself and you're not going to say a word until I finish, and *then* you can make up your mind about me."

"I don't have to—"

"Damn it, Kip!" I cut him off, desperation slipping through my voice as it cracks. "Let me fight for you!"

My heart squeezes, tears stinging my nose, but I don't let them show.

"If you don't want me after you hear me out, I'll let you go," I concede, swallowing the awful possibility of that like a jagged, dry pill. "But I'm not going to do that until I know I've fought to keep you."

Kip's jaw ticks, his eyes flickering over mine. I wait, wondering if he'll shrug me off, if he'll turn back around, but when he just stands there, I take a deep breath and a step closer.

To which he takes a step back.

I roll my lips together, closing my eyes as I confess. "It's true," I say, and instantly anger shades his face. "But it's not what you think," I add quickly. "The night I met you, Kip, I wanted you. For *me*. You completely captured me. And then when I saw you in class, I knew it would only be a matter of time before you would be mine."

"Cocky, are we?" he clips.

I narrow my eyes. "Right after that, I went back to the sorority house and Erin called us into her room. She told us the story about you guys that summer and then she dropped the bomb that you were here. And when she said your name, everything changed. She came up with this..." I wave one hand in the air. "Sick game, and like a fool, I agreed. But Kip," I plead, stepping closer again. "I *tried* to get out of it. I gave Bear's Little money to buy me at the auction. I tried to stay away from you. I tried to make you not want to be around me, but the more I tried to avoid you, the more I fell for you. And that?" I smile, just barely, a reaction of the heart. "*That* was not a game. That wasn't fake, it wasn't a lie, it wasn't pretend."

My hands shake as I confess everything, washing my slate clean yet revealing all the inky smudges forever left behind. My eyes flood with tears, and I have to take a calming breath to hold them there.

"Kip," I whisper his name as I take another step. He doesn't move, doesn't back away this time. "That night at the dance, it broke me, too. And seeing you with Erin? It..." I shake my head, and it releases the tears I was trying so desperately to keep at bay. "I can't even explain what it did to me. I've never cared about anyone the way I care about you. I would have just let any other guy go without so much as a second glance." The truth of that rings like a bell in my ears, and I realize another truth as the words slip from my lips. "But you have changed me."

He's changed me.

The weight of that sits on my chest, but not like an uncomfortable pressure. No, more like a blanket, like a warmth, a comfort, a piece of me that had been missing and now is found.

"You've opened up the side of me that I have tried so desperately to hide and I'm not even sure why," I confess, thinking about my time at PSU, how I've tried so hard to just fit in and blend. "You like me when I'm being *me*, no matter what I'm wearing or who I'm with or what I'm doing. You care about my love for poker and no one has ever taken the time to appreciate what I love the way you have."

His face morphs at that, a shade of something coloring his anger. Is it remorse? Sympathy? Whatever it is, I take it as my cue to slip through the crack in his walls.

"You made it impossible to play Erin's game because you came at me so fiercely and without apologies and you..." I choke. "You made me love you, Kip."

Oh my God, I said it. I said I loved him.

I don't have time to panic, because it's true, and the truth is all I can offer Kip right now.

"And I'm sorry. I'm so, so sorry for what I've done," I continue, tears streaming, heart squeezing. "But I'm not sorry for loving you."

Kip's hands snap out for me and in the next instant, I'm in his arms, his body engulfing mine as I melt into him and completely break. I fist my hands in his shirt, my tears soaking his shoulder as relief pours through me like sweet champagne.

"I'm so sorry," I repeat, words muffled by his shirt.

Kip kisses my hair, his lips lingering there as he forces a long exhale. "Stop, it's okay. It's okay."

"It's not okay," I argue, pulling back. "None of it was okay and I knew it then just as much as I know it now. But it's over, and I promise I will never lie to you again. I don't want to keep anything from you. Ever. You've always given me nothing but honesty, and that's what I want to give to you. I'm sorry. Please, please forgive me."

Kip's nose flares, his own eyes glossing over as he pulls me back into him. It's indescribable, what I feel when his arms are wrapped around me, when my ear is pressed against his chest, his heartbeats connecting to mine.

"I do," he says softly, stroking my hair back as he kisses my forehead. "I forgive you."

I didn't know I had more weight to give him until those words slipped free, and I melt into him even more, my knees weak, hands gripping onto him for dear life. Kip takes my weight easily, his stance never wavering. Slowly, he pulls back, his eyes searching mine.

"I love you, too," he whispers.

My lip quivers, more tears slipping free, but this time from a different well. I smile, shaking my head as Kip wipes them away with his thumb.

"I don't deserve you," he adds. "I'll never be good enough for you, but I love you, nonetheless."

He presses his lips to mine before I can argue, and I kiss him hard in return, sealing our vows of love in the only way we really can. Kip's hands slip to frame my face, his own kisses coming harder as heat builds between us. We're all hands and grips, breaths and groans, and when he presses my back against the railing, his grip tight on my hips as he trails kisses from my lips to my jaw and down my neck, I whisper the only thing I want in the world right now.

"Take me back to your room."

<hr>

"Get out," Kip says firmly when we burst through the door of his room.

Kade smirks, his eyes bouncing between us before he hops off the bed. That smirk grows to a shit-eating grin as he swipes a flask off the dresser and tips it at us with a wink on his way out.

I smile back, a blush shading my cheeks. Kip just rolls his eyes and shuts the door as soon as Kade is gone.

When we're finally alone, that same electricity that always exists between us buzzes back to life, charging the room with a familiar, magnetic heat. Kip slows his movements, making his way to a phone plugged in by the bed with a long exhale.

"Do you like Ed Sheeran at all?"

I shrug, taking a seat on the edge of his bed and tucking my hands under my thighs. "I don't know, I've never really listened to him, honestly."

Why am I so nervous?

The answer to that hits me almost as soon as I think to question it. I'm not ashamed to say I've had plenty of sex in my short twenty-one years of life, but I've never made love.

I've never had sex with someone I loved.

Truly loved.

I swallow when a soft melody fills the room, and Kip turns the volume up a few pegs, his eyes hot on mine when he turns around again. He reaches for me, pulling me to stand easily before slipping his hands to frame my face again. He searches my eyes, lips finding mine with a tender, delicate pressure that makes my knees shake.

When I open my mouth, his tongue slides inside, stealing both of our next breaths. When we let them go, it's on a sigh that mixes between us, my hands finding their way up into his messy, wind-blown hair. Kip reaches for the hem of my hoodie, fingering it softly at first before breaking our kiss long enough to strip it over my head.

He smiles when he sees I'm in nothing but my bra once it's gone. "Were you planning on taking this off at all tonight?"

"I was hoping you'd be the one to do it."

Kip smirks, his eyes hungry as he slowly unbuttons my jeans. He takes my mouth with his before tugging them over my hips, my ass, my thighs. They fall to my ankles and, keeping my eyes on his, I slip my thumbs in the band of my panties, peeling them down my legs next.

His eyes follow the movement, Adam's apple bobbing hard in his throat as I step out of them, snapping off my bra in a fluid motion next, and then I'm standing in front of him completely bare.

Completely ready for him.

Time slows, dancing with us to the soft croon of Ed Sheeran's voice as I cross the space between us. I slip my hands under his shirt, moaning in appreciation at the hot, hard muscles underneath. I remember all too well how they feel, how they look... how they taste.

Kip's eyes roll back when my fingertips trace the line of his boxers, his hands reaching for the back neck of his shirt quickly. He discards it as I untie his board shorts, my heart beating in my throat with every move. I've touched

Kip before, felt him inside me, witnessed his head buried between my legs. But every touch is amplified this time — slower, more purposeful, with a weight only three little words can add.

He loves me.

He *loves* me.

I smile, that thought on repeat as Kip pulls his shorts and boxers down swiftly, shoving them to the side once they're on the floor. And then, it's just us, body to body, skin on skin.

We stare.

His eyes devour me, racing over every curve before locking back on my eyes. I see the same blue of mine reflected in his, like two oceans meeting, joining as one. There's no rush, no frantic urgency. Tonight, we take our time, letting the music pace our touches, our breaths, our love.

I reach forward, fingertips brushing his jaw before I drop them to his chest, tracing that valley between the muscles of his abdomen. I let them rest just above the line of his hips, waiting.

"You're so fucking gorgeous," Kip whispers, our foreheads brushing.

I just smile, holding onto him as I lower myself back down to the edge of the bed. Then, slowly, I crawl my way up the bed to the pillows, watching him over my shoulder as I move. His eyes on me are like the strongest shot of espresso, the caffeine buzzing through me as I spread myself across the bed. I touch one edge of the bed with my left toes, and then the other with my right, legs wide open as I beckon Kip with one finger.

He shakes his head, like he can't believe I'm real — that *this* is real — that we are real. Time stretches as he kisses his way up my body, starting at my ankle and touching every inch he can with his lips until he reaches my mouth. He sucks my bottom lip between his teeth, grinding his stiff and ready member against my clit with just enough pressure to make me moan into his kiss.

Kip slows, circling his hips, the friction a perfect tease for both of us. When I reach down, gripping him between us and pressing him to my wet entrance, we both pause, inhaling a breath and locking eyes as just the tip of him slides between my folds.

A beat in time.

A second.

A breath.

And then, slowly, with his eyes still on mine, Kip pushes forward, filling me in one, slick flex.

Just like that, everything fades away.

The music is gone, the lights extinguished like match flames, the ship and the bed and anything that isn't our bodies, our hearts, our souls — gone. We're floating, suspended in a moment, in a body-consuming, earth-shattering, life-altering speck of time where everything changes. Kip is a part of me now, and I, a part of him, and neither one of us will ever live without that part being with us ever again.

I moan, dragging my nails down his back as he presses all the way in. Our bodies are sealed together in a seam, sweat slicking our movements as Kip withdraws and flexes, over and over, again and again. He plants kisses as I breathe and moan, his lips brushing my neck, my collarbone, the swell of my breasts. It's all I can do to hold onto his biceps, feeling each rock of his hips like an earthquake of pleasure and powerful emotion.

And for the rest of the night, we make love. Like two virgins, discovering each other in a brand-new light, a brand new way. It's my first time making love like this, and I know without a doubt that it's his. I see it in the way his eyes search mine, in the gentle touches of his hands, in the soft melody of our breaths mixing together.

I laid my cards on the table, and I lost my heart in the bet.

It belongs to Kip Jackson now.

It belongs to him forever.

Cassie

LAST TIME I WAS in Key West, Adam kissed me.

I close my eyes, feeling the salty ocean air breeze across my face as that night comes back in blinding color. I remember the way he looked at me before his lips met mine, that crease in his brows, like he knew he shouldn't but he couldn't help himself. I remember the way we both exhaled, the way my stomach flipped, how my hands shook as I climbed to straddle him on that dark, secluded beach.

All we did was kiss.

But it wasn't *just* kissing.

It was an exchange of souls, a trading of hearts. I gave him mine, and he handed me his, and even though things were complicated then — I was with Grayson, he'd just broken up with Skyler — we made a silent promise not to hurt each other.

And we both lied.

My eyes flutter open, and I sigh, leaning over the railing and letting my eyes drift lazily along the different vendors set up at Mallory Square below us. It's the last day of our cruise, and we all spent the day frolicking on Duval Street before retreating to the boat just in time to push off from shore. I watch as the last few people board the ship, the door shutting, and the captain announces we'll pull away in just ten short minutes.

There's a party on the pool deck, and all of my sisters are down there making the most of their last night. They're day drunk and happy, celebrating an incredible trip, and I should be with them.

But I can't be.

I can't fake a smile anymore, or shove another shot down my throat when everything I taste makes me want to vomit. The truth is, I can't stop thinking about Adam, about last night, about what we said and what we *didn't* say. Everything's a mess.

First and foremost, me.

So, I snuck up to the very top deck, and while the party rages on just below me, I watch the coastline below, thinking of the last time I was in Key West and how I'd been just as much of a mess then.

Yet, somehow, I'd been happier.

Being with Adam, no matter how wrong it was, always made me happier.

I sigh, trailing one finger over the cool railing. Suddenly, there's a loud clanking noise behind me, followed by a curse muttered under someone's breath. I turn, one brow cocked as I take in Adam shuffling toward me, a giant, black duffle bag hanging from his shoulder. It hits his thigh, bouncing off awkwardly, and he curses again before dropping it to the deck when he's standing a few feet away from me.

My instinct is to laugh, to smile and ask him what the hell he's doing, but as soon as the thought passes my mind, my smile dies before it's even born. His messy hair, his dark, intoxicating eyes — shadowed and dark, as if he hasn't slept — they make me want to forget what happened. They make me want to throw my arms around him, kiss him, hold him, spend the night in his arms.

But I refuse to do any of that.

Instead, I cross my arms over my chest, leaning one hip against the railing as I face him.

"I've been looking everywhere for you," he pants, running a flustered hand back through his hair as he eyes the duffle bag at his feet. He points to it like a curse. "Dragging this sonofabitch with me."

I shift, glancing at the bag before I take in his haggard appearance again. Though I know it's impossible, it almost feels like he's lost muscle mass since yesterday, like he's shrunk three inches, his entire body shriveling away before my very eyes. He hasn't slept, that much I know.

He can join the club.

"I just needed some time to think," I answer softly.

Adam swallows, nodding just once. "Good. I'm glad you're up here, away from everyone." He pauses, wringing his hands together. "Cassie, I am so sorry for hurting you. Again."

I close my eyes on his words, pressing my fingers to my temple. "Adam…"

"No, please. *Please,*" he begs. "Just, I know you said I have to earn it. Earn *you*. And you're right. Can you please just give me the next five minutes to try to do just that?" Adam's shoulders fall. "Or at least, to try to *start*, anyway."

I don't nod, don't give him a verbal agreement, but I also don't turn away. I just fold my arms over my chest again, eyes falling to the bag at his feet before they settle on his tired eyes once more.

Adam sighs, his shoulders tugging back like he's preparing to deliver a speech he's practiced for years. His eyes level with mine, tender and soft, just like they always are when he looks at me. They're like home, that familiar, comfortable peace that exists in no other place, in no other person.

Just him.

Always.

"Ever since we met, we've played games with each other's hearts," he starts, reaching into the bag at his feet.

He pulls out the board game, Clue, and holds it between his hands. "At first, I didn't have a clue how to handle what I felt for you."

A smile threatens to break on my lips, but I cover it with my fingertips, trying with all my might not to let the fact that Adam is insanely adorable affect me.

"If I'm being honest," he continues. "I think I did know, I think I always have. But, I was scared."

He reaches into the bag again, this time pulling out the board game, Snakes and Ladders.

"Our entire relationship has been full of ups and downs. It seems like when I climb a ladder to reach you, you slide down into a pit of snakes." He coughs. "Clay, Grayson." He coughs again.

I smirk.

"And just when I slide down to you, just when our hands touch, it's like you climb a ladder, and you're out of reach again." He pauses, shaking his head. "It's like we're always just out of reach."

He drops the box, reaching in to pull out Chess, next.

"So, I try and try to set up a strategy, to put all the pieces in place. I convinced myself if I waited, if I let Grayson fuck up on his own, you'd be with me in the end. But I couldn't stop myself from interfering. And even though, in time, he did end up proving that he was a douchebag," he says, holding up one finger. "I shouldn't have tried to rush that. I shouldn't have been wishing for him to hurt you, Cassie, just because I wanted the chance to have you."

My heart twists with the thought of Grayson, that wound still tender, still healing.

"As if that wasn't bad enough," he says, reaching in the bag for a little foam football. "When I finally had you, instead of being your teammate, I tried to be your coach, instead. I tried to tell you how to run your plays, how to live your life, how to find yourself — when, honestly, it was just because I was scared."

I frown, tilting my head to one side.

"I was," he repeats, nodding. "*God*, Cassie, I was petrified to be with you. To love you. Because I knew that somehow, some way, I'd fuck it all up and I'd lose you. Up until this point, I've never had the chance to make you mine — not truly. And the fact of the matter is that even though it's all I've wanted since the very moment I met you, it's also my biggest fear. To have you, *really* have you, and then lose you. For good."

I roll my lips, fighting against the tears blurring my vision as Adam pours his heart out to me. It makes sense, that fear, because I know I've had it, too. But the more he talks, the more he explains, the more my heart retreats.

"And I know," he says, dropping the football and pulling a small, wooden bat out next. "That I haven't just had three strikes. No, I've had three strike*outs*. I haven't lost just one at bat, I've lost an entire game."

He rears back, holding the bat high above his head before slamming it down on the deck.

I jump, he screams, the bat staying fully in tact as he drops it to the deck and rubs his right wrist.

"Oh, my God, Adam, are you okay?"

I move toward him, but he holds up one hand to stop me, gritting through the pain.

"Stop," he grunts. "I'm trying to grand gesture here, okay?"

I chuckle, shaking my head and leaning back against the rail to let him finish.

Adam shakes his head, cursing as he shoves the still-whole bat back into the bag. "What I'm trying to say is,

I'm done playing games, Cassie. With your head, with your heart, with our relationship. I want to be with you. *Really* be with you — no matter what the risk, no matter what the odds, no matter what the future might hold."

He's shaking now as he bends to retrieve one last box, and he holds it up with a sad, hopeful smile.

"I don't know everything. I don't know if we'll make it, or if you'll change your mind, or if I'll be a perfect boyfriend or fuck up time and time again." He shrugs. "I can't predict what will happen. All I *do* know is that I love you, Cassie McBee."

I choke on a sob, the tears flooding my eyes and spilling over without a chance to hold them at bay.

"I *love* you," he repeats, stepping forward, the game still between his hands. "And if we are stuck in the game of Life," he says, tapping the box. "There's no one else I want to play it with."

Smiling, I cover my mouth with one hand, glancing at the box as he drops it at his feet and steps toward me. His hands reach for mine, both of us shaking, and when his thumbs smooth over the skin of my wrists, I sigh.

"I can't take back anything that I've done, but I can tell you that I am sorry. And I can promise you that I will do everything I can to not be so fucking stupid anymore," he says, and we both chuckle. "If you will give me the chance, I will love you like you deserve to be loved."

More tears slip from my eyes as my head falls forward, and he meets me in the middle, our foreheads touching, eyes closing. Adam rubs my hands with his, pulling me closer, his arms slipping around me and pulling me into him.

And I want to stay.

I want to stay right here, in his arms, in the comfort of his words forever. I want to plant a flag, plant some roots, and settle down for life. Because in my heart I know that he's it — he's all I've ever wanted, and he's everything that's wrong and right and all that I desire. Adam Brooks is my soul mate.

But he's my Kryptonite, too.

I reach around my back, unlacing his fingers and dropping them at his side before I step back. My heart aches in protest the moment we break contact, but I stamp that little sucker down, letting my head lead this time.

"I'm sorry, Adam," I whisper.

I glance at him with the words, and immediately wish I hadn't. The way his face breaks, the slump in his shoulders, the tremor of his hands as he reaches for me again, shake me to my very core. But I step back, away, swiping the new tears from my cheeks.

"I don't believe you."

Silence.

Not just between us, but in the entire world. It's like with those four words, I stole time and space, created a vacuum that took everything away. There are no breaths, no sun setting off in the distance, no music playing below, nowhere to exist after this moment.

It's all gone.

Adam's eyes well, and I can't even beg him not to cry, knowing it will break me, before one tear slides down his cheek, running the length of his jaw and falling to the deck below.

"You don't mean that," he croaks, shaking his head. "You don't... you can't..."

"I do," I say, swallowing down a fresh wave of tears. "I'm sorry, Adam. I'm sorry. I just can't do this anymore."

The vacuum breaks, the noise crashes back in all at once, the sun sets in the distance, and I turn away from the boy I've always turned to.

Then, I run.

Legacy takes place during the same semester as *Black Number Four*. Whether you've read it before now or not, you'll get a wider view of what was happening at Palm South University (especially between Kip and Skyler) if you read *Black Number Four* as you read this season. I will help guide you, letting you know which chapters to read before moving on to the next episode.

FOR THE FULL READING EXPERIENCE FOR THIS EPISODE, READ **CHAPTERS 16-18** IN *BLACK NUMBER FOUR* BEFORE CONTINUING ON TO EPISODE SIX — THE FINALE. (You'll get to see Skyler and Kip sneaking around in the library before Spring Break, witness the black number four roulette scene from Kip's POV, get even closer with Kip and Skyler after the piano scene, see the break from Skyler's POV and the apology from Kip's, and find out what Kip's plan is to handle the secrets *he's* hiding, now that Skyler's are all out in the open. DRAMA. ;))

EPISODE 6

season finale

Adam

"COME ON, MAN," JEREMY says, kicking my foot where it hangs off the side of my bed. "You've got to stop moping."

"Fuck off."

He chuckles, sitting at the foot of my bed with a sigh. "Look, you pulled out all the stops and it didn't work. So, you didn't get the girl," he says, shrugging. "I hate to tell you, but you're not the only one in history for that to happen to. You're not the first, and you definitely won't be the last."

"Is this supposed to make me feel better?" I ask, eyes glued to the ceiling. I'm still in the same flannel pants and white t-shirt that I changed into when we got home from the cruise. It's a little more dingy yellow than white, now.

"It's supposed to let you know that this won't kill you."

"I beg to differ."

Jeremy sighs again, and I just let out another painful breath. That's how every single breath has been since I watched Cassie run away from me on the top deck of that cruise ship.

I don't believe you.

My chest shrinks again, as if the bones of my rib cage want nothing more than to puncture each one of my lungs and put me out of my misery.

"Have you tried talking to her?"

I shake my head.

"You should."

"She ran away from me, Jeremy," I say, not taking my gaze from the ceiling. "*Ran.* Like the thought of being around me for even a split second more would make her crawl out of her skin."

"She's scared."

At that, I laugh, though the whole situation is anything but funny. "She should be. I'm an asshole. I've done nothing but hurt her when all I want is to make her happy."

"You're being such a chick."

I don't acknowledge that. There's nothing more to say.

Jeremy punches my leg in a brotherly way, standing and shoving his hands in his pockets. "Alright, man. I'll leave you alone. Just... try to take a shower before Chapter tomorrow night, okay?"

The door to my bedroom opens and closes, and then I'm alone — the way I'll likely stay forever.

God, I really am pathetic.

But I can't help it. I was barely putty in Cassie's hands the day I went to her, putting my heart on the line — putting *everything* on the line. I was held together by bubble gum and hope, and she popped both.

I've gone through every emotion since that day.

At first, I was devastated. I cried. *Cried.* I'm a man, one raised by a grandfather who warned me that men don't cry. And yet, I did. Then, once the sadness had faded, I got angry. How could she walk away from me, from us, when I apologized for *everything*? How could she just throw it all away?

Guilt came next, because I knew *exactly* why she could throw it all away. I told her to listen to my actions, and then I let them speak loud and clear. In my mind, I was showing her my love, but in reality, I was only showing her time and time again that she was never the number-one priority in my life. Even though she *was*, I didn't show it.

I wished I could go back, go back to the dance and not chase after Skyler. I wished I could take Cassie in my arms instead, twirl her around the dance floor, remind her I would always be there. I wished I could go back to the poker tournament, let Skyler go on her own, wait for Cassie and go to her and Skyler's room *together*.

So many mistakes. So many moments I wish I could re-do. So many things I wish I could take back.

And after that guilt subsided, I landed in some sticky kind of acceptance. Except it wasn't the healing kind. No, the kind of acceptance I found myself in was the kind that swallows you whole, that pulls you into a deep, tar-like darkness, its hands around your throat, suffocating you with your new reality.

I've laid here inside it ever since.

Right now, it's still cold. It's still dark and unfamiliar, like a reality that couldn't possibly be mine. But over time, I imagine it'll come to feel like home.

Over time, I imagine I'll have to learn how to let her go.

My bedroom door opens again, and I sigh, closing my eyes on that painful exhale. "Jeremy, just drop it. Please. Let me wallow in peace."

"Whatcha wallowing about?"

My eyes snap open at the sound of her voice, almost as if it's a dream, as if I just realized I'm sleeping but now I'm half awake, wondering if I want to stay in the dream or shake myself to consciousness.

Slowly, I raise up onto my elbows, and when my eyes land on Cassie, my chest tightens, heart jumping to life at the sight of her.

Her ginger hair is piled into a curly, messy bun, a few tendrils framing her face in a haphazard manner as she folds her arms over her middle. Her eyes skate the floor before those emerald gems lock onto mine, and her brows bend, pink lips pulling to one side.

"Can I sit?" she asks, nodding toward the bed.

I scramble up to the headboard, scooting over and making room for her. "Of course. Here, sit. Please."

She smiles, sitting at the edge of the bed, one leg propped on the sheets while the other remains grounded. Her eyes search mine, taking in what I'm sure are dark, sleepless circles by now. Cassie's face breaks, tears glossing her pupils before she blinks them away.

"Adam, I'm so sorry. I shouldn't have run from you, I shouldn't have left you like that."

"Stop," I say quickly, holding up one hand on a breath. "Trust me, I deserved that. And more. I don't..." I swallow. "I don't blame you for leaving, for not believing me. You don't have a reason to, not after all I've done."

She smiles, but it falls quickly, eyes still glossed as she whispers, "That's just the problem, though. Even though I shouldn't, I can't help it." Cassie shrugs. "I do."

I frown. "You do what?"

"Believe you," she says it on a whispered laugh, a shake of her head like she can't believe it's the truth. Then, she lowers her voice even more. "Want you. Need you." She pauses. "Love you."

I gape at her.

Full on, eyes wide, mouth open gape.

"What are you saying right now?"

She smiles, shaking her head with something between a shrug and a shiver touching her shoulders. "I'm saying that it doesn't matter what you've done to me, what I've done to you. It doesn't matter if we've both hurt each other, if we've both messed up. It doesn't matter that we can't go back in time and make this story — *our* story — perfect." She sniffs, her eyes flooding again as she watches me. "What we have is the messiest, stupidest, most fucked-up thing I've ever heard of and yet, I can't let it go."

I let out a breath, reaching for her hands, my fingers wrapping around hers as two tears slip from her eyes.

"I can't let *you* go, Adam. Not even if I wanted to."

I steal her next words with a kiss, tasting the salty wetness of her tears on her lips as they meet mine. She chokes — whether on a laugh or a sob, I can't be sure — but her hands reach around my neck, fingertips slipping into my hair as she pulls me closer.

"Don't let me go," I whisper, kissing that plea as soon as it leaves my mouth and touches hers. "Please, Cassie. Don't let me go."

She laughs, climbing into my lap and kissing me harder. My hands slip into the back pockets of her jean shorts, and she gasps, pushing her hands into my chest.

"But, if we're doing this, we're *doing* it." She says, one brow raising. "I mean like I'm your girlfriend, you're my boyfriend, there is no other girl above me and no other guy above you."

I cock an eyebrow back at her. "You act like any of that is a deal breaker."

"And, I want to take it slow," she says, resting her hands on my shoulders. "We've rushed through so much, made decisions without thinking... that stops now. From here on, I want to be a team."

"Me, too."

"Okay," she says, as if she's stood her ground. Her brows are set, eyes determined.

"Okay," I agree, and I can't help but smirk. "Can I kiss you now, boss?"

Her eyes soften, a smile touching her lips, too, before she lowers them to mine.

"It's like you said earlier this semester," she whispers against my lips. "You never have to ask."

And just like an 80's movie, I thrust my fist into the air, earning me a chuckle before I steal her next laugh with an even deeper kiss.

I got the girl.

Thank *fuck*, I got the girl.

Erin

A BLINK.

A breath.

A blink.

Repeat.

I stare at my planner, willing it to clear itself, or to check off the items highlighted in a dozen different colors without me having to participate. All I want to do, all I can manage, is to blink, breathe, blink, repeat.

Classes start back up tomorrow.

I should have stood tall as a leader tonight, running our post-Spring Break Chapter, but I cancelled it.

Because I couldn't stand up there in front of all my sisters and pretend like I deserved to be there.

Not after what I did.

As soon as the words slipped from my mouth, I regretted them. I almost stopped mid-sentence, almost turned and left Kip standing there wondering what the hell I was going to say. But it was like word vomit, unable to stop once I started upchucking the truth.

My parents never told me it was right to tell the truth, but somewhere along the way, I learned that. Church, maybe? A teacher? A friend? Wherever that lesson came from, I'm sure there was a little asterisk somewhere that said, "Always tell the truth — *if* that truth is yours to tell."

And what I told Kip? That was not my truth to tell.

Sure, I was a part of it — the "plan." Hell, I was the source of it. But, I knew just as well as everyone else after seeing Kip and Skyler that night at the piano bar that they were in love. I was out of the picture. There *was* no chance for me and Kip anymore.

But I couldn't stop.

I wanted him so badly, wanted *happiness* so badly, that I couldn't see reason.

And now, I have to own up to that. To *my* truth.

A blink.

A breath.

A blink.

Repeat.

Somehow, I peel myself out of my office chair and let my feet carry me on autopilot down the hall to Skyler and Jess's room. The girls all freeze inside when I swing the door open, my eyes gracing each one of them.

Ashlei, Jess, Cassie, Skyler — all snuggled up, spending a lazy Sunday watching movies.

Without me.

"Little," I finally say, my voice a croak. "Can I talk to you?"

The realization of how bad I must look sinks in as the girls' brows bend in pity, their eyes skating over my worn and tired features. I cross one arm over my stomach, holding the elbow of the opposite, feeling like an injured bird on display at a zoo.

"About what?"

Skyler's voice is a clip, her jaw set.

I just watch her, silently begging her to give me the chance to explain.

She sighs, throwing the covers off her and Cassie in a dramatic fashion before hopping off the bed. I don't even look at the other girls before I turn, and Skyler follows me back to my room.

Skyler pauses at the entrance, her arms crossed, body language as closed off as I imagine her heart is to me right now.

"Come sit down," I try, gesturing to the bed.

"I'll stand."

I sigh. "Leave it to you to make this even harder than it already is."

As soon as the words leave my mouth, I internally curse. They aren't *my* words — they're my mother's. I hear her more in every move I make nowadays. But, for once, I understand her.

Easier to point a finger at the other person than admit my own part in the game.

Only, Skyler isn't me. She won't just sit back and let me speak to her the way my mother speaks to me. She won't let me — won't let *anyone* — talk to her like that.

She crosses the room in less than a second, and yet I feel the palm of her hand against my cheek in slow motion, the sting of it somehow lost by the time I register what happened. My hand flies up, covering the cheek she struck, and while my immediate reaction is to strike back, I simply nod.

Skyler stands there, chest heaving, face beet red as she dares me to get mad, to lash out. But she and I both know I won't.

"Fair enough," I say, rubbing my cheek. "I deserved that. But I'm not the only one at fault here, Little."

Skyler laughs, throwing her hands up and turning to leave without another word.

"Wait!" I plead, stopping her just before she hits my door. "Please, let's just talk about this. I'm not saying it was your fault, I know it's mostly mine, but just let me speak. We have to work this out." My chest squeezes. "You can't be mad at me forever."

"The hell I can't."

Her face morphs in that moment, a darkness I've never seen in my Little emerging like a dragon.

"You're a *bitch*, Ex."

Her words are like another slap to the face, and I stagger back at the force of them.

"I'm your Little. Your *Little*. You're supposed to take care of me, to help me through college, to be my mentor in all things. Instead, you wrapped me up in this twisted game that you *knew* I was uncomfortable playing."

The more she speaks, the more my brain scrambles, quickly building my defense. I should be listening to her, should be heeding her words, but I can't help but hold up my mirror to reflect back at her.

"And when it was all finally over," she continues, "and we could move on, you gave me one last jab with your knife like the last thing you wanted to see was for me to come out of this whole mess alive. I don't owe you anything, Erin. Nothing."

"I know that, okay?!"

The words burst from my lips in a high-pitched, desperate scream. I step toward her, hands out in a plea for understanding.

A blink.

A breath.

A blink.

Repeat.

Except this time, with the blinks, my cheeks are wet. With the breath, a sob.

"You think I don't see that what I've done is pathetic and disgusting?" I choke out. "I can't even talk to anyone I know about how I feel because I'm ashamed to admit what I asked you to do. And on the cruise? Yeah, I made one of the worst choices of my entire life, Little. I fucked up."

My next breath is stolen, chest stinging painfully as I gasp for air on another sob.

"And I am so, so sorry," I croak. "I'm sorry for what I asked you to do, for the way I've treated you, for what I did earlier this week. I'm sorry for all of it. I love you, Little."

Skyler swallows hard as I succumb to another wave of tears, my skin hot and itchy with emotion. Sniffing, I inhale a deep, cleansing breath, wiping the tears from my cheeks with the back of my sleeve.

"But you hurt me too, Little," I say, finally looking her in the eye again. "You could have stopped this. You could have told me from the beginning that you couldn't do it, that you didn't want to. At the auction, I told you before it even started that we didn't have to do this," I remind her. "You could have stopped it."

That seems to sober Skyler, and she blinks, holding her chin almost defiantly high.

"And when I was getting caught up in Kip and thinking everything was working," I say, voice thick with emotion again at the realization that everything I thought I felt from him was all a lie. "You could have warned me that it wasn't. You could have told me the truth. But instead, you snuck behind my back and pulled him back to you. You played our own little game so that you could come out of this whole thing unscathed."

"You threatened me with the presidency!"

"And you knew that with or without me, you could get elected!" I throw back.

Skyler's jaw clenches, the air thickening with a hot, electric charge.

"Stop trying to make it sound like you were defenseless in all this, Sky. You didn't stop it, and you damn sure didn't do anything to make it right in the end. You would have never told Kip. Yeah, it wasn't my place to tell him," I admit. "But he deserved to know. If you two are going to be together, he should be able to choose to be with you knowing the truth."

"God, do you hear yourself?" Skyler throws her hands up, exhausted. "You manipulated me, Erin. You know what, I will give you one thing — I should have stopped it," she confesses. "But I couldn't. I didn't have the strength — not until after Kip made me realize to stop caring so much about what you and all the people on this campus think of me."

She shakes her head as I digest her words, wondering what intention lies beneath them. Does she think I judge her, that I don't love her for who she is? Because that couldn't be further from the truth. If anything, I look up to her. I wish I could be more like her, not the other way around.

"I don't know if I want to be president next year," she adds, voice softer. "But *if* I run, it will be because *I* want to. Not because our family has been in this room for as long as anyone can remember, not because everyone would talk if I didn't run, and damn sure not because you want me to."

Skyler points at me with one straight, damning finger. When she lets it drop again, she just stares at me like I'm a monster.

And I can't even argue that I'm not.

I nod, sniffling. "Look, I don't want to fight anymore," I say pathetically. "I'm sorry, okay? I'm sorry for everything. I know it's not going to be like a light switch for you to forgive me, but please just tell me you'll try," I plead, eyes searching hers for the same girl I sat with on pledge night, the same girl I helped become the young woman she is now. "I'm human, I made a mistake. But I love you, Sky. And whether you think I do or not, I love you regardless of what you wear, or who you're with, or what position you hold."

Skyler's bottom lip quivers at that, but she just holds her chin higher.

"We all do," I add, gesturing to the girls down the hall. "We're your sisters, Skyler. You may think we judge you based on those things, but we don't."

She swallows, nodding a bit as her eyes gloss. "I love you, too, Big. And I forgive you." She pauses. "I'm not ready to move back to where we were before, but I'm willing to try if you are."

A smile splits my face, and I nod.

"But don't ever put me in this kind of position again, Ex," she warns.

"Never."

Skyler nods. "Okay."

"Okay," I agree, still smiling. But as soon as she turns and leaves my bedroom, that smile dissipates, like cotton candy in a bowl of cold water.

What the hell is wrong with me?

She's only just left the room, and yet I can't help but replay my so-called apology — one that she gracefully accepted even when I didn't deserve it. I can't even *apologize* right. I can't even accept fault for the mistakes I've made without pointing two fingers right back at the person I'm apologizing to.

My mom has hardened me into the same kind of woman she is.

Cold.

Heartless.

Selfish.

In my attempt to heal, to survive what happened to me, I took advice from the one woman I never wanted to be. And just as I suspected, it's lonely in her shoes.

It's lonely in mine.

I don't even realize what I'm doing until I'm halfway down Greek Row, tears still stained on my cheeks, hair pulled up in a messy pony tail and shoes not matching my sundress. A few girls gape at me as I pass, no doubt wondering if it's even me. Surely, that can't be Erin Xanders, the most put-together girl on campus.

Surely, those can't be her tears on her cheeks.

Surely, that can't be her hair, thrown up haphazardly over a face completely void of makeup.

I shove through the door of the Omega Chi house, and on my way down to Clinton's room, I run into him in the hallway. His cologne invades my senses before his full body comes into view, and I can't help but scan him — hat to matching sneakers. He looks incredible, like he's going on a date, like he's ready to make panties melt off with one little second of eye contact and a smirk.

I should leave.

I should leave him alone.

I should let him be happy.

But one glance at me has his brows furrowing, his hands reaching for me before I can stop the tears from pooling in my eyes. They slip over easily as he pulls me into him, dampening his button-up shirt.

He just kisses my hair.

"I'm here," he whispers, holding me tight. "I'm right here."

A blink.

A breath.

A blink.

Repeat.

And then, I break.

Skyler

WHEN WEDNESDAY ROLLS AROUND, the first week of classes post-Spring Break back in full swing, Kip and I finally get together for the first time since he kissed me goodbye after the cruise ended. We've texted, but he's blown me off every time we had plans to hang out. He kept saying he was dealing with something, and though I told him I was there to help, he just asked for space.

So, I gave it to him.

But now that I'm finally with him, I can't help but feel uneasy as one thought repeats like a record in my mind.

Kip is different.

I don't know how else to describe it. He's *physically* here — he cooked me dinner, held me close while we watched a movie, kissed me just as slow and sensual as ever before loving me between his sheets — but mentally, he's gone.

And for the life of me, I can't figure out how to pull him back to Earth.

"Are you sure we're okay?" I ask for what has to be at least the tenth time. I'm sure it's annoying, but it can't be half as frustrating as him avoiding whatever it is that's bothering him.

We're still lying in bed, our bodies tangled up together. He pulls me in a little closer and kisses my forehead. "We're fine, babe."

"Just fine?" I lean up to look at him, taking in his messy blond hair — the hair I had my hands in not too long ago. He sighs, gently moving me off of him as he stands and pulls on his boxers. I watch as the muscles in his back ebb and flow with the movement, like a hypnotizing song lulling me into a trance.

"Sky, please, I'm asking you to just not push right now."

My stomach aches at his words. I hate this. We're not fighting, but something is off and he won't tell me what. And perhaps the feeling souring in my stomach the most is that this is uncharted territory for us.

We've never been here before.

We've been pissed at each other, sure, but all *those* times we were apart. Now, we're together and something is wrong, but what?

"Are you still mad at me? For the Erin thing?"

He laughs a little, running his fingers through his tousled hair. "No, Skyler. I told you I forgave you for that and I meant it. I'm not even thinking about it anymore. It's done."

I swallow, hating the possibility of his answer to my next question. "Are you done with me?"

His eyes grow wide and he crosses the room to sit on the bed with me again. "What? No, baby. Are you kidding me? You're the only thing keeping me grounded right now, the only thing getting me out of bed in the morning." His diamond eyes are pained, his jaw tense as he lets out a long breath. "I don't deserve you, Skyler."

"I don't understand, why do you keep saying that?"

He opens his mouth to say something, but then stops himself, shaking his head. "I can't get into it tonight, okay? I love you, Skyler." My stomach still flutters at those words. "I do, *so* fucking much. But I'm going through a lot right now. And I want to tell you, I *will* tell you, but I can't tell you tonight."

My stomach drops.

"I know that's not fair, but I'm asking you to be okay with it. For me."

Kip lifts my hand in his to his lips and kisses my fingers, waiting for me to reply.

I nod softly. "Okay."

He smiles and pulls me in for a long, slow kiss, and that's all it takes for every thought to blur.

"I'm going to jump in the shower real quick. Want to join?" He winks, and for just a second the playful Kip is back, but even still, he's hidden behind sad, hooded eyes.

"I have to turn in that paper before midnight. Let me finish and submit it real quick and then I'll be there."

"Don't keep me waiting too long." He leans up and kisses me again before turning toward the bathroom, shutting the door behind him.

I sigh, leaning over the bed for my bag and retrieving my laptop. I don't like that he won't tell me what's going on, but whatever it is, it's something he's not ready to deal with just yet. I can respect that. I've been there before.

And when he *is* ready, I'll be here.

With my mind made up to just let it go and let him come to me when he wants to, I shift my focus to the paper I should have turned in *before* I let Kip distract me in his bed all day. It's written, and ready to go for the most part, but I have to add a few finishing thoughts and get it submitted before the clock strikes midnight.

Cinderella essay, ladies and gents.

When I open my laptop and click the power button, nothing happens. I try a few more times and curse under my breath when I realize it's dead. I didn't bring my charger with me, and my stomach sinks when I check the clock.

Twenty minutes until midnight.

Shit.

I scan the room for Kip's laptop and find it set up on the small desk pushed against the far wall. Quickly, I grab my computer and take it to the desk, pulling the cord from his laptop and trying it in mine.

Nothing.

Double shit.

I knew it was a long shot that it would work for mine, too, but it was worth a try. I have the paper in my email, I just need to format it and add a few sentences in the conclusion. Why didn't I just do this before I left the house? Idiot.

Can brunettes have blonde moments?

"Kip?" I call out over my shoulder, opening his laptop. "What's the password on your laptop? Mine's dead and I forgot my charger."

He doesn't answer, the shower muting my question. I go to open the door to ask him again when his home screen pops up without asking for a password.

"Perfect," I murmur, double clicking the Internet Explorer icon. I log into my email and pull up the paper before quickly formatting it and typing out my final thoughts. By the time I send the email to my professor, there's less than two minutes left until midnight.

Talk about a close call.

"Sky?" Kip calls over the shower.

"I'm coming!"

I exit the browser window and start to close the laptop screen again when a folder in the right-hand corner of the desktop catches my eye.

It's labeled with my name.

I glance back over my shoulder at the bathroom, but the door is still closed, the shower running as an unsettling feeling finds home in my chest.

I know it's wrong, snooping through his stuff, but my curiosity overwhelms my conscience and I double click the folder until a list of documents pops up.

I squint at the screen, taking in the contents like I'm looking through text messages that prove my boyfriend is cheating. But there are no emails from other girls, no nude pictures — though there *are* photos.

Of me.

Playing poker.

I scan through them, noting how serious I look with my hoodie pulled over my hair. I recognize the video that he took that night I blew the tournament downtown, right before we came back here and he blew my mind.

I breathe a sigh of relief.

It's just the research he's been doing to help me prep for May.

Wow, he made an entire folder for me. He wasn't kidding about wanting to help.

I click on the Word document labeled FILE and when it fills the screen, one large photo pops up. It's the headshot I took for a blog site last year. Written above my head in bold letters is my name in all caps.

Okay, this is weird...

I scroll through the file, reading the text under each category.

CLASS SCHEDULE.
PAST RELATIONSHIPS.
HOME LIFE.
HOBBIES.
TOURNAMENT STANDINGS.
BLOG ARTICLES.
SOCIAL MEDIA.

VIDEO RESEARCH.
LIVE FEEDBACK.

The more I scroll, the faster my heart races. Under the regular text in each category, there are short notes written out in red.

Wears sunglasses to hide eyes – possible tell?

Lip quivers slightly when she has a pocket pair.

Easily distracted by emotions – work her up before tournament?

Bothered by blogs referring to her looks. Pay blogger for racy interview/find pictures?

Main reason is for family – parents not well off. Cares a lot about what other people think.

My throat constricts, my attempt at a swallow thwarted by the sick feeling that everything I think I know about Kip Jackson is a lie.

I scroll and read and scroll and read until I feel I might throw up. When I reach the end of the document, there's a small line of text written in bold.

Remember, Son – head in the game. Get her close, but don't get caught up. Break her down, find her weaknesses, and beat her in May or give it hell trying. You help me with my dream, I help you with yours. UCLA is waiting. – Dad

I stand so fast I knock the top of my thighs on the bottom of the desk, but the pain is masked by the panic racing through me. I cover my mouth, shaking my head as tears rush to my eyes.

No.

Oh my God, please, *please* no.

"Sorry, Sky, but I was turning into a raisin in there," Kip says, opening the bathroom door as steam floats up around him. He's relaxed and smiling, a navy blue towel wrapped around his waist.

But the only color I see is red.

Kip stops short when he sees my face. "What happened?" He moves toward me but I back away, shaking my head violently. "What's going on?"

My eyes find his computer and he follows my stare, swallowing hard when he sees the file pulled up on the screen. For a moment, he says nothing, and it feels like the entire world has stopped — like everything and everyone is waiting for what will happen next. My heart drums loud in my ears, my hands shaking, eyes blurred from tears.

"Skyler," he finally says, moving toward me with his arms outstretched, palms facing up like I'm a wild animal and he knows the slightest move could scare me away. "I can explain."

"Don't." I shake my head more, the room spinning as my stomach lurches. My voice is low, too low. Scratchy. Weak.

He takes another step toward me and it's like he crossed over the force field that was holding me back.

I back up to the wall, doubling over as I scream at the top of my lungs. "Don't fucking touch me!"

My breaths are ragged, strained under the pressure of my world collapsing. When I look back up at Kip, his jaw is clenched and his eyes laden with pain. "I wasn't going to go through with it, I was going to tell you and call the whole thing off," he says quickly. "Yes, that's why I came to Palm South, but when I met you, I knew I could never do what my dad was asking me to."

"Then why didn't you tell me?"

He swallows. "It's complicated."

"Are you serious?" I ask, incredulous. Not even a full week ago, we agreed — no more lies, no more games. It was supposed to be us. It was supposed to be *real*.

I've never felt more foolish in my entire life.

Shaking my head, I lift myself from the wall and stand straighter. "Whatever, I don't even care. Just tell me you aren't registered for the tournament. Tell me this was something stupid you were involved in when I was being stupid with Erin. Tell me we can put all this stupidity behind us and move on."

Kip doesn't respond, his nose flaring as he presses his lips together in a hard line. I watch as the muscles over his abdomen flex with every breath. "I can't."

My heart slows, the beats coming at a reduced pace but with more force than I've ever felt. Every thump knocks me forward a little, jerking my body with it.

"What?"

He swallows. "I am registered for the tournament."

"But you're not going, right?" I press. "Not anymore. Not after you promised me you wouldn't hurt me. Not after you told me you loved me. Not after we became *us*. Right?" I ask the questions without breathing. Breath doesn't exist in my body at this point. "*Right?*"

Kip doesn't move. He doesn't swallow or blink or flinch, but one single tear rolls down the left side of his face and under his cheek.

And I know that one tear is saying more than any words can.

"I'm sorry, Skyler."

He doesn't look away from me or hang his head. He just kills me with his baby blues, keeping me locked in their glare as he waits for my next move.

And I don't know what to do.

I want to throw something at him, I want to kill him, I want to cry and scream and rip his apartment to shreds.

But more than that, I want to run to him.

I want him to hold me and make the pain tearing my chest apart disappear. I want him to fix it. To fix me.

But he won't.

Because he can't.

Because he never loved me enough to care in the first place.

The reality of everything crashes down on me in one large, soul-crushing wave. I start breathing faster, inhaling the water instead of oxygen, panic washing through me as the wave takes me under the current, pulling me down, down, down.

I look at him one last time, memorizing the words I read in the file and relating them to his face. His beautiful smile ties into his lies, his lips into his broken promises, his eyes into the pain I feel right now in this moment.

Without another word, I turn and run out of his apartment, flying across the parking lot and across campus. He doesn't come after me and I don't wait to see if he will. I just run. I know I'll have to send someone back to get my stuff tomorrow, but I couldn't stay in that room one second longer.

For minutes, or maybe hours, it's just my feet against the pavement. It's just the air assaulting my lungs, every breath burning more than the last. It's just image after image of Kip — of his eyes, his stupid glasses, his panty-melting smile. A torturous cycle of images and touches on replay, but now, with flashes of the truth between them.

The file.

My face.

His father's words.

The tear on his cheek that told me all I needed to know.

Kip betrayed me, he lied to me — I was just a means to an end.

When I reach the house, my legs are burning and my feet are raw from running on the concrete. I put my hand on the doorknob but don't turn it. Everything hits me and I fall to my knees, leaning my forehead against the door as I give in to the flood of tears escaping my eyes. I squeeze them tight, trying to will the tears to stay away, but they seep through the cracks and pull me down further into the dark hole Kip shoved me in.

Everything was a lie.

Helping me with poker, asking about my past, about my dreams. Kissing me, touching me, making me want him and making me think he wanted me, too. The words, the promises, every single feeling.

This is the game changer.

This is the part where everything I thought I knew about the game gets shattered into tiny pieces and I'm left reeling, trying to pick them up and glue them back together, to force them to make sense to me again. I thought I had it in the bag, I thought I was sitting on Lucky Street with nothing but good days and smooth sailing ahead.

But I'm in stormy water.

Deep, treacherous, Kip-infested water.

And I don't think anyone is strong enough to survive this storm.

Ashlei

BRANDON IS LOOKING AT me like a dog he's about to put down.

His eyes are laden with concern, brows pinched together, jaw tense and lips thinned into a flat line to keep him from saying the multitude of things I know he wants to. He rests his hands on my shoulders, gently rubbing — up, and then down — like he wishes he could somehow change my mind with that touch.

"Stop looking at me like that."

"I'm just not sure about this," he confesses, swallowing hard, his dark eyes searching mine. "We have no control over how that room will respond. It could be a disaster."

"Or, it could be the end of all our worries," I counter.

He rolls his lips together, skepticism rolling off him in waves.

"Look," I whisper, stepping closer to him. "Whether they react the way I want them to is irrelevant at this point, because the truth of the matter is that Kimberly knows. Okay? She knows about us, and she's going to out us."

"She hasn't yet."

"Because she's been waiting for the perfect time, for the opportunity that would hurt us most."

Brandon frowns. He knows it's true.

"And I'm not going down like that," I finish, sneaking a kiss on his cheek before pulling back and straightening my blazer. "If anyone's going to tell my story, it's me. Period."

"You could ruin your career," he says softly, solemnly.

My rib cage squeezes, but I just smooth my hands over my skirt next, holding my shoulders back, my chin high.

"Trust me, I've been through much worse than this." I blink, Xavier's face flashing behind hot lids. "I've been through real ruin. And if I can survive that, if I can rebuild from ashes, I can damn sure rebuild from sexist, judgmental assholes."

I sniff, grabbing my folder and clipboard from Brandon's desk.

"Ready?"

But he's just watching me.

A smile spreads on his face as he makes his way around his desk, framing my face with his hands. "This," he whispers, eyes flicking back and forth between mine. "*This* is why I can't leave you alone."

I let out my next breath on a sigh, smiling a little as I lean into his hand. I kiss his palm, stealing another breath before holding out my arm not wrapped around my binder.

"Well," I say. "How do I look?"

"Like a woman on a mission."

"Perfect." I nod, swallowing down any doubt or fear that's left. "Let's do this."

My knees don't shake as I strut my ass out of Brandon's office, ignoring the curious stares that I'm sure sprouted from us being in there alone — with the door closed. But I don't care, because I'm about to set the record straight.

Kimberly falls into step right beside me, a wicked smirk on her face as she lowers her voice.

"You're going down, Daniels. Hope you've enjoyed this semester, because it's the last one you'll ever have at *Okay, Cool*." She laughs. "Or anywhere, if I have it my way."

I fake fear, coming to a complete halt as she stalks past me. She spins, raising her eyebrows at me as she walks backwards.

"Nice knowing ya."

Then, she rolls her eyes and laughs, continuing on into the conference room.

Once she's gone, I smile.

Good luck with that, sweetheart.

I hold back for as long as I can, filling my tumbler with water and stopping at a few desks on my way to the meeting. It's two minutes past ten when I swing into the giant conference room, already packed wall to wall with virtually everyone in the company. I offer a few smiles and hellos, but mostly keep my head down, not even acknowledging Mykayla when she waves me over to sit by her.

And it's her unassuming smile that gives me my first jolt of guilt.

She's my friend — one of my closest — and I've kept this from her for almost a year now. Even if I *do* keep my job, will I have any friends left here?

I don't have time to answer that question, to get sad, to talk myself out of my decision before Brandon stands at the head of the table.

"Welcome, everyone," he says, his signature smile in place — though I know him well enough to see he's forcing it. "We're nearing the end of the semester for our interns, and, thanks to them, we just secured the *Palm South Luxury Suites* account. Please, help me thank and congratulate them."

Everyone politely claps, Mykayla letting out a few rowdy hoots that earn her some laughs and elbow nudges. She catches my eyes from across the table, holding both of her thumbs up, her mouth open in an ecstatic smile.

I smile back as best I can.

"As they prepare themselves for summer break and the next step in their event planning career, I invite them each to speak a little about their time here, what they've learned, and what they hope to accomplish in the future," Brandon says, unfastening the button on his blazer before taking a seat.

Kimberly smirks at me, hands braced on her chair to stand when Brandon speaks up again.

"Ashlei," he says, eyes on his folder and not on me, one leg crossed over the other like it's just a casual day in the office and I'm not about to completely expose us. "Why don't you start?"

Kimberly pauses, already half out of her chair. "Sir, I thought I could—"

"Thank you, Mr. Church," I say louder, cutting her off as I stand.

She sits back down with a murderous glare locked on me as I clear my throat, shuffling through the papers I wrote notes on. But once she's sitting again, she smirks, as if she knows there's nothing I can say to get myself out of the hole I dug.

And honestly, she very well could be right.

But I hold onto the small, feather-light streak of hope I built my plan on, and I tuck my notes away in my binder.

"I had some notes," I say, gesturing to the pile of paper I just tucked away. "I had all these things I wanted to say, but the truth is there really aren't any words for all this company — and you all — have done for me."

I'm met with smiles, Mykayla even giving a soft *awww* as she clutches her heart.

"The truth is, I was in a dark place before I started my internship last semester. And throwing myself into event planning, into a company and a task that makes me happy, it saved me in more ways than I can ever explain. I turned everything around — my attitude, my life — and I found purpose again."

I glance at Brandon, just long enough to catch his understanding eyes, and I hold onto the burst of energy they give me as I clear my throat again.

"You know, what I love most about this company is that we're not really like an office," I say. "We're a family."

I scan the faces of all the people around me, some I know well and others who I've only just met. Regardless of how *well* know them, my statement is true — the *Okay, Cool* crew is a family, and the moment you start for them, you're part of it.

"We work hard together. We celebrate together when one of us succeeds, and we buck up and pitch in to help when one of us is down. We don't turn our backs on each other, and we don't try to climb over one another." I direct my gaze at Kimberly with that point. "No matter what, we always see that the team is bigger than the individual, and I truly believe that's why we continue to win account after account, and award after award."

"Hear, hear!" my manager says, and everyone chuckles.

My hands tremble a little, and I fold them together in front of me, willing the bad ass, confident bitch who just stood in Brandon's office to stay with me a little longer.

"As a woman in this industry," I say. "Well, in any industry, really — I have been faced with a lot of choices." I laugh a little, lifting my brows on a joke. "My mother's voice is loud in my head every time I step off those elevators. 'Don't be too firm, they'll call you a bitch. Don't be too emotional, they'll say you can't handle the pressure. Don't wear clothes that are too masculine or baggy, you want to command attention. Don't wear clothes that are too tight, or too low cut, they'll say you're sleeping your way to the top.'"

The room grows quiet as soon as the word *bitch* slips from my mouth, and I feel the solemn weight overtake us all. A few women nod as I speak, a few others smile knowingly.

Kimberly just glares at me.

"And we're not alone, you know? Guys," I say, gesturing to the men in the room. "I know you face your own kind of hell, your own kind of judgment, especially when it comes to *being a man*, as my father likes to say." I shrug. "There's no room for anxiety or feelings when you're supposed to be dominating everything with masculinity and power every day."

"Preach, honey," Mario, one of our other interns, says. He snaps with the words, which lightens the mood a bit, earning a chorus of laughter from the room.

I smile, but my stomach rolls as I take one last breath and say what I need to say.

"That judgment," I start. "That expectation is what makes it hard for me to tell you what I'm about to."

Mykayla eyes me curiously, leaning forward in her chair as the rest of the room falls silent again.

"Mr. Church and I are in a relationship."

I hold my head high as those words tumble out, my shoulders back, spine straight. And I don't blink or close my eyes or let any tinge of color shade my cheeks.

But the whole room goes nuts.

"*What?!*"

"Oh, my God."

"No way," I hear Mykayla's voice mutter, almost a whisper. I glance at her with an apology in my eyes as Kimberly stands up.

"I knew it! I knew it all along!" She smiles, pointing her finger up at the ceiling. "I was going to tell you all. I saw them together. In his office!"

That earns another gasp, all eyes turning to Brandon, who just sits calmly at the head of the table. His eyes find mine, the worry there thicker than before as he holds up both of his hands to silent the room again.

"It's true," I say, voice loud, commanding the attention back to me. "Kimberly did see us, and she did threaten to out us. She's been using it as blackmail, as she is so proud to claim."

That shifts the judgmental eyes to her, and she sits back down slowly, a cowardly shade of red on her neck.

"Because, come on," I say with a scoff. "*What* a stereotype, am I right? The CEO hooking up with the intern. Classic." I press my hand to my chest. "I clearly *must* be a whore, one who doesn't offer anything to this company other than how far my legs can spread. And, obviously," I add, pointing to Brandon next. "Mr. Church *must* be a mysoginistic, horny predator taking advantage of the women who work underneath him."

That shuts the room completely up, and I watch as one by one, eyes start to turn from judgmental to ashamed, from angry to sad.

"Right?" I press. "There's no way we could have actually have found a genuine connection, or that what we've built together has been completely outside of the realm of where we work, and what position we hold. I mean, that would make us human." I scoff again. "How ridiculous, right?"

Mykayla frowns, her eyes falling to where her hands lay in her lap.

It seems no one else can look at me anymore, either.

"Joanne," I say, calling on one of the women in accounting. "Has Mr. Church ever made a pass at you?"

Her eyes bulge. "What? Of course not." She shakes her head. "Mr. Church has always been nothing but professional and caring toward me."

"How about you, Valerie?" I ask next, pointing to a younger associate from marketing. "Surely, he's cornered you, offered you a raise for a blow job, right?"

Brandon raises a brow in warning of my language, but he doesn't understand that this is how the punches hit hardest.

Valerie shakes her head. "No. Never." She sinks a little lower in her chair. "In fact, he helped me once, when I was behind on rent. He gave me an advance and let me pay it back over time." She smiles at him then. "He didn't ask for a single thing in return."

I nod, tracing the other female faces in the room.

"Can any woman, or man, in here stand and say that Mr. Church has made them ever feel uncomfortable? That he's ever approached them with sexual intention or tried to use his power in a way to get what he wants?"

Silence.

Kimberly's eyes sweep the room, too, only hers are shaded with horror, like she's watching her entire plan burn down like a flimsy house.

"And what about me?" I ask, my eyes glossing over a bit. I inhale a stiff breath and hold those fucking tears back like a boss bitch. "Have I done nothing valuable for this company, for any of you?"

More silence, heads hanging, eyes averted.

"I know this is shocking, and Mr. Church and I both realized when we first got involved that it was a dangerous idea. We tried to stop, several times, but the fact of the matter is that you can't tell love to live within the boundaries you draw for it." My heart skips at the fact that I mentioned the L word, but I don't let anyone dwell on it — least of all Brandon. "We care about each other, and because we work in an office of *family*, we didn't let the fact that he is my boss stop that.

"Now, you can say what you want about me, about us, and you can call me all the names in the book if that will make you feel better. You can cast your stones at me, and I promise, I will not cast them back." I swallow, sniffing back the threat of emotion. "But I am not ashamed of the work I've done here, nor am I ashamed of the way I feel for a man who, just like this job, saved me in more ways than he'll ever know."

My heart surges with that, like the power of that simple truth is enough, no matter what happens next.

"I want to apologize to all of you," I continue. "But not for how I feel for Mr. Church, or how he feels for me. I apologize for hiding it, for not respecting you all enough to tell you *before* we were caught and threatened. I should have come to you sooner, and for that, I am sorry."

I try to capture Mykayla's eyes again, but she refuses to look up, and I'm left staring at the only person in the room who can stand to look at me.

Brandon.

"I am a good woman," I say. "And he is a good man. And we are human. I hope that our family will understand that, but if you don't, there's no need for any drama. I will quietly pack my things and I will leave, without even one word of argument, if *any* of you are not okay with what I've told you."

"And I will step down as CEO, and revert to being only a silent owner," Brandon chimes in.

I balk, his statement not part of our plan. "Brandon, you can't—"

"I played just as big a role in this as you did, Ashlei," he says, eyes hard on me as he stands. His chest is broad, stance powerful as he refastens his blazer and straightens his shoulders. "And if you have to lose something you love, then I should, too. Just because you're a woman, you do not own the fault. Just because you're a woman, you do not go down in this alone."

I've never wanted to fuck him more in my life.

God*damn*, feminism is sexy.

I smile, eyes watering more than I want to allow as I watch him stand up for me — literally.

With nothing more for either of us to say, we stand defenseless in front of our peers, waiting. The room is quiet, nothing breaking the silence other than the occasional shuffling of papers or cough. After what feels like a weighted hour, Mykayla finally stands — though she's just barely taller than the woman sitting next to her even when she's on her feet.

"I just want to say something," she says, eyes on the table before she lifts them to me.

I hold my breath, preparing myself for the verbal lashing. She's my friend, and I left her in the dark. She's my friend, and in a way, I betrayed her. Not only did I not tell her, but I mishandled her trust, and I know a simple apology would never fix that.

Mykayla shakes her head, her brows furrowed. But then, she sort of smiles.

"That was the bravest, most amazing act of womanhood and humanity that I have ever witnessed in person."

My chest tightens, and I cover my mouth with one hand, stifling my need to cry.

"Ashlei, you are *such* an amazing woman. You're powerful, and courageous, and you get shit done and you balance a million different things on your plate better than I can balance three." A few soft chuckles as Mykayla sweeps the room with her hand. "There isn't a single person here who could say that you are nothing but a *whore* or whatever, because it'd be a bold-faced lie. You have done more as an intern than most of us have done with years of being fully employed."

I smile, dropping my hand back to clasp with the other one in front of me. "Thank you, Mykayla."

"And, Mr. Church," she says, turning to him next. "Excuse my language, but to be frank — whatever gets your dick wet is none of our business."

My jaw pops open as Brandon fights to hide a smile, and the mood in the room lifts again, notch by notch. More people lift their eyes, a few of them smiling, a few laughing.

"You are the best boss any of us could ask for. You're here every day, usually longer hours than we are, and you do whatever it takes to make sure your work family is okay. No, *more* than okay. You're our friend first and our boss second, and you run one hell of a company, if I do say so myself."

There's a chorus of head nods and soft claps to that.

"So, no. I'm not going to pass judgment on you. I appreciate you telling us, even though there honestly is no reason you should ever feel like you have to." She turns to Kimberly then. "And any woman wanting to out you for the disgusting reasons you just listed is the only person, in my opinion, who should have to answer for their actions. We should be building each other up and moving forward," she adds, eyes hard. "Not tearing each other down and setting us all back fifty years."

The women in the room cheer at that, a few of them clapping Mykayla on the back as she sits down again, a shit-eating grin on her face.

Kimberly just shrinks down farther into her chair.

"So, are we done here?" Mykayla adds. "We still have five other interns to hear from and this girl right here is ready for lunch."

A few more laughs ring out, and Brandon and I smile at each other before glancing around the room. No one else speaks, just smiles and nods, letting us know we're still in the family.

Not a single stone is cast.

Kimberly swipes her binder from the table, hurrying out of the room as Brandon and I take our seat again. She doesn't look up from the floor until she's out the door, and though I should feel like I've won, I can't help but feel bad for her, too.

Meh, she'll be fine.

Glancing at his folder, Brandon folds his hands together on the table, sliding me one last smile before he addresses the room.

"Alright, then," he says. "Who's next?"

"I'll just be a second," I say, hopping out of Brandon's convertible and jogging toward the apartment building. I pop up the steps with a smile on my face, rapping my knuckles on the door.

As I wait, I run over my plan in my head. There are only a couple weeks of classes left, and now that I have my drama handled, I can finally start being a better friend to my sisters.

Starting with Skyler.

The poor girl has been moping around the sorority house like a lost kitten for weeks now, and I can't sit back and let her be sad anymore without trying to fix it. Something happened with her and Kip — though she won't tell us *what* — and I'm determined to make them get out of their own way.

God knows they fought hard enough to be together in the first place, it doesn't make sense for them to throw it away now.

The door swings open, and Kip doesn't show a single ounce of emotion or any kind of reaction when he sees it's me. He's sweating profusely, likely from another run — he's been running all over campus since the break up — and his hair is a damp, blond, ratted nest. I trace his features, noting how hollow his cheeks are, how his eyes sag, the skin beneath them shiny and purple like he's been in a fist fight. He's got a full chin of stubble, and as soon as the door opened, I could smell him.

And not in a good way.

"You look like shit," I say, letting myself inside his apartment. He's still standing at the door as I survey the space — dishes piling up in the sink, clothes strewn everywhere, trash overflowing. "So does your apartment."

"What do you want, Ashlei?" he asks when the front door is closed again. "You already go all of Skyler's things out of here."

I nod, eyes softening a little as I take him in again. Poor sap. Skyler sent me back the day after she'd left his apartment in a hurry. She wouldn't tell me why she couldn't go back, and I tried my best not to pry. Still, he looked shitty that morning, his questions aimed at me like bullets as I gathered up her things. But now? He just looks... void. Void of light. Void of happiness.

Void of life.

"I came to check on you," I say with a sigh. "I figured if you were half as bad as Skyler, you'd probably need me to force you into the shower. Which is kind of what it's looking like right now," I add, eyeing his dingy clothes.

Kip glances down, but doesn't respond.

"Kade says he never sees you anymore," I continue. "And you won't talk to anyone. You can't hold yourself up in here, Kip."

Kip blinks, but other than that simple, automatic body reaction, there's nothing.

"I can do whatever I need to do to get through this, Ashlei," he finally says, voice hoarse as he gestures to his messy apartment. "And this is part of the process."

I shake my head. "I don't understand, what exactly happened between you two? Skyler won't talk about it, and you're both acting like you still *want* to be together... so why not just *be* together?"

Kip swallows, his eyes sad. "It's complicated."

"Sounds familiar," I murmur with a roll of my eyes. "Listen, the KKB formal is on Saturday. Come with me."

That gets a reaction.

Kip cocks a brow, his eyes wide. "Are you serious?"

"Not like that," I clarify. "I know Skyler wants you there, but she's not going to ask. Maybe if you come with me, you can talk to her and figure this shit out. You're both making yourselves sick, and it's not healthy."

He crosses his arms, seemingly considering the offer. "Is she going with anyone?"

"Bear," I answer. "As *friends*."

I know I'm overstepping, putting my nose deep in Skyler's business when she asked me to just drop it. But, I know my girl, and she's in love with this kid. She's trying not to be, trying to just let him go and be the tough bad ass she always has been, but she can't help it. She's head over heels, and from what I can tell, he feels the same about her.

If I've learned anything, it's that life is too short to let stupid games get in the way of love.

Kip is quiet, thinking. After a moment, he shifts his weight, eyes finding mine. "It's Saturday?"

I nod.

He watches me for a moment, like he's checking to see if I'm setting him up with some kind of trap. Finally, he sighs, running fingers back through his hair. How he manages to get them through without getting caught in a tangle is beyond me.

"Okay."

I smile, feeling more victorious than I should, considering I have no idea what will happen once he's actually at the dance. "Wear something nice, it's formal attire. And for Pete's sake, take a shower. You smell like complete ass."

Kip chuckles.

"We don't need to ride together or anything," I add. "Just meet me at the venue. I'll text you the address."

Kip nods, moving toward the door as I make my way that direction. But once it's open, I pause, holding one hand on the knob as I face him.

"Skyler loves you, you know?" I say, watching how those words wash over him. His face breaks, his fist clenching at his side like it kills him to know it. "Whatever is happening between you two, I can see that hasn't changed."

I watch him for a moment longer, but when he doesn't respond, I decide my job is done for the day. I got him to agree to come to the dance, and that will set up his chance to make things right. So, I smile once more, close the door behind me, and jog back down the steps.

"All good?" Brandon asks when I slide back into the passenger seat.

I take a moment just to stare at him before I reach for my seatbelt, taking in his smooth skin, his soft, crooked smile, his relaxed posture as he grips the wheel with one hand, the other already reaching for my thigh.

Swoon.

"Yep, all good. At least, for now."

"Do I even want to know what you're getting yourself into now?" he asks once my belt is clicked.

"Probably not."

Brandon just smirks, throwing the car in drive and cruising down toward the dock. With the semester coming to a close, we planned one last day on the yacht to relax before my finals kick into high gear. I've been looking forward to this day all week, but now that it's here, I can't help but feel a sinking in my stomach.

It says with me all the way to the dock, and well into our day on the yacht. I feel it niggling at me as we lounge by the pool, let it keep me from eating much when we sit down for dinner, and barely manage to fight past it to get an orgasm when Brandon takes me from behind on the top deck, my chest hanging over the railing, hair swinging.

But when we're back in bed, curled up together and softly running our fingers over one another, I can't ignore it anymore.

Now that the cat's out of the bag and we're no longer keeping our relationship a secret, I can't help but wonder what we are. It seems like the most juvenile thing to ask, even before the words make it from my brain to my mouth, but I have to ask.

I have to know.

"Brandon," I whisper, fingertips dancing on his bare chest.

His eyes are closed, a sleepy smile on his face as he plays with my hair. "Mmm?"

"Can I ask you something?"

"No, I'm not ready for round two yet."

I smack his chest playfully before lightly running my fingertips over the skin again. "I'm serious."

"So am I," he says, still smirking.

I roll my eyes, finger stilling as I swallow down the nerves. "I was just... I was thinking, about us. About how we don't have to hide anymore. And, well... I just, I don't know how it works at your age, but at mine, everyone plays all these games. It's like, you can be dating someone but not actually *dating* them, like not *just* them. It's all this open-ended *are we, or are we not* nonsense and..." I pause, forcing a breath. "I'm rambling."

Brandon finally opens his eyes, cocking one brow. "What's your question, Ashlei?"

I frown, biting my lower lip. "Are we... are we exclusive?"

He watches me a moment, his brows tugging inward. And then, he laughs.

Laughs.

And not just a little laugh, but a full on, head thrown back against the pillow, one hand over his stomach laugh.

"I'm serious!" I say, rolling away from him defensively. But he snags my wrist with one hand, tugging me back into him and wrapping both his arms around me.

"I'm sorry," he says, still laughing as he kisses my hair. "It's just, it's so ridiculous that you think I have even done so much as *think* about another woman since the day I met you."

The stiffness I held against his hold melts in an instant, my entire body molding to fit his as I let out a sigh of relief. My cheeks flush, and Brandon pulls back, returning my smile.

"Are you saying you want to be my girlfriend?"

I shrug, keeping my eyes on the fingertip I run over his chest again. "Do you want me to be your girlfriend?"

"Honestly," he says, thumb brushing my cheek until I look at him again. "I kind of thought you already were."

That earns him a wide smile, and the corner of his mouth pulls to the side before he leans down, pressing that smirk to meet my smile in a perfect kiss.

And just like that, I have a boyfriend.

One who actually cares about me, who wouldn't hurt me, who wouldn't use me. And, most importantly...

One I don't have to hide.

Jess

"WHAT A SHIT SHOW."

I shake my head, taking another sip of my old fashioned, rolling the amber liquid around in the glass as I watch Kip on the dance floor.

To say I was shocked when he showed up at our formal tonight would be an understatement. For reasons I *still* don't understand, even after Ashlei explained her plan to me, she invited Kip to be her date. Of course, in her mind, it was a way for Kip to be able to talk to Skyler, for them to work out whatever has been going on between them.

But I know better.

I know my girl Sky, and she's on a mission tonight. Mission Forget Kip Ever Existed. These types of missions are dangerous, and usually consist of large volumes of alcohol, kissing random guys who *aren't* Kip, and blacking out by the end of the night.

So, I can't help but sigh in pity as Kip watches Skyler walk away from him. She had just been dancing with him, but from where I'm standing, it looked more like she was chewing his ass and reminding him that his chances to be with her are long gone.

Poor sap.

As if it isn't already bad enough, Erin slides up, asking Kip to dance next. I can't even watch that disaster.

Waving a hand like I can't be bothered, I turn toward our table, ready to make my way to a chair so I can kick off my high heels for a bit. But instead, I'm met with a goofy smile and two full shot glasses.

"Well, if it isn't Venus herself."

I flatten my lips, blinking twice at Kade before I answer. "What does that even mean."

"It means you're the goddess of sex, of course," he says. "And love and fertility and some other shit, too, but that's not the point."

I shove past him, rolling my eyes and draining the last of my old fashioned. I drop it on the first table I pass as he jogs to catch up to me, spilling a little of the two shots he's balancing.

"Come on, look at you. That gold dress, the vine headband. You *do* look like Venus."

"Stop talking."

"Fine," he grinds, stepping in front of me so I can't keep walking away. "How about we drink, instead."

Kade holds a shot toward me, and I eye it suspiciously before taking notice of how good he looks in his tuxedo tonight. All his tattoos are covered, which I actually hate, but how tall, dark, and handsome he looks somewhat makes up for it. His usually unruly hair is gelled and styled, curling a bit at the top. He's sporting an all-black suit, his beige dress shirt and gold pocket square matching me a little too much.

He looks down at the shots again, waggling his brows in an annoyingly adorable manner. "Eh? Come on."

"Ugh, fine," I say, but when I go to snag a shot glass from his hand, he pulls both away.

"First, a toast." His brows furrow. "Or, rather, a proposition."

I groan, slapping one hand against my forehead and dragging it down dramatically.

"Just, hear me out," he says. "You're here this summer, right?"

"I am... creeper, how did you know that?"

He ignores my question. "I've been thinking about what you said on the cruise... about my game. And as much as it pains me to say this... you're right."

At that, I stand a little straighter, folding my arms over my chest. "Okay, you said the magic words. I'm listening."

"I *am* eager, and I spit a bunch of cheesy lines because, frankly, it's all I know. I was raised by two older, bonehead brothers who treat girls like absolute garbage. I learned how to flirt from them, how to land a date, how to hold a relationship. And, as you can see, that's working out just peachy for me."

"Please tell me they didn't also give you advice on how to fuck."

He cringes.

"Jesus Christ."

"I know," he says quickly. "I know. It's bad. Which is why, I was thinking..." He steps closer, a stupid smirk on his face. "What if you helped me? What if you were my teacher of sorts."

I balk, jaw flopping open as my eyes double in size. "You're kidding," I say, but Kade just stares, biting his lip and bouncing on his toes a little. "Wow, you're actually not."

"Look, I know it sounds..."

"Stupid? Crazy? Like there's absolutely nothing in it for me and it's never going to happen?"

"Out of the ordinary," he finishes. "But, you're wrong about there not being anything in it for you. First of all, you get the satisfaction of taking an over-eager puppy under your wing and turning him into a panty-melting beast of a dog."

I roll my eyes.

"And, you get free, no-strings-attached sex whenever you want it."

At that, I laugh. "Because that's so hard to find."

"I'm clean, there's no danger in banging me. And we're friends."

"News to me."

Kade narrows his eyes. "Fine. What do you want in exchange. What will it take for you to say yes?"

I'm tempted to just tell him to get lost, but something about his little proposal piques my interest. Here's this massively built, incredibly sexy, young kid asking for me to help him get better at flirting. And dating. And fucking. He may be annoying as hell, but I saw the bulge in his swim trunks on Spring Break, and I know that equipment is *more* than enough to help a girl get by.

And there's something about his eyes, about his tattoos, about his bulging biceps that remind me of Jarrett, and I wonder if he could fuck me like him, too. With a little training, of course.

My thighs clench at the thought. I need to get laid, *bad*, but that's not reason enough to say yes to these kinds of shenanigans.

... Is it?

"Do you have a car?" I finally ask.

"I do."

"What kind?"

He quirks a brow. "A Camaro."

"Convertible?"

"Uh-huh."

"Good, it's mine now," I say. "You can drop the keys off tomorrow. I had to sell mine to help a friend out, and I need wheels going into the summer and my last semester."

I wait for him to argue, sure my request is too steep. But, to my surprise, he grits his teeth and nods with a somewhat genuine smile.

"Fine. Car's yours. Anything else?"

"You have to actually listen," I say, holding up one manicured finger. "And at least *try* not to completely annoy me every time we're together."

"I'll do my best. So, we have a deal?"

I narrow my eyes, but finally sigh, snatching the shot glass out of his left hand. "We have a deal. Here's to your helpless game, and my sanity in trying to fix it."

Kade chuckles, clinking his glass to mine before we both throw them back and seal the deal.

Lord help me.

Skyler

I'M GOOD AT THIS game.

The *"ignore him, get wasted, dance with every other guy and make him want to crawl out of his skin with jealousy"* game.

It's the most natural, comfortable thing, slipping into that role tonight. I didn't expect to see Kip at *my* formal, the one place where I was supposed to be able to let loose with my sisters and Clinton and just forget about Kip for a while.

But of course, he showed up.

At first, I tried ignoring him. Then, I got so annoyed by his presence that I pulled him into a dance and demanded to know why he was there.

"I wanted to see you, to talk to you. I feel like I owe you an explanation."

Oh, you fucking think?

Just remembering his stupid, sad eyes when he tried to explain himself makes me throw back another shot angrily. Then, I'm grabbing another guy and dragging him to the dance floor. I have no idea who he is. It doesn't matter. All that *does* matter is that he's got his hands on my hips, his crotch pressed against my ass, and Kip has to watch it and know there's nothing he can do about it.

Take that, asshole.

It's petty, and childish, but I can't help it. All semester long, Kip preached to me to stop caring what other people think of me, to stand up for myself and be who *I* want to be — regardless of what anyone else has to say about it.

So, to find out he's letting his father play him like a puppet because *he's* afraid of disappointing him?

He's a hypocrite, and now I'm determined to drink and dance until I forget he ever existed.

My head rushes, vision fuzzy and legs heavy as I try to keep up with the swaying rhythm set by the guy behind me. His hands crawl up my ribs, grabbing the silk of my dress as I lean more of my weight on him. I kind of feel like throwing up, kind of feel like taking someone home — and in the back of my mind, I hear my dignity begging me to come to my senses.

"'Scuse me," I slur to the guy, shoving off him and stumbling toward the stage. The DJ claps his hands and changes up the beat when I make my way up to stand next to him, and there's a crowd of guys below me, hooting and hollering, my own little fan show.

In my mind, I try to convince myself that they want me because I'm such a catch, because I'm such a great dancer and my dress looks amazing. But I know the truth. Somewhere deep down, I know they just see a drunk girl who they can easily get in their bed.

But no one is getting in my bed. Not for a long time. Maybe not ever.

Not after Kip Jackson.

I let him in, let him obliterate my walls like they were made of paper instead of stone. I trusted him, confessed all my lies, thought we were starting over with a clean slate. But all this time, he was playing me.

All this time, I was just a game.

The sting of that drives me as I dance, the cheers from below fueling my pettiness. And when I look up past the crowd and see Kip's back, see him walking away, I know I've won. He can't take anymore. He's leaving.

Why do I suddenly want him to stay?

I shove that thought down, throwing my hands up and closing my eyes as I dance. I sway my hips, spinning slowly to the beat. But my foot slips, and then there's no floor beneath it, and the next thing I know, I'm falling.

For a moment, it's almost as I I'm suspended in time, as if my body is floating down to the hard ground below the stage like a feather. I watch the faces twist around me, the eyes growing wide, the mouths closing into tight *o's* as they watch in horror.

But I feel nothing.

Not when my body hits the floor.

Not when my vision goes dark.

And not when I come to again, however many minutes later, and see Kip's ocean blue eyes staring down at me.

"Fuck, Skyler," he says, pulling me to his chest. I'm still on the floor, but he's holding me in his arms, my head on his shoulder as he wipes my hair from my face. "You scared the shit out of me."

My heart skips a beat, warmth crashing over me as my traitorous body clings to Kip like he's my only lifeline.

"Ouch," I manage, and there's a little ring of laughter around me. I can't even focus my vision enough to see who's there. Someone presses a cool washcloth to the back of my neck and I sigh, head spinning, body aching.

"Let's get you home," Kip whispers in my ear, and all I can do is nod, holding onto him tighter as he lifts me.

I hear my sisters telling him to let them know we made it home safely, but I just curl into him more. I feel hands touching my back, but I just curl into him more. Clinton tells me to call him in the morning and I nod, but then, I curl into Kip more. And when we're in a cab, the engine humming me to sleep as we make our way across town, I hold onto him, wishing I never had to let go.

Wishing he was still the boy who loved me, instead of the one who caused me pain.

I don't know how far we are from the venue when I lift my head, my eyes struggling to focus on his as he stares back at me. And I don't know what I'm thinking when I lean into him again, this time pressing my lips to his, my entire body buzzing to life with the electric charge that's always existed between us. Kip inhales a breath, and I do, too, holding it in my burning chest as I try to deepen the kiss.

But he breaks it.

"Skyler," he says when he pulls back, and just the way he says my name is the worst rejection I've ever felt.

I swallow, waiting for him to take it back, to kiss me, too. But his brows pull together, his eyes searching mine.

"You're drunk," he finally says, shaking his head. "You don't want to kiss me."

And I wish he was right. I wish that were true.

But no matter how he's hurt me, no matter what I *should* feel, I can't help it.

I still want him.

"Yes, I do," I whisper, eyes blurring from tears instead of alcohol as I push off his lap and slide across the back seat to the opposite window. I stare at the car lights passing on the other side of the road, rolling my lips together to keep from crying.

How did I get here?

I can't wrap my head around it, how I started the semester with only one thing on my mind — the tournament — and yet ended it with a boy somehow ruling more of me than poker ever has. I just want him to take it all back, to tell me he's not entering the tournament, that he loves me more than he loves playing me for his father's entertainment. I don't even understand it all, what his dad wants from him, why it means so much.

I want answers, and yet I don't want anything else from Kip at all.

Other than maybe for him to go back in time and never come into my life at all.

"You know," I say after a moment, sniffing. "This just might be the worst downswing I've ever experienced."

I turn to him again, waiting until his eyes are on mine before I continue.

"I never could have expected I'd lose so much of my self betting on you."

I know the words cut him deep. His eyes sag, brows pinching together. One of his hands twitches, like he wants to reach for me, but I just turn away again, staring out the window and waiting for the ride to end.

But Kip is just like me.

He can't let go.

"I love you."

His words fly into space without warning, and I choke on a sob I didn't expect, shaking my head and trying with all my might to fight off the wave of tears. But I can't fight anymore, and as the first tears wet my cheeks, my heart twists in defeat.

"Well, I fucking hate you."

"No, you don't."

I face him again, my chest tight, tears hot on my face. "I want to."

God, do I want to. I don't think I've ever wished for anything more than to disconnect from my feelings in this moment, to take his face and associate it with pain and betrayal instead of love and comfort.

Kip just swallows, his mouth opening like he wants to say something before he snaps it shut again. And when we pull up to the KKB house, he jumps out, quickly making his way around to my door. In an instant, his arm is around my waist, mine over his shoulder as he peels me out of the cab and helps me up to the porch.

"Are you okay?" he asks when we make it. "Are you going to be sick?"

And I just laugh, because the irony of the boy causing me the most pain asking if alcohol is going to be the reason I have a shit night is just too much.

"I'm fine," I bite, pulling out of his grasp to stand on my own. "I've been drunk a few times before, you know."

"I just want you to be okay."

"I find that hard to believe."

Kip swallows, stepping back with a slight nod as he shoves his hands in his pockets and stares at his shoes. There are so many words hanging between us, suspended in a void we can't quite reach. There's so much still left to say, and yet, there's nothing more to say at all.

A fresh tear streaks down my cheek without warning, and I swipe it away, wishing I could do the same to the love I feel for Kip. Glancing at my phone, I see it's just past midnight — on a date I know I'll never forget, not since the cruise when Kip had me figure out what his lucky number was.

"See you in Vegas," I say, reaching for the door handle when I turn. But I pause, heart squeezing as I look back over my shoulder. "Oh, and happy birthday."

I close the door behind me, climb the stairs, and crawl into bed still in my dress, hoping sleep will kill the pain.

Thankfully, I don't dream of Kip.

That's the only mercy I'm shown.

When I check into my room at the Aria the night before the tournament, I can't help but feel like a bird in the pouring down rain — so desperate to fly, yet with no means to get off the ground.

I'm broken, and I just wish the only thing that could fix me wasn't the one thing I need to stay away from.

The past month has been absolute hell.

I somehow managed to make it through the rest of the semester and finish out my classes, but just barely. Practicing for the tournament has been nothing but me playing like complete shit. I'm off my game, and it's not a secret, anymore.

I drop my luggage and sit down on the bed, looking around at the beautiful room. I have an incredible view of the Strip from my window and the bed is luxurious. Whites and purples cover the room and every amenity is top of the line and brand new. The Aria is one of the newer hotels on the Strip and this is the first year they've hosted the American Poker Club Tournament. I just wish I had someone here to celebrate this amazing room with me.

I thought it would be Kip here with me.

I planned on asking him to join me before everything happened. My Little was going to come, but I knew she wanted to get a head start on her summer classes, so I told her it was okay. I'm sure the other girls would have come, too, but to be honest, I was tired of them asking if I was okay.

Why is it that I can hold everything together until someone asks me that one question? I'm fine... until you ask me if I'm fine.

Then I'm not fine, at all.

It's the exact same feeling when I think about Kip calling me. He checked on me the day after formal, and I basically told him to fuck off. And though part of me wished he would fight me on it, he didn't.

He's left me alone just like I asked him to.

Isn't it funny how sometimes we tell someone to fuck off, but then wish more than anything that they would just call?

I sigh, still looking around the room as I try to prepare myself for the night. They're hosting a tournament pre-party tonight downstairs, and even though I don't want to go, I know I need to make an appearance.

For one, everyone in the blogosphere has been talking about how I've been off my game, so I need to try to fake that I'm fine so they see I'm still here to compete.

And two, I want to scope out my competition. A lot of people register last minute, just like I did, and I want to see who I'm going to be facing the next two days.

I pull out the black cocktail dress I packed for the party and slip it on, curling my hair and touching up my makeup before heading downstairs. The party is already packed and I run into a few friends from past tournaments almost immediately. When I say *friends*, I mean either competition or other female players. For some reason, we all gravitate to one another. I guess because we all understand what it's like to be on the "hot or not" list.

Stupid sexist magazines.

I grab a plate of hors d'oeuvres, even though I haven't really eaten anything in the past three weeks, and snag a glass of honey whiskey from the bartender before finding a table near the back of the room. The lights are off, but there's multicolored uplighting and lights that move with the music from the DJ. On any other day, I would be stoked to be here. I would be taking in everything and how amazing it is here in Vegas, one of my favorite places in the world, but right now I just can't. I need to get myself pulled together before tomorrow.

I just really don't know how.

"This seat taken?" he asks, and I know it's Kip without even looking up from my plate. I shake my head and he sits down. For some reason, I still can't look up.

"Hi," he says softly, and I find the strength to pull my eyes to his. He's dressed in a long-sleeve, white button-up and black vest, and of course he's wearing his glasses.

Perfect.

The sleeves of his shirt are rolled up to his elbows, his hair styled perfectly, and his skin is a beautiful bronze. Maybe he's been lounging by the pool living the good life. I don't know, but whatever he's been doing, he looks amazing.

And I know I look like shit.

"Hi."

He takes a pull of his drink, surveying me. "You look beautiful tonight."

I really want to make some smart-ass comment back to him, but I just don't think it's worth it. And I need my head on straight tomorrow. I can't let him faze me tonight.

"Thank you. So do you."

He cocks a brow. "You think I'm beautiful, huh?"

I roll my eyes, but a smile threatens at the corners of my mouth and it's the first time I've had that urge in a while. "Like a shark before he eats his prey."

"So, what you're saying is that I'm like Sparky?"

I laugh a little at his reference to the little stuffed shark I won him on our first date, forgoing playing with my food on my plate and taking a drink instead. "Sparky is fluffier than you. I think I like him more."

"Hey, I've put on a few pounds. I might be fighting Sparky for that fluffy title here pretty soon."

He doesn't look like he's put on even a single ounce. In fact, he looks like he's lost weight — especially in his face. It's then that I take a closer look at him — the bags under his eyes, the tired expression behind his smile. Maybe this hasn't been as easy for him as I thought.

"Skyler, I need to talk to you."

I close my eyes, setting my drink on the table. "Please don't do this, Kip. Not before tomorrow."

"It's not about us," he clarifies, but then he bites the inside of his lip a little. "Well, not entirely. I just need you to know something before tomorrow, before we start this tournament. I want you to understand."

Pulling the glass to my lips, I drain the rest of my whiskey and cross my arms on the table, bracing for impact. I have no idea what he could possibly say to make me understand why he's here, why he's doing this to me. But, I remember running to him on our cruise, desperate to make him understand the whole Erin situation when I knew I didn't even deserve him listening to a word I said.

I owe him the same courtesy.

"Skyler," he starts, and the way he says my name is almost too much. It's almost enough for me to get up and walk out. "I did come to Palm South to seek you out. My dad has been watching you play for years and when he found out you were entering this tournament, or well, rumored to be, anyway — he made me a deal. If I came to this school and got close enough to you to learn how to take you down at this tournament, he would pay for me to go to my dream school — UCLA."

He pauses, probably reading the confusion on my face. *Why the hell would his dad target* me *of all players?*

"Please don't take it personally," he says quickly. "My dad doesn't have a vendetta against you or anything, it's just that he thinks you're the best in the game right now. And you're also one of the youngest. I don't know," he says, scratching the back of his neck. "I guess he felt like if everything he's taught me about the game could help me beat you or at least keep up and compete, he would be 'beating the best', in a way."

I'm oddly flattered, but still can't understand how Kip could go through with that deal — not after he actually met me, after we fell in love.

Or was it only *me* who did the falling?

"He even made that crazy fucking file that you found." Kip says, running his fingers through his hair. "It's like he's living through me. And I didn't understand that before, not for a long time. But I get it now."

He shakes his head, almost as if he's jumping to something too quickly — something he's not ready to say yet.

"Anyway, I've been going to community college the past couple of years because I couldn't afford anything else without my dad's help. And I know there are loans and I could work, but to be honest, I just didn't think it through. I was lazy, I was selfish, and I wanted my father's help. So, when he offered it, I jumped on the chance."

I inhale a deep breath and lift my glass, trying to suck the remaining whiskey from the ice cubes. Kip pauses for a moment, his attention falling to my mouth as I swirl the cube around inside. A surge runs straight through me when I realize why he's distracted. And no matter how much I try not to like it, I love the power I still have over him.

So, I grab another cube.

But he tears his eyes away, continuing. "When I met you that night at rush, I didn't know who you were. You have to know that," he pleads earnestly. "I found out that night when I went back to my apartment. That first night between us was all us — you didn't know about Erin, I didn't know about you — it was just us and the way we felt together."

My chest squeezes, stomach tightening, too, at the thought of seeing him for the first time that night. I can close my eyes and still feel his tongue on my stomach, licking up the tequila before he kissed me.

I shiver, but don't say a word.

"When I did find out it was you my dad had sent me to Palm South for, I almost called it off then," Kip says, licking his lips. "I fell for you that first night, Skyler. The first time my eyes found yours. When you called me a nerd and said I looked like a Matthew." He laughs a little and I do, too. "You had me. Right then."

We both sit silent for just a second, just a split second after that laugh before he takes a breath and continues.

"But it's my dad, and this was his deal. For a while, I let that drive me. Then, when I was close to calling everything off because I was starting to fall for you, you ended it at the dance. And then I was more determined than ever to take you down. But then things changed again, and fuck." He runs his hands through his hair again and lets out a puff of air. "Everything was just such a mess, Skyler. My head was fucked up. But I tried calling my dad to tell him the deal was off before the cruise."

I sit up a little straighter at his words. "You did?"

He nods. "Yes. But, he didn't answer, and I should have known then that something was wrong." Kip swallows hard and his eyes grow darker. "But I called him as soon as we got off the boat, Skyler. And my mom answered. And once again, when I thought I was done with his game, shit got more complicated."

I inhale, waiting for him to continue. Something tells me what he's about to say is difficult for him, and even though I still feel that little pang of anger deep in my stomach, I try to give him the time he needs to gather the words.

"My dad is sick, Skyler." He chokes on the words a little, his façade breaking. "He has lung cancer. And he's not going to live much longer."

And just like that, there's no oxygen left in the room.

My chest tightens again, this time from a completely different kind of pain. I think of my own dad, of what I would do if the same were true for him, and it's too much to bear. Tears immediately sting the backs of my eyes, but I hold them back, because this isn't my time to cry. This is my time to listen and be there for Kip, even if I'm not sure I can be.

His dad is sick.

And now, suddenly, everything between us seems so small.

"Oh my God, Kip." I shake my head, reaching out to grab his hand in mine. He flinches at first, but then he takes mine in his and squeezes like it's the last thing in life he has to hold on to. "I'm so sorry. I'm such a bitch. *God*, I'm sorry."

He shakes his head. "No, you're not. I didn't tell you. I was going to that night at formal, but you weren't exactly in the best state."

He eyes me for a second and I blush, looking down at the table. I made an ass of myself that night and I know it.

"I know this doesn't change anything between us. I know I still betrayed you, lied to you, earned your trust when I didn't deserve it. I know that," he says, his voice fading. "But, I wanted you to understand. I needed you to be able to look at me from across the table tomorrow and know that I'm here for my dad, not because I don't love you. Because I do. I love you, Skyler."

He pulls me across the table and our lips meet in the middle, his hands moving to either side of my face. I let him kiss me and I kiss him back, but my heart is still torn. I still don't know what to believe. I don't know what was real between us and what was an act.

I'm still broken.

I wish this kiss alone could put me back together, but it can't.

When he pulls back, he runs the pad of his thumb over my cheek once before dropping his hands. We both stand there for a moment, and I know this very well could be the last time I stand this close to him. We'll be at the tournament together, but there's no telling if either of us will even make it far enough to sit at the same table together. And after this, he'll be gone from Palm South.

From me.

"Is your dad here?"

He hangs his head. "He can't travel right now. He's watching from home."

A pain shoots through my heart and I bite my lips together. "I'm sure he's proud of you."

Kip nods, trying to smile but failing. Finally, he looks up at me once more, his diamond blue eyes glimmering in the soft light. "For the record, I hope you win tomorrow."

I cock my brow and he leans in, kissing my forehead.

"I want to win for my dad, yes," he says, eyes still on me. "But, more than anything, I want to see you happy. And if that means you kick my ass tomorrow, then so be it."

My skin stings from where his lips touched my head, and my fingers move to the spot as he reaches into his pocket, pulling out a long, slender case. He hands it to me and I know what it is without even opening it.

"Good luck, number four."

He winks before turning and walking away. I watch as he walks across the room until he disappears behind the doors and I lose sight of him. Then, I grab what was left of his drink and down it, open the case, and try not to show any emotion.

Inside are the same glasses he got me before, though I know he smashed that pair, so this is a new one. On the top left of the left lens, there are four gold dots, just like my freckle tattoo. I swallow hard, closing the case again before sitting back in my chair.

For some reason, I find myself wondering if Kip has a tell.

What is the sign that he's bluffing? I can always spot it, a person's giveaway. Always. I can read every single human being I meet.

But not him.

Why? When he tells me he loves me, why do I believe it's true? Yet, there's still something warning me that maybe, just *maybe*, he's bluffing.

But what could his tell be?

Is it the way he kisses me? The way he runs his hands through my hair? The way his eyes shift from dark blue to sky blue? The way he smiles when I touch him?

What is it that will give me the true answer?

I need another drink.

I head back to my room not too long after that, exhausted from our conversation. My heart and soul ache for him and what he's going through. I can't imagine losing either one of my parents, and knowing what a big part his dad played in his life, I know this isn't easy for him.

As if I'm a glutton for punishment, I pull his oversized black t-shirt from my bag and slip it over my head, taking everything else off. I don't know why I packed this, why I kept it after all this time, but there's something about it that brings me comfort.

Wrapping up in the covers of the bed, I pull the shirt to my nose and inhale his scent, closing my eyes as tears start to gather again. I hate crying, and I hate crying over him more than anything else. But, lately, it seems it's all I can do.

I don't know what to think. I don't know what to feel. He told me he loved me tonight and I believe him, I just don't know what that means. I understand why he's in the tournament still, but how do I know what was real between us and what wasn't? Does he really love me, or did he just get caught up in his game?

As I drift off to sleep, I think about love. Love is like the wind, someone once told me, because it's felt and not seen. But I think you actually can see it. You see love just the same way that you see the wind — by the way it moves other things. Love has moved me, it's changed me, and I can see it more clearly than the sun in the sky. Clearly, love has moved Kip, too.

The question is, will love move us together, or sweep us apart?

Cassie

"REMIND ME AGAIN WHY I agreed to let you torture me."

Adam chuckles, smacking my ass as I pass him on my way up the stairs. He's on his way down.

Bastard.

"You agreed to let me *train* you," he corrects, turning all the way around to face me, but he keeps jogging down the stairs, anyway. Backwards.

Bastard.

"And, for what it's worth, your ass looks great in those shorts."

I smack that ass he's referencing before flipping him off, and he just laughs harder, turning the corner down the next set of stairs.

It's summer, which is usually my time to go back to Arizona and be lazy by the pool. But with my biology major picking up speed and medical schools getting tougher to get into by the day, I don't have time to mess around anymore. I signed up for a full set of summer classes, and since Adam was elected to be president for a second term — an achievement never before seen in Alpha Sigma's history on campus — he decided to stay with me to gear up for the next year.

He also agreed to train me, when I chopped half my hair off and said I wanted to add a fitness routine to my study schedule so I wasn't inside sitting so much.

Mistakes were made.

So, here we are, at nine o'clock at night on a Thursday running up and down the stairs of the tallest parking garage on campus, stopping on every floor to do different body weight reps.

And, here *I* am, dying.

After the last round of dumbbell squats on the top floor, I flop down on the warm concrete, chest heaving. There are a few clouds in the sky tonight, the moon casting a magical glow through them, and I watch them float by as my breathing steadies.

"You okay, there, Red?" Adam asks, taking a seat next to me.

"If I had the energy," I pant. "I'd punch you so hard right now."

"What? It's your favorite nickname."

I just glare at him.

He chuckles, leaning back until he's lying next to me. His hand reaches for mine, but I yank it away.

"I'm sweaty and gross."

"More like sweaty and adorable," he argues. "Come here."

He reaches for me, trying to pull me into his chest, but I wiggle free.

"Seriously, I'm soaked. And sweaty."

Adam gives me a pointed look, one brow cocked as he taps his chest. "Your sweaty, smelly head. Here. Now."

I groan, but give in, letting him pull me into his warm body. He somehow still smells like soap, even after an hour of working out, and as much as I want to hate it, I can't help but inhale his scent and snuggle into him.

"That's better."

For a while, Adam just holds me while we watch the clouds, his fingers playing in my new, short hair. I chopped it all the way above my shoulders, the curly edges of it framing my chin, and it's too short now to even bother trying to put it in a pony tail.

"I can't believe we're here," Adam muses, his voice soft.

"On top of a parking garage?"

He smirks. "I mean *here,* together. Really together. No other guys, no other girls, no one and nothing between us. We're just... us."

At that, I sigh, snuggling into his chest more. "It is pretty crazy."

"Did you ever think we'd actually get here?"

I snort. "Honestly? No."

"Really?"

"I was wrapped up in Grayson," I say, trying to defend my thoughts. "And you had the presidency, and before that, you had Skyler. I don't know, I just kind of felt like it was never in the cards for us. Half the time I wasn't even sure how you felt about me."

"Well, then you weren't paying attention."

"More like you're harder to read than my biology books."

Adam leans up on one elbow, his brows bending together slightly as his eyes search mine. "I always knew we'd be together. Eventually. When the time was right."

"You did?"

He nods, a little smirk climbing on his lips. "I did."

"How could you be so sure?" I ask, pushing up to sit with him.

Adam stares off in the distance, his lips pressed together in thought. Then, slowly, he smiles, and a shrug finds his shoulders. "I don't know. I guess the best way to explain it is that when we weren't together, you were always on my mind — even when I was busy, or dating someone else, or mad at you for choosing Grayson."

I blush at that, but Adam keeps going.

"You were always what I was thinking about. And when I was with you, when I could see you, it felt like this piece of me that was missing when you were gone just snapped back into place. Now, don't get me wrong," he says, cocking a brow as his eyes find mine again. "That little piece of me shook with anger when I had to watch Grayson with you."

I bite my lip, cheeks flooding with more heat.

"But," he continues, thumbing my blushing skin before pulling my chin up. "I only felt like me when that piece was alive, when I was with you — even when it hurt." He lowers his mouth to mine, and after stealing one small kiss and my breath along with it, he smiles. "*That's* how I knew."

Adam kisses me again, this time pressing into my lips until I opened them to let his tongue inside. He smooths his over mine, one hand cradling my neck as he deepens the kiss. My body reacts automatically — leaning in, heart picking up speed, stomach fluttering. By the time he pulls back, my desire to take things slow that I've managed to hold onto since we made up after Spring Break is depleted to dust.

"Well, now that you know," I whisper. "And *I* know, where do we go from here?"

Adam's dark eyes sparkle in the low light of the moon, and he pops up onto his feet without warning, hands wrapping around his mouth to make a megaphone.

"I LOVE CASSIE MCBEE!"

His scream echoes off the walls of the parking garage, so loud I jump and my heart picks up for a completely different reason. But he just keeps going.

"CASSIE MCBEE IS MY GIRLFRIEND, AND I'M HER BOYFRIEND, AND EVERYONE ELSE CAN JUST FUCK THE HELL OFF!"

I laugh, scrambling to my feet and ripping his arms down to break the megaphone. "Oh, my God. Shhhh, stop."

My entire neck lights with heat as he screams again, megaphone or not.

"CASSIE MCBEE IS MINE, MOTHERFUCKERS! *MINE*. YOU HEAR ME, BOYS OF PSU?"

Thrusting up onto my tiptoes, I press my lips to his, shutting him up the only way I know how before I blush so hard I get a sunburn. Adam laughs against my lips, wrapping his arms around me and swinging me in a circle before he lets my sneakers touch the ground again.

"There," he says, kissing my nose. "Now, you know, I know, and so does everyone else." He brushes my short hair behind one ear, shaking his head as his eyes trace the features of my face, like he can't believe the words he's about to say. "You're mine," he whispers, bending until our foreheads meet. "And I'm never giving you up. Ever."

I giggle, kissing him again as I wrap my arms around his neck. "Take me home, stupid."

"Yes, ma'am."

Adam takes my hand, stopping to pack up the small equipment we brought with us and shove it into his duffle bag on our way downstairs. We're laughing and talking as we make our way across campus, but when we turn onto Greek Row, something shifts.

The energy around us picks up a static charge, one familiar and yet different tonight. It's that same electricity that lets me know when Adam is around me before he's even said a word, but tonight, it feels powered by an unstoppable magnetic field. I lean into Adam, and his arm wraps around my waist, and as we walk down the silent street, most of the Greek students already gone for the summer, we fall silent, too.

And I know.

I know tonight is the night I give myself to Adam, and he gives me another piece of him, too. Tonight, we'll make another promise.

And this time, I know we'll keep it.

The Alpha Sigma house is quiet when we step inside. There are only a few other brothers staying in the house over summer, and all of them are upstairs in the second-floor rooms. Adam drops his duffle bag by the front door and holds my hand tight as we walk down the dark hallway to his room.

Once we're inside, I slip out of my sneakers and socks, and Adam strips his shirt over his head. I trace the lean muscles of his abdomen, a flash of last semester hitting me hard. I remember running into him rush week when I had to bring him a file from Erin, and how even then, when I was with Grayson, I couldn't help the way Adam affected me.

His eyes meet mine when I trail my way back up, and he smirks, crossing the room until his hands rest on my hips.

"Shower?" he asks, voice low. The only light in his room is from a small, bedside lamp, and it casts his skin in a warm, orange glow.

I nod, and Adam fingers the hem of my tank top before peeling it from my slick skin. I lift my arms, keeping my eyes on his as he strips the fabric over my head and lets it fall to the floor. He swallows, eyes flashing to my breasts, and I keep my hands in the air until he peels my bra off, too.

When the cool air hits my nipples, they peak, rushing a wave of goose bumps down my arms, my ribs, my legs, all the way to my ankles. Adam watches them, chest heaving as he steps closer, his fingertips reaching for my shorts next.

I close my eyes, trying to savor every touch, featherlight or bruising, like I can store this moment and relive it anytime I want. So long, I've wondered what it would be like. So long, I've hoped it would happen — one day, just me and Adam.

And when someday becomes tonight, it's almost too much to bear.

Adam drops to his knees, his eyes on mine as he slips his fingertips beneath the band of my shorts and pulls them slowly over my hips, my ass, letting them fall down to the floor once they're free from my thighs. I step out of them, and when Adam stands again, I'm completely naked in front of him.

For the first time.

He lets out a shaky breath, hands reaching for me before he stops himself, rolling his hands into fists at his side, instead. His eyes roam over my exposed flesh, his erection straining more and more beneath his shorts as he does. And as much as part of me wants to hide, wants to skip the shower and jump under the covers of his bed, instead — it's the way he looks at me, the way he's *always* looked at me, that makes me stand tall and confident, welcoming his appreciative stare.

"Now I remember why I never let you get naked in front of me before," he whispers.

"Why's that?"

"Because I knew if you took off all your clothes, I wouldn't be able to let you leave without taking all of *you*."

I swallow, stepping closer to him, my trembling hands reaching forward for his shorts. I slip one hand beneath the band, the other sliding over his bulge as his eyes flutter shut at the contact.

"Take all of me," I whisper, meeting his gaze when his eyes open again. "Here. Tonight."

He opens his mouth, but I shake my head, kissing him to stop his words.

"Don't ask me if I'm sure," I breathe against his lips. "I want you. Now. And I wouldn't say it if I wasn't sure."

With that, I push his shorts over his hips, taking his briefs with him, and in seconds, he's naked with me.

I don't look down, don't let myself see what I've always wanted to until Adam leads us into his small shower. He runs the water hot before stepping inside, and then he reaches back for my hand, pulling me in with him. I step under the stream, and then — only then — do I let myself look down.

My walls clench at the sight of his stiff member, the size of it even more than I expected. I've felt it under sheets and clothing, felt the warmth of it pressed against me when we made out. But to see it, to see *him* fully exposed from head to toe, every muscle in his body hard and wanting, with me as the desired target... it sends a rush through me so powerful, my knees buckle at the force.

Adam's arms wrap around me just in time, his chest pressing against mine as he sweeps my wet hair from my face. His eyes search mine, that heavy, magnetic charge descending on us even under the water.

"Do you remember what I said to you earlier this semester?" he asks, voice low in my ear as he spins me to face the faucet. His erection presses into my lower back, and my breath catches, eyes shutting on a sigh. "When you let me touch you, do you remember?"

My head is foggy, thoughts nonexistent as every molecule of my brain focuses on how his hands feel sliding with the water over my hips, up my ribs, his warm palms cupping my breasts. "Um... you said... you said..." I try, but my breath is too ragged, my heart beating too fast for a single thought to catch.

"I said before we went any further, I wanted you to know that every single chance I get to touch you, every chance I get to put my hands where you don't let any other hands go, it means everything to me."

"Yes, that." I pant.

Adam chuckles, his hands still massaging my breasts under the warm stream. When he rolls my nipples between his thumbs and pointer fingers, I hiss, arching my back off his chest and leaning into the touch.

"I just wanted to remind you," he says, sucking my earlobe between his teeth. One hand keeps rolling over my left breast, but the other slides down with the water over my navel, down below my hips, his hot fingertips slipping between my thighs easily. "I want to make you feel good, Cassie," he whispers. His fingers slide farther between my legs, the tip of one of them slipping inside me, and I moan, the sensation of it rocking me from head to toe. "I want to make you *come*," he says a little softer, and my knees shake, legs parting wider to let his fingers press inside me more. "But first, I had to make sure you remembered."

"I remember," I pant, one hand flying back into his hair behind me while the other braces on the wall. "Now *please*, Adam. Touch me."

My voice is light and raspy, more seductive than I even knew I could manage, and it drives a growl out of Adam so deep I feel it rumble through his chest as his two fingers finally slide inside me. The way he enters me, my back pressed against his chest, his arms wrapped around me — one between my legs, one flicking my sensitive nipple — it's so much more than anything I've felt before.

It's like he's completely consumed me, like we're one together. When my hand slips behind me, gripping his hard on and pumping in time with his hand, I can't decide if I'm touching him, or still touching *me* — because I feel everything I'm doing to him, too.

"Fuck," he draws out, biting my neck with another groan. His fingers dive deeper inside me, and I squeeze my hand over him tighter, relishing in the feel of the water over his soft skin as I pulse. I remember how I felt the first time Adam touched me, the first time his fingers were inside me, his mouth on my clit — but it's nothing compared to my first time touching *him*.

And now that I've had a taste, I want more.

Adam's fingers slip from inside me when I push away from him, spinning and holding onto his arms as I lower to my knees. His eyes widen, hands gripping my arms like he wants to pull me back up. And when I'm level with his hard, wet cock, I realize I have no idea what I'm doing.

"Cassie..." he warns.

"I want to taste you," I whisper, looking up at him through my lashes from where I sit on my knees. "The way you've tasted me."

His nose flares, hands pulling my wet hair back as I grip him firmly in one hand. The water streams down Adam's back, his chest, dripping down his abdomen to where my hand grips his shaft. I pulse once, wrapping around him at the base, and then slowly, I lower my lips to his tip.

He tastes salty on my tongue, and as I swirl it around his tip and lick down to where my hand rests, I wonder what I tasted like to him. The memory of his head between my thighs, his magical tongue licking and sucking my clit, makes my thighs clench. And when I look up at Adam again, my tongue running along his base, and watch his eyes flutter shut as his head tilts back, a new wave of want pulses through me.

"Is this okay?" I ask, flicking under his crown with the tip of my tongue. "Am I doing it right?"

Adam pauses, his head lifting slowly as his eyes find mine. "Is this... is this your first time?"

I nod. "Doing this, yes. I've never... can you help me? Tell me what you like."

Adam shakes with a guttural moan as I wrap my mouth around him again, this time taking him in my throat as far as I can. It's not far, and I gag a little, eyes watering as I withdraw and suck his tip.

"Is that okay?"

"God, Cassie, you're going to make me come in this shower before I've even been inside you if you keep looking up at me like that."

He groans, gripping my forearms tight and pulling me to stand again. Then, his mouth is devouring mine hungrily, like his last breath exists somewhere inside me and he's on a mission to steal it back.

"We can revisit that another time," he breathes. "Right now, I need you."

He reaches behind him to kill the water, thrusting the shower curtain back and hastily wrapping a towel around him. He pulls one out for me, but when he turns to face me again, it's as if time completely stops.

Adam pauses, holding my towel in his hand, and our eyes stay connected without either of us taking another step. Water drips from his hair down his jaw, to his chest, and I know he's watching the same waterfall over my own body. He swallows, as if he's just realized what we're about to do, and then slowly, carefully, he wraps me in the towel and helps me out of the shower.

I'm still dripping as Adam lowers me into his bed, my wet hair splaying out over his pillow, hands clutching the towel over my chest. I was just naked and on my knees for him, but suddenly, I'm more exposed. Suddenly, it's not just his fingers inside me, or me going down on him. It's not just a shower. It's not just sex.

It's me, and Adam, for the first time.

It's years of wanting, of never knowing, of always hoping. It's an immeasurable time of hurt, of pain, of broken promises — and an equal amount of time making that right. It's late nights eating pizza, him being there for me when Grayson wasn't. It's our first kiss on a dark beach in Key West, his hands on me when they shouldn't have been. It's him knowing better than I did what I needed this semester, and holding back on what *he* wanted just to make sure I was okay.

It's love.

And that's more intimate than the touches, the kisses, the feel of his body against mine. It's what makes this time different than any other.

It's what makes tonight *more*.

Adam swallows from where he towers above me, balancing on his forearms. He shifts his weight to one of them, kissing my hands where they clutch my towel before slowly peeling them back. I fist them in the sheets, instead, as he drops the edges of my towel to each side, and then his eyes are on me, his mouth descending.

He kisses my neck, my collarbone, the swell of my breast. His hands grip my ribs, my waist, my hips and my thighs. It's like he can't kiss everywhere he wants, can't grab me tight enough, and when his hips settle between mine, the slick, hard tip of him pressing against the wet, swollen entrance of me — we both stop.

Kissing. Breathing. Feeling.

For that one moment, we're suspended in time, and nothing or no one else exists.

Adam's hand shakes as he reaches past my left shoulder and into his bedside table drawer for a condom. I just hold onto his shoulders, watching the mix of nerves and desire play across his face as he slips it on. When his weight is back on his forearms, his hips pressed against mine again, and his eyes float to mine, we both inhale a deep breath together.

"I love you," he whispers, and his entire body trembles with the words.

"I love you, too."

The laughter is gone. The playfulness? Left behind in the shower. It's all heat and love and wonder as Adam presses his lips to mine, and slowly, with intent and care and purpose — he pushes inside me for the first time.

He fills me with our mouths fused together, stretching me inch by blissful inch with each withdrawal and flex of his hips. My nails dig into his shoulders, his back, my toes curling under the sheets. When it's too much, I gasp for air from our kiss, eyes closing as he plants gentle kisses down my neck.

It's nothing like I expected, feeling the weight of him between my legs. It's more — *so* much more. It's the love behind his eyes as he watches me, the tenderness of his shaking hands as they cradle my face, the careful way he enters me each and every time, pressing deep, but not too hard, letting us each feel every single centimeter. It's everything I've always wanted sex to be, and everything I thought it never *could* be.

"Are you okay?" Adam asks, eyes finding mine.

I nod, kissing him again, my heels digging into his behind to press him deeper inside me. When he fills me again, I gasp, a rush of heat warming my entire body. "Yes," I breathe. "More."

And he delivers.

More and more, flex after flex, moan after moan, until I'm so ready to come I almost don't want to. This feeling — this rush of pleasure right before it all ends — *this* is what I love the most.

Adam shifts his weight to one arm, wrapping the other around my thigh and lifting it until one leg is on his shoulder. In the new position, I'm even tighter than before, and both of us groan at the sensation.

"Adam..." I breathe, nails dragging down his back. He thrusts a little harder, the friction catching my clit in the perfect way, and I pull him closer, down into me, like I can't come until we're seamed together. "Yes. Oh, God, *yes.*"

Moans I've never heard before somehow spill from me, my cries loud and unabashed as I come harder than ever before. My vision goes black, a rush of blood flowing from every vein in my body straight to the pulsing need between my legs. I shudder, gripping Adam tight as I spiral out into space, and my moans drive him over his edge, taking him down with me.

He buries his head between my neck and my shoulder, his breath hot on my skin as we find our releases together. My name leaves his lips in a sigh, his falls from mine in a prayer, and when we emerge on the other side, in a new time, a new place, a new existence.

It's the after, the now, the impossible that somehow slipped within our reach.

And we take our first breaths together.

The next night, I'm ridiculously happy and deliciously sore, crowded into Erin's bed with her, Jess, and Ashlei as we FaceTime Skyler in Vegas. She just wrapped up the first day of the tournament, but we're all more focused on what she just told us about Kip.

None of us knew what happened with Skyler and Kip after the cruise. We all thought everything was smooth sailing once the Erin drama was out in the open. But, they had a big blow out, and now that she's revealed *why*, none of us can wrap our heads around it.

Kip's dad sent him to PSU specifically to meet Skyler, to get to know her — to get to know her *game*. He wanted Kip to beat her at the tournament in Vegas, and Skyler found a file on his computer detailing the whole thing. It makes complete sense to us now that she blew him off and wanted nothing to do with him, but as soon as she dropped that bomb on us, she dropped another.

And this one has more kick.

Kip's father has cancer.

So, what started as a deal between them, as a way for Kip to get the tuition money he needed for his dream school, turned into his father's dying wish. And suddenly, nothing is black and white.

I'm beginning to learn that nothing in life is.

"Not to sound like your mother," I say after a while, the subject changed. "But you look too thin. Are you eating out there in Vegas?"

Skyler laughs a little, bringing color to her ashen face. Her eyes are tired, hair in a messy bun, and I can tell she hasn't been sleeping as much as she needs to to win a tournament.

"Trust me," she says. "It's just the camera. I've eaten at like five buffets already."

"Sounds like heaven to me," Jess pipes in. She takes a swig of the bottle of wine we snuck in and passes it to Erin. Skyler salutes us with a drink from her own bottle on the other end.

"I just wish we could be there," Ashlei says, her face falling. "You should have someone there to cheer you on."

"I know you girls will cheer me on at the watch party tomorrow, and honestly that will probably be more fun than the viewing section here. Send me pictures! I want to see everyone."

"You know we will," Ashlei says.

My phone lights up with a text from Adam and I blush, smiling as I tuck it under the covers.

"Bear has been planning this thing for months. I'm pretty sure he bought enough kegs for the entire city instead of just the school. Which, by the way, literally the entire school will be there." Ashlei smiles, shaking her head. "We are all so fucking proud of you."

"Thanks." Skyler says with a small smile, but it falls a bit when her eyes land on Erin. "What are you thinking so hard about, Big?"

Every time Skyler addresses Erin, or the other way around, we can't help but all get a little stiff. Things are still tense between them after everything that happened. I'm glad they apologized to each other and agreed to make amends, but something tells me it won't be anything they can resolve overnight. Or even over a summer.

Erin sighs. "I just can't get over what you told us about Kip's dad."

Jess and Ashlei exchange glances, their eyes wide. *Why is she bringing up Kip again? We just moved past this.*

"What do you mean?"

Erin shakes her head. "They were just so close when I knew him back in high school. His dad was everything to him. He was so afraid to be who he was because he wanted to be everything his *dad* wanted him to be. I was in the process of finding myself that summer, but Kip couldn't join me in that because he was trying to find how he fit in his father's picture." Erin pauses, her brows pinching together, eyes on her hands. "I know he's come a long way from that, but I also know this can't be easy for him. I just can't believe he's even there."

"Well, isn't that precisely *why* he's there?" I point out. "I don't think he would be if this wouldn't have happened."

"Can we not talk about this?" Skyler pinches the bridge of her nose, her eyes closing on the other end of the video call.

Jess gives Erin a pointed look before jumping up from the bed, pulling the wine bottle with her.

"Whatever," she says. "Forget all that. To you, Skyler Fucking Thorne." She lifts the bottle to the screen. "Kick ass tomorrow and then get back here so we can throw a huge rager with all that money."

We all laugh and Jess takes a pull of her bottle as Skyler lifts hers, too. "I love you girls. Thank you."

Ashlei shrugs. "That's what we're here for."

"Do you guys mind if I talk to Little alone?"

Skyler's eyes find mine in the screen, a silence falling over us as the other girls nod in understanding. They all blow kisses at the screen and offer various forms of advice before leaving the room. Then, it's just me and Skyler.

She inhales a shaky breath, her eyes watering, and I immediately shake my head.

"Do not cry on me, Big."

She blows out the breath. "I'm trying not to. Little, I don't know what the hell I'm doing. This tournament means everything to me, or it *did*, anyway. But now, I'm not sure what matters most to me anymore." She buries her face in her hands, as if admitting that out loud scares her more than anything ever has in her life.

"I think you do know."

I offer Skyler a soft smile as she looks back up, wishing more than anything that I could say what I'm about to say to her in person.

"Skyler, you were going to pretty much be done with tournaments after this, right?" I ask, remembering what she'd told us last semester. She just wanted to get enough to finish paying off her tuition for her remaining time at PSU, and to set her family up a little more. After that, she wanted to focus on *her* future — on what that looked like.

Skyler nods, blinking against the tears pooling in her eyes.

"You want this more than anything not for the title, but for your family. You want to pay off school at Palm South and help your parents out. I get that, I totally do," I say. "But, Sky, it's not up to you to set your parents up for life. And you and I both know that it wouldn't take first place for you to be able to pay off your tuition. Don't let the pressure of winning get to you. Just play like I know you know how to and let the cards fall where they're meant to fall."

Skyler bites her lower lip, considering my advice. Maybe she hasn't thought of that before, how winning at almost *any* point now would give her a great pot of cash to come home with. Or, maybe she's known all along, but she doesn't know how to handle her new feelings. Poker has been everything to her for so long. She's never put a boy above it.

Sometimes, love makes us forget who we are. But others? It shows us who we've wanted to be all along. I've felt that with Adam, and just by looking at my Big, I know she feels it, too.

Poor girl. Here's hoping she doesn't have to go through what we did.

"What are you going to do about Kip?" I ask her after a moment.

She shrugs. "What is there to do? It's over."

"I call bullshit."

Huffing, Skyler takes a long drink from the bottle of wine. "It is! How could I ever forgive him for what he did? How do I know what's been real and what was just a game?"

I roll my eyes, because I remember those exact same excuses coming from my own mouth. "Oh, please. Every single moment between the two of you has been one-hundred percent real and you know it." I lean in toward the screen. "Look at me, Big. I have known you for two years now and I've never seen you like this with a guy. *Ever.* You may not be sure about what's happening between you and Kip, but I am. When he says he loves you, he means it — and I think you know that, too."

"I don't though, that's what's so hard!" Skyler practically yells, slamming the wine bottle down on her bedside table in frustration. "I would never have guessed he was playing this game, Little. Never. Everything with him felt so real, so genuine, so unlike anything I've ever had before. If it was so easy for him to pull off this whole scheme without me knowing the difference, wouldn't it be just as easy for him to make me believe he loved me when he didn't?"

I shake my head. "But then why would he still be trying to convince you? If it was all just a game, why would he bother?"

Skyler scoffs. "He's probably trying to get under my skin for tomorrow."

"You and I both know that's complete crap," I say firmly. Leaning in more, I make sure her eyes are on mine when I say my next sentence. "You're scared, Skyler. I know you are and it's okay to be scared. But remember, some of life's best experiences are masked as terrifying leaps of faith."

Her face softens at that.

"Just please, *please* — think about what you want before tomorrow," I beg her. "Think about what matters to you. What *really* matters."

Skyler nods, and I can only imagine how she must feel with all the thoughts in her head warring against each other. Poker used to be simple for her, it used to be the *only* sure thing. Now, everything she thought she knew about what she wanted, about *who* mattered in her life, has been flipped upside down.

But she can do this, she can make her way out. She just has to decide what result she wants in the end.

"I love you, Big," I tell her. "We'll all be watching tomorrow. Just know you have a team rooting for you, no matter what happens."

And with that, we end the call, and all eyes at Palm South University are watching Vegas.

Bear

"**COME ON, SKY.** Come on."

I press my fingertips into the bridge of my nose, my hands steepled around my mouth as I pray. It's the final table in Vegas, and at almost eleven our time — about eight o'clock theirs — Skyler just went all in.

There are three players left — her, Kip, and some douchebag named Brandon who just stood up to challenge her. Honestly, Brandon probably *isn't* a douchebag. For all I know, he could be a sweet country boy from Missouri trying to win money for his high school sweetheart to go to college or to get his sick grandma the care she needs.

But right now, he's up against my best friend.

Therefore: douchebag.

"Is this how you get during football season?" Becca teases from beside me, popping a Dorito in her mouth. "If so, I might be busy for like all of fall."

I smirk, blowing out a breath and leaning back on the couch. I throw my arm around her, pulling her into me.

"It's just Skyler. She's like a little sister to me, and I know how bad she wants this."

"Well, from what you told me, the guy she's been dating all semester wants it just as bad. Wonder what she'll do about that."

I frown, eyes flicking to Kip as his face fills the screen. Then, the camera is back on the cards, and I don't have time to think about how I'm torn between ripping Kip a new asshole and giving him a Bear Hug. My parents are shit humans, but I've seen what good family can look like. It looks like Mac and his family, like Skyler and hers. And I can't imagine being in Kip's shoes after what Erin told me about his dad.

Luckily, it's none of my business, and I'm completely content in staying the hell out of it.

The dealer reveals a Jack of spades, and everyone in the room groans. At least, everyone who's paying attention. The rager ended up being bigger than even *I* expected, and half of the crowd is gathered around the various TVs in the house while the other half plays drinking games, dances, and parties outside.

"Fuck," I murmur, running my free hand back over my head.

"So, what does that mean?" Becca asks. "Is she done?"

"Not yet, but he has three Jacks now. She needs a heart on this last card or she's fucked."

Becca turns back toward the screen just in time for the dealer to turn the river, and when I see it's a nine of hearts, I jump up from the couch at the same time Skyler thrusts her fist in the air. The entire house cheers, even people not paying attention knowing something good must have happened. It's a deafening roar, one I hope Skyler can hear from Vegas.

"Atta fucking girl, Sky!" I holler, and Becca holds up both hands for a high ten.

"That's so crazy!" she says, running her hands through her hair, eyes wide. "So now it's just her and that guy? Like, one of them is walking away the winner of this whole thing?"

"Yep," I say, still buzzing off the win. Skyler shakes hands with Brandon, but then her eyes focus on Kip, and I can see her jaw tighten on the screen. My stomach falls. "It all comes down to this."

There's a mad dash to the kitchen for beer refills and

snacks before the last round starts. And in my rush to get back to my spot on the couch with a fresh beer for me and Becca, I nearly run over Erin.

"Ooof!" she exclaims as I hold the beers out above her head, doing my best not to spill them all over her.

"Shit, Erin, I'm sorry."

"No, no, I'm sorry. I wasn't looking where I was going," she says, and then she starts giggling. Erin Xanders, who I haven't seen laugh in over a year, is *giggling*.

"Uh..." I bend down to look into her glazed eyes. "Are you okay?"

"Oh, I'm *fantastic!*" she says, clapping her hands down on my shoulders. She kisses each one of my cheeks and pulls back with a grin plastered on her face as she runs her hands back through her hair. "I've had a few beers. I can't remember the last time I had *beer*," she says. "And Skyler is doing so good. And Kip is there, so that's super fun. And I had the best brownie of my *life* and now I'm going back to get more."

"Brownie?" I follow her gaze to the plate of baked goods behind me in the kitchen, and my eyes double in size when I look at her again. "Oh, shit, Erin. Those are pot brownies."

I expect her to freak out, to go into paranoid mode about being within even twenty feet of drugs. But she just smiles, and shrugs. "Ah. Well, that explains why I feel so great then, doesn't it?"

"Um, yeah..." Glancing behind her, I see Becca watching us, but she pulls her gaze away as soon as mine finds hers. "Are you sure you're okay? Maybe you should come sit down in the living room for a bit."

"I will. I'm just going to get some water," Erin says, smacking her tongue to the roof of her mouth. "I'm thirsty."

She grins again and I can't help but chuckle. "Alright. See you in there."

Erin makes her way into the kitchen as I take my seat next to Becca again, handing her the beer I managed to save. She takes her first sip as a new hand is dealt to Kip and Skyler.

"You missed it," she says, licking her lips as she sets her cup down on the table. "They had these hot bitches bringing out piles of money and shit."

"Damn it!" I say, making a big deal of it even though I could care less. I prop my arm around her shoulders on the couch. "Maybe you can get half-naked later and give me a replay."

"Only if you get *all the way* naked," she says, brow arched.

I just laugh, bending to kiss her full, nude lips before turning my attention back to the screen. Erin plops down in one of the chairs down the couch from us, spilling a little water as she giggles and tries to focus on the television. I watch her for a moment, caught somewhere between happy for her that she's smiling and worried for her because I know drugs can become an addiction when it feels like there's nothing else happy in life. And for Erin, right now, I know that's how she feels.

She finally came to me.

After all this time running, after all this time saying she was fine, she finally came to me after she and Skyler made up. And I held her, and she talked, and cried, and even though we haven't figured everything out yet, it's a step.

I feel like she can get better, like she can be okay again.

I feel like I can help her get there.

"She okay?" Becca asks, noticing my gaze.

I clear my throat and take another sip of my beer. "She's good. Just ate a pot brownie by mistake."

Becca laughs. "Oh, God. Been there." She leans into me, her eyes on mine while I keep my gaze on the screen. "Hey... I don't have to worry about her, right?"

"What?" I snap my eyes to hers, immediately shaking my head as I drop my beer to the table again. "Of course not."

"Okay," Becca says, fingers playing with the hem of my t-shirt. "I just wanted to check. I know we're not official or anything, but... I like you, Bear. And I've been second place before." She swallows, her eyes on where her hand twists in my shirt. "Too many times, actually. And I'm not doing it again."

I tilt her chin up with my knuckle, making sure her eyes are on mine when I say my next words. "Hey, you're not second place with me. You're first. Hell, you're the *only* place, there aren't even any other competitors."

She smiles, leaning into my touch.

"I know we're taking it slower than either of us is used to," I say, searching her golden eyes. I let myself trace the smooth features of her face, the curls of her hair. "But, it's not because I have feelings for anyone else. It's because I have a *lot* of feelings for you, and I want to take my time exploring them. Just like you've been second place before, I've rushed in and felt safe sooner than I should have," I admit, a flash of Shawna hitting me out of nowhere. "I just want to do it right this time."

"Me, too," Becca says. She leans up, pressing her lips to mine. "Just keep it real with me, okay?"

"Always."

She snuggles into my side, and then the entire house is sucked into what's happening in Vegas.

A little past midnight, the stacks are almost completely even in Vegas. It's easy to see both players are tired, even with the jokes they've been throwing back and forth at each other, and we all know it's going to be over soon.

"I better piss now or forever hold my peace," I murmur, slipping my arm from around Becca.

"Gross. Did not need to know."

"Hey, you said to keep it one-hundred."

"For future reference, that doesn't include your digestion status."

I shrug, throwing her a wink as I make my way toward the hall. "Your loss."

I jog down the hallway first, but the bathroom in my room is in use — and not in the way I need to use it. I smirk when I hear the moans and thumps, tapping the door with an, "Atta boy," before heading for the bathroom upstairs. It's usually the cleanest, and after the kind of party we've had tonight, I know the co-ed ones downstairs have to be a mess.

I don't bother locking the door behind me, knowing I won't be long. I realize that was a mistake not even a full minute later when I'm still zipping up my fly and the door bursts open.

Erin flies through, shoving me to the side just in time to drop to her knees and vomit in the toilet I just pissed in.

"Jesus Christ, Ex," I say, rinsing my hands quickly before drying them and bending to hold her hair back. I reach her just in time for her to heave again, and I cringe at the sight, looking away but still holding her hair and rubbing her back. "It's okay, get it all out."

"I don't understand," she groans, leaning her cheek on the toilet seat.

"Don't do that."

I try to get her to sit up again, but she swats me away, groaning again.

"I felt fine, I felt great."

I chuckle, dropping to the floor next to her. "Yeah, well, you drank and *then* ate a pot brownie. The spins were inevitable."

She opens her eyes, blinking a few times. "So, you feel the room spinning, too?"

I don't have time to answer before she's head in the toilet again, dry heaving. I just smile and rub her back. *Poor girl.*

"It's okay, just get it all out and you'll feel better after a night of sleep."

Erin doesn't get anything up that time, so she rests her cheek on the toilet seat again. Her eyes are glazed and out of focus as she looks up at me, and a smile splits her face. Then, she giggles before full on laughing.

"Still high, huh?" I ask with a smile.

"No, no, it's just..." She shakes her head, waving her hand at me before it lands on my arm. She squeezes it tight, her warm hand smoothing over my bicep as her eyes search mine. "It's just, the last time I was throwing up in this bathroom, it was because I was pregnant with your baby."

There's a loud commotion downstairs, a mixture of cheers and groans, but all I hear is ringing. All I see is Erin's smiling face, staring back at me without a single ounce of embarrassment or regret over what she just said. She doesn't realize it. She probably doesn't even remember it, and it just happened.

But I'll never forget it.

"What did you just say?"

Suddenly, her eyes go wide, like her words finally registered. Her breathing accelerates as I drop my hand from her back.

"Erin. What the fuck did you just say to me." I shake my head, grabbing her wrist and pulling her up to look at me. "Was that a joke?"

"Oh, God."

Her eyes bulge again just as the door swings open, and my Little grimaces at the sight of Erin's puke in the toilet before his eyes find mine.

"Shit, man."

"Get out, Josh." I point to the door he just came through, my voice firm.

"I'm going, man, trust me. I just thought you should know. Skyler lost," he says.

My stomach drops even lower, head falling back a bit as a sigh leaves my chest. *Shit*. She lost, and I wasn't even there to watch it.

Josh shrugs, his eyes sympathetic. "Sorry, man. It's all over."

He shuts the door, and as soon as we're alone again, Erin finds a little more to throw up.

Skyler

I stare at Kip's text when I'm fully dressed, debating if I should actually meet him or just crawl back into the hot bathtub. His message is the only one I've looked at, choosing to ignore the multitude of other texts and calls until the morning when I can face them. They'll all want answers, they'll want to know what happened, they'll want to congratulate me on second place even when they're secretly wondering why the hell I didn't take first.

Only Kip and I know that.

I'm already late, if I do want to meet him, but I still don't rush. Instead, I sit on the bed, replaying the night. I close my eyes, see Kip sitting across from me, see his eyes widen when I go all in with a pair of black fours on the table. It's my cursed hand in poker. He and I both knew it was over right then, but what *he* doesn't know is that was the exact moment I realized it didn't matter.

The title didn't matter.

The only thing that did was *him*.

The second-place check is plenty to pay off my tuition, set my family up, and then some. It was what I came for. The title would have just been a bonus for me, a decorative medal for my ego. But to Kip? It was everything.

So, I went from being his opponent to being his teammate, and we won the tournament *together* — for his dad.

I sigh, opening my eyes again to stare at the black television screen hanging above the desk. Not even an hour ago, I watched Kip's face fill that screen, his eyes tired but his smile wide as he talked to the reporter.

"I'm not really sure how I feel just yet," he'd said, laughing.

It was a charming laugh that I was sure was melting panties across the country.

"I just..." He'd paused, biting down on his bottom lip and looking up for a second to compose himself. *"I just want to dedicate this to my father, Oliver Jackson Sr. Thank you for sacrificing your dream so that I could have mine. I didn't win this tournament today. You did. I love you."*

The announcers went on and on about Kip's dad and his condition and I wondered how they found out. Did Kip reveal it in one of his pre-tournament interviews? Had they been talking about it while we were at the final table? Regardless, I know one thing is certain — this will make for one of the best headlines in the tournament's history.

FISH TAKES HOME GRAND PRIZE, HONORS FATHER WITH WIN.

I smile, finally standing and inhaling a long, slow breath. "Okay. Let's get this over with."

I take my time making my way downstairs, and don't rush as I walk the Strip to the Bellagio. It's not too far from the Aria, and my stomach flips with every step as I let myself overthink what he wants to talk about. Does he want to know if I threw the tournament? Does he want to know if I'm okay after the loss?

Does he want to tell me he still loves me, that he wants to be with me?

I shake the possibility from my head, trying to remind myself that everything between us was just a game for him. It was a means to an end, and even if *I* still love him — and perhaps, always will — it doesn't mean he feels the same.

And that's okay.

For once, I'm not asking what's in this for me. For once, I care about someone else's happiness more than mine.

To me, that's what love really is.

The strip is alive as I walk toward the fountain, the lights bright and energy buzzing. Groups pass me in a blur, smiles and laughter blending together with the distant dings from the slot machines to create the Vegas symphony. I just smile, tucking my hands in my pockets and scanning the crowd for Kip. A warm breeze tickles my neck when I find him, and suddenly my feet are lead. All I can do is stand and stare.

He's facing the fountain, his shoulders slumped like he's convinced himself I'm not going to show. His hair is mussed, and even from the back, I spy the black frames of his glasses — those stupid glasses that proved to be such a weakness for me.

Kip turns, looking over the shoulder farthest from me, his face searching the crowd. When he turns over the other one, his eyes catch on mine just as another breeze whips through my hair.

A minute stretches between us, dancing like a year, with his diamond blue eyes locked on mine.

My breaths are shallow but steady, and I finally force my feet to move, carrying me toward him without our gaze ever breaking. He stands straighter as I make my way toward him, wiping his palms on his dark jeans. He's nervous, and suddenly, I am, too.

When I'm just a few feet in front of him, Kip's face washes over like a ghost, like he can't find a single word to say now that I'm here. So, I let out a breath, and I say the first word.

"Hi."

My voice is barely above a whisper, but it visibly stabilizes Kip. He finally breathes again, though his eyes are still heavy, never leaving mine.

"Hi."

I tuck the blowing strands of my hair behind my ear, chewing the inside of my lip. "Congratulations," I finally offer, smiling a little.

"Thanks."

He returns the smile, but it doesn't stick, doesn't warm me from the inside out like his smiles used to do. Instead, it settles us into a long moment of silence, the two of us standing and staring, not knowing what to do.

Kip shoves his hands into his pockets, shaking his head just slightly as his eyes continue to search mine, like he's sure he'll find all the answers there. "Skyler..." He says my name like a curse. "Why did you do it?"

My heart skips a beat before kicking back into gear, but I don't let an ounce of emotion show on my face.

"Do what?"

"Don't make me say it. You know what."

I shrug. "Maybe I was trying to have more faith in our lucky number."

"You knew before he even dealt those fours in the flop that I had a pocket pair. Don't act like you didn't," Kip says, his eyes level. Then, his brows bend together, his eyes still on mine. "Why did you let me win?"

I sigh, crossing my arms over my middle. "Because, Kip," I say, wishing I didn't have to explain. It was easy to make the decision, but to defend it? Not so much. "I knew you wanted this for your dad, and, frankly you deserved it."

"And you didn't?"

"I didn't say that." I huff, anger surging up inside me.

Can't he see it? Can't he see the real reason I made the decision I did?

"My reasons for wanting to win were no better than yours," he says, stepping a little closer. "Skyler, this was important to you and your family."

"Well, maybe it wasn't as important to me as you!" I yell, and as soon as the words leave my mouth, I know there's no going back now.

A few bystanders glance our way before skittering apart, and I shift my weight, pulling a strand of hair between my fingers. I don't want to look at Kip, don't want to see his face after what I just said, but I can't look anywhere else.

"Are you saying you're not important to me?"

"No," I answer. "I'm saying you didn't have a choice. I did. The runner-up prize is plenty for me to pay off school and set my family up, Kip." I shake my head, still playing with my hair. "And even if it wasn't, it wouldn't matter. You did this for your dad, for his dying wish. If it were me in your shoes, I know you would have done the same."

Silence.

I can't take my eyes off his, no matter how badly I want to find comfort in staring anywhere else but at him. His blue pools are wide with wonder, like he can't believe I would do that for him.

Like he can't believe I'm real.

"So, what does this mean?" he finally asks.

I shrug. "I don't know. It means you won and I lost, I guess."

"I don't know if I agree with that."

His answer is so quick, so sure, that I can't do anything other than tilt my head as I try to digest it.

"I may have won the tournament," he breathes, taking another small step toward me. "But did I lose you?"

For the first time tonight, I let myself look at the ground and away from him. My heart thumps hard in my chest, the beats echoing in my ears.

"I don't know where we go from here, Kip," I whisper, tears stinging behind my eyes. "I don't know if we can come back from this. We lied. Both of us. We played games and even though all the cards are on the table now, I don't know if this is a game we can finish playing and still survive."

I look up just in time to see Kip's bottom lip quiver as he looks up to the sky, willing himself not to give into his emotions. Slowly, he levels his gaze with me again, his chest deflating on a long breath.

"I'm sorry, Skyler. For everything," he says, voice raspy and desperate. "And I know those two words won't do anything to heal the fucking hole I've punched in you, but I mean them. And if you let me, I will spend the rest of my life making sure you know that nothing in this world is more important to me than you are. Nothing."

He pauses, debating his next words as I try to swallow the ones he just said.

Did he just say the rest of his life? As in, forever? As in...

"You've changed everything about my life," he says, pulling me out of my head and back to the moment. "Every dream I thought I had means nothing to me now if you're not a part of them, too. I've never opened myself up to love, I've never let anything get in the way of my career. But you came in and turned all that into nothing. You obliterated everything I thought was important. All that matters to me, Skyler, is you."

My heart flutters to life, like a hot air balloon being fired up into the sky. But my biggest insecurities are still standing on top of it, digging their heels in, and I let them win as my eyes fall to the ground again.

"How do I know what was real and what wasn't? How do I know when you were getting to know me because you wanted to, as opposed to when you were just playing a game?"

Kips moves closer but I step away, keeping the space between us. I know he wants to pull me into him, to wrap those perfect arms around me and make me melt into him. But I can't. The moment he touches me, it's all over.

And before I let him touch me again, I have to be sure.

"Everything was real, Skyler," he breathes. "It was real when we kissed the night we met and the electricity shocked us both. It was real when I asked you about your past. It was real when I helped you figure out who you really are and told you not to be ashamed of her. It was real when you ripped my fucking heart out at the Valentine's Day dance," he chokes, as if just the memory of that night is enough to make him want to throw himself in front of a train. "When I touched you for the first time, when we fought because we cared too much about each other, when we made sacrifices and decisions we weren't proud of — all of that was real. This," he says, stepping toward me. I don't back away this time. "*We*, are real."

Listen to him, my heart screams. *You love him, you idiot.*

But my walls are still up, the wire on top buzzing with an electric charge as if to remind me how bad it hurt the last time I let them down, let him inside them.

My heart and my brain are at war, and I don't know who I want to win.

"Let's let Fate decide," Kip says after a moment, and then his hand is in front of me, a shiny, black die balanced on his palm. "Roll the die. If it's a four, we give this game another round. If it's anything else, we walk away."

I eye him, doing the easy math in my head as he stands there with his heart on his sleeve. "You know those odds are really terrible, right?"

But Kip just shrugs, his eyes calm. "I'm confident in our number."

I study him for a long moment, eyes sweeping over the stubble on his jaw, the messy ends of his blond hair blowing in the wind before finding his eyes again. Then, slowly, I take the die from his hand.

This is crazy, I think, shaking my head as I roll the die around in my hand. But I let it go anyway, the black plastic sliding across the concrete at our feet.

Time warps again, as it always does with Kip, and we both watch that plastic bounce around from side to side until it knocks against a man's shoe. When it finally falls, I close my eyes on a sigh, my heart squeezing hard in my chest.

Six.

When I open my eyes again, I will Kip to look at me, but he can't look away from the die on the ground. He just stares at it, as if he can change what number is showing with his glare alone. The crowd continues to grow around us, laughter and conversation floating in as we exist in our own little bubble of silence.

And just like tonight in the tournament, I have a moment of clarity.

The devastation on his face, the bravery it took to ask me to meet him tonight, to say the words he has… it's all the proof I need. What happened between us *was* real, and no matter how badly my walls want to protect me, the truth is that he's worth the risk.

I'd feel the pain all over again, if it meant I got to be with him in the end.

So, I bend, retrieving the die from where it rests between us. I offer it to Kip at first, but he doesn't move for it, and just when I see his hand twitch forward, I rear back, throwing it with all my might and sending it sailing over his head.

Whipping around, Kip watches the die splash into the fountain while I watch him, knowing this is the moment when it all changes. He turns to face me again, eyes wide, brows bent together in question.

"I'm done leaving my life to chance," I say, smiling and shaking my head as the tears that threatened before blur my vision. "Black number four can suck it."

I close the space between us in the next breath, Kip's arms wrapping around me as I crash my mouth to his. His hands slide into my hair, pulling me closer, deepening the kiss as I fist my hands in his shirt. We're completely lost in the moment, in each other, when suddenly music spills out from the fountain speakers and the show begins.

Neither of us look up to see it.

We lose ourselves in each other, touching and feeling and kissing as the water shoots up into the night sky until someone near us clears their throat, pulling us back to reality.

"I love you," Kip breathes, the pad of his thumb skating over my bottom lip as his eyes flick between mine. "I'm so fucking sorry, Skyler."

"Stop." I shake my head. "We both played a stupid game."

"I promise to never gamble with your heart again, Ella Mae."

At that, I smile, remembering that night of our first date. We were both hiding so much, fighting our own demons, and yet we couldn't help it even then.

We were destined to be together, to love each other.

It was always in the cards for us.

"Deal," I say as Kip grabs my hand. He pulls me away from the fountain and toward the Strip, walking me back to our hotel without even asking. We both want to be alone, away from the crowds, away from anyone who isn't us.

"I can't believe you let me watch that die roll like that, when you knew it didn't even matter."

I laugh. "It was fun to watch you sweat."

Kip squeezes my hand.

"That was super cheesy, by the way," I add, glancing back at the fountains still going off.

"What? You're not impressed with that impeccable timing?"

"How did you know I wouldn't be dumping your ass when the fountains went off like that?"

Kip frowns, pulling me into him and knuckling my head. I laugh and push him off, smile fading a bit when his blue eyes lock on mine again.

"I knew you couldn't resist this."

I roll my eyes. "Please."

But when he presses his lips to mine again, his fingertips skating down my arms to grip my waist and pull me into him, I know he's right. He sucks my bottom lip between his teeth, biting it gently and eliciting a moan from deep within me.

"You couldn't resist me if you tried."

I smile, pulling back just enough to take in those stupid black frames surrounding his eyes. Looking back on the semester, on all the games, I can't wrap my head around how far we've come. He was just supposed to be a blond-haired, blue-eyed boy to play with, a new toy to keep me occupied on the weekends. And somehow, he got under my skin. Somehow, he became so much more.

He became my everything.

And I can't resist the urge to bring everything full circle.

So, I lean in, eyes mischievous and hands around his waist as I whisper against his lips.

"Wanna bet?"

Jess

"I'M SO OBSESSED WITH your new haircut, Little," Skyler says, pulling on one of Cassie's curls and letting it bounce back into place.

"Same. Makes me want to chop mine," I chime in. "But, you know, that means less to pull on when I'm getting banged from the back. So... priorities."

The girls all laugh at that, Ashlei tossing a handful of popcorn at me.

"I'm going to miss this," Cassie says, leaning her head on Skyler's shoulder. We're all piled together on the sorority couch, enjoying one last movie day before we split up. Cassie and I are both sticking around for the rest of the summer, but the other girls are leaving, and it'll be two months before we see them again.

"I love summer," I say. "But, I wish I could spend more of it with you girls."

"Me, too. It's been an... *interesting* semester." Erin's cheeks flush. "Thank you for not completely disowning me after the major bitch I've been."

Skyler shifts uncomfortably, not saying anything, so I lean over and pull Erin under one arm. "Ah, we've all had our period before. Rest assured, we'll pay you back sometime in the future."

She smiles, leaning her head on my shoulder.

"So, Cassie, you're sticking around here for summer classes... and Adam is here, too?" I waggle my brows. "Bow chicka wow wow."

She flushes a deep red, pulling her blanket up to her chin. "You just can't go a day without trying to get me to divulge the details of my sex life, can you?"

"My lady blue balls need rubbing, Cass." I flex my hips toward her and the girls all laugh while she swats me away.

"Thought Kade was rubbing those balls for you," Ashlei points out.

"Oh, please," I scoff. "More like I'm trying my best to teach him how to even get a girl to talk to him for more than three minutes. We're so far away from bang town, it's not even funny."

"I still can't believe you agreed to train him," she says.

"Yeah, well, I can't believe you're officially dating the hottest, richest CEO this side of the Florida-Georgia line."

"Seriously!" Erin chimes in, smacking Ashlei. "How the hell did you keep that a secret from us for almost a year?"

Ashlei just smiles, popping a kernel into her mouth. "Some things are too good to share, my friends."

"Selfish whore," I murmur, and the girls all burst into laughter again.

"Skyler, are you going up north with Kip?" Erin asks, and the weight of his father's illness settles over us like a cloud.

"I am," she says, eyes on her hands as she picks at a stray string on her blanket. "I'm a little nervous, a little scared, but mostly, I just want to be there for Kip. It's going to be weird, meeting the man who sent him here to take me down, but at the same time, I understand him. And at the end of the day, being a support system for Kip is what matters most to me."

"He's lucky to have you, Little," Erin says, sincerity in her eyes. And when she reaches over to grab Skyler's hand, Ashlei and I exchange a worried glance.

For a moment, Skyler just stares at it, like she's debating flicking Erin's hand away and immediately flipping her off. But instead, she sighs, squeezing her Big's hand with a soft, resigned smile. "Thank you."

I let out a breath of relief.

"And what about you, G Big?" Cassie asks. "What are your plans for the summer?"

Erin swallows, her gaze finding the television screen. "Therapy."

"*What*?" We all gasp in unison, eyes locked on Erin as we wait for her to explain.

"There's a lot I've been through in the past year that I haven't talked to anyone about..." she says, her voice soft. "Not even you girls. And, it's time. I need to work through it if I'm ever going to move forward."

"What happened?" I ask, leaning into her. "You can tell us."

"I know, I know I can," she says, finally returning our gazes with a slight smile. "But, it's not the right time. When it is, when I'm ready, I'll come to you. I promise."

Ashlei leans over my lap, squeezing Erin's knee as I try to search her eyes for some sort of answer.

"Well, when that time comes, we'll be here."

"Thank you."

For a while, we're just silent, staring at the television screen without even registering what's on it. Finally, Skyler jumps up, clapping her hands together.

"Alright, enough of that shit." She skips away and up the stairs, returning moments later with a half-empty bottle of whiskey. "We're ending this semester on a high note. Time to belly up, bitches."

"Oh, God. I can't even *think* about alcohol right now," Erin says with a wince.

"You don't have to think about it," Skyler says. "You just have to drink it."

"I'll grab glasses!" Cassie sprints off to the kitchen, and when she's back, she lines up five shot glasses as Skyler tops them off with the amber liquid. We each grab one when they're full, holding them together over the coffee table with a mixture of sadness and joy in our eyes.

"We only have one more semester together before you three bitches graduate," Skyler says, eyes flashing over me, Ashlei, and Erin. "So, here's to making the most of it — the Kappa Kappa Beta way."

Ashlei thrusts her glass higher. "To parties."

"To movie days," Cassie chimes in.

Skyler pushes her glass in next. "To love — in all its forms."

"And to sex, because... well, it's us."

They all laugh at my addition, and then our eyes are on Erin, hers on her glass, like her thoughts are far off in space. Finally, she blinks, swallowing a little as she joins our glasses with hers.

"To friends," she says, her voice light. "Who are always there for us, no matter how bad we fuck up."

Skyler's eyes soften, and she clinks her shot glass to her Big's. "Hear, hear."

We toss the liquid back, me throwing my hands up in the air with a *woo* and Skyler joining in with a high five while the rest of the girls grimace. We all laugh, stacking the glasses and piling back on the couch just in time for a new chick flick to start.

And as another semester comes to an end, I glance around at my sisters, heart squeezing at the thought of living a life without them. I only have one more semester with them, and in less than a year, I'll be graduated — thrust into the real world whether I like it or not.

But the truth is, I know I don't have to worry, because I'll never have to live without them.

My Kappa Kappa Beta sisters are my sisters for life — through college and beyond.

So, for now, I vow to make the most of the time we have left. I'll have a kick-ass summer with Cassie, recruit some more bad-ass bitches in the fall, and when my time as officer is over and it's time to walk across that stage, I'll do so holding hands with the girls who matter most.

In the meantime, there are parties that need raging, kegs that need draining, and boys who need banging. Those are my duties as Jess "J-Love" Vonnegut, and I can't wait to honor my university.

Buckle up, Palm South University.

You ain't seen nothing yet.

To be continued...

Legacy takes place during the same semester as *Black Number Four*. Whether you've read it before now or not, you'll get a wider view of what was happening at Palm South University (especially between Kip and Skyler) if you read *Black Number Four* as you read this season. I will help guide you, letting you know which chapters to read before moving on to the next episode.

FOR THE FULL READING EXPERIENCE FOR THIS EPISODE, READ **CHAPTERS 19-24** IN *BLACK NUMBER FOUR*. (You'll get to see how Skyler felt during Erin's apology, get inside Kip's head in the aftermath of the break up, hear what Erin says to Kip when they dance at formal, watch the tournament go down from Skyler and Kip's point of view, and live the fountain scene in Kip's head. Sigh!) *Please note: if you read the epilogue, there are slight spoilers for the 5th installment of Palm South University.*

Tweet as you read using #PalmSouth and join the Facebook discussion group here: https://www.facebook.com/groups/712042985606913/?ref=br_rs

More from Kandi Steiner

The Red Zone Rivals Series
Fair Catch
As if being the only girl on the college football team wasn't hard enough, Coach had to go and assign my brother's best friend — and *my* number one enemy — as my roommate.
Blind Side
The hottest college football safety in the nation just asked me to be his fake girlfriend.
And I just asked him to take my virginity.
Quarterback Sneak
Quarterback Holden Moore can have any girl he wants.
Except me: the coach's daughter.
Hail Mary
(AN AMAZON #1 BESTSELLER)
I used to love Leo Hernandez, but that was before I hated him. And now, I have no choice but to move in with him.

The Becker Brothers Series
On the Rocks (book 1)
Neat (book 2)
Manhattan (book 3)
Old Fashioned (book 4)
Four brothers finding love in a small Tennessee town that revolves around a whiskey distillery with a dark past — including the mysterious death of their father.

The Best Kept Secrets Series
(AN AMAZON TOP 10 BESTSELLER)
What He Doesn't Know (book 1)
What He Always Knew (book 2)
What He Never Knew (book 3)
Charlie's marriage is dying. She's perfectly content to go down in the flames, until her first love shows back up and reminds her the other way love can burn.

Close Quarters
A summer yachting the Mediterranean sounded like heaven to Jasmine after finishing her undergrad degree. But her boyfriend's billionaire boss always gets what he wants. And this time, he wants her.

Make Me Hate You
Jasmine has been avoiding her best friend's brother for years, but when they're both in the same house for a wedding, she can't resist him — no matter how she tries.

The Wrong Game
(AN AMAZON TOP 5 BESTSELLER)
Gemma's plan is simple: invite a new guy to each home game using her season tickets for the Chicago Bears. It's the perfect way to avoid getting emotionally attached and also get some action. But after Zach gets his chance to be her practice round, he decides one game just isn't enough. A sexy, fun sports romance.

The Right Player
She's avoiding love at all costs. He wants nothing more than to lock her down. Sexy, hilarious and swoon-worthy, The Right Player is the perfect read for sports romance lovers.

On the Way to You
It was only supposed to be a road trip, but when Cooper discovers the journal of the boy driving the getaway car, everything changes. An emotional, angsty road trip romance.

A Love Letter to Whiskey
(AN AMAZON TOP 10 BESTSELLER)
An angsty, emotional romance between two lovers fighting the curse of bad timing.
Read Love, Whiskey – Jamie's side of the story and an extended epilogue – in the new Fifth Anniversary Edition! (https://amzn.to/3FB1B7E)

Weightless
Young Natalie finds self-love and romance with her personal trainer, along with a slew of secrets that tie them together in ways she never thought possible.

Revelry
Recently divorced, Wren searches for clarity in a summer cabin outside of Seattle, where she makes an unforgettable connection with the broody, small town recluse next door.

Say Yes
Harley is studying art abroad in Florence, Italy. Trying to break free of her perfectionism, she steps outside one night determined to Say Yes to anything that comes her way. Of course, she didn't expect to run into Liam Benson...

Washed Up
Gregory Weston, the boy I once knew as my son's best friend, now a man I don't know at all. No, not just a man. A doctor. And he wants me...

The Christmas Blanket
Stuck in a cabin with my ex-husband waiting out a blizzard?
Not exactly what I had pictured when I planned a surprise
visit home for the holidays...

Black Number Four
A college, Greek-life romance of a hot young poker star
and the boy sent to take her down.

The Palm South University Series
Rush (book 1) FREE if you sign up for my newsletter!
Anchor, PSU #2
Pledge, PSU #3
Legacy, PSU #4
Ritual, PSU #5
Hazed, PSU #6
Greek, PSU #7
#1 NYT Bestselling Author Rachel Van Dyken says, "If
Gossip Girl and Riverdale had a love child, it would be
PSU." This angsty college series will be your next guilty
addiction.

Tag Chaser
She made a bet that she could stop chasing military men,
which seemed easy — until her knight in shining armor
and latest client at work showed up in Army ACUs.

Song Chaser
Tanner and Kellee are perfect for each other. They
frequent the same bars, love the same music, and have the
same desire to rip each other's clothes off. Only problem?
Tanner is still in love with his best friend.

Acknowledgments

BEFORE I GO INTO the people who helped bring this book (and series) to life, I want to start by thanking you — the reader. As you've probably gathered by now (if you've read the other acknowledgements in this series), PSU is my passion project. It's my baby. And man, have y'all been taken on a ride! I want to thank you for always reading as soon as the new installment is live, for tweeting and posting on Instagram and Facebook, for spreading your love for this series at every possible opportunity. YOU are what makes this series what it is. I'm so thankful you love these characters as much as I do, and I can't wait to continue their adventure with you.

As always, my beta readers were absolutely fantastic for this season. And man, talk about a BEAST of a book! Y'all had the job of reading a book that is the size of TWO full-length novels, and you provided amazing feedback that helped me more than I could ever say. So, thank you Kellee Fabre, Patricia Leibowitz (Queen Mintness!), Ashlei Davison, Danielle Lagasse, Jess Vogel, Haley Sue Brewer, and Sarah Green. I literally could NOT do this without you. Besos!

I also want to give a special shout out to the lovely ladies who the KKB girls are named after — Ashlei Davison, Jess Vogel, Erin Spencer, and Cassie Graham. Circle of Trust forever and ever!

My life would be a living, breathing disaster if not for my amazing PA – Christina Stokes. You have no idea how helpful you have been to me through the writing of this book (which took WAY longer than anticipated, given the surprising length!). Thank you for your continued support, your love and generosity, and for always knowing what I need to breathe a little easier. You're the best!

Shout out to Staci Hart, Brittainy C. Cherry, Karla Sorensen and Kathryn Andrews, who have all been a part of this series for so long they're practically honorary students at PSU. Thanks for letting me gab to you all about the characters, this world, and for bouncing ideas whenever I need to. More than anything, thank you for being the best friends a girl can ask for. Love y'all.

Momma Von and Sasha Whittington always get shout outs, just because HELLO — mom and bestie. ;) Thank you both for always cheering me on, for sharing my posts, for geeking out over new covers with me. I love you both more than I can say.

Also, thanks for all the wine in Italy. Totally helped write this book. ;)

Editor of the Year goes to Elaine York with Allusion Graphics, for putting up with my deadline being missed... again... and again... and one more time just for fun. LOL. Thank you for being so patient and understanding with this ever-growing book, for rushing to format the new paperbacks and eBooks when we rebranded the covers, and for helping polish this baby up to a spit-sparkle shine. You're amazing, and I never want to live in a world where you aren't a part of my team!

To Nina Grinstead, Chanpreet Singh, Hillary Suppes and the rest of the team at Social Butterfly PR, thank you for always helping me spread the word about new releases. PSU was a challenge, and y'all have handled it with such grace.

There's a special man in my life right now, some of you may know him from social media as #MysteryMan, and I have to thank him most of all for this one. He was there to rub my shoulders and work on my wrists after long, grueling days of writing, to listen to me as I worked through my deadlines being missed due to higher word count, to give opinions on the rebrand, and best of all, to kiss away the anxiety when it crept in around release. I don't know where our story goes from here, but I do know that I am forever grateful for the way you've loved me, and for the time we've had together.

Lastly, but never least, thank you Kandiland and Palm South University Discussion Group. You guys keep me going when I feel like I can't, and it's because of you that I get to do what I love for a living and live a dream I've dreamed for so long. I love you. Let's be best friends forever.

About the Author

KANDI STEINER is #1 Amazon Bestseller and whiskey connoisseur living in Tampa, FL. Best known for writing "emotional rollercoaster" stories, she loves bringing flawed characters to life and writing about real, raw romance — in all its forms. No two Kandi Steiner books are the same, and if you're a lover of angsty, emotional, and inspirational reads, she's your gal.

An alumna of the University of Central Florida, Kandi graduated with a double major in Creative Writing and Advertising/PR with a minor in Women's Studies. She started writing back in the 4th grade after reading the first Harry Potter installment. In 6th grade, she wrote and edited her own newspaper and distributed to her classmates. Eventually, the principal caught on and the newspaper was quickly halted, though Kandi tried fighting for her "freedom of press."

She took particular interest in writing romance after college, as she has always been a die hard hopeless romantic, and likes to highlight all the challenges of love as well as the triumphs.

When Kandi isn't writing, you can find her reading books of all kinds, planning her next adventure, or pole dancing (yes, you read that right). She enjoys live music, traveling, playing with her fur babies and soaking up the sweetness of life.

CONNECT WITH KANDI:
NEWSLETTER: kandisteiner.com/newsletter
FACEBOOK: facebook.com/kandisteiner
FACEBOOK READER GROUP (Kandiland):
facebook.com/groups/kandilandks
INSTAGRAM: Instagram.com/kandisteiner
TIKTOK: tiktok.com/@authorkandisteiner
TWITTER: twitter.com/kandisteiner
PINTEREST: pinterest.com/authorkandisteiner
WEBSITE: www.kandisteiner.com

Kandi Steiner may be coming to a city near you!
Check out her "events" tab to see all the
signings she's attending in the near future:
www.kandisteiner.com/events